INTERNECINE

Also by David J. Schow

NOVELS

The Kill Riff
The Shaft
Rock Breaks Scissors Cut
Bullets of Rain
Gun Work
Upgunned (forthcoming 2011)

SHORT STORY COLLECTIONS

Seeing Red
Lost Angels
Black Leather Required
Crypt Orchids
Eye
Zombie Jam
Havoc Swims Jaded

NONFICTION

The Outer Limits Companion
Wild Hairs (columns and essays)
The Art of Drew Struzan

AS EDITOR

Silver Scream
The Lost Bloch Volume One: The Devil With You
The lost Bloch Volume Two: Hell on Earth
The Lost Bloch Volume Three: Crimes & Punishments
Elvisland (collection by John Farris)

DAVID J. SCHOW

INTERNECINE

THOMAS DUNNE BOOKS   ST. MARTIN'S PRESS   NEW YORK

This is a work of fiction. All of the characters, organizations, and events portrayed in this novel are either products of the author's imagination or are used fictitiously.

THOMAS DUNNE BOOKS.
An imprint of St. Martin's Press.

INTERNECINE. Copyright © 2010 by David J. Schow. All rights reserved. Printed in the United States of America. For information, address St. Martin's Press, 175 Fifth Avenue, New York, N.Y. 10010.

www.thomasdunnebooks.com
www.stmartins.com

Book design by Jonathan Bennett

Library of Congress Cataloging-in-Publication Data

Schow, David J.
    Internecine / David J. Schow.—1st ed.
        p. cm.
    ISBN 978-0-312-57136-8
    I. Title.
    PS3569.C5284I67 2010
    813'.54—dc22

                            2010013059

First Edition: July 2010

10 9 8 7 6 5 4 3 2 1

INTERNECINE

DAY ONE

The briefcase was a stainless-steel Halliburton, attaché size, exactly the sort you see used in countless movies with drug deal scenes, only this one was matte black, and I knew for a fact it cost at least eight hundred dollars, new.

Here's what I found inside:

Two matched SIGARMS semiauto pistols, model 229. A hundred rounds of boxed ammunition in .357 caliber and four clean 12-round clips. Two glasspack silencers, threaded to muzzle size. Each silencer was nearly a foot long.

One five-shot .44 caliber Charter Arms Bulldog revolver with rubber grips and fifty rounds of ammunition. The barrel was a hair over two inches long. This type of gun is what I've heard called a "snubbie."

One dispenser containing ten pairs of disposable, left- or right-hand surgical gloves, unpowdered, size large.

One Telemetrix cellphone with a booster antenna.

One laminated, letter-perfect FBI ID featuring a man's face that's not mine. A stranger to me. It smelled fake.

In the sleeve pocket of the case lid were two more items: An envelope containing two 8 by 10 photos of a woman I also didn't know, but whose name was Alicia Brandenberg. I learned this from her fairly detailed itinerary. There was another envelope containing—to near-bursting—$25,000, in used, nonsequential tens and twenties.

No serial numbers on the guns, the phone, anywhere. No lot numbers on the ammo boxes. No product plate on the briefcase. The slugs were heavy-grain cartridges packing maximum muzzle velocity, intended to do a great deal of damage to whatever got in their way.

Not a single fingerprint on anything. It was as though the contents had been boxed by a machine, factory-fresh, untouched by human hands.

There were three numbers programmed into the cellphone, no names or designations attached. I didn't want to use it to call anyone; I think I was slightly afraid of it.

The briefcase wasn't mine. I came across it by accident.

Perhaps I should back up a little bit.

My name is Conrad Maddox. For the past twelve years I've worked as Vice President in charge of development for Kroeger Concepts, Ltd., an advertising firm in Los Angeles on the Valley side of the hill. My boss is the fellow who founded the firm, Burt Kroeger—a "superior" who has nonetheless managed to remain a friend, or at least an ally. I'm one floor below him and we see each other for drinks; that kind of friend. Burt headhunted me, for which I remain grateful. I've always tried to merit his absolute trust in business.

My job earns me a fair amount of frequent flyer travel miles, thanks to several hops a year to Chicago, New York, Seattle, Houston, Mexico City and, occasionally, Beijing or London. Berlin three times; Paris twice so far. I can afford a couple of weeks per year in St. John or Bimini to get away and, you know, unwind.

I'm divorced. Don't ask about the ex–Mrs. Maddox because: (1) she never took my name, and (2) we don't stay in touch. I've had maybe ninety liaisons, affairs, trysts, and "relationships" in the eddy-rings surrounding my marriage, which lasted three years and then evaporated. It was the only time in my life I've been completely faithful to one woman.

I try to resist involvements with co-workers, but as you can guess there's always an exception. It's human nature. In fact, I'm breaking my own protocol in my mind right now.

I drive a fairly decent car, a Benz CL600 with blackout tinting everywhere, except on the windshield, which would be illegal. I have a variety of what could be called friends and acquaintances (I differentiate between the two), but more often than not, I veg out after work and pop in some DVD, just like you do when you need a break. I see my girlfriends frequently enough to maintain the delusion that I have a healthy outlook.

I was coming in late from Pittsburgh on American flight #183, non-stop with dinner service. The first-class dinners were better than those in coach; I had steak au poivre and three glasses of a middling Cab. You could still get the heated nuts, the hot towels and such; company credit cards never feel the turbulence. My Benz was in the shop in Manhattan Beach for a leaky coolant hose, so I had Danielle, at the office, hunt me up a decent rental.

She booked me into a midnight-blue Pontiac Sebring convertible, a car with a nice, solid suspension. I dumped my junk in the minimal trunk and when I settled down to orient, I noticed there was something in the passenger seat next to me.

A locker key.

(Since 9/11, storage lockers had vanished from LAX as too tempting, but guess what—they're still there if you know where to look and don't mind being eyeballed by security. The coin-lockers used to be beyond the scanning points and X-ray pass-through. Now they're inside the terminal near the check-in counters, far ahead of where your individual freedoms evaporate. But they're still there.)

So I sat there for a moment, inventing assorted scenarios to explain the wayward locker key, subdivided across two general categories— "accidental" versus "intentional." Assuming the first, it might have been left by: (1) the previous rental customer; (2) one of the guys working at the car agency; or (3) it might have fallen inside . . . somehow, which would have been a complete caprice of chance.

Assuming the second, I wondered, was the key left (4) on purpose for me, or (5) for someone else? Big joke potential, there. *What a riot on old Conrad. Let's see what he does.*

At the time it never occurred to me that there might be a (6).

I could have stuck the key in the glove compartment and forgotten it. Or turned it in at the Hertz lost and found. But guess what: I'm not so dead inside (yet) that I'm not curious. I like that evil thrill you reap from a privileged peek into stuff that's none of your business. You do, too. At the same time, I'm also cautious enough to know that maybe the whole temptation is a setup. Maybe the locker, if it is to be found in the airport at all, is staked out by two dozen undercover cops, waiting for some Colombian coke lord, and wouldn't *that* be embarrassing? I mean, in addition to making me late and all.

I picked up the key and looked it over. I even smelled it. Number

202. Ultimately, I drove away with it. But over the weekend and into the problem packet of a new Monday I looked at it a thousand times.

Generally I take a lot of work home. Sometimes I just sleep at the office. There's an executive washroom with a shower and amenities, and my corner office (right below Burt Kroeger's corner; sometimes I can hear him stomping around up there, working late, like me) has the world's best sofa for crashing. For thinking things out. Doping out small mysteries. Or positing possible scenarios such as (6) the key might have been left for me, specifically, on purpose.

I mean, what would *you* do?

I volunteered to collect Katy Burgess at LAX on Tuesday afternoon because: (1) Katy is undeniably attractive, (2) Katy is competent and fun, (3) I sensed a work-related entanglement that I want to toy with avoiding, and (4) as an excuse to stop thinking about the locker key.

Yes, Katy is the co-worker that interested me, despite myself.

Yes, I was baiting myself with the proximity of the airport.

Yes, I was already aware that I had whomped up a wicker basket of lies as perforated as a sieve—a desperate cover story that any intelligent scrutiny could smack to pieces—but at this stage of our budding relationship, Katy would be professionally polite enough not to question it. I told her that when I had gone to Pittsburgh, I remembered I was carrying a pocketknife, so I stowed it in a coin locker rather than risk a public panic, an evacuation, and a lockdown of the airport when the metal detector revealed me as a potential terrorist. Don't laugh; this kind of childish, overreactive shit happens all the time (and usually gets on the news).

With this backstory in position, I had an excuse for reaching inside locker #202. If I did not like what I saw—a human head in a trash bag or something like that—I could withdraw my hand, palming the knife I'd already brought along.

When I saw the flank of the Halliburton, I pulled it out, casually said, "my briefcase, too," and stashed my decoy knife in a single smooth move. Misdirection works. Katy assumed the knife in question was on top of the briefcase; she wasn't more inquisitive than that. Airport security guys watched me approach the bank of lockers. They saw a business-looking guy remove a business-looking case. Normal, almost dull. No platoon of gun-wielding DEA agents sprang forth.

Katy and I strolled out looking like the most boring couple in the world. Then I did something more difficult: I locked the case in my trunk and tried not to think about it for the next six hours or so.

Why did I even have to lie to cover this? Good question. Apart from the justification that I lie for a living, this was the only moment in this entire process that I could try to contain a possible future spill. It was a note of unexpected excitement, and I wanted to keep it to myself until I learned more. My excitements, up to this point, had all become predictable and dull. This was new, and I didn't want to share.

"Katy" is a collapse of "Katerina," and is pronounced *KAH-tee*, with the accent on the first syllable. Get that wrong and you don't have a chance at conversation of any sort. People sometimes try to curry intimacy by calling me Connie; I can't seem to stop them. Katy runs sales for Kroeger; we're like chessmen of equal value inside the company. She likes Bombay Sapphire martinis and never gets tipsy with co-workers (that I've ever seen). As we walked to the car, she indicated that a recreational beverage or two was just the thing she needed to unscrew her spine from the flight, ex–New York after a full workday on the far end of the country. We could plot strategy and swap mild professional gossip. Then I could drop her off at her condo in the Marina.

The lounge we went to was one of those places redolent of "yuppie flu" run epidemic: too much brass, wood, and foliage, all fake, with high stools posted at little round tables, like pedestals. When she scooted up to her seat I noticed she was wearing stockings, not panty hose, and I felt a little tug inside my rib cage. I thought, *Caution. You wouldn't be so instantly randy if she were wearing a revolver strapped to her hip. In this business, wardrobe is often a weapon.*

Without the Blahnik heels Katy was probably five-foot-eight, with a lot of wavy brown hair she usually wore down, reminding me of forties movie sirens in soft focus. She had slender hands with long fingers, like porcelain sculpture, and frank blue-gray eyes with a thin, natural brow arch. She didn't use a lot of makeup; she didn't have to, and knew exactly where the line was to be crossed. Subtle gloss was all she wore— lipstick would have been overdoing it. Small fine teeth and a body full of promise. You'd never know she was a hotshot in the field, and ruthless at her job, which is what I really liked about her, in addition to the obvious.

Come to think of it, she'd probably look *more* sexy wearing a gun; who was I kidding?

We had tacitly agreed to buy the persona each of us was selling to the other. That's the first step in any relationship, right? You buy the vision, then deal with the reality later.

Katy's big deal, today, was our impending acquisition of a PR package for a hotshot politico named G. Johnson Jenks. He had the California governorship in his sights after emerging from private industry and logging the usual community service time as a councilman and ecological paladin up north, where people still get uppity about topics like old trees, or ozone. Kroeger Concepts was in the running to sell Mr. Jenks to the voting public in a salubrious fashion. Katy was the point person on the deal, and brought all this up because she wanted my assurance that I would be onboard, armed with enthusiasm and ideas, if we actually did score the gig. We'd have to pull long hours, "in close and tight," as she put it.

I dropped smoothly into work mode, admiring myself because I now had a secret and was comporting myself extra-slick. Jenks's opponent in the gubernatorial slapdown was an equal-but-opposite talking head named Theodore Ripkin, and our task as good Kroeger soldiers was to demonstrate Mr. Jenks's vote-worthiness and overall moral superiority. In other words, anticipate every single gob of mud that might be hurled against our gladiator, and emplace damage-control strategies while hunting for the one subterranean factoid that might knock Theodore Ripkin right off his high-ass horse. Put another way, employ the usual misdirection and surgical strikes. Votes matter in theory but not in practice; what matters is grabbing the gold in the big popularity contest. All's fair!

The Jenks campaign was well-heeled enough to promise all of us a lot of pull and cash flow; the sort of thing that almost always spins me to attention and a full salute. But I had not become involved enough yet to bring myself up to speed on the actual personalities involved in the campaign. That was more Katy's jurisdiction, and thus we had plenty of aboveboard excuses to huddle. Beyond that, I wanted a chance to beguile and amuse her.

She spun off anecdotally enhanced details. When you're about to plunge into an intimate client-provider relationship for money, the first phase is deep background and research, the same as basic coursework for a final exam or rehearsal for a performance. The ongoing data stream of a client's history, as it evolves, is frequently incomprehensible to outsiders who might eavesdrop in midconversation. It begins to sound like a foreign language. Katy had that brightness in her gaze that said she was about to dive, and dive deep.

My brain caught up with her in midsentence.

"The real prize seems to be Jenks's campaign manager," Katy said as she killed her second Martian. "You might have to talk to your guy about her. The ferret guy."

"The Mole Man," I interjected. He was a slightly shady broker of information I sometimes used in my pursuit of Kroeger greatness. "Why?"

"Because past a certain date I can't get any background on her. She seems to have sprung fullblown from the forehead of Zeus or something." She paused for effect. "Just like Jenks."

"Whoa, wait a minute. Candidates are supposed to have nothing to hide."

"Mm-hm. . . . And it is our sacred job to find out otherwise. Don't get me wrong—Jenks has a personality file that goes back three generations. But there's something fishy about it, and it didn't occur to me until I checked his campaign manager, who doesn't seem to exist on paper before 2003. Could be something like Jenks legally changing his name a few years back and then covering it up. Fair enough. Might be innocuous. Might be a minor scandal in the woodpile. Any public profile can survive a minor scandal if it's twirled correctly. But if so, what is there to hide? And now his prime mover's history hits a brick wall at almost exactly the same time. As if the storytellers fabricated a watertight pocket history for Jenks but were less discriminating with his accomplices, do you see?"

"What's her name?" I said.

"Alicia Brandenberg . . . apparently."

No bells rang then; I hadn't yet opened the briefcase.

Katy was good. Right out of the gate she had unearthed a bit of suspicion. It took on the zest of a serial and made anticipation of next week's chapter more exciting. "All I'm saying is that if they're making up backstories, we have to know. If they're covering something up, we have to know, before we get in deeper with them, agreed?"

"Absolutely."

"And if Jenks isn't being straight with us, why'd he pick us to publicize his campaign?"

"That's too much to wrap my brain around right now," I said, indicating my drink, as though it was to blame, although we both knew better.

"We'll stick a pin in it for later," she said, graciously relenting, and allowing me my chance to be charming and funny. Katy even reached over to touch my hand, several times, to make a point or to mock some lame in the bar. And you know what? Past that, I don't remember a thing we talked about, because all I could think of was that briefcase, sizzling away in the trunk of my car. I acquitted myself dazzlingly, which means I hung on for an hour past the time we had originally allotted for our pit stop. The plateau of our gestating relationship beyond our mutual jobs was broadening, and she seemed willing, but cautious (which was very smart) . . . and it was all pointless because I knew what I really wanted to do. I guess she was a little confused when I dropped her off.

File it for later. We mutually promised to "do this again, soon."

I knew I was lying, but not because I wasn't attracted to her. A stronger attraction refused to vacate my brain.

After another paranoid moment wasted in thinking about suitcase bombs, I went ahead and opened my prize, in private.

If it had blown up in my face, I might have been better off.

The dossier inside the briefcase was a detailed look at the daily movements of the aforementioned Alicia Brandenberg, current campaign manager for G. Johnson Jenks, Kroeger political client, and possible phony-baloney. The kind of detail that suggested not merely rich resources, but enemy surveillance.

Every other item inside the Halliburton presented myriad possibilities. It seemed like a toyset for contract killing, as least as far as I understood such things from espionage fiction. But what was it for? Attack or defense? Was Alicia Brandenberg a target or a player? Maybe she was supposed to pick up the kit? Maybe the guy on the phony FBI card was supposed to kill her? Or shield her? Were the cellphone numbers for one, or both of them? If I called one of the numbers, would I tumble into some sort of bureaucratic panty-twist? The guns were dense and compact, their heft testifying to their serious reality. Real guns, real bullets—hollow-point bullets, in fact—dropped off at the airport with no more concern than a FedEx envelope full of invoices.

I've been on a shooting range once or twice but don't own any firearms. Toying with them, now, was a queer, macho thrill. *Take that. You're history. You talkin' to me?* I played to my reflection in the window glass, trying to stand tough. If you don't know how to entertain yourself, or enjoy your own company, then nobody else will like being around you, either.

(I thought only cops could buy hollow-point ammo in the state of California; it turns out ordinary citizens can, too. I checked. Being detail-biased is part of my job. People who don't sweat the small stuff, in my book, are called "unemployed." I don't have much sympathy for people who are content to slide by, with minimum effort, toward the easiest way out. They become the voyeurs of *other* people's lives.)

The itinerary for Alica Brandenberg was specific enough to suggest that she employed handlers to keep her dance card jam-packed. Visits to a gym or a salon were shoehorned between public appearances and inner-sanctum think-tanking: *Address assoc. hotel managers + reception. Meet researchers for update on Cal Pablo landfill/reclamation. Lunch w/ Ripkin rsrvs. Bistro Garden 12:45 P.M.*

Full stop. *Ripkin,* as in Theodore Ripkin, our political nemesis in the Jenks campaign? Rewind: Ripkin, as in our current lieutenant governor, noted by papers and newscasts as being in our fair town for most of the week? I knew he owned a house down here, somewhere expensive and private.

And apparently he was having lunch with the campaign manager of his opponent.

Guns, ammo, Alicia Brandenberg. Add Ripkin, however peripherally. Stir, shake, pour intrigue. Better: This might be the hangnail-edge of something that could be turned against Mr. Ripkin, for the benefit of all of Burt Kroeger's employees, not to mention his opponent, Mr. Jenks. A peek behind the curtain only I knew about, so far.

I had to give Katy Burgess a peek at this stuff, at the first opportunity.

Unless it was a setup. A trick, a trap, a gag, an advanced marketing scheme, or maybe one of those advertising role-playing games. There are some people I would not put this past, but I hoped Katy was not one of them.

Pedicure/private session w/Molly. Molly might also have been a masseuse; either way, Alicia's schedule bespoke plenty of loose petty cash to make all her running around more convenient. She was being chauffeured from gig to gig, too: *Confirm BLS pickup 7:30 A.M. (310) 576-0020.* BLS was a high-end livery service, and it looked like the car and driver were Alicia's for the entire day, at $120 per hour, less tip.

There was also a page subheaded *Profile Action Items* that more or less blurted outright that Alicia was romantically liaisoned with somebody named Garrett J. Stradling, corporate bigwig. Another page solely about Stradling revealed that he was the president of a company called Futuristics, Inc., which name I *did* know, from my job at Kroeger— Futuristics had been heavily involved in selling the Metro Rail subway project to the whole of Los Angeles at retail plus a million percent. Stradling had owned half the companies under the construction contract. After Metro Rail was a fact, I think Stradling went into private enterprise; I did not recall a mental picture of him. His profile had settled into the fog of past history. He had probably traded up, into anonymity, and what was left of Futuristics was most likely being run by somebody else. Executive turnover is one of the best ways to mint cash in a dicey economy.

Okay, this was getting interesting, in a Lifetime Channel way. Big money, power games, sex, and intrigue. Somebody phone Harold Robbins.

Wait . . . Harold Robbins is dead, right? The guy who once proclaimed himself to be the "world's best writer" is dead. (I know some movie producers who would say, "call him anyway.") Man, what a dated reference. For decades, Robbins was conversational shorthand for best-selling glitterati soap opera, the kind involving power-grabbers and lustful indiscretions. Beach reads. You know: Universally accessible melodrama about common human concerns as suffered by incredibly rich people. Always remember your cultural talking points. The problem comes when your topical shorthand spoils on the shelf and you haven't bothered to stay current on what has slid into their place. Voilà, you're old, and past it. Okay: Somebody call John Grisham. Great; in a few years nobody will get that one, either. Ever heard of William Shakespeare? Same deal.

I need to catch up on my reading.

It was mildly exciting to look at these puzzle pieces as a lurker, the way you try to suss out a detective movie because you have the comfort of not being at risk yourself. You try to catch the trick or the twist, and if you are like most ordinary people, you wind up resenting the story either way: If it fools or outfoxes you, you conclude that it is too murky or dense; if you guess the snap, you dismiss it as too easy. The story isn't allowed to be smarter than you or vice versa. It has to be *just right,* like most porridge, and indeed most blockbusters and best-sellers. Sorry, but that's the way the normal world works, and I should know because, like you, I think I'd never get fooled that way—because that's the luxury of living life as a bystander, where you never risk anything.

Paycheck junkies always admire brash criminals until the bad guys get caught. Commuters dismiss the flamboyant as pretentious children of privilege. Ordinary people cluck about revolutionaries, broadcasting their disdain for any kind of boldness. At some point, dreams are lost because the day-to-day fight to hang onto to what you've already got is too exhausting. You console yourself by talking about all the traps *you* would never fall into; all the ways *you* would never get fooled.

I wondered if I had become one of *them.* It happens while you're not looking.

I had to call Katy. Risk the embarrassment of the case being some elaborate gotcha. Cross the line of calling one of my fellow professionals during their free time. The Halliburton was weirdly crazy, but also very normal in its reassuring weight and reality. The guns sure seemed real . . . and if they were, did that mean the dossier spoke true? The FBI ID card evoked stability and reminded me that there were agencies and authorities trained to deal with crazy weirdness.

And if Katy started laughing at me, or got mad, then at least I would know more than I knew now, and that was an excitement I had not honestly felt in a very long time. I had to know.

It was still before midnight. It took four rings and I got a machine.

Beep. "Katy? It's Conrad. I know you're probably already asleep, but—"

"Conrad . . . ?" Her voice was a little blurry, but she had picked up, live, terminating the auto-answer. She screened her calls the same way I did.

"I woke you, didn't I?"

"No, I was asleep anyway."

I will admit that I admire people who can be sarcastic right off the pillow.

"Is this one of those heavy-breathing, middle-of-the-night phone sex things?" she said. I pictured her groping around in the dark by the glow of a nightlight.

"It's about Jenks and the campaign," I said. "Something I just realized, spun off something you said."

"Oh, Conrad . . . shelve it till tomorrow, huh? I don't wanna work now; I'm naked. Just talk dirty to me or something for five minutes and let me go back to sleep."

"I know; I'm sorry—"

"You know I'm naked?" I heard her emit a congested little snicker.

You can imagine the pictures that were now forming in my brain. Some DNA codings go all the way back to the dawn of time.

"No, of course," I spluttered. "I mean I'm sorry for the lateness of the hour and the rude awakening and all that, but I found something you need to know about . . . I think."

"Is it important?" More serious now; a bit more awake. "Are you okay?"

"Yes to both. Yes, I think it's important. Five minutes?"

"You're going to pay for this, big-time. Five minutes. Go."

I thought of her propping herself up in bed, clearing wisps of hair, maybe lighting a cigarette, settling in for this bedtime tale.

But I never got started because somebody was banging on my front door and calling my name.

I jumped like a teenager caught jerking off. My heart was trying to bend my ribs outward.

The door muffled the voice, "Conrad? You home? Oh, please be home . . . Conrad, come on, it's me, Celeste, from down the hall? 307? Conrad? Open up, *please* . . ."

"Hang on a second, Katy," I said to the phone.

"I'm hanging on."

"Be right back."

I left the unit rocking on the table (to put it back on the base station would be to hang up), slammed the Halliburton (almost guiltily), and hustled to my front door's security peephole.

First off, I live in a security building. That's (1). (2) was easy: I didn't know anybody on my floor, not by name. Which suggested: (3) that I had just crossed some invisible line and the game was on, whatever it was.

I wondered if there was a (4), dangling. Something I was missing.

I didn't know any Celeste from 307. I'm 318. Come to think of it, I not only didn't know anybody on my floor, but every soul in the building was a mystery to me. Not "neighbors"; that's why you pay for the security. Through the peephole I saw . . . well, cleavage. A hint of leather binding it all together. A woman's face, vaguely Asian, distorted by the eighteen-millimeter vantage of the spy lens. Black unbound hair. Kind of pretty. Stranger in distress. When I first heard the door, I'll admit I engaged in a brief fantasy that Katy had sought me out and shown up unannounced, naked beneath a trenchcoat or something, with a plaintive speech prepared about how she couldn't let our evening go without just one kiss. This wasn't that. Katy was still on hold, miles away.

"Can I help you?" (Why do people always say that?)

"Conrad? It's Celeste, from down the hall. Three-oh-seven. I know you don't know me, but oh God, she's not breathing and the goddamn cellphone went dead!" Her panic seemed genuine and her sentences were rear-ending each other in urgent need. Tears on her face. "I know your name from the mailbox please *please* can you just call 911 you don't need to let me in and *nobody else is home, oh my god*—"

Even before I got the door completely unbolted she seemed ready to grovel, saying *oh thank god* over and over. I have a steel Sentry crossbar lock with a hand crank. I like the Industrial Revolution look of it, and it can forestall a battering ram. The door is solid-core and cross-girdered. Nobody gets in, unless I want them to.

If nothing else, I wanted a better look at her. Sorry.

She was wearing black calfskin trousers and engineer boots, a kind of bustier-corset thing, and a silk wrap over that to cover her bare shoulders. Bright gray eyes the color of aluminum dust. Now she looked more exotic; Brazilian, maybe. And she kept talking in a torrent before I could interject.

"Oh, great, great, good, I *so* knew you were home, you're really a lifesaver, Conrad, I'm sorry we don't really know each other, but like I said I'm from down the hall—"

"307," I said. She had a roll of black duct tape in one hand.

"—yeah and I've got this, like, total *problem* that I just know you can help me with, right? Please?"

I was working on the reply when she hit me smack in the forehead with the center of her palm, and I blacked out before I could hit the floor.

My first name isn't on my mailbox. That was the missing (4).

I remembered the wet, beefsteak sound my skull had made against her palm and the feel of head-butting a concrete post. Then my dreamy attention was diverted by a sensation comparable to being stabbed in the brain with a stiletto made of dry ice. I woke up in a rush, with the stench of an ammonia ampoule flooding my nostrils, and there she was, looking at me the way you'd look at roadkill on your stoop.

"C'mon, wake up, goddammit. Stop pretending you're asleep. People do that at the dentist all the time; they pretend to be gassed out when they're awake. I *hate* that."

My eyes hurt to open. Rusty hinges. I definitely had a headache. I imagined scores of burst capillaries above my eyebrows. "I don't—"

"Spare me," she overrode me with a wave of her free hand. "Don't ask who I am, or what I'm doing here, et cetera, because that'll just waste time. I don't care if your name is really Conrad Maddox or not. It doesn't matter."

She had used my downtime to relock the door and familiarize herself with the contents of my wallet. The phone was cradled. Good-bye, Katy.

"You're a mess that needs cleaning up, and don't ask why, because you fucking *know* why." She cocked a thumb toward the Halliburton, still on my dining-room table.

Open, now.

Missing one of the guns, which accounted for her free hand.

"Stupid," she said dismissively.

I was mummified by black duct tape into my Dansk leather recliner, my ankles, wrists, and throat bound tight. It was hard to breathe.

She screwed a silencer onto the business end of a SIG SAUER. The size of the suppressor made the gun unwieldy, no good for anything except close-range work. I already knew about the bullets, and my mind painted nasty pictures. She pointed the gun at me, almost experimentally, testing for balance.

"Shouldn't mess around with things that don't involve you, Conrad. Shoulda stayed in your nice, safe, normal world of the walking dead. Curiosity, the cat, Pandora's box, all that? Bad idea."

What could I say? That I had the briefcase by accident? That I was not the guy she was looking for, whomever that doomed soul might be? Either way, she'd probably shoot me sooner, based on the quality of my excuse. This was a million times worse than *hey officer, you've got to be kidding, I know my rights, I pay your salary*. This woman's attitude said there was no room for negotiation—or stalling. In her mind, the jury had come back, and nobody was smiling.

"And you read the fucking files. Jesus. Y'know, if you'd've kept the case shut, you might have had a chance. Not now. So sorry."

She was wearing a pair of gloves, from the case. She flipped the bogus FBI ID wallet open right in front of my face.

"See? That's not you. So what are you doing here?"

"I live here," I managed to say.

Worse than the *worse* I'd just thought of, what if the case *was* meant for me? I didn't understand any of it. That made me the de facto biggest idiot in my area code. If the stuff in the case was meant to stimulate some revelation that might keep me from getting blown away right now, that magic golden punch line was staying under cover, sure as hell.

She shrugged. "See? Makes no sense. You're going to die for a reason that makes no sense. That's really dumb."

I abruptly understood what she meant about wasting time with fruitless, obviously desperate explanations. The sheer uselessness—mine—encompassed in her contemptuous use of the word *stupid*.

She snapped the action of the SIG SAUER, which set the hammer to full cock, and aimed directly between my eyes from about nine feet away, probably to avoid getting my brain matter on her boots, which looked expensive. "Thanks for the fingerprints on everything, though. Makes my part easier."

She smiled, holding the gun in a two-handed grip.

My mouth was constricted into an *O*-shape (think of Munch's *The Scream*) and my throat dried up as I tried to formulate some half-assed protest I couldn't think of anyway, and my whole body flinched and flinched again, trying to contract, and time really does expand, like they say, during stress or torture, and *bang*.

I don't know what happened.

There was a blinding flash of hot, solar-white, phosphorescent light, and a harsh blast of sound that seemed to punch all the air out of the room. I thought it was the gunshot, never mind the silencer. The sound of death is always loud, and for five, maybe ten, seconds, I was certain I was paid in full, or at least mortally perforated. My heart tried to break my ribs and pole-vault out my throat. All I could see were milky, purple sunburst globes. My nerves were screaming. I had an itch in my lower back that was driving me nuts.

The curtains were still wafting around, from the blowback. And Celeste, whatever her name, was sprawled on the floor, writhing feebly. Her right hand was gone and her face was a voodoo mask of blood, still steaming from the heat flash. Some of her hair had cooked into vapor and her eyebrows were gone. When I saw her track and grope around, I knew she was blind. When she grimaced and tried to roll herself to a crouch, I saw gaps where two of her front teeth had vacated. Her top was shredded and her blood-streaked breasts were exposed. Not implants. Pierced nipples; single posts. She made it halfway to standing, then collapsed and went still. I thought she was dead but after an instant I could see her still breathing—shallow, autonomic respiration. Not dead, not yet.

I could do exactly nothing. Duct tape is tenacious. What could I do? Manfully rip myself free at the cost of my own flesh, not to mention ruining a lot of Danish leather? Call the cops? And say . . . what? Help her? Why? Fifteen seconds ago she was getting ready to blow me away with a sharklike smile.

My skull was really pounding, now. What a riot on old Conrad.

Well, my deft verbal skills had sure gone on unpaid leave. Talking people into or out of things is one of my big guns, and I had just completely blown it.

This so-called Celeste person, by contrast, had come in like a total pro, even telling me I did *not* have to open the door—so I *would* open it, you see, to prove what a swell, okay guy I was at heart. A guy competent and self-assured enough to see poor little Celeste as no threat at all. She sold me a persona I was eager to buy.

And like a coward, I found myself wishing for the calm pool of how things had been just a tiny while ago, before the locker key.

Now it was gruesomely apparent that there were entire universes from which I had managed to insulate myself. We've all done it: Go for the pay hike, stay in the moribund job, seek and acquire the material things guys like me instruct you to value. Ever since my divorce, I realized, I had willingly given myself over to life in a bomb shelter. Touch nothing, and make damned sure nothing touches you. When you get very good at it, nothing will move you, either, and pretty soon, you're checking your own wrist to see if there is still a pulse. Then you contemplate opening a vein to ascertain whether your own blood is still in there.

I mentioned movies before; I watch a lot of movies and would deny the accusation that I experience anything vicariously through them. Los Angeles is an industry town in the way Pittsburgh is a steel town (or was) or Detroit is an auto town (or was). LA's product is visual media—movies, TV, Webisodes, dancing billboards. The raw material, the local "ore," if you will, is stuff of the imagination, which means that this industry, unlike all the others, is based on *making shit up*. That's too mysterious for most ordinary people to handle, and they disqualify the notion that Hollywood's "industry" is different or special in a variety of down-home, salt-of-the-earth ways . . . because to keep the world at large un-special is a great way to deny your own lack of individualism or status.

The point is this: In order to sell people things, you have to be movie-literate, because movies provide pocket homilies that roll smoothly off the tongue instead of any sort of cogent philosophy. Movies tell Blue State folks to beware of the Red States, and vice versa. Hell, movies even tell people what clothing to wear; what's hot and what's not. The reason we don't have royalty in America is because we have celebrities.

Which includes our politicians. Which was why it was so critical that Kroeger Concepts was chosen to paint the correct portrait of G. Johnson Jenks, so the electorate would buy it the way we told them to.

Katy Burgess always called them the "electo-*rat*."

So everybody logs their time, pays their tributes, keeps their heads down, locks their doors, and worries about pedophiles or what commercials will be on during the Super Bowl. It all works, after a fashion, providing a simulacrum of life . . . until you unlock your door of your own volition.

It had been nagging at me ever since I regained a soupy sort of consciousness. It was almost as though I had *willed* that goddamned key into existence to stir up the turbid compost of my life, which had become buffed, shined, rigorously arranged, and allergen-free, festooned with the correct car, the proper tank watch, the desirable living quarters, and an utter lack of oxygen. Friends? I had conditionalized them according to their usefulness. Lovers? I had used and disposed of them according to contractual double-talk.

Some sainted wiseass once said that you recognize the turning points in your life only in retrospect.

I had done my job and done it well—so well that I had pulled a kind of cell door shut behind me and saved everybody else the trouble of locking it. Did I want to shove someone like Katy Burgess into that grinder, where all the product emerges the same? I didn't think so; I kind of liked her. Talking with her, I was aware of being entertaining instead of forthright. My rule was never to discuss my past. There was only the *now*.

Was this just standard-issue, middle-aged cynicism and boredom? The kind of joy two decades of white-collar skills can bring?

Some other sainted wiseass once said that dramatic events accelerate your thinking. I'll say . . . especially when your life is thrown into jeopardy.

Like in the movies: The jeopardy is the turning point.

Here was the jeopardy: gunfire and bloodshed. Suspense, too—I was tied up firmer than a tree engirded by killing vines.

Like the weekend gambler, I had indulged a tempting little risk and lost my bucket of quarters. Would I moan about my superficial damage and retreat, having learned my lesson? Or would I take a bigger risk and chance learning something that could bust me out of the cage my life had become?

There's this guy I know—Katy had mentioned him back at the bar—who calls himself the Mole Man. He's an information conduit for Kroeger and a total eccentric. Nobody knows anything about him, not really. Sometimes he tries to talk me into coaching him on fine wines. It is his sheer lack of background that makes him fascinating; he just *is,* in all his weirdness. He doesn't care what's hot and what's not. He only cares about what's interesting. He *knows* things; all kinds of obscure linkages and arcana. I imagine you could sit down with him, no preamble or conditions, and within five minutes be swept away into some place you never thought you'd find worthy of note.

Once, when he brought up the topic of wine yet again, I thought: *He's inviting me in*.

But I didn't pursue it. I had work to do.

The Mole Man is a short bald guy—nobody would ever want to look like him. But to get inside the finely machined clockwork of his mind and live there awhile, that might be the key to making sense out of life. If not adventure, then at least answers, the kind that could liberate you from the dictates of mass manipulation.

All we ever need is a key.

An hour later, by the stereo clock, and I was still in my seat, needing more than anything to go to the bathroom, when I enjoyed another nighttime visitor. Another un-invitee. Celeste had not moved and was still breathing.

To yell for help from some Samaritan from another of my unknown neighbors would have been in vain. One of the selling points of the building in which I live is the soundproof walls. I was nowhere near a telephone, and in no position to manipulate one. Given help of any sort, I would have to wrestle the challenge of explaining the bloody, maimed woman currently spoiling the resale value of my Stahls carpeting. The duct tape held me, powerless, viselike at all points.

I wished I could backpedal; maybe ask Katy what was so god-damned *interesting* about this Alica Brandenberg person. I had plenty of time to wonder that myself. Ridiculously, the briefcase that might be hiding an answer, or five, was on the other side of the room, beyond the grab of some schmuck tied up in a chair.

Some admen call them bullet points. Some call them action items. Others call them flags (a term which, interestingly enough, comes from the pharmaceutical industry). In the movie biz they're called loglines. Their purpose is to boil away flowery filigree and get right to the steak. What did I know, right now, without the garni du jour?

Somebody wants Alicia Brandenberg dead.

Subterraneans are involved.

Alicia Brandenberg may or may not be lying about her past, according to Katy. She might have more than one name, history, dossier.

Best guess: Alicia Brandenberg was straddling the political fence, playing both candidates, Jenks and Ripkin. Or, she was a mole for Ripkin.

The rest was conjecture, and I was still firmly immobilized.

That's how it remained until a new intruder came in via the sixth-floor balcony. Like I said, I live in a security building.

He was just *there,* filling air that had been tenantless a moment before, a black silhouette through the sheers of my Odelay drapes. He appeared like a ghost, ninja-quiet, unmoving. I thought I was freaking out or hallucinating until he tickled the sliding door (silently defeating the Sentry lock there, too) and stepped inside.

Oh christ, this one was wearing a black ski mask. Black everything else, and what looked like dancing shoes. He stepped over the inert form of Celeste like it was no big deal. When he spotted the open case on the table, he muttered *goddammit to hell* and immediately slammed it shut.

Then he saw me, across the room, as if for the first time, as if I was the least of his worries.

"Lucky you," he said.

I can spin-doctor verbal pitches like a fighter pilot doing Immelman turns. I can go silver-tongued with zero prep and talk nearly anyone into nearly anything; it's part of my job. I can commiserate with clients and give voice to their inarticulate objections with the psychiatrist's trick of prompting trust. I am extremely skilled, verbally. And right now I couldn't dredge up a thing to say. At least half of my body was still convinced I was dead, and seeing all this from the ceiling, or a tunnel of light. I was mute with fear, and it was embarrassing.

The intruder stooped to pick up something behind my Donatelle quilted pillowback sofa. Celeste's hand. He held it gingerly between two fingers, like dead vermin from a trap, turning it this way and that. He, too, wore surgical gloves, snugged into the wristlets of a black, military-style brigade sweater. He emitted a tiny *humph* and walked to the kitchen to drop the hand into my vegetable-washing sink, the smaller one that was part of the marble butcherblock centerpiece. He rinsed off blood and something that smeared like lampblack, and dried his still-gloved hands on a paper towel from a chrome spindle I'd bought at Smarter Image.

He stood looking at the case again, and shaking his head. "What a classic," he said. Then he turned to me. "Are you shot?"

I shook my head no, rattling my forebrain.

"Are you sure?"

I shook my head yes.

"Are you *mute,* or something?"

Getting my voice to work was like trying to crack ice with a banana. I forced out a dry croak. "No." I swallowed. It hurt. "I'm not."

"Fucking amateurs." I didn't know whether he meant me or the still-motionless Celeste, or both of us. "Bet this was all a big surprise for you, am I right?"

I nodded again. "You could say that."

"Oh, I *could*? That's priceless. You're all tied up in a chair with a soon-to-be corpse in your lap, and do you *really* want to play stupid games? Maybe you should just go back to nodding, ace."

"She's not dead," I said.

He nodded, now. Better answer; no drama. He stepped toward her and pulled his own silenced automatic from a spine holster. The gun was black, the rig was black; I didn't even register it. He gave her two shots to the head, point-blank. The gun made a coughing sound like someone punching a cardboard box, one-two. The body on the floor jigged with the hits, expelled its final breath in a watery gasp, then settled, as though deflating.

"She's dead now," he said. "For sure." He moved closer, gun in hand, hands on knees, leaning down to inspect me. "She hit you in the head?"

I nodded. "Why?"

"Because your forehead is the color of a pluot."

"A what?"

"Pluot. You know—plum and apricot, a hybrid. Fruit. Look it up."

No, I didn't know that.

"You got anything to drink around here? I'm as dry as sand. Sure you do." He rummaged around inside my refrigerator (a KitchenAid double-wide in stainless steel that cost over four thousand bucks, new, and was mostly for show) until he found a bottle of sparkling apple juice. "You?"

"No, I'm good," I said, as though deferring another drink at a cocktail reception. Glib. Terrific. I needed to purchase a spare hour somewhere just to wrap my brain around the concept of this ninja-looking sonofabitch now standing in my very own living room, and until I found my voice I was going to sound like a complete tool.

He leaned against the counter. "Suppose I cut you loose? You going to cause any trouble, you think?"

He was making it my responsibility, and the implied threat was already lying dead on the floor. Smart.

"I really have to go to the bathroom."

"Don't want to leak all over your Danish cowhide? The reason I ask is because I have to decide what to do with you, and we have to reach an accord rather quickly, and—what's your name?"

"Conrad."

"And, Conrad, time is of the essence, and I need you to promise me that you don't have a hogleg hidden in the bathroom, or something equally laughable. I'll know if you lie, and I'm faster than you, and a better shot, too." A lockback knife appeared in his grasp as magically as the gun had. He snicked it open by thumb, without looking. It was narrow and mean, probably of German manufacture, with a clip-point blade.

"Try not to cut the chair." My follicles, from the back of my head to the cleft of my ass, were standing sharply to attention. Cold, sickly sweat had popped from my pores. I couldn't play cool, even faking it. My whole body would betray me, and I knew this man would see it, smell it, just *know*.

"Don't worry about the chair."

I saw him use a fingertip as a depth guide and he slit the tape around my wrists, again without really looking. I peeled loose and he handed me the knife.

"Well, go ahead, Conrad."

He had given me the knife and I clumsily freed my neck, then legs. It was a test, to establish fake trust. Dammit, that was one of *my* tricks.

"Does this have something to do with Ripkin? With Jenks? With the election?" I'm afraid I babbled.

"Don't know any of them," my intruder replied.

I closed the blade and handed the knife back to him, leery, as though feeding a treat to a surly alligator.

"Go. You've got two minutes."

I always try to default to levity. "Sure, I can have a nervous breakdown in two minutes."

"I mean it. Hurry." He was really loving that apple juice.

I walked like a zombie to the bathroom on numb, unresponsive legs. Closed the door. Didn't lock it. Made the mistake of staring at myself in the mirror. A huge crimson-violet cloudbank of bruise joined my eyebrows and the moisture on my upper lip was not perspiration, but thin drops of blood. My lying bladder mustered a dribble that would barely top off a shot glass. I flushed anyway. Rinsed my face. It hurt to touch my head. I leaned on the counter and tried to remember how to breathe. Hurry.

When I came out, the intruder was still in the same spot.

"Good," he said. "Now, Conrad, listen carefully because I don't have the time to explain things in detail or repeat myself. If you came out of that bathroom with anything in your pants besides your dick, tell me now."

"I'm not armed," I said. He patted me down regardless.

"Okay. Do you have any guns in the house I should know about?"

"Just what's in that thing." I indicated the Halliburton. "Can I please get some water?"

I saw his eyes and mouth compose a frown, through the holes in his mask. "Fuck, Conrad, it's *your* house; you don't have to ask. I thought you said you didn't need a beverage. And don't play that phony courtesy shit just because I have a gun. That gets on my nerves."

I poured and drained a crystal tumbler of seltzer, imagining I could feel his gaze boring into my shoulder blades, or maybe the horripilation of a gunsight, trained there. But when I turned around, he wasn't even facing me.

"Conrad," he said peevishly. "You're not my fucking *hostage,* okay? I ran a fast meditation unit while you were in the can and I've decided I can't neutralize you the way I did the kindergartener over there. You have inadvertently stuck your weenie into a fan, but you may also have saved my life tonight. For that, I have to break tradition and discuss a couple of things with you. Hot button items. Like these fellows Jenks and Ripkin—who they might be, I mean beneath and behind all the schmooze and persona, and how that involves you, because according to the crap in the briefcase you're part of their mix, in some mysterious switchback way. But in order to explore this like civilized human beings, we have to leave, like, five minutes ago. Unless you want to wait around for Celeste's pals, who will probably be storming your lobby by the time the news comes on."

It was three minutes till 11 P.M.

"You can stay here and try your luck with the, ahem, authorities, if you want. But I guarantee you won't see any real police for days, during which time you'll be detained by grim people who aren't very giving. Like her."

"She gave me a hell of a headache," I said.

He snorted. "Hmm. I guess she did. So let's you and me make like a tree and get the flock outta here. We have to dispose of *that*."

He meant the briefcase, not the corpse.

And he had not mentioned Alica Brandenberg at all, not once.

"Expect not to come back here for a while. Take some aspirin and we go."

I gulped some leftover Vicodin and killed another whole glass of bubble water. So much for my Katy fantasy. A brief vision of her, at home and safely asleep (alone, I hoped), made my sinuses throb. When I looked back, the gun was gone, the knife was gone, and my living visitor was holding the Halliburton.

"Shall we? After you."

He had also removed his stocking mask. It was the guy whose photo was laminated onto the FBI card.

There was a helicopter idly buzzing the building when we exited through the stairwell fire doors. It made me feel like a fugitive, already. My keeper pointed at a Pontiac Sebring parked in the visitor lot and keyed the doors open with a fob remote.

I could run away, sure, but the point of that would be . . . what? I'd spend the rest of my life (however short) wondering what the bejeezus had just happened to me. I mean, what would *you* do?

"What do I call you?" I said.

"You can call me Dandine," he said, as though he'd thought the name up on the fly.

"Well, Mr. Dandine—please tell me what the hell is going on?"

"In a minute." He shrugged into a black jacket and fired up the car, identical to my airport rental, except this one was not a convertible but a black sedan, with a sunroof. "First, we get clear of the hot zone. Second, we lose that fucking case."

That seemed wrong to me. The mystery, the questions, were all tied

up in the briefcase. To get rid of it seemed somehow counterproduc-
tive.

Dandine sensed this, apparently. "Here's what you failed to know
about that case. The center button, the one above the handle? It's a
microcamera about the size of a penny, with a 54-millimeter lens and a
DC power supply that activates when you open the lid. The second you
opened that thing, they had your face. How long after that did your
killer girlfriend show up?"

"About an hour?" I wasn't sure. "She said her name was Celeste."

"Whatever." He tooled us onto the eastbound 10 freeway. "Looks
like one of Varga's freelancers, which might explain a lot."

That didn't track for me, but I behaved as expected. Waited for
more.

"Interesting thing about that model," he said, meaning the briefcase.
"The inside is a polymer sleeve designed to present a bogus profile to
X-ray. Instead of guns and ammo, the scope sees a digitized representa-
tion of papers and folders as the contents of the case. That's handy until
some nosy baggage rat opens the case, but sometimes, it's handy enough
to get you to the next step."

"Does it blow up, too?" The damned thing was sitting on the seat
right behind us.

"Nah. Don't see those much, anymore. Drug runners still use 'em."

"Are you a real FBI agent?"

He smiled. "No. But that ID is the tits, ain't it?"

Dandine looked vaguely European to me, maybe it was his hairline,
or chin, or nose, or something. He had green eyes but wore contact
lenses that might have been tinted. Later, I saw him use eyedrops. Clean
shaven, maybe eighteen hours from the razor. Conventionally handsome, yet almost nondescript. That's hard to get across, that sense that
he could make you remember him, or make you forget him; always by
his choice. It was mostly in the eyes. Even now I can't summon a clear
mental picture of him, or tell you which movie actor he most looked
like.

"I've got an idea, Conrad, " he said. He was using that negotiator's
tactic of constantly repeating my name for emphasis. "You tell me
what you think is going on, and I'll butt in as needed. That'll be more

fun than us playing the license plate game while we're on the road, yeah?"

Around us, the fast-motion traffic of the 10-East zoomed. We passed some of them; some of them passed us; everybody changed lanes at high speed with impunity. Normal people on normal missions. Night shifters, speeding toward clandestine hotel affairs, or a late beer and indifferent sex at home. People on first dates. People on last dates, in separate cars. Road diggers headed to and from hole-patching work. Stoned kids in muscle cars. Rice rockets that were all bass hip-hop and no horsepower. Mexicans in pickup trucks that looked like they had driven through Armageddon en route to some leaf-blowing or janitorial gig. Tharn soccer moms up too late, driving too slow in SUVs too large, wandering lane-to-lane and pissing off everyone as they tried to manipulate mobile devices, texting, Tweeting, eyes on screens instead of traffic. Limos and taxis from the airport, inbound. We were inarguably the weirdest story on the road that night, I believe.

"All right," I said. "I got off my plane and found the key in my rental. I sat on it for a couple of days. What can I say? My curiosity got the best of me."

"Possibly fucked up the remainder of your life," Dandine said, not taking his gaze from the road . . . but also reminding me of my probationary status.

"I didn't open it until I was at home. It looked to me like . . . well, you know, an assassin's toolbox. With the lady in the envelope as a target."

Dandine chewed the inside of his cheek and nodded. Then irritation creased his face. "Fucking Zetts," he said.

He caught me looking.

"Oh, nothing. Just that some guy I trust, who possibly got bought out from under me, but more likely, fucked up a simple drop. Apparently he can't perceive the difference between a blue convertible and a black car with a sunroof." He thought about it for two seconds more. "Nah. He wasn't in on it." He glanced to meet me eye to eye. "You ever use marijuana in a recreational capacity, Conrad?"

I shook my head no.

"Don't start," he said.

I began to form a fuzzy picture of Zetts. "So this guy, Zetts, put the key in the car?" I asked.

"Yeah. Not time to kill the messenger, at least not yet. Knowing Zetts, I'd bet that he's not what you and I would call a 'complicitor.' Still, it was sloppy. Might have been more fun if you'd just turned the key in at lost and found, but then your life would still be full of badges right now, and that's no place anyone wants to be. If you'd've played it safe and tossed the key, you would be at home, asleep in your secure building under your nice Milford comforter, or maybe making some fashion model or wannabe actress swallow your DNA. Am I boring you, Conrad?"

"No way." I felt fatigued, but wide awake.

"What do you do?" he said. "This being Hollywood and all, I guess I should ask what you *really* do. You look like a studio executive to me. A Suit."

"I work for an ad agency."

"That's kind of like working in the movies, now isn't it? Your own company? If not, I'll bet you're pretty far up the ladder. Benefits, per diem for travel, perks, deductions, all that?"

"I'm a vice president."

That seemed to disappoint him, as though it made me predictable. I hate people who judge by first impressions. Who judge *me,* before I get a chance to charm them.

"A lot of cross-country jumping? Shit, man, you could be a courier and not even know it."

"No. I pack my own bags, like they say at the airport."

"Squeaky-straight, am I right? You ever cheat on your taxes, Conrad? You know—amp up those business dinners, run double receipts, pad the expense account? You ever lie to a woman to get her heels-up in the sack? Ever take stuff without paying for it? Oh, wait—guess we've answered that one, already."

I tried to cross my legs in the narrow footwell. I worried my hands, having nothing to do with them, playing thumbeldy-peg, interlacing my fingers compulsively, broadcasting my nervousness.

"The hit-kit you intercepted was for me," he said. "You opened it. They saw your face, not mine, and sent little Celeste to erase the op."

"Just like that?" I said. "See a face, shoot a guy?"

"Exactly like that. Tainted ops are immediately expunged. Better to start over from GO. Understand?"

It was similar to the mercenary tactics commonly used in advertising, politics, and food processing: the slightest pollutant could queer the whole pitch. One botulin-infected can of tuna fish could deep-six your entire commercial line, leading to a costly recall and an even more costly promotional flourish to prove how socially responsible you are; how much you care for your customer. Better to just flush everything and resurrect under a new label. Consumers did not like being dismissed as collateral damage.

"I think I get it," I said. "They have to act fast and decisively."

"This is the twenty-first century—you can't just hang up on a wrong number anymore and expect to skate."

"Yeah, but wrong numbers don't usually overreact and murder you."

"These numbers do."

"Then they need to work on their people skills," I groused. "If a deal goes south in my business, everybody in the office knows who dropped the ball."

The man who called himself Dandine winced . . . maybe at my use of two vile clichés in one sentence. "Doesn't work that way," he said. "Janitorial is immediately vetted to subcontractors."

And I was immediately in danger of drowning in a whirlpool of argot. If I didn't learn to speak this new language in a big hurry, I was going to flail-and-fail—a bit of in-speak I learned from Burt Kroeger. Better to let Mr. Dandine continue as interpreter.

This man rarely said anything he did not think over first.

"I assumed the case would have a tracking device on it, which is why we're getting rid of it," Dandine continued. "Sort of LoJack, with basically the same recovery window. That's how your dream date found you. She came in like a pro but went out like a piker."

"I don't follow." (*Always encourage clarification.*)

"She came to you dolled up, with no weapons. Let your glands unlock the door for you. She probably could have eliminated you with her bare hands. You had the case, so she thought you were me. She's never seen me, never seen you, so the fake ID didn't matter. Am I going too fast for you?"

"I'm with you so far."

"I mean, the car. Am I driving too fast? You seem touchy."

My teeth were locked from grinding. "Well, excuse the piss out of me."

He waved a hand. "Save it. You're going to complain that you fell into a rabbit hole and you don't know what the fuck is going on, that you're an accessory to a murder and you've just been abducted, and you're scared. I'll give you the last one. But for the rest, you wouldn't have seen that lady come apart if you had minded your own goddamn business. And you came with me of your own free will. So calm down. You want to stop for some herbal chai, or something?"

"No." Now my bladder was about to explode, from all the seltzer.

"Okay, to continue. Our darling—what'd she say was her name?"

"Celeste."

"Doesn't matter; probably a pseudo. She got cocky and decided to terminate you with one of the guns from the hit-kit. But they were booby-trapped with firebacks."

"You mean backfires?"

"No. Firebacks: burn charges designed to cripple and blind the shooter, not the shootee."

"Intended to hurt . . . you?"

"Mm-hm. Except I would have stripped the rigs and checked them, and found out when I eyeballed the ammo. Hence, our Celeste was an amateur, probably a freelancer."

"From someone named Varga. A subcontractor."

"Glad to see you're paying attention. Yep, I owe Mr. Varga a visit, and it might be ugly. But Celeste's employers either didn't know about the firebacks or neglected to tell her. Either way, that's uglier. I'm beginning to think she was hired by Alicia Brandenberg, or possibly her creatures, to roadblock me. Which throws an uncomplimentary light on my contractors."

There were too many balls to juggle. "The people who hired you to . . . er, kill Alicia Brandenberg?"

"Never use terms like that," he said. "Too definitive. Could give people the wrong idea."

"About what? Assassination by contract?"

"One of my friends used to call it 'maximal demotion.' It all means the same thing—to purge."

It was no worse than advertising argot, I thought. Vague terms designed to cloak and mislead. Potent adjectives, wrongly directed. The art of saying one thing and meaning another. Politician speak.

"Are you some kind of black ops guy?" I said.

"You seem to be a fairly literate man, considering your profession," Dandine said. "Right now you're thinking of terrorism, counterassassination, military coups, dirty tricks, Watergate, spy-spy, murky secret organizations, that sort of thing, am I right?"

"Well . . ." I fumbled. "What would *you* think?"

"It'd only be funny if you were wrong," he said. "You're in the ballpark. So I'll skip the smoke screen. You know why? Because it might be fun trying to explain it to you. There's a reason subterraneans call people like you the walking dead. You live blissfully unaware lives in an overworld that pays taxes. Sometimes you are collateral damage, and that almost *never* matters, in the scheme of the real world. But we'll save that for later."

"Any special reason?"

We had sailed north from the freeway and were now in the center of Hollywood. Dandine wheeled the car into a parking slot at a 24-hour drugstore.

"Because, Conrad my lad, we have arrived."

It was absurdly like a stilted, chaperoned date. I waited in the car while Dandine picked up decongestants from the drugstore. He said his allergies were bugging him. I correctly interpreted this as another test of my trustworthiness. As if I had anywhere to flee. As if I had more pressing business to conduct.

"If you do get out of the car," he said, "do not, I repeat, do *not* phone anyone. *Anyone*. They had a pull sheet on everybody you know or work with, as soon as they had your face on camera. That's important. I don't care how remote you think they are, or how much they love you. No calls, no contact with anyone. Agreed?"

I shrugged helplessly and concentrated on not pissing my pants.

Pull sheet? I confess I instantly wanted to know: (1) what was on mine, (2) what was on everyone else's, and (3) how I could access it. What Dandine did not know, and what I was thinking about now, was that there was literally nobody I cared to SOS or shoot an emergency holler toward. Not Burt Kroeger, my boss, therefore an assumed ally. Not my ex-wife. Certainly not Katy or any other lady friend. Not often do I admit to myself that the way I really work is by getting impatient once people have fulfilled the uses I require of them. A shrink would call it cold, emotionally isolationist.

But I couldn't picture Dandine having Friday night two-for-one drinks with a gang of *his* "co-workers," either. Maybe if I saw a gang of the type of pull sheets Dandine had referenced, I might know who to trust.

He returned and dumped a plastic bag in the seat. "Come on." He lifted the Halliburton out of the rear.

"Where?"

He pointed next door, across a parking lot. "Bus station."

"Why?"

He looked me up and down and cracked another of his almost-grins. "Because they have a men's room there, Conrad."

Checkmate, I thought, feeling idiotic.

"You're asking yourself, *why is this guy letting me roll with him,* am I right?" said Dandine. "I need to talk to you. About politics. I don't keep up with elections and candidates; it means almost nothing to me. Here."

He pressed some cash into my hand. "What's this for?"

"Go buy a one-way bus ticket to Denver."

"Am I riding the bus?"

"No."

"Can I hit the restroom first?"

"Make it fast." He was already scoping out the losers hanging around the vending machines, and the transients and bummers-of-change in the parking lot. He obviously knew what he was looking for.

"Go ahead," he told me. "Meet me back here in five."

I'd never spent time in jail, but the bathroom I located stank the way I always imagined a cell would. Urine, diseased shit, Lysol, ammonia, mildew, and more candidates for Dandine's review, though these were drugged out or unconscious. The sink mirrors were those metallic plates that are supposedly unbreakable. I saw sprawled feet in a locked coin stall, and heard snoring. There was water—well, moisture—all over the black-and-white tiled floor. Dried blood, or barbecue sauce, on one of the sinks.

God, I just said *I've never spent time in jail.* Just wait—that part gets better in a bit.

When I emerged, I queued up and bought a ticket. By then, Dandine had found what he was looking for—a man with that "help a homeless veteran" look. He was about fifty, sandy gray hair, with an occluded eye. Threadbare jeans, fatigue jacket, sneakers bound up with packing tape. He was holding the Halliburton.

Dandine was loitering near the storage lockers, leafing through a copy of *USA Today.* "Now," he said, "Go give that man your ticket and we're outta here."

The man sized me up as I approached, maybe wondering if he should ask for a few loose bucks. But he took the ticket as though expecting it and muttered, "Semper Fi."

Dandine had already walked out of the terminal. I had to hustle to catch up to him. "What the hell?" I said. "That guy won't even get on the bus—he'll try to trade the ticket back for cash."

"Doesn't matter," said Dandine. "He gets on or he doesn't—doesn't matter. He rides to Denver or finds a hidey-hole and tries to jimmy the case—doesn't matter. I basted the locks so he'll find it a mite difficult without tools."

"'Basted?'"

"Yeah, you know." He showed me one of those blister-cards that pack four tiny tubes of Super Glue. One was missing. "These are great. Pop the cap, one shot, throw away."

"Why?"

"He's a random factor. Control freaks hate random factors. If anyone is following the case, he'll toss 'em a few curves. Can you imagine how comic it would be if a black SUV pulled up and a bunch of secret agents jumped out, yelling *drop that case?*"

It was no longer our problem, but I did not feel *done* here, and Dandine smelled it.

"If you're waiting for a shoot-out or an elaborate strategy to outfox the people after the briefcase, forget it," he said. "It rarely works that way in the real world."

The man probably wasn't even a bona fide soldier, ex- or not. Nobody was who they appeared to be. He'd stand up to the best interrogation because he really, truly didn't know a damned thing. Buying the ticket was itself pretty smart. Pursuers, enemies, would waste more time trying to figure out why, connecting all the wrong dots.

Real operatives in real crises don't stand around waiting for ordinary citizens to appreciate how cool they are.

"I trashed the guns, swept the phone—it's bug-free—and kept the envelopes. No tracking shit on the paper. So the leash is slipped and now it's your turn to make yourself useful."

"I really don't know any more about these political guys than—

"Yeah, yeah." He seemed annoyed, aware of my obvious smoke screen. "Consider yourself my fucking captive if you want. You could have ended this evening strewn all over your living room. Or you could shut the hell up and let me ask my questions, and maybe you might learn something."

I had to remind myself that this man was armed all the time.

His personality seemed to speed-shift again, so it was a surprise when he asked, "You hungry?"

He was batting my brain around like a paddleball. The bus station lockers brought memories that made my gut lunge. The tape on the Nam guy's shoes reminded me of the duct tape with which Celeste had trapped me. The newspaper made me think of the big lie, the stage role we were both performing. Ordinary objects, unnerving new associations.

"Don't glaze out on me, Conrad," he said. "I need to ask you some questions about those politician buddies of yours, strictly for my own intel. If I'm going to quiz you, such good pals that we are, I should also offer you some disposable information in return that might make you see things differently. You know—value received. It's an ad concept."

The way I was looking around, any cop would ask to scrutinize my pupils.

"Conrad, look," he said. "I'm not going to hurt you. I am going to *use* you. Now, once again: Are you hungry?"

He next conducted me to Café 101, a glorified coffee shop near the Franklin onramp to the Hollywood Freeway. We commandeered a dark booth. The joint was fairly packed with people shouting over medium-loud music. The noise made me feel safer; we were hiding in plain sight. A caffeinated waitress with hair dyed a virulent magenta brought her cheery manner to our table. Her pants were low-slung and her starched white blouse, tied high, exposing a bare midriff of pale skin. I bet a lot of customers tipped her abdomen.

"What happened to your head?" she asked me.

"Birthmark," I said.

Her face narrowed into a sidelong glance. She had brightly indicated cursory interest in her customers, then I had set off her bullshit alarm. Fine, then—just serve 'em and forget 'em. When she bounded away I saw she had some sort of elaborate tattoo on the small of her back. *Tramp stamp,* Katy would have said.

"Now what?" I said to Dandine.

"Now we make like real Americans and do the burger and fries thing," he said. "And if you'll shut up a minute, I'll try to answer your question."

I ordered a milkshake to calm my stomach. Better than eating a pound of antacids and washing them down with Alka-Seltzer, and maybe some strychnine.

Dandine doodled on a napkin. "Ever hear of these organizations?"

He spun the napkin so I could read it. He had written: CRASH. I/KON. MORG.

"Nope."

"Most of them were deep cover phalanxes. The usual freak show— sociopaths supervising psychopaths. They'll always have a high burnout rate. The whole protocol of espionage changed after the 1960s and Kennedy. It hasn't been James Bond land for decades, but most people don't know, or give a shit. At one point in the early seventies there were a hundred and thirty-seven subgroups in the basement of America's power structure, and like rats infesting a tenement, they spent more time devouring each other than they did accomplishing anything useful. Mostly they headed off assorted scandals while causing others, and purged the odd foreign leader who might be getting too feisty."

"Maximally demoted" them, he meant. *Killed them.* In my business, when you were beheaded or chopped off at the knees, it was called "administrative leave."

"The hundred and thirty-seven ratpacks got winnowed down to a hundred and two, after which the umbrella designation for all of them was CII—not an abbreviation, but a Roman numeral." He wrote it on the napkin under the others. "One operative quite rightly called it a 'bureaucratic malignancy.' There was a similar mirror organization in Great Britain about the same time."

"Another hundred and two . . . spy groups?"

"And just multiply by country, as needed. To shut them all down meant the excision of hundreds of chains of command. Thousands of jobs, evaporated. It was like the French Revolution. Heads rolled."

It was an industry unto itself, I thought. And when industries become top-heavy and wasteful, they cave in or self-destruct. I've read Marx. Rather, Lenin.

He dunked the napkin in his water glass and the ink blotted away to a Rorschach abstract. He balled it up, wrung it out, and pushed it aside.

"Like a whole bunch of businesses competing for a tiny market."

"You've got it. Today there's only a few cells left with any power or leverage—the meanest, the cutthroats, the survivors. After I/KON and MORG became 'subpotent,' as they say, this week's winner was something called NORCO."

"Like the Impossible Missions Force?" I said.

Dandine wrinkled his brow.

"You know—" I said, flustered. *"Your mission, should you decide to accept it . . . ?"*

"Oh. TV." I suppose it was irrational to expect someone like Dandine to be fluent in what is oxymoronically termed "television culture." More reminders of other worlds, coexisting invisibly with what *he* called the walking dead. Parallel planes, like the gaps in a venetian blind. Head-on, it looks solid, but there are all kinds of slats to slip through.

Our meal materialized with admirable speed. It really was an impossible mission *not* to look at our waitress's navel, and she knew it. A sterling silver stud lived there, to catch the light and prompt the show. I cursed my male coding while she slid Dandine's plate into place, casually touching him on the shoulder and calling him *doll*. I thought about alpha wolves and swirling clouds of pheromones.

"Think of it this way," he said. "Most ordinary citizens' concept of enforcement goes like this: Cops, detectives, undercover cops, FBI, then CIA . . . and after that, it gets hazy. Maybe they've heard of the Division."

"What does it divide?" I tried, but he didn't laugh.

"Sits between the FBI and CIA. Now, think of all the subterranean cells as being in the same order, but starting with the CIA at the *bottom*. It helps to remember all the clubs essentially mistrust and despise each other, and that's a chink that can be exploited."

"What about the National Security Agency?" I hazarded a bite of club sandwich, and I don't know why it *bothered* me that it tasted pretty damned good.

"Not players. Remember, the NSA started out as 'codebreakers and codemakers,' ever since the end of World War Two. They umbrella SIGINT and INFOSEC. Did you know the NSA employs more mathematicians than anyone else? People got the NSA confused with subterranean ops back at the turn of the century—all that so-called 'terrorist' shit."

"It's sexier now," I said. "Now that we live in a world of red, white, blue, and yellow alerts."

"Bottom line: The more agencies there are, the more time they have to spend spying on each other instead of doing any sort of sociopolitical work. Then they have to police themselves for suborganizations *within* their own clubs. So you stand a decent chance of getting misfiled, or slipping through some loophole, I know not what."

It sounded as though he was trying to soften some blow, or set me up for worse things coming. "So . . . where is NORCO on the food chain?"

Dandine filled his glass with Rolling Rock and drank half in one swallow. "Ever wonder what happened to the jobs the Impossible Missions Force turned *down*?" He chuckled at his own gag. "That's NORCO."

"What does that stand for?"

"I have no idea." He destroyed most of his turkey burger with the relish of good hunger. (My mom used to tell people that *hunger is the best seasoning;* at least, that's what I tell people. *Amusing personal maxims* build client trust.) "Rather, you might say that whatever they *say* it stands for; it probably stands for something else entirely."

I sipped my milkshake. It was pretty good. I watched our server gallivant from customer to customer. Her whole manner was probably a front, too. It worked, what can I say?

"So . . ." I tried to gather thoughts in air, like invisible sand. "Somebody, somewhere, needs to erase somebody else named Alicia Brandenberg. Somebody, somewhere else, pays you to do it on a kind of work-for-hire basis. A whole bunch of other somebodies fuck up the plan, and I'm stuck with a dead body in my apartment, and . . . crap, I can't believe this is happening."

"Because we're not on the same page yet," said Dandine, finishing off his beer and refusing a second. "Here's how I see it: Miss Alicia and I are supposed to dance, one quickie, done deal. But the plan leaks, and moves are made to counteract it. Now the shooter is supposed to blow up, sparing Miss Alicia in the process, and making the whole setup look like an abortion—a failed attempt on Miss Alicia. I was supposed to be the patsy, the fall guy. Then you came along. You're the most valuable thing I could ask for in a situation like this: A totally random factor with no knowledge and no experience."

"Gee, thanks, now I *really* feel insignificant."

"No, thanks to you I have a better chance of doping this out."

The dregs of my shake tasted dead and flat; tacky, too sweet. "Couldn't I have just handed the case over to some TopGuy, or the Chief or something? Apologize and forget about it?"

Dandine was nailing me with that look of pity, again.

"Sure, you could have—that's why I removed the option. Then you *could have* wound up with a gang of mystery doctors, who *could have* jabbed a syringe full of Freon into your brain, selectively erasing your memory centers until you forgot what they wished. Along the way, you *could have* forgotten how to stand up, or not shit yourself, or keep from drooling." He worked his incisors with a toothpick and I saw a thin line of blood from his gums. "You don't grasp how this inevitability works in the world. Your comparative guilt or innocence is no longer a factor. After all, you chose to open the box. Past that, you're a wart, and it's easier to just *X* you out."

You think your entire existence can't evaporate in an instant? Think again. At the very least, I had to acknowledge my low status in the food chain.

"Listen to me," he said. "One thing; if ever you do find yourself explaining this to an important looking functionary in an overpriced suit, and he smiles and tells you it's all just a 'misunderstanding' . . . brace yourself for a bullet to the head."

Our waitress caught the tail of Dandine's last line and arched an eyebrow. She scooped up the check and the money Dandine had laid out, a total pro, still too cute to live. I automatically reached for my billfold and Dandine made a face.

"Nah, I got it. This is rough enough on you, I bet."

I had to say it, "Your treat?"

"We might as well spread around some of this currency before we have to toss or burn the rest of it. Before they nail the serial numbers or tip to the tracking ink."

(This was just after the Treasury had changed the look of the $20 bill . . . again. First it had become what I called "big head money," with amplified, hydrocephalic presidential profiles spilling past the borders. Now it was a riot of hidden watermarks and foil strips, sprinkled in a snow of golden numbers as if for a remedial child—*now look, honey, this is a twenty, see? Twenty-twenty-twenty*—with a deranged inking scheme that appeared to me to have been run through the wash cycle in a pocket alongside a leaky blue pen. Our money had changed so much in the past few years, my thoughts were: [1] indecisive government, [2] field day for counterfeiters, and [3] we win the goofiest currency on the planet award. You could have three different forms of this one bill in your wallet at the same time. Yeah, that makes everything easier.)

I stared at the spot where two twenties had been a moment before. "That was from the briefcase?"

He dipped his head once; affirmative. "All they'll know is some landed at the bus station, and forty bucks more landed here, a couple of blocks away. They're waiting for us to try swapping out the whole bang for clean cash."

"And . . . we're not going to do that?"

Another dip of the head, like a teacher approving of a satisfactory test answer. "And we're going to be best pals, until I can amass some more data. Remember not to whip out your credit cards for anything, either."

"You have a charming way of diverting the question of what's going to happen to me."

He rose and returned the waitress's passing appraisal, with just a hint of heat. She would remember he was handsome; she would remember her substantial tip, but she probably would not be able to describe his face. I had been staring at it for hours, now, and I knew it would turn to fog if I tried to describe it to a sketch artist. His face was . . . "uninhabited."

"Conrad—as for what's going to happen to you, I don't fucking know. But you're stuck. We can get there easy, or hard. Pick one."

Introspection has never been one of my bullet points.

My head was still swimming with an alphabet soup of sinister organizations, as reeled off by Dandine. If it was a smoke screen of noise to hide a larger lie, it sure worked. Looking at this man whom I still can't describe in terms of facts and figures, I saw a man looking at me the same way. He was wondering who the hell I really was. Which meant *I* was now wondering who the hell I really was. In pro wrestling, this is called a "reversal." Who was Conrad Maddox, this skin I wore?

Hunger is the best seasoning. Thanks, Mom.

The person I presented to the world had no parents, no relatives, no ties that could not be clipped if they got messy or personal. This person, this version of me, was notably different from the person he once was. Blame was always assumed by others—*oh, he had a bad marriage, another failed career, a rebuilding year, a crappy childhood, a personal tragedy.* You take all those possibilities and toss them off in a no-big-deal way, and no one will ever press you for details. They will simply assume you have the same retinue of damage that everybody else pretends to carry around as a life burden. It's sleight of hand at its best, and we all do it. . . . Why?

To make ourselves *appear* more interesting than we really are. To be the spy at the airport, like in that old George Carlin routine. In the airport, surrounded by total strangers, you get to pretend to be mysterious. *There's a spy at the airport! Your job: FIND HIM!*

To pretend to be characters like Dandine. . . . Why?

Have you ever seen one of those action flicks where ordinary people more or less just like you are suddenly plunged into a whirlwind of conspiracy and have to spend the next hour running away from helicopters and black SUVs? The thrills, if they work, are vicarious. Try taking it on the lam for twenty-four hours with no food and no rest and tell me it's something your inner hero craves.

No, people want to entertain the fantasy that anyone's life can become exciting and dangerous in the blink of an eye. The sticking point is that nobody wants to actually risk anything. Not the paycheck, not the family, not life as we know it in these United States.

However, a vast majority of *those* lives do not constitute "living."

Hence, the world of the walking dead.

Guilty.

You mate suitably, pay the bills, and wait around to die. The rest is just buying stuff. You buy the stuff you've always wanted, then you upgrade to more expensive stuff. Until you die.

You consume movies and books and art, because those can dream for you, when you've lost the fashion of dreaming.

And I haven't dreamed of anything for a long time.

What I do instead is target the next conquest—the next job, the next lover, the next mark. It's an atavistic hunter-gatherer gene that still fires because it's got nothing left to aspire to.

Now, walking with Dandine is dreamlike, unreal. But I can taste the air, smell the city pulsating all around me, and see my reflection in the windows of the coffee shop. It's me. My blood is alive. I literally have no idea what I might be doing five minutes from now.

So, who am I?

Try this question on yourself, sometime.

Outside the coffee shop, he lit a cigarette from a burnished ebony case in his jacket pocket. It was whisper-thin, about the size of a business card case. Two cigarettes leaned against each other inside like sad sentries. Having nothing more intelligent to offer, I said, "You need more smokes?"

"No. I allot myself five of these a day. They're best right after a meal."

"Smoking less and enjoying it more?"

He was taking his time strolling back to the car, practically sauntering. "Something like that."

We were about the same height, I noticed. Part of my mind was busily indulging a paranoid whim involving Dandine's substitution of my own dead body for his, in some elaborate bait-and-switch scenario, which would explain why he was keeping me close. It was tough to think about this and force idle, personal chat—the kind I normally use to massage a client—while not barfing up the white-hot ball of worry that sizzled between my lungs.

"Is Dandine really your name?"

He chuckled, to himself. I wasn't included. "No comment."

"Mr. Dandine . . . are you going to kill me?"

He stopped, turned, and faced me, his smile clicking off as though on a motion sensor. "Don't try to tell by looking in my eyes," he said. "Get in the car."

This was a negotiation, a contract conference, and it was time for me to haggle. To strengthen my position via objection and contraindication. "The world's nicest hit man," I said. "Why is he so pleasant and forthcoming? In my business, people use honesty and familiarity to hide the bigger lie. So I'm thinking, what's the lie, here? Could it be that you're going to cancel my ticket? I've been beaten up, home-invaded, bound and gagged, shot at and practically kidnapped. But you say it's all smooth, don't worry. When people insist on telling me not to worry, *that's* when I start to worry."

He pitched his smoke and spread his fingers across the roof of the car. "You give up and go home. Aim for a good night's sleep. You won't get it. You'll have an ass-full of NORCO agents in your way. Try to walk back into your life with your head high. Just make sure you have your estate in order, because there won't be a funeral, because they'll never find your corpse. See ya." He shook his head again and got into the Sebring.

"Wait a minute!"

He started the car.

"Unlock the fucking door, goddammit!"

He idled just long enough to rile me, then buzzed the passenger window down. "Can I help you?"

"Just wait a minute, will you? God!" My heart was racing and I had broken a new sweat.

"I don't need you anymore, Conrad. The briefcase can't do anything except lead back to you, and you're a dead end. The rest, I can do myself. You can blab all about me, all you want—it's just the usual mess of conspiracy theories any paranoid schizophrenic could have made up. Secret agencies with funny names. A laugh riot. Best of luck with your career."

He started to roll up the window and I hit it with the palms of both hands.

Understand something: I did it impulsively, already angry that I was spending so much time beating myself up. I had the sudden, taboo urge to hit something, and I just did it—practically a first.

The safety glass bowed and shattered into a crescent shape, a shark-mouth, and suddenly my wrists were gouged and bleeding. When I looked toward him, it was down the muzzle of a pistol.

"Think first," he said.

It wasn't fair. He wasn't sweating. I doubt if his heart rate had even changed from when he was calmly smoking.

Again, the smile, but this time, it was actually connected to his eyes, which glinted with mischief. "Conrad Maddox, Man of Action," he said.

Then the son of a bitch started laughing. It started as a stuttering exhalation that turned into a chortling cough. Then the dam broke. He laughed out loud. He smacked the steering wheel. He clutched at himself. He had to mop his eyes with his gun hand. "I'm sorry," he tried to say, and this propelled him into another paroxysm of mirth, at my expense. He put a hand into the air to steady himself, like an actor trying to wipe his expression clean for a new take. No good. That busted him up again. This paragon of control was out of control.

"I'll just stand here and bleed," I said, brushing glass cubes from my arms.

"No, no . . . it's not you, it's . . . ohh, hoohoo . . . !"

Terrific. If I had been hit with a cream pie, Dandine couldn't be more hysterical.

"It's . . . ahhh . . . you *broke the window ohhaaaahahaha!*" He stuffed the pistol into his crotch and tried to compose himself. "You looked so fucking *serious,* man!"

"Shut up."

"I . . . can't. Look, Conrad, what do you want?"

"That shit you were running about guys in JCPenney's suits swarming over my apartment? Prove it."

He really was just going to drive away and leave me; exit my life, fast as a finger snap. But something in his eyes told me he might consider indulging this stranger, this member of the walking dead, for a few moments more just because it seemed exotic to him. And look at me: begging my captor to hang onto me, in a sort of ultimate perversion of the Stockholm syndrome.

Good god, maybe he felt *sorry* for me.

"You opened the door," I said. "I don't want to just stand on the threshold. If some of the things you said are even remotely true I can't ease back into whatever I was before tonight. I know you understand that much. I need to understand more. Please."

It was a sales routine, and we both knew it.

He huffed out a sigh hinting at some of the things I suspected inside him. He could keep me for a few more minutes or take me to the pound.

Or euthanize me, if I pestered him enough.

Finally he said, "All right, climb aboard, but mind the . . . *glass* . . ."

That shoved him down the fun-chute again, and I willingly got into a high-powered vehicular deathtrap with an armed man who was apparently a gibbering lunatic. What the hell, it wasn't even 2 A.M., yet.

He handed me a fairly expensive looking pair of Zeiss binoculars. "Four down, three over from the west face of the structure," he said. "See it? That's your apartment."

The magnification screwed up my ability to count, and I had to resist trying to squint and see the display through one eye. "How'd you get onto my balcony?"

"Trade secret."

I craned up to the top, then down, then over. Windows, mostly dark, rushed past in my amplified view until I found my balcony. Funny; I'd never bothered to place it before, from the outside of the building. Now it seemed as obvious as a billboard—more so because my lights were on, and I knew I had turned them off when we first left Celeste's body there, cooling off.

Somebody (just a black cutout shape against the light) came out onto the balcony, lit a cigarette, and was joined by another black shape.

"NORCO," said Dandine.

"Shit," said me.

"You don't have any, like, nasty Polaroids of yourself hidden up there? Incriminating evidence about your secret, gay double life? The infamous 'second set of books'?"

"No." I felt weirdly embarrassed that my home life offered no evidence whatsoever that I was cutting edge. The knives from my De Vries butcher block barely ever got food on them. The most provocative thing in the kitchen was a few bottles of pretentiously priced Cabernet, alongside some higher-class gift wine. There were five or six photos of my ex-wife shoved away in a drawer, in exile, and she had her clothes on in all of them. We had never been huge snapshot hounds. Most of the stuff in the kitchen had been bought out of catalogs. There were one or two framed prints on the walls, practically screaming my lack of personal character. My home looked like an upscale hotel room, anonymous and functional. They're weren't even any intriguing stains on the 300-thread count sheets.

The ultra-dull catalogue of my previous existence. Like, from birth until . . . yesterday.

"They're turning the place over," said Dandine, "trying to get a handle on where you'd run away to. It's important for you to avoid anything familiar. If you've thought of it, they'll know it. Including people. You want to get closer, or you want to take a side trip to your office so I can show you *that's* open for business, too, right now?"

Strobes of flash starkened the balcony shell at regular intervals.

Pictures of things being captured for analysis and discussion. Maybe some of them would be suitable for framing, as urban studies. Still lifes.

"See the van?"

"Where?" I lowered the binoculars.

"Double-parked over there, no running lights, no trim. That's where our friend Celeste will be dumped, like baggage nobody will claim. They'll have a hand-to-hand team watchdogging this place for a while, hoping you'll think the heat is off, and come back for something valuable. They go to training seminars to learn how to be inconspicuous. It's a growth industry."

Dandine eased back in his seat, like someone used to long stakeouts. "The best smugglers look like accountants. No sharp edges on their personae that would stick in your mind. That's been going on for so long that the bland outward face has itself become a template for a potential smuggler, for all those VICAP and profiling obsessives. Back and forth, like a seesaw, and you always have to know which end you're on today."

"Civilians," I said. These ghosts had to *rehearse,* to look like the walking dead. "What media define as ordinary people."

"Exactly; now you've got it."

Pause now, for my insanity defense.

It had been hectoring me ever since I noticed Dandine and I were the same height: the notion that he might not exist, that he was a projection, my doppelganger, an idealized, spy movie alter ego. An invisible man in the "real" world. Dandine's commentary emphasized how un-special I was, then he trumped the game by noting how un-special he *had* to be, in order to succeed. I quit smoking five years ago, but when Dandine whipped out his little case (augmenting it just enough with the history hinted at by his nicotine diet), I felt the old jones for a butt slam in harder than ever. I knew without asking that he would not smoke another until the next stage of our nighttime mission had been accomplished. He used the cigarettes, as I would have, as punctuation in his workday. I would mention that maybe I was losing my mind and that he was me, like that guy in that Brad Pitt movie . . . and Dandine would say he'd read the book, but not seen the film. Stuff like that. He avoided talking about himself *(always make the client sell himself),* but much of what he did offer made him sound like an alien observing Earth culture from afar, or a visiting animus from some parallel spirit plane. He seemed to know the score and had all the answers, the way I would expect him, as a fictional character, to just *know* things not apparent to the rest of us.

Or maybe I was just exhausted, free-associating myself into a padded room.

"It's time to go visit Mr. Varga," he said, wrapping the topic of my apartment, is-it-is-or-is-it-ain't.

"Maybe I should just curl up in the backseat, you know," I said, "and cry myself to sleep."

"No. I need another set of hands and eyes, and right now is ideal for a social call. You hit them at night, when they're tuckered out or perhaps have had a couple of cocktails. It hampers their menu of reactions."

"What you meant when you said you were going to use me?" I said. "Does that mean you're using me now instead of Celeste, back there?"

"No. It means I want you to pay attention, and alert me if something smells funny. Something I wouldn't notice. I'm serious."

"How?" How was I supposed to become sensitized to a world I barely understood?

"I can't explain it, Conrad—it's the sort of thing you'll know when you see it. Why you? Because you're here. Besides, you have yet to tell me what I want to know about those politician fellows, remember them?"

"You didn't ask me."

"That's right," he said knowingly. "Celeste is academic."

Fair enough. "What about the window?" I said. "There's glass all over your car." I still felt sheepish about it.

He said exactly what I thought he would say. "Don't worry—it's a rental."

We took the freeway downtown and wound up near the top edge of Compton, a confusion of railroad switch-tracks and warehouses lit by harsh, sodium vapor lamps, in the middle of Ramparts Division, locally notorious with the LAPD as gang central.

On the way I explained what I knew or could cobble together about the cryptic G. Johnson Jenks, as referenced in the hit-kit folder on Alicia Brandenberg—the same bullet points I had uselessly amassed while tied up. I slammed into the brick wall of how little I actually knew about Kroeger's political client, and Dandine glanced at me with an arched eyebrow, as though I had just made it all up. My big hole card of presumed information was useless.

"This is why you never get involved with a contract client beyond their dossier," he said. "The water just gets muddier. Kind of the opposite of your line, come to think of it."

He had a point. One of my job skills, borne of necessity, was the cultivation of bogus intimacy, the ability to read between the lines of a dry printout and extract the one personality quirk that would make your target believe you were on the same frequency, that you were simpatico.

It hit me like a bolt of heat lightning in the desert: I needed something I could *sell* Dandine. And he was allowing me a bit of latitude to find out just what that might be. In a way, I had reinforced his latent need to *give* me that latitude . . . or so I deluded myself.

I used to think I was a lot smarter than I was proving to be now. And Dandine was a world-class expert at teasing a fish, this capacity exacerbated by what I was coming to see as a weird disposition toward the oblique. He was definitely one of those adverse to authority or stated rank, a condition common to thinkers. He enjoyed bumping the rulebook out of true. He was doing it now, by allowing my ride-along, and leaking more of his psychology to my inner salesman. I could not go passive; he'd smell it.

"So you missed the case," I said, "and found me. How does *that* work?"

"I had to access the car rental records," he said. "Which delayed me. Almost too long."

"Kroeger rented the car, not me."

"Kroeger's records led to yours. You know that dossier on Alicia Brandenberg? You should see the piles of data that was condensed from. In fact, you should take a look at *your* life-file, one of these days, if you ever get the chance."

The secret records that sum up your whole life, that big imaginary file folder with the stamps and seals? You've always suspected its existence while shrugging it off—*naahh, there's nothing interesting about* me *anybody would want to know.* But that's two different things: the facts, in excruciating detail, versus someone's desire to know them, justified or not. The facts, the file, remains . . . and Dandine had just said that one of those mystery folders, in some secret place, had my name on it.

Privacy is another illusion, like national security.

Dandine took a few labyrinthine turns inside a huge lot populated with equal numbers of big-box trucks, vacant slots containing parts trailers or other on-hold junk, and automobiles that appeared to be bombed-out, forsaken, or at least had been sitting there long enough to get dusty.

"Do I sit in the car again?"

"Negative," he said. "They already know there's two of us."

"How do you figure?"

"We've been dogged since six blocks back. Varga uses spotters." I saw his eyes check the periphery and mirrors with metronome relentlessness. "But something's cooking. I'm sensing a lot more spotters than he needs for simple security."

"What?" I said. "You're telepathic, now?"

He snorted. "No, just observant. You learn to see how controlled spaces are monitored. Shadow profiles. Negative movement. Maybe the watchers are being watched, and maybe they don't know it, but I know it. Rather, I sense it. Unconfirmed. You ever hear that expression about growing eyes in the back of your head? Now would be a good time to start."

Every time Dandine answered a question I felt more in the dark than ever.

He made sure to park with adequate cover from multiple angles; I did notice that.

"Now," he said. "Do you want to continue to play?"

Flashbacks of game shows crowded my head. Door Number One, Two, or Three? Dandine would know that, then wait for me to ask what he was talking about, then tell me that I couldn't afford the luxury of dissipate fantasy. I could impress him by skipping the obvious. I nodded, feeling my own reluctance.

51

He sketched it out for me, "You're my associate. You don't have to say anything unless somebody addresses you directly. Just stand behind me about two paces, with your hands folded in front of you, and try to avoid direct eye contact, like it's all beneath you. Think you can manage that?"

"Hell," I said. "It's exactly the same as a bid conference."

"A what?" Dandine paused in midexit.

"Your company's got a bid on an account, but so does another company. They're the enemy, and you have to out-macho them by pretending it don't mean nothin'."

He rolled that around in his brain for a moment. "I think you'll do fine." What he did not say was *I want to toss you onto the firing line and see who flinches,* because that might have made me bolt outright.

He led the way up a roll-off ramp to a metal staircase. There were lights on in the office, about three stories from ground level. The shutters were cocked halfway, and they looked very sturdy; probably bulletproof. He rapped exactly three times on an all-metal door, and we were quickly sized up through a view slot even though there was a surveillance camera mounted behind us, up high, painted black. Dandine's knock was businesslike. I hate it when people try to knock "cute," or do shave-and-a-haircut. I hate it when people try to compose creatively adorable and individual outgoing messages on their answering machines. Grow the fuck up. Most people are un-special and untalented, and always will be. Otherwise, I'd never be able to sell them anything at all.

The door unbolted and we were admitted by a gigantic guy who looked: (1) Samoan, and (2) born without a sense of humor. Oh, and (3) He was holding an automatic pistol that dwarfed his big hand. He nodded with recognition at Dandine.

"How's the music biz, Thule?"

"Sucks, man. Who's the bread sandwich?"

"My associate." I tried to duplicate Dandine's deferential nod, and look anywhere but into Thule's deep-set, unblinking, judgmental eyes.

"We gotta do the thing," said Thule.

"Absolutely," said Dandine, raising his arms for a poke-and-pat. It was no different than going to the airport, these days. When Thule

was done with me I was sure he could name the brand on my underwear.

(American Male, full briefs, gray. As good as Calvins but less expensive. I'm glad I don't usually have to go into this much detail. Now, I
thought, I could get wiped out by a speeding bus, and the only way paramedics could identify me was by checking my underwear, and they'd
write *American Male* in the box for my name. In the last few hours, I
had thought about death more than I ever had before. Personality Modification Checklist Item #1: I really needed to shunt more effort into not
being ridiculous.)

Dandine had made a point of wearing a single gun for the benefit of
Thule's search, leaving the rest of his personal hardware in the trunk
after shuffling some of the payoff currency into separate envelopes. I
had neglected to ask why. I was learning to save my tyro-sounding
questions for, you know, the good stuff.

We were ushered past a few more homicidal-looking dudes with a
lot of piercings and tattoos—half of them looked mildly high—into an
office where most of the furnishings were stacks of paper and boxes.
The dust layer was nearly an inch thick. This was the room with the
window shutters. The centerpiece was a banged-up, metal office desk
the size of a big refrigerator laid on its side. There were seven separate
multiline phones on the desk, and what I took to be some "drug para-
phernalia," based on what I'd seen in movies.

Seated behind a fly-vision bank of security monitors was Varga, who
resembled a generational dime-a-dance mix among Asian and Mexican partners, with some of our darker brethren stirred in to cool his
gaze. The sclerae of his eyes were completely yellow. He was shaved
bald (you could see the pattern lines on his pate) and had a gold stud in
his upper lip, as though to plug a small-caliber bullet hole.

"You the last motherfucker I expected to see," said Varga, not standing. His hands were knobby, callused, and prearthritic; he kept both in
plain view on the desk blotter. "Who's the luggage?"

"This is my associate, Mr. Lamb."

I realized he was talking about me. I stood back, partially in shadow
from the feeble throw of the desk lamp, folded my hands, and tried to
hang tough.

"What'd you do to his head?"

"Bizarre flossing accident." Dandine indicated the monitors. "You expecting celebrities?"

Varga was keeping his gaze on the multitude of tiny TV screens, speaking to us without looking at us a whole lot, his eyes scanning left to right, giving each screen about three seconds in succession, then back to one.

"Things have been weird for a couple hours now," he said.

Dandine got right to it. "Alicia Brandenberg—I need to know everything you know about her."

"Who?" Varga grinned, finally looking at Dandine for the first time that counted. It was part of the jockeying.

"Shit," said Dandine, looking to the side, disappointed. "I didn't want to waste any of your time, and here *you* are, wasting it anyway." He blew out a long sigh and sank both hands into his pockets.

"Careful," said Varga. Two goons appeared to bracket the door, like djinn, gently summoned from a bottle.

Dandine withdrew his hands and showed them in the light, front and back. "Anyway. Alicia Brandenberg, spelled the same as the town. A political pain in the ass that needed tweezing. Except she found out, and she called some guys, who called you. And you sent home delivery right before midnight. Extra sauce. Sorry, but the service was lousy, so no tip. It all smells like NORCO to me, and you know what we say about whatever NORCO says."

"Yeah." Varga grinned. "Do the opposite."

"Now, you can catch me up on the details, all of which I don't know. But I'm a good guesser. Or, you can be an asshole. Please don't be an asshole; if it's NORCO, you're so far down the pecking order that it won't hurt you."

"Cost me a good little worker, looks like."

"Yeah. Otherwise I wouldn't be standing here with Mr. Lamb. I'm here to make good on that. All I need is a contact."

"Fuck you. Why should I help you now? You owe me from before; you got too big for your *pantalones,* dick-suck. Get the fuck outta here before I shoot you in the ass and make Thule eye-fuck your faggot lover, there."

Dandine refused to rise to the bait. "C'mon, Vargs, you're just pissed about your little honey. I understand that."

"Man, she was the bomb, and you just fuckin broke her in two before I could really run her."

"Not true. The delivery itself was spoiled and inedible. I didn't unplug her. Neither did Mr. Lamb. The delivery was suckered. You were lied to. They used firebacks, Vargs. Not pretty. Mostly what we did was clean up the mess. NORCO got there before there was time to say good, Catholic last rites. Check out what I say. Or just wait for NORCO to show up here."

That was what Dandine had whiffed back in the car; why Varga was on paranoid watch right now. They were waiting for the intrusion of NORCO to throw a spooky shadow. Like the moment in a slasher movie where you finally catch a glimpse of the mystery killer, who might or might not be supernatural.

"Fuck," said Varga. "I don't need that political-governmental bullshit up in my backyard. I hate fucking politics. Religion, too."

"That's why I think they used an intermediary to contact you. You're out of the loop. You didn't know. For now. I could mention your name, if you want."

"No fuckin way. So I give up the middleman to you, and you go on some fuckin rampage, and what do I get? Shit-fire, dude, I'm out one of my little worker bees, and the contract was blown, and I wind up holding dick."

"That's why I thought about it."

"Poor Marisole. She was a sweet little piece. Lotta potential."

Conrad, come on, it's me, Celeste, from down the hall? 307? Conrad? Open up, please . . .

"No, Vargs, she was a beginner you let free-range too goddamned early."

I was still puzzling "deliveries" and "spoiled food." Dandine and Varga had just had an entire conversation about contract killing without once mentioning it.

"Doesn't your amigo there say anything?" Varga was looking at me.

"Ask me a question," I said, making my own heart punch me in

55

the chest. I wanted to break another window. Then I thought: *Dandine brought me in order to unbalance them. Why not really throw a wrench?*

Varga was now staring directly at me, like one of those lizards with no eyelids. "It go down like our man here said?"

My mouth was functioning independently of my brain. "Yeah—I'm the guy she tried to kill."

Without a sound, the room filled up with drawn guns.

Thule had appeared in the doorway behind an enormous double-barreled shotgun, flanked by two of the giants outside, who drew pistols so large they looked science-fictional. Varga was leaning across the desk pointing some kind of revolver at me. The cylinder was the size of a soup can. All my eyes could see were the guns, and all the guns looked gigantic.

I missed Dandine's move. The space he had occupied was vacant.

Somehow, Dandine had folded behind one of the big enforcers by the door, coming at him head-on but *rolling* around him *en passant,* like a dance move. He now held the roughneck by the larynx in midbreath, and had the guy's pistol leveled at Varga.

And still, amid all this, Varga kept watching his screens. The guy was good at multitasking, if nothing else. Or he was really afraid of something bigger than a mere crowd of tough dudes with guns.

Thule was too large to get completely out of the way, jostling the other watchdog off target as he tried to point the shotgun at Dandine. No good; too much gun. He'd have to back up two paces and blast through his partner's skull to hit Dandine, and he looked like he might do it anyway.

"We don't have to do this," said Dandine, as calmly as ordering extra fries.

"Tell me a little bit more," said Varga, his eyes turning red.

I could have been naked or wearing a clown suit. No matter what the humiliation level, it was showtime.

I imagined the desk as a conference table. Varga's thugs as attorneys. The guns as deal points.

"You're the victim of an information gap," I began shakily. "Your contact told you as little as we knew, and when that happens you get collateral damage. It's nobody's fault—you were just doing your job.

That's clear from what happened to your . . ." What the hell was a good word for Celeste? Worker? Employee? Independent contractor? ". . . your girl."

Varga's gun dipped a quarter of an inch.

"And it was me or her, believe that. You already suspect it's true because you're not stupid. And we came here to put things right, not kill each other in a blaze of glory. If you were truly in the loop, you would have known my face. You didn't. I saw it when I walked in. That means you've been lied to. So have we." I spread my hands wide, the only guy in the room without a firearm. "That's it, man."

Varga lowered his weapon. "See, that's what I'm talking about—respect," he said to Dandine. He waved a hand and Thule backed off. Dandine handed the pistol back to his gasping cohort with a wry little smile.

"See, *this* guy," said Varga to me, meaning Dandine, "I never know what to think because he's always trying to play me. If he'd'a told the story, it would have been all prettified with made-up shit designed to fool me. The way you tell it, it was so simple it *had* to be a fuckup."

"If he'd made a mistake, I would have said something." I couldn't believe I was saying this, as though I had rank.

"All we want is the contact," said Dandine. "You're out, you're clear, you're away from it."

Varga's yellow-red gaze narrowed. "So what do *I* get?"

Dandine stepped forward. "Ten thousand, cash, now."

Varga sniffed. "Twenty."

"Deal." Dandine didn't even blink.

"You got it on you?"

Dandine permitted himself a small, deadly smile. "Amigo, I might let Thule take my gun and play with it awhile, maybe shoot off a couple of his own toes, but I'm not going to let him take my wallet, you hear what I'm saying?"

"So . . . what the fuck?"

Dandine opened his hands toward Varga in a broad gesture, raising his eyebrows. Just like I had. *You be fair, I will, too, and we both walk away conscious.*

Varga expelled a hiss of disgust. "Dude's name is Butcher. I'm not kidding; that's his fuckin name."

"And you met Mr. Butcher . . . where?"

Varga was rubbing his head, confessional, resigned almost. "Union fuckin Station."

"Okay, we're almost done. Now you hook me up. Can I ask you a question?"

Varga shrugged. "Nine and a half inches, soft." His primary focus of attention was back on the little screens. I noticed Dandine noticing this.

Dandine ignored Varga's interpretation of levity. "How much did Mr. Butcher arrange to pay for little Marisole's contract?"

"Aww, you *suck*, man!" He moved things around on the desktop, uselessly, caving in. "Ten K."

"Well, then, you just made yourself an additional ten, for answering a single question. Come with us and I'll put it in your hand."

Eyes still dancing across his monitors, Varga said, "Don't insult me by assuming I'm *that* stupid. Thule can go. I can watch from right here."

He pointed at the fifth or sixth screen, presumably a shot of where Dandine had parked the car. I couldn't see it from where I was standing.

Dandine turned while grunting a small assent. "Sure you can." His eyes found mine, and suddenly I believed in that mule-shit about telepathy, because I swear we had the same thought at the same time: *Look at how much Varga is sweating right now.*

Mystery movement in the loading yard, the "parking lot." Something fishy about the sentries. Varga's refusal to lift his ass from a chair for an easy twenty thou. Conclusion: Varga was no longer in charge here.

Somebody else was, and the whole exchange had been hijacked by something less noble than Hoyle's rules for games.

"Hey, Thule! You go with these dudes. You come back here with twenty large, damn quick, or I shoot your ass multiple times."

Thule filled up the doorway and nodded, like an Easter Island statue being subtly repositioned.

"Call our dear Mr. Butcher. Tell him you're aware of the screwup and you'll send a man to make it right. I'll meet him at Union Station on the Metro Rail Red Line platform in one hour. The place where the train changes to Hollywood. Good?"

"What if Butcher's like, a NORCO dude, and they wanna wax your ass?"

"Oh, I guarantee they won't recognize me. My problem. Your profit."

"I'm still out Marisole."

"Life sucks, what can I say?"

"Use my phone," said Dandine, handing Varga the secure mobile from the Halliburton just as he was reaching for his landline. "Then throw it away."

Varga made the call and it sounded level, but he eyeballed his monitors even more. Sweated more. Then he popped the battery and cracked the phone in two against the desk edge. "Happy now?"

"Overjoyed," said Dandine.

"Goddamn-goddammit, I knew this wasn't gonna be easy. Get the fuck outta my sight."

Somehow it was Varga's last-minute fake bluster that convinced me we were in deep danger, despite the drug-deal atmosphere of cautious partnership. This part wasn't over—it was just starting.

We strolled out as we had strolled in, with Thule hulking at rear-guard. I still remember Varga, sitting in the middle of his dark spiderweb of a room, behind slug-proof shutters, posing himself as a kingpin, trapped in there by his own machinations. It was no caprice that he refused to accompany us and back, even with a bodyguard, to the parked car in the dark. He probably never saw daylight.

More honestly, he would probably never see daylight again.

Back in the industrial parking lot, my adrenaline soured into a flood of nervous perspiration. I had expected uncomprehending savagery and likely violence, a firefight or perhaps an exploding car . . . and Dandine and Varga had just talked in obscure code like two old homies.

False alarm, maybe. *Maybe.*

It was then, when my guard had been relaxed, that the violence I had fantasized paid a call. It had been there all along, waiting to be invoked. And it wasn't done with me yet.

Thule handed Dandine's gun back to him as though passing a bag of chips. Dandine gave him the fatter of two envelopes from the trunk. Before he closed it, he grabbed a rucksack (his gear) out of the back.

Calm and loose, Dandine touched my shoulder to make sure he had my undivided attention, and said, "Hit the ground now."

He said this simultaneously with the first gunshot as he shoved me down.

Thule spun like a big fat carousel as several holes the size of my fist blossomed in the trunk lid. Dandine had already disappeared from the space he had occupied, taking me down with a forearm smash-dive that piled us both between the Sebring and a tarped trailer (the small kind you rent at U-Haul and hitch to your car, only this one was olive green). He landed on top of me.

Gun out, Thule fired several useless, unaimed shots into the sky as he died, one big arm hanging him up on the trunk so it looked like he was sitting down for a break. I struggled to rise but Dandine pressed me back down to the gritty pavement.

"Stay flat," he said, lunging past me and hugging the car.

More shots, from across the lot, I couldn't tell where. Hard, fast slugs zinged off the car and the tarmac near my feet, and I curled up into a ball with my nose smelling the Sebring's radials. The ricochets sounded like someone trying to tune a stringed instrument; low rubber-band hums. Hits disintegrated the taillights and holed the fenders with metal-work punch-through sounds that stung to hear. The tire next to my head hissed and the whole car sank toward my face.

The playlist of my life's ups and downs did not unreel behind my squeezed-shut eyes, but I did hastily redefine my concept of violence, as opposed to "action." This was the real thing. All I could see was Celeste— Marisole—with half her head blown off. Exciting gunplay? No thanks. I thought I craved it, or needed it. I wasn't thinking that now.

Dandine's grasp on my collar dragged me into a stumbling run.

"They can't see us—come on!"

I expected Dandine would pop up near the hood, having produced some hidden weapon of awesome firepower, to eliminate the threat in a hot barrage of special killing projectiles. Nope. He stayed low and hustled us both out of there. He didn't fire a single shot.

About the time I was going to note some of this, or protest, or tender a comment about our situation, his hand clamped over my mouth. His voice in my ear was barely a whisper, but audible. "Shut up—not a word—this way."

I wish I could say I *participated*. I wish I could say I was brave or manful. I had hit the deck hard enough to dislodge my fillings and had stayed curled up on the ground with my hands over my ears. This isn't happening, *no-no-no-la-la-la I can't hear you.*

Like kids sneaking through a graveyard, we bought ourselves some distance. Then Dandine halted us in the shadow of a tractor-trailer. "Give 'em a minute," he said. I saw a vague glint of his tongue, working his teeth. We were subvisible.

He had the key fob for the Sebring in his hand. When he pressed it, the car alarm chirped twice and then the car blew all to hell in a mushroom of eye-searing orange-yellow light. It illuminated several hostiles who became midair silhouettes as they were flash-fried. Doors, trunk, and hood exploded from their moorings, cartwheeled afire, and clattered. I imagined Thule's abundant lipid tissue, beginning to sizzle to medium-rare. Flames curled up to lick the night sky, halating ground zero, and huffing a fogbank of laterally rolling smoke. The sound thunder-clapped my skull, like a batter swinging his lumber into my ear for a homer. I recoiled and came down on my left knee, hard enough to make standing back up even harder.

Dandine marched me farther away like a corpsman dragging a casualty. "Now *that's* a car alarm!"

"Who are those guys?" I said, forgetting my admonition to myself about my budget of stupid questions.

"You mean who *were* they. NORCO shooters. Dumb sonsabitches must've forgotten their night-vision."

"How do you know?"

"Pattern of the first hit. They were shooting at shadows."

"How do you know it's NORCO?"

I could sense him smiling in the darkness. "*Size* of the first hit. C'mon, Sancho, they've got other worries right now."

"How do we get out of here?"

He sniffed. "We *walk* out. Follow the tracks."

"What about the car?"

He held up the rucksack. "I've got my gear. It was time for new wheels, anyway."

"You jumped before the first shot. Did you see them?"

"One of them forgot to take off his glasses. I saw a glint."

This was not the glamorous, gadget-laden getaway I had imagined.

"Come on, Conrad, walk tie-to-tie. You know a better way to get to the train station?"

We humped along railroad tracks in the dark, the city lights washing away all detail. I had to shade them away with my hand to see where my feet were.

Had I helped Dandine, back at Varga's? He had not said anything.

Were Varga and his crew past tense already?

Did it matter?

Was I lapsing back into my corporate pattern, trying to please the boss, so to speak? Had Dandine become the new boss of my existence?

Had I "played" well?

(*Always seek approval indirectly. To ask for reinforcement point-blank will only get you a placating lie.*)

It was a classic executive strategem: Don't encourage or discourage, but allow the client to overcompensate on his or her own initiative since their fear is that they can never do enough, or could have done more.

What a revolting goddamned business we were both in.

Union Station, downtown, is pretty dead at three in the morning. But even then, the Metro Rail cars are running. Some people have to be at work at 4 A.M., commuting the span of the line, from Long Beach to the Valley. The grand old train palace has undergone a lot of expensive remodeling, but still retains the woodwork and brown leather look of bygone glory days. We could hear sirens outside—LAPD, fire trucks—but you always hear sirens in this part of town, most any hour. None of the loiterers around the station even bothered to look.

Dandine had a mouthful of Milky Way when he handed me a rail map.

"What's this for?"

"Prop," he said. "You'll see. Stare at it like you're lost and can't figure it out."

Except for security cops and a guy nodding toward sleep on the platform steps, we were alone on the northbound side.

"Hey," he said. "You did good at Varga's."

"Yeah, and when those guys shot at us, I did everything but cry."

He shrugged again. I was coming to learn this gesture was, for him, a matter of disqualifying things that did not matter. Small shit he did not sweat. "How many times have you been shot at, Conrad?"

"Exactly never."

"Point. At least you kept your head down, and you're still with us. Pretty chipper for a guy who was about to hit the sack before midnight, after a full workday." He finished off his candy bar. But it was *Dandine* finishing off a candy bar—even mundane gestures, by him, seemed fraught with portent. He broke a half-smile. "And *where* did you get that speech?"

Already, it seemed like it had happened a week ago.

"Come on, man!" Dandine twisted his face into an imbecilic tough-guy expression I gathered was meant to be me. *" 'That means you've been lied to. So have we. That's it, man.' "* He even duplicated my open-palms gesture. "I mean . . . *damn*. I may have to reassess my whole picture of you."

"Listen, if you're trying to make me feel good, I *don't* feel good, okay? It's my right *not* to feel good." I said the words but didn't believe it. Dandine's world might have further use for me, and queerly, that did make me feel . . . better.

"Next you're going to say it's a free country."

"No—I wouldn't go that far."

"See? There's hope for you, yet." He went to fire up his next-to-last cigarette, noticed the NO SMOKING sign on the platform, and stowed it with a pained expression. NO SMOKING. NO RADIOS. NO FOOD. NO WEAPONS. NO ROWDY BEHAVIOR. *No, No, No!*

I thought of the gun nestled in his armpit; the other weapons most likely inside the rucksack, and said, "Maybe if we had a boom box and some corn dogs, we could break all the rules on that sign at once."

He chuckled at that, and it somehow made me feel more stable.

Careful, a little voice warned in my brain. *That chuckle is for you, precisely to reassure you. It's not real.*

Warm, oily wind began to stir us from the tunnel. An incoming subway train honked. Dandine peeled a cuff and checked his watch. "This might be us. I'm going to point you at a stranger. When I do, you approach them—use the map as an excuse—and ask if they're Butcher. Then, if they say yes, tell them they're covered; the very next thing you say. Okay?"

I swallowed. My mouth was extremely dry. "Okay."

Los Angeles has the newest subway system in the world, and the cars are a wonder to behold, sleek and silver. The Red Line train zoomed in and shushed to a stop, making the air smell pneumatic.

Dandine scanned the occupants. "Second car, the woman with the newspaper. Go." He shoved me off and headed for the next car back.

I stumped toward my target, again, like a zombie. The walking dead. The doors dinged and withdrew. *Oh, I guarantee they won't recognize me,* Dandine had told Varga. Now I knew why. He had a spare warm body to throw toward the fray. Guess whose.

I itemized what might be the final thoughts of my life, and they were depressingly mundane: (1) This was the first time I had ever ridden the subway. (2) I wish I had taken Dandine up on his offer of a candy bar, five minutes ago. (3) I've seen this goddamn movie—*Strangers on a Train.* Maybe Hitchcock's ghost would help render me bulletproof, so I could indulge more dumb thoughts like these.

The doors closed and the train lurched. Showtime.

I wobbled my way toward the woman sitting midcar. Her paper was open and there was a full page of ads in red ink, reading *Meat Specials at Ralphs.* There were four other people in the car, seated as far away from each other as possible: a ragbag, asleep in the corner; a Hispanic lady who looked like a domestic maid, her stare abstracted, her ride long from over; a black man in a business suit, wearing headphones, paging through *The Wall Street Journal;* and a sleepy looking banger, probably trying to stay vertical long enough to get back to Van Nuys after overdoing Ecstasy at a rave. I glimpsed Dandine standing by the interlock door to the next car as I took the seat beside the woman. She seemed surprised that I'd crowd her . . . but she did not have that auto-reflex, flatline expression that said she was getting ready to deflect a commuter come-on.

She had designer-cropped spiky blond hair and a model's cut of jaw. Her eyebrows were blond, too. Eyes, brown. Fatigue pants, sweatshirt, Timberland boots.

"I'm looking for Mr. Butcher," I said.

"Ms., actually," she said, and then her eyes widened almost imperceptibly. "Oh, christ—it's you. I mean—"

"I'm supposed to advise you that you're, um, covered."

She blew out a breath (no lipstick, I noticed), but didn't look around to check. "Behind me, I suppose."

"Mm-hm."

She looked me up and down, from my bruised forehead to the hasty bandage job I'd done on my wrists from hitting the car window. "You get beat up?"

"Sort of."

"And you were so depressed you tried to kill yourself."

"No."

"So what do we talk about?"

"Let's talk about Mr. Varga, and how you knew *oh-christ-it's-me.*"

"Varga's been dealt with by now. You're not supposed to be riding the train in the middle of the night."

I tried my best not to fear this woman. I tried to flash back to my demi-date with Katy, to use the way I'd played *her* in seemingly innocuous chitchat. "That's not only a good start, but it's very, very interesting. Do go on."

"Look," she said, at odds with what she thought she knew. "Some bigwig set up a job. Independent contract, strictly à la carte. A one-way deal. Signed, delivered, done. Except somebody else, I don't know who, found out about it, took the job at face value, and tried to stop it. Somebody on the inside, because they tried to stop it by doctoring the hit-kit. Except Varga, who was contracted to stop what he believed was a genuine job, didn't know that part. Now bigger wheels are involved, so the ins and outs don't matter anymore. That's why I came—damage control."

I became sick of this argot—the dance-around—in record time. All of her words needed translation. My rage—at everything—touched off and burned bright, all in a microsecond. I grabbed her upper arm. "I need a better story. Less vague . . . and in English. I think you're going to have to talk to my associate, Ms. Butcher."

I realized she assumed I was pointing a weapon at her already.

"You unplug me, it still doesn't stop them," she said, eyes front.

"Yeah, I know—it's not your fault. Maximum deniability, and all that."

"I just came because Varga called about the gig. What do you want from me?"

I wasn't sure, exactly, but by that time, Dandine was behind us. The train pulled smoothly into the stop at the intersection of Sunset and Vermont.

"This is our stop," announced Dandine, startling her.

Now we were three.

Slight pause for a snapshot of me, admiring my own cool.

Mr. Butcher had turned out to be a Ms. In a world where nothing happened by accident, I had accounted for this ploy in several phases. First, I made sure not to repeat the stupidity of being distracted by anything feminine. I did not want to make the Celeste mistake again. I had not hesitated to threaten or grab roughly, instead of hanging back with fake courtesy that could cost me my life. I had tried to channel Dandine instead of defaulting to the helplessness that makes people call the police too late to do any good.

Still, this woman's manner reminded me of myself just hours earlier. Unsure of what she had stepped in; positive she did not want it on her shoe. I had to caution myself not to cut her any excess sympathy that might provide her with an unfair advantage.

Of *course* she looked great. She was *supposed* to look great.

Now consider the last human being that caught your eye. We poor Homo sapiens have nothing to go on, no place to start, except our genetically ingrained mating checklist. The attractive stranger in the restaurant, the hot number hailing a cab. You flash forward through whole scenarios in an instant—what would they be like? How do they look naked? It's always the same.

Except. Add the notion that this delectable stranger made a call or had a meeting earlier in the day, a decided plot whose purpose was to erase you. Kill you. Now how would you feel?

Only a fool tries to charm a rattlesnake.

Hollywood isn't a city. It's another subsection of Los Angeles, distinct from downtown, which retains the old 213 area code. With the Los Feliz district to the east, it ends where West Hollywood and Beverly Hills begin, both of which are incorporated as cities and have their own police forces. In Hollywood, if you call the cops, you're calling the LAPD. Every so often, a secession is attempted for assorted pocket-lining political reasons. I always thought it would be cool to see actual "Hollywood police"—just think of the uniform patches, and imagine what the patrol cruisers would look like.

Dandine laid out the rules as we approached the first of the subway stations actually inside the boundaries of what is called Hollywood.

"Listen carefully," he told the woman. "You can alert police on the platform or in the station, but if you do, they're history. They'll hit the ground a couple of seconds after you do, because your life will be done. I'm not trying to frighten you. I am frightened for my own life. All I want to do is ask you a few things and try to get a better map of what has happened to me tonight. Now, answer *yes* or *no*. Do you understand?"

"Yes," she said. No protest. No excuses.

"Do you work for Varga?"

"No."

"But you contacted Varga and paid ten thousand dollars?"

She swallowed, but didn't falter. "Yes."

"Are you working on behalf of Alicia Brandenberg?"

Another pause, barely perceptible. "Yes."

"So your job was to act as intermediary for a slightly less-than-legal assignment in order to protect Ms. Brandenberg?"

"Yes."

Dandine cut her no mercy, and would not permit her to avert her gaze, or otherwise dissemble. "If you're telling me the truth, you have absolutely nothing to be afraid of." That didn't prompt her, so he encouraged, "Go ahead, speak your piece."

"Varga wasn't supposed to contact me again. Now I'm afraid the whole job has been compromised. Zero integrity. So, when Varga called, I had to come see for myself. All I did was play middleman. Middlewoman, I guess."

"So Alicia Brandenberg wouldn't get any on her?"

Ms. Butcher nodded. "All it was, was . . . somebody threatened her, or was planning to hurt her, and she wanted them taken care of. You know—neutralized."

"*She* came up with this plan?" Dandine seemed incredulous.

"No, no . . . she met with some people . . . I don't know who they were. Like, advisors."

"Staff?"

"No. Outsiders. I've never seen them before."

The train glided to a stop and the doors racketed open.

"I apologize, Ms. Butcher. My intention was to let you go home, stay on this train. But you haven't talked fast enough or deep enough. Unfortunately, we need to continue our conversation. So we'll be leaving, together. Remember what I told you about raising a ruckus. My partner's job, here, is to deal with you exclusively, should anything go astray. Do you understand?"

She closed her eyes and nodded. "Yes."

He winked at me. "Let's go, Mr. Lamb."

We walked off no differently than college buddies, all three of us. Two dicks and a chick. Ordinary citizens glanced and saw a woman enjoying the protection of two male friends. This neck of the woods, females couldn't be too careful. Lots of rapists and robbers in LA. No street loudmouths or thugs would molest this woman. Not from the way one of her boyfriends was holding her by the biceps, almost possessively.

We rode three escalators up to street level, and emerged on Sunset Boulevard, with a huge medical complex across the street. There was a sprawling Scientology building a block away, off a side road that had been granted its own stoplight and renamed L. Ron Hubbard Boulevard. That structure, too, had once been a hospital; I knew people who had been born there. (The street was originally called Berendo, and still is, to the north and south, a safe distance from where money talked.) By the time we came up out of the earth, Dandine had secured Ms. Butcher's wallet. Pretty slick; I never saw him dip it. We were alone on the corner, smelling night air, maybe oncoming rain.

"Ms. Butcher's actual name seems to be—" Dandine scrutinized her billfold. "Choral Anne Grimes, is that right?" He frowned. "What was it before you changed it to Choral?"

She shot him a hurt look. "Linda. Big fucking deal."

He handed me her mobile. "Take out the battery and throw it away."

Over a hundred million cellular devices in use right now contain the essential guts of a GPS system which cannot be activated by the user. That tiny circuit can be turned on, long-distance, and used to track you even when the mobile is turned off. Best of all, people carry their leash with them voluntarily.

Dandine's breakdown of Choral's wallet was professional, not obvious, and swift, with the concentration of a Vegas blackjack dealer practicing a fast shuffle. "A Ralph's card," he said, meaning a supermarket discount card. "PETCO. You have a little whiny dog, I bet."

"You want to know *his* real name, too?"

Dandine cracked a half-smile, indulgent, avuncular. "A library card; that's kind of rare. Video Aces rental card. Coffee Bean & Tea Leaf freebie card—look, you're one punch away from a free espresso."

He was dissecting her via billfold. It's ridiculously easy for most people you know. I kept mum because I was supposed to be the hang-tough enforcer guy, and yes, I'll admit that I enjoyed the cheap thrill. As I watched this woman's existence spill out of her wallet, I was reminded that most people scribble down their PIN numbers and other vital data on other cards in their wallets. Most people kept ancient, smelly photos as some kind of goofy ritual—I was glad that I never did. It separated me from the walking dead a little bit; perhaps a little bit that could buy me negotiating time or room to lie. One thing was for certain: After tonight I was going to make sure my own wallet could never betray me again.

But Dandine had access to secret files and dossiers. How much of your life, or mine, is really a secret from anybody? Your "personal information" is anything but. I watched Choral's eyes follow Dandine's every violation of her personality. It was obvious that the whole

"Mr. Butcher" thing had been a one-off for her, a quick and easy dodge, because her contact with Varga had likewise been intended to be a quickie. A dip into the dark side, like kissing a stranger in an elevator. Her every twitch and blink told me that she was not used to this business. She was an errand girl.

I stopped short of making her as "innocent" as I was supposed to have been. But the deadly magnetism, the attraction for a strange woman who was now being squeegeed through a ringer almost identical to mine, was present and insistent, working on autopilot to erode my composure. Charm the rattler? No, you don't. But maybe you wonder what even a viper might be like.

"Here we go," said Dandine. He pulled out a MasterCard (not gold or platinum) and an AmEx card (entry-level green, not corporate). "How're these, Choral-Linda?"

"Why?"

"Because we three hardy travelers are going to the airport, to rent another car, since mine just blew up a little bit ago." LAX was practically the only place around where you could still rent a car at three in the morning . . . and not be subjected to a lot of undue scrutiny. "Oh, wait . . . even better," he said, discovering another card and holding it up for me to see like a brass ring. "Hertz Travel Club. This is going to be smoother than I thought. You got this by working for Alicia Brandenberg, didn't you?"

"Whatever you say." Her composure was chipping. Soon enough she'd either have an outburst, or try to take action.

He spun her to get her full attention. "Hey! Let me fill you in on something, Choral-Linda. You got a woman killed tonight. Her hand was blown off, then her face, in roughly that order. Ten seconds after Varga called you, his place was swarming with narcos, and *he's* probably dead now, too. Please understand that the night is young, and the body count can get a lot bigger while you worry about splitting a fucking fingernail or being inconvenienced. You're probably safer with us, right now, than you would be in your own home with a guard dog and a machine gun. Clear?"

His tirade put the shakes into her. Her eyes began darting about. I knew the feeling too well—looking for an exit. An excuse to resume whatever less thrilling thing she was doing before her phone rang, and she was foolish enough to pick it up.

"Not a dog," she muttered, eyes down, submissive and hurt. "Cat. His name is Horace."

That almost derailed Dandine; I saw it in his eyes. *"Horace?"* he said, caught between doubt and absurdity. "That's a *terrible* name for a cat."

"Rough night," I said, mostly to contribute.

This was clinical, bug-under-the-microscope stuff. I was watching Linda a.k.a. Choral Anne react the same way I had when Dandine first showed up in his ninja suit. Except now I was on the other side of the fence, watching her and judging her weak, full up with denial. Now I was one of the good bad-guys. Dandine shot me a glare, already knowing what was going on inside my head. *Don't protect her,* the glare said. *Not worth it.*

"Those guys you said, you know, the narcos?"

I realized Dandine had not made a mistake; he had said "narcos." If Choral had responded by saying NORCO, then she would have been lying to us. Normal people weren't supposed to know about NORCO.

"I think they may have been the same guys Licia had some meetings with. Closed-door stuff. I wasn't invited."

"You call your boss Licia?"

"Better than calling her Horace," I said.

"Stop making fun of my cat," she said.

"Choral, what did the guys look like? Government bodyguard types, identical suits, too tight?"

"Yeah. Short hair, no smiles, a lot of sunglasses."

"Some fashions never change, Choral."

She was on the verge of tears, but I had to marvel at Dandine's tactic. He had started off ridiculing her name; now he was using it normally—the same way he'd used mine, when he began talking me into shit. We were already moving north.

"Where are we going?" I asked.

"Cab stand, a couple of blocks up," Dandine said. "One of the few places in Hollywood you can actually grab a taxi right off the street without phoning for an appointment."

I trooped along behind them, trying to remember that I was supposed to be holding down on Choral with a firearm, all business.

"Choral," said Dandine, "you don't happen to know a gentleman who might have given his name as Gerardis, do you?"

"No. Why?" She was back to monosyllables.

"Not important. But here's how I think you were lied to: Somehow, some way, your boss found out there was a plan to do harm to her. You drew the scut-work duty of securing Varga and his hirelings to pull a short-term cleanup. I think your boss—Alicia—mentioned this to her secret advisers, because when we went to see Varga to get *your* name, all of a sudden we had a lot of gunners shooting at us. You see how this all sifts out? Your boss doesn't give a shit about you, and if she needs to sacrifice you, she will . . . because she answers to someone higher up."

"That's crazy," she said, actually stopping to look at him. "If everybody's in on it, and she doesn't get hurt, then what's the deal?"

And why is NORCO *so concerned?* I thought. Assuming that NORCO even existed. After all, I only had Dandine's word for it . . . and his name probably wasn't even Dandine, not for real. I tried to listen to what he told Choral with fresh ears, displacing myself from my own recent nightmare, testing the alternate perspective for leaks.

All he said to her was: "Now *that's* an intelligent question." To me, he added, "I've got to think about this. You sit in back with her."

There were several Checker cabs congregated around a traffic triangle at Hollywood Boulevard and Vermont. ALL PASSENGERS RIDE FOR ONE FARE, a sign in the backseat advised. It was a flat fee to LAX, plus surcharges, plus an extra $2.50 for making the trip at night, which I've never understood. Dandine made sure there was enough cash in Choral's wallet to cover us.

Most of the forty-five-minute ride passed in eerie silence, on nearly empty surface streets. Choral was scared, moping, catatonic, or all three. Dandine was folded inward, running more meditation protocols or whatever it was he did to clear his head. Processing data. And what was I going to do, talk to the Russian driver about the fucking *weather*?

"I've been having this really bad dream," Choral said, her gaze defocused out the port window of the cab. We had ridden together, about a foot apart in the backseat, in silence for nearly half an hour. Just as she spoke, rain droplets began to pelt the glass, smearing backward from our speed. "I'm trying to put together this outdoor party thing, to call a lot of people at the last minute, and it starts to rain. I get frustrated and run away, down a very long staircase to a city street. There are security gates on the staircase; I have to climb around them. Then I look down and the stairs aren't stairs, but those round wooden things—you know, dowels. They hurt my feet. I jump around the last security gate and land on a city street, and a Chinese photographer snaps my picture and tries to sell me a copy, but we both have to move out of the rain. I don't have any shoes on and my feet are soaked. And I'm huddling under an awning near a newsstand, and a Persian man tries to sell me a self-published book explaining how Allah is really running things, and that Allah isn't such a bad guy, for a deity."

During our transit time I had been formulating my own fantasy about Choral—pondering whether she was for real, loading up options in case she wasn't, trying very hard not to make her a castaway in the same boat as me.

Maybe I didn't want to share the boat. I had convinced myself I was caught up in Dandine's slipstream and pulled along blameless as drift-wood, but how necessary was I now that he had achieved the newest link in his logic chain? I could have resisted harder, or told him no two dozen times between here and his home invasion, but frankly, I didn't want to. I wanted to believe I was *part* of whatever was going on. Conrad the player.

I had chosen this. It was outside my skin and I hadn't fully admitted it yet, but the pick was mine and Dandine, for whatever reason, was letting me ride. Maybe he was curious as to my exterior world versus his interior one, but that was hopeful me, still kidding myself. Maybe he had grown a sprig of conscience and was looking for a confessor. No, that was still too rosy. More likely, he was some kind of demented chaos theoretician who reaped a perverse glee out of mixing in random factors. He'd said as much back at the coffee shop.

I could have resisted harder. Oh, yeah—sure. You try it.

Choral Anne was what Dandine had called a "complicitor." She was connected to Alicia Brandenberg, and hence the briefcase that had impelled me on my own wild ride, so I did not want to feel sympathy for her. Since she had failed as the be-all, end-all Answer to my questions, she had become the Enemy. But my increasing sense that she was in the dark, too, did nothing but elevate my sympathy for her. She would have to clean up the mess Dandine would make of her credit cards, and probably wasn't well-paid enough to just have some stranger vacuum her wallet of cash without feeling it on some other level. Maybe poor Horace, the cat, would have to go without fresh litter and kitty treats. If Horace really existed at all, if he wasn't another of those smoke-screen details that belie a story being told as overspecific hooey.

It wasn't rainshadows, but tears that streaked her face.

"Why 'Choral'?" I said. It was kinder than grumbling *that's the stupidest fucking dream I've ever heard,* and asking about her issues.

"It was my maternal grandmother's name. Really."

"Why not 'Cody,' or 'Brittany,' or 'Ashleigh,' or one of those designer names?"

She chewed on a knuckle. "Because some women over thirty grow up, I guess."

Or maybe not, since she was apparently considering the consequences of her actions for the very first time . . . and they did not please her.

I started to speak again—you know, keep them talking, add disposable bricks to the illusion of a client relationship—when Dandine overrode me, from the front seat, having resurfaced from his Zen trance, if that's what it was. "Mr. Lamb."

I took a beat for me to recall he was talking about me.

"No chitchat," he said. He knew where I was headed—disposable chitchat land—and aborted my infield play. "T-one," he told the cabdriver, as we sped up the airport ramp from 96th Street.

Terminal One was the local hub for US Airways and Southwest, less likely to be overpopulated with cops or soldiers all het up about terrorists. Very few red-eyes to Phoenix at this time of night; downstairs, in the section for arrivals and baggage claim, it would be relatively quiet and nonprovocative. Hell, they didn't even bother to check your bags for tags anymore, down there.

Dandine "helped" Choral rent a Lincoln Town Car with full options while I stood near a rack of pay phones, holding my imaginary "gun" inside my jacket. The car was a good choice; sturdy, maneuverable, yet anonymous. When I asked why, anyway, Dandine just said, "It's heavier."

"Okay?" she said, seeking some minimal approval for her complicity.

"Okay," said Dandine.

Choral seemed a degree brighter, tired and put out, but resigned to a program that needed to play out, like a grinding machine, or a record on a jukebox, trapped in the groove. It could have been worse. It could have been fatal.

"I just can't figure it out," she said to me, quietly enough not to attract Dandine's ire again. "It doesn't make any sense."

"What?" I said.

"I've been working on it and rolling it over and over in my mind, but why would Licia be involved in something that required so much deployment of effort, and resources, and like you guys say, even *people?* When it doesn't appear to amount to anything?"

"Yeah." I still couldn't track it, either. "A lot of sound and fury, signifying nothing."

"Jesus," she said. "Did everybody have to read *Macbeth* in high school?"

"I didn't start quoting it until college." Normally, to keep the conversation going, I would've launched into an amusing anecdote about the quotidian foibles of chasing a university degree. Obscure the more prickly realities with entertaining details that sounded like facts, and made for a better story. Dandine would have said merely to reveal nothing. Innocent factoids could be turned against you by malefactors.

She didn't look to me like a ringer. She looked like she simply wanted an honest answer. If it was a spy trick, it was a good one. But my own Trickster, no doubt, had long preceded Choral to the same destination, and would advise me not to step into a potential mantrap. I also knew that Dandine was no Outlaw Josey Wales, and had scant intention of vagabonding through the landscape, collecting enough informants to form a caravan, suffering them all with detached yet humorous fatalism.

A safe distance from the rental counter, Dandine handed Choral forty of her own remaining dollars, folded double. He pointed past the automatic doors of the terminal, toward the cabstand outside. "Go home," he said.

"What about my cards?" said Choral, not willing to be cut loose so ignominiously. "What am I supposed to do about—?"

"Shhh," said Dandine. "Go home now."

She looked from one of us to the other, expecting something more climactic, or needing a more definitive closure, or perhaps fearing the long-threatened bullet. All drama, too far gone in the day. All the patterns we endlessly replicate, without thinking. Pretty soon the sun would rise and it would become the *next* day. She couldn't stop her gaze from seeking the doors; the EXIT sign might as well have read ESCAPE, and she gravitated toward them despite all her unanswered questions, or her due of outrage at the rough use we had made of her life.

"Sorry," I said. I don't know if she heard it.

Dandine did, and poked me with an elbow. "Aww. That's sweet."

"On top of everything else, we're *muggers,* now."

His eyes indicated that we should walk briskly to the rental car bay and blow the hell out of there, posthaste. "You're mistaking your attraction to her for an innocence she does not possess. She's tied up with Alicia Brandenberg, don't forget."

"So you cut her loose. She'll be on a phone in five seconds. Sooner, if the cabdriver has a cell."

"I think she was only involved as far as contacting Varga. It's obvious that she's been kept in the dark. I think she is only realizing that, now, and it will impact how she approaches her employer about what happened to her tonight. It's more useful to set her free, and gauge the responses to what she does, to try to form a clearer picture." He consigned her credit cards to the nearest trash can, after wiping them down.

"So everybody's still in the dark, you included."

"Less so," he said. "This operation, this plot, is so shielded as to suggest NORCO's internecine machinations. It's the way they work."

"NORCO again." I sighed. I had a right to feel strung out. "What's inter-ness . . . *what* did you say?"

"Internecine," he said. "Look it up."

*   *   *

Dandine drove the Town Car to one of the airport hotels, *any* of the airport hotels. They, too, were comfortably anonymous. He tooled around until he located a gang of private cars from assorted rental outlets, and switched out the license plates. Then he checked into a suite, apparently on his own dime, again.

Right when I was feeling victorious because Dandine had "chosen" me over Choral Anne Grimes, he nailed me.

"Stay or go?" he asked me.

"What do you mean?"

"Stay or go—you. You're not my prisoner. I've apprised you of the consequences of trying to innocently resume your life. I don't need your help, and you don't have any additional information. By now you have some appreciation of the risk factor. So . . . stay or go?"

Part of me bristled at being so baldly useless. In the world of the walking dead, at least, I always had *something* to contribute. It all seemed peripheral now, less important. I could shrug it off and say the feeling was due to the innate nosiness that normal people have about what goes on behind the scenes of their reality, but what rankled me was the suggestion that it might be preferable, for "somebody like me" (a norm), to re-don blinders and go about my life of un-willful ignorance.

Where, in the next twenty-four hours or so, I was likely to be detained, roughly interrogated, and possibly murdered, because it was cleaner for all the puppet masters—that maddeningly faceless *Them,* the people that *really* run everything. You've always suspected *They* exist. You and I complain about *Them* a lot, without considering their actual shape, or scope. "Why don't They just provide socialized medicine?" we grouse, sipping overpriced boutique coffee. "Why don't They just give us electric cars?" Or, "What They should have done is bartered grain for petroleum," or "lowered taxes," or, in short, "solved my problems for me." Well, *They* do . . . and we all pick up the check. *They* have trained us so that it's easier and more convenient to just pay the bill, take it up the ass, and eat our gruel with a smile.

And I'm one of Them. My job is to talk you into footing the bill every time. And you love all my little seductions. But in a merchant economy, the only true god is profit, and I'm on bended knee, just like you.

People love venomless risk. The saccharine danger of amusement park rides and the catharsis of fiction. The torpor of narcotics and the exercise of loveless sex. Bungee jumping cheap thrills for the walking dead, to lend an illusion of "life" to that which is not alive. You can buy all that and more, in the marketplace of distraction. You can be entertained to death, when you are defined by what you consume. Anyone who dares confess a desire for spiritual growth is mocked into marginalization. I'm not talking about religion; I'm talking about being more than the products you buy, and living a life instead of just hanging on and hoping for the best, like a chimp swinging vine to vine. It's dangerous for someone in the advertising business to be thinking like this.

They ought to do something about that.

We *prefer* to admit we're trapped in forceful waters we cannot control, and find success and fulfillment in just being swept along on someone else's tide. It abrogates our responsibility and makes our lives someone else's fault. It's a relief not to be accountable, and we love palliatives. Our whole culture is built on the sand of excuses, excuses. Not my fault; not your fault. *Their* fault.

Some people define success as dying, to beat creditors. Tell me that's not fucked up.

Why me? I thought yet again. If Dandine was for real, I was being offered an opportunity to acid-test values to which we all pay lip service as ideals. Step up, or step off. You don't confront yourself without doubt, or excuses. Why *not* me?

"What would *you* do?" I asked Dandine. "If you were me? Stay or go?"

Dandine pinched the bridge of his nose. It was pleasing to see him admit a little human fatigue. "Fair enough," said this man who usually didn't give a shit about fairness. "You handled yourself well with our confused little Choral. At Varga's, too. You probably feel in over your head, but you stuck to my rules and didn't make any frivolous contacts."

"Because I'm scared to death to call anybody."

"You're examining real fear for perhaps the first time in your life," said Dandine. "But you haven't run gibbering into the night."

"You mean like I could right now? Supposedly?"

"Sure you could. But you're selling yourself on the idea that you just might learn something about how the real world works. You're not my squire and you're not indentured. Yet, you're still here."

Brilliant. All along I was trying to saddle Dandine with the burden of blame and here he was—exposing me to myself.

"I told you about NORCO because your reactions were intriguing and useful to me. You paid me back by rising to the challenge at Varga's— you acted like you'd surprised even yourself."

"I'm surprised I didn't fill my pants and run around like a decapitated chicken."

"No, see, you're still trying to do that huckster thing: shrugging off credit and deferring blame. Like you did with Varga; *that* was a super-sized order of boardroom bullshit. You knew to pretend to kiss his ass because that was what would unlock him. With me and him, it would have been threats and counterthreats."

"I also know how to deflect the issue with backhanded compliments," I said, zeroing in on him. "What about NORCO?"

"Old news I thought was resolved," said Dandine. "Apparently, it's not. Otherwise, neither of us would be here right now. As far as you go . . . well, you decide. I'm willing to let you continue this ride-along because it's worth it to me to see your perceptions, and I think you're game because you want to unravel these invisible things that impact your existence. If you don't like that one, how about this: It's weirdly fun. I've never had a partner before."

This was far more revealing than I expected Dandine to be.

"Partners usually share intel," I said. "So far this is pretty one-sided. Need-to-know stuff that only *you* need to know."

"Here's what you need to know right now: Some faction inside of NORCO has decided to sacrifice me to cover some kind of political play distantly connected to a client of your ad agency. In the process, you accidentally blundered into their crosshairs, but I can insulate you from them—for the time being, and only if I keep my eyes on you. I'm willing to bet some answers can be found if we poke into who's screwing whom in the election snake pit, and you can help with that."

"*We* . . . ?" Jesus good goddamn, were we a duo, now?

"Sorry. Slip of the tongue."

He went toward the elevator, walking the room card across his fingers like a magician.

"Let me put it this way: Tomorrow, I plan to visit the Sisters. That's exposure, which means escalation. Like the way flak, in World War Two, was always followed by fighter planes. Tomorrow, it gets serious. So if you need to bail, do it now."

I sensed he wasn't just going to hand me a gun, pat me on the head, and send me on my way.

I mean, what would *you* do?

I left the TV on, sound off, for company, and for the calm blue glow of the screen. From a desk, the hotel telephone tempted me a thousand times.

I imagined the world's nicest hit man, in his own room on the other side of the suite, stretching out on his queen-sized, smoking his final cigarette of the day, organizing some sort of battle plan, calm, his heart rate steady.

I conducted a raid on the minibar to force myself to become pleasantly fuzzy. I put away some potent vodka, thinking of it as medicine. My brain was redlining, but my body finally copped to exhaustion. I managed the civilized, proactive move of balancing a plastic bag of hotel ice on my tender noggin, but I never made it out of my clothes.

I slept better that night than I had for years.

DAY TWO

H ere's a scenario:

I wake up in a strange hotel room, jostled back to the land of the living by strangers in severe business suits. I've lost over a week of time. My handlers say nothing as they escort me past the bullet-riddled corpse of Dandine, in the next bedroom. Our headquarters is in the basement of the Federal Building out in Westwood. You have to insert a special key and tap the elevator buttons in a certain pattern for access—the same way you search out "hidden menu features" on a DVD supplement. Back at HQ I am debriefed by some Man in Black, which is funny because the man himself is also black, one of my darker brothers. He is an absence of light in a cold and unforgiving room.

"The programming technique worked beyond our expectations, Connie," he says, using the diminutive as though he knows me; but I say nothing, because he is my superior. "We knew Dandine would use the trigger word sooner or later."

He fills me in: I have been hypnotized using something called the Deep-Trance Method of Mental Parallels, in which fabricated details serve as memory blocks for the bitter truth, and thus, shield my actual identity like bricks in a wall. To the world of the walking dead, I am an advertising executive named Conrad Maddox . . . until my target cues mission memory by utilizing a certain word or phrase. By then, I am inside his trust, and defenses, and can easily purge the target. Dandine was a tough nut indeed, and this was the only gambit that could possibly breach his defenses. Set up a false playbook to draw him out, then saddle him with an apparent norm to whom he will feel some sense of atavistic responsibility.

"As your reward," says the black Man in Black, "we have decided to grant you administrative leave." Then he shoots me in the face with a wad-cutter, to cover the possibility that someone else might recognize me.

Some people will lie to themselves, invent anything to make their lives appear more interesting.

Struggling toward the surface from deep REM sleep is more difficult than waking up on schedule, according to habit. My tendency is to awaken, eye on the clock, usually about thirty seconds before the alarm goes off. Even my body knows how predictable I am. There was a fleeting, dreamlike phase that preceded my memory of recent events. Then my brain reminded me of what had gone on in the real world, and woke me up with a stab of worry.

In the main room of the suite was a room service tray of coffee, croissant, fruit, yogurt, cereal, and toast. The toast was kept warm, but not dried out, by a special, covered silver tray. Dandine had damaged the repast and left me half, which I ravenously gobbled up in no order.

I redressed my wrists with gauze and a little packet of antibiotic ointment, the first probably procured for me by Dandine, the second part of the hotel's thoughtful cache of toiletries. Shampoo, shaving cream, razor, all one-shot and disposable. Lacking identity. No one would ever know I had passed this way.

Later Dandine told me that he had risen after four hours of what he called meditative sleep. Then an hour of isometric exercises, which he could do practically anywhere there was a fixed and stable vertical surface, like a door molding. Then he used the hotel gym and baked in the sauna for twenty minutes. He was halfway into an overloaded day and I was still trying to figure out how to pour coffee directly into the fissures of my bleary brain. He walked in wearing a hotel robe and slippers, hair damp with condensation, skin reddened from basting in steam.

"Doc Savage," I said.

He gave me what was becoming a familiar look, quizzical.

"Doc Savage used to do a regimen of two hours of special scientific exercises, mental and physical calisthenics, every day, no matter where he was."

His gaze tried to flatten me. "You're staring at my nipples, aren't you?"

Was he saying I was gay? I was staring, all right—Dandine did not *have* any nipples. His chest was as blank as the molded plastic of a doll, with two smears of shiny scar tissue where nipples would normally be.

He realized he couldn't blow it off. "It was sort of a shaving mishap," he said. "At least, it involved a straight razor. Understand?"

Someone had removed Dandine's nipples with a razor, like planing cheese with a girolle. Someone had tortured him, once, and he had survived. I suffered a fast local wince. I wondered if he had cracked—talked—and what he might have said, or not said. I wondered what my own tolerance for pain might be, and whether I'd have to find out, soon. Someone edges a razor against your nipple and asks you a question. Wrong answer, and they move to your eyes. I mean, what would *you* do?

He watched me figure it out, then said, "Okay. I shower, then we go. Last chance, Conrad."

"Everybody in the hotel has used up all the hot water by now."

"I don't want *hot* water." I knew he'd say something like that.

We blazed eastward on Washington Boulevard, Dandine piloting the Town Car like a fighter plane during war games. He had good "cop radar" and knew how to get someplace fast, with a minimum of left turns. I'd learned to use a seat belt all over again, to avoid being dumped all over the cabin, since I didn't have a steering wheel to hang on to. The vanity mirror on the visor revealed my forehead, in daylight, had mellowed to a sick ochre color, mottled with impact spots in darker sienna.

"I look like I've got the plague," I said.

"Is your nose still bleeding?"

"No."

"Headache?"

"You have to ask?" I kept touching my head, as though it belonged to someone else, or feeling up a mystery object in a dark room with cautious dread.

"I think you're okay," Dandine said. "How many fingers am I holding up?"

He was flipping me the bird.

"Tell me about the Sisters," I said.

"They're what I'd imagine you'd call brokers of information. I obviously can't work with what I've got unless I make direct contact with NORCO, and I'm not ready to do that, yet."

"Last resort?" I said. He pursed his lips and jigged his eyebrows briefly; I took that as a "yes," subcategory: *desperation measures.*

After Dandine's profession (at which I was getting my first good look in—still—fewer than twenty-four hours), information theft is probably the country's number one subterranean industry. Remember my Kroeger spy, the Mole Man? Nobody knew *his* real name, either. But he'd sell us the skinny on a competitor's bid ceiling or reveal which players were about to check into detox, and the Mole Man's truth record was spotless. He had saved our collective butts more than once by divulging weak links in the chains of large companies, brand names of which you are probably still a loyal customer. That whole "New Coke" thing? The Mole Man kept us from taking a dive on that account by advising that the three-person team who had conceived the idea were one baby step shy of seeing their faces on *America's Most Wanted,* and their original plan was to sneak the coke back into Coke, so to speak. New Coke was *intended* to be a disaster, to cover the chemical changes worked on the original before it was hurriedly reintroduced as "classic." The only thing classic about it was the sleight of hand, and having bought the illusion, consumers forgot it was ever an issue, and my outfit dodged that bullet. Same deal with the whole Blu-Ray fiasco. Whatever the Mole Man charged Burt Kroeger, it was worth it. I think it was Burt who came up with the moniker, because the Mole Man was, well, talpoid. Soft, round, balding, with downy hair on his cheeks and forearms, like a boiled-egg man with rheumy eyes, bespectacled like a wise woodland critter in an Arthur Rackham painting.

Dandine took Overland, north. We were lost somewhere between 20th Century Fox and MGM, if that means anything. A few more turns and he parked behind a courtyard apartment group that had been sinking into the ground since the 1950s, a lot of stuccoed archways engirded by overgrown eucalyptus trees, surrounded by a security fence.

"We have to go through a metal detector, just so you know," he said. "You could always wait in the car."

"Lead on," I said.

"Lose your belt first. The buckle."

"Right." I knew that. I still felt like a first-grader, fucking up the simplest things.

We were buzzed through a locked gate and Dandine led the way through a well-tended garden, almost Japanese in its severity and specificity. There was a modest pond with tuned stones. A sun-browned, skeletal man frowned up at the morphing clouds in the sky. He looked like somebody's older Mexican uncle. He nodded as we passed, and resumed reading his copy of ¡*Alarma!* Amid a scatter of gardening tools on the ground, I was sure I spotted the butt of a shotgun.

A narrow, stoop-shouldered hallway led to a room tricked out like a parlor frozen in time from a century earlier. Lace and antimacassars, wingback chairs and dainty little spool tables. A rolltop writing desk with a cane chair, starkly varnished. Floral draperies.

"What happened to the metal detector?" I said.

"We're already through it." His gaze cut past me. "Ah, Sister, my heart swells with joy."

Our hostess beamed, open-armed, as she emerged from an alcove I had failed to notice, behind me.

"Oh, Mr. D, how delightful to see you again after all this time." The woman in the nun's habit was gnomic and resembled a classic babushka, even down to her unfortunate hair distribution. Her dark eyes glittered. She embraced Dandine warmly, and because she was about four feet tall—including her clunky, thick-soled shoes—Dandine had to stoop. "Welcome, welcome. Please introduce this new face," she said, her expression rounded with thick, peasant bonhomie. She shot me a genuine, yellow-toothed smile that struck me as overly hungry.

"This is my friend, Mr. Lamb," said Dandine. I shook hands with her, working my grasp around a rosary. She wore a plain silver ring on her middle finger and her grip was like a trash compactor. "You are most welcome," she said. "Oh, it's a pleasure to meet you, Mr. L. You won't mind my using the initial, I hope. It's the way of things, here."

"What do you do when you have a roomful of people and all their names begin with the same letter?" I asked after she relinquished my dented hand.

"Oh, my, that *is* amusing, isn't it?" she said, as her hands vanished into capacious sleeves. The matriarchal penguin folds its wings. "May I offer you nice gentlemen some refreshment?"

"Not today, Sister," said Dandine. "Although please accept some from me. I saw it and thought instantly of you." He presented her with a bottle of Haut-Brion, which she examined owlishly.

I hadn't even noticed he was carrying it, and didn't bother to wonder where he'd gotten it. But I knew it was in the three hundred dollars-per-bottle range. I've been there, done that.

"Oh, very, *very* good. The 'eighty-two, in perfect condition. To decant this properly would require a little time. Perhaps for your next visit?"

"That's what I was thinking, as we're kind of pressed for time, today."

"Oh, dear boys, so are we, so are we. As a matter of fact, the Sister and I were right in the midst of something when you were so thoughtful as to call. If you don't mind—?"

"Please," said Dandine, waving away decorum.

"But first," she said, "does our new friend, Mr. L, require any sort of . . . ah, medical attention?" She pointed at my forehead.

"No, Sister," said Dandine, gracious enough to field what was becoming a recurring gag that wasn't funny. "He was in a strange place, you know, and he . . . walked into a mirror."

"Oh, you poor dear. Are you all right?"

"I'll live," I said, rubbing my head to demonstrate it was no biggie. Lancets of pain shot from my eyebrows to my jaw. Still tender. She had taken note of my gauzed wrists, too, but tastefully refrained from asking if I had recently attempted suicide.

She waddled off down a hall to the back of the structure, crooking a finger for us to follow. "Attend," she said, all smiles. "Our Mr. L may find this instructive."

"Oh, yeah," Dandine said, sotto voce.

The Sister levered open a heavy door and indicated that we should enter. I caught an ambient, fishy odor my nose did not enjoy.

Dandine ushered me through first. "This is probably one of the most bug-proof rooms in Los Angeles," he said.

I expected to see—surprise!—a soundproofed, hi-tech chamber

where we could shuck the niceties and get down to business. A bunker of safety tucked amid the chintz and religious bric-a-brac. I was half-right.

A gridded steel staircase led down to an unsuspected subfloor of the house. The main room was at least twenty by twenty feet, tarted up as a medieval torture dungeon. There were two vacant cells in one wall, each about the size of a toilet stall, with barred doors. Another door on the opposite wall led to a bathroom. Most of the equipment—the stretching rack, the X-shaped inverted cross (with padded wrist and ankle cuffs), a gymnastics horse augmented with restraints, and a Frankensteinian dentist's chair—were wheeled back out of the center of the room to clear a large, general space of floor, carpeted in thin, but durable, all weather stuff like tweed. It was a harsh, deep crimson color, varying enough to reveal the traffic areas, and wheel impressions from the assorted machines.

The other Sister, virtually a clone of the first, stood in the center of the room, next to a footstool holding an open can of cat food and a spoon. Slick morsels littered the stool and the floor around it, and I identified the stench as minced mackerel. (My stepmom used to feed it to a bloated, glassy-eyed, catlike thing she called a pet; I've always hated that smell.)

Connected to the ceiling girders by a steel cable was a middle-aged, red-faced man wearing a too-tight Cub Scouts shirt (Troop 183) and nothing else. Smears of cat food had chunked around his mouth and spattered his naked thighs, making him look as though he had vomited excrement (I'm sorry, but that's really the only way to describe it, and if you'd seen it, you'd agree). He was just struggling to stand as we entered, and the Sister closed the door behind us. Around him the carpet was darkened and wet; sweat was pouring abundantly off of him and as he managed to climb to his feet (freehand, since his wrists were bound behind him by a buckled leather strap), a rope of drool escaped from his mouth. The cable looped from a choke chain around his neck to the ceiling. He stood there, swaying, with his feet planted apart.

"Please do continue, Sister," said our Sister. "I believe we were on Number Three."

The other Sister nodded, stepped back for swinging room, hiked her habit, and kicked the captive man in the groin as hard as she could with those big, clunky shoes. The man folded up and collapsed with a huffing noise as his leash (the cable) unreeled a predetermined length from its pulley. His genitalia were deep purple, the color of blisters filled with blood. I flinched.

Our Sister pulled a stopwatch out of her habit and clicked one of the studs, monitoring the sweep hand.

"Who've we got here, today?" said Dandine, hands in pockets, no more casually interested than if we'd walked in on grannies watching a soap opera.

"Oh," our Sister said, "our Mr. G, here, devoutly hopes that one day he will become a U.S. senator. Or is it a congressman? Which one is more important?"

"Fewer senators than congressmen," I said, amazed I'd found the breath to speak. The mackerel aroma was killing me. Past that there was a stale, locker-room smell that wasn't an olfactory bouquet, either. Something was venting from the pores of the guy on the leash that stank like nerve gas.

"Oh, I believe you are correct, Mr. L. In that case, our friend here would be a congressman who wants to be a senator. Sister, may I have the honor of presenting our new friend, Mr. L?"

The other Sister was panting with exertion as she humped over to greet me. When she had pulled back to cock her kick, I'd noticed that she had a clubfoot. Otherwise, the Sisters could have been . . . brothers. It had taken me this long to twig to the fact that these two were little old men, in nun drag. You'll understand that I had a few other things to occupy my immediate scope of attention, but Dandine should have warned me, goddammit. Not that it made a scrap of difference.

The other Sister's handshake was not so vibrant. "Do excuse us, Mr. L," she chirped. "We were right in the middle of this when our dear boy, Mr. D, gave us the pleasure of this social call. Normally, we would deflect such an interruption, but after all, this *is* for Mr. D, isn't it?"

She squeezed Dandine's cheek between thumb and forefinger and gave him a matronly hug.

"So what is this, Sister?" asked Dandine, amused. "Atonement for bad highway services?"

"Oh, no," said the first Sister. "The gentleman there, Mr. G, was *very* specific in his requests. He even brought his own waivers, which was *very* considerate. Time." She clicked off the stopwatch.

Mr. G thrashed around on the floor, trying to secure one knee so he could hoist himself anew. He grunted and snot spurted onto his chin. Veins bulged from his scarlet face, and his eyes were bloodshot, rimed in white. It hurt to look. I could feel my cock and balls trying to contract, to hide behind my lungs.

"If he stays on the floor for less than a minute," said the second Sister, "then we get another 'go,' as they say, until we've each had three tries. One would think that the urge would be to hold back, but he insisted we use all our might and kick as hard as we possibly can. The sensation is quite liberating, actually, for the good Sister and I. The urge to kick harder, every time, is somewhat empowering. . . . He has stood up, inside the minute, every time. So now we move to the next phase."

She smiled sweetly and returned to spoon more cat food into Mister G's slack mouth. "You can lie down now, dear," she said.

Mr. G fell forward onto his face and rolled until he was spread-eagled. The Sister gingerly taped his violet, malignant-looking penis to his stomach, and separated his testicles as though arranging a lace doily.

Then she stomped down hard on his left ball, using her heel.

I felt a black hole swirl open from the top of my rib cage to mid thigh. I think my own mouth was hanging agape.

Mr. G folded together like a flimsy lawn chair, convulsing.

"Ow," said Dandine. His bemused expression had not changed.

"It is Mr. G's wish," said the first Sister, "to ultimately become handicapped through this abuse, in order to somehow curry sympathy with his constituents." She leaned closer to us. "Personally, I think that part might be just a *story*." She winked.

Mr. G gradually flowered open again, and the other Sister stomped on his opposite gonad, this time with the club heel of her orthopedic shoe.

"Oh, it's *my* turn, now," said our Sister. They exchanged places, her compatriot in the Calling clumping back over to us.

"Now, my delightful Mr. D," said the second one. "How may we serve you?"

"I'm afraid it's rather indelicate, Sister," said Dandine. "Please know that I would not impose unless it was absolutely necessary."

"Tish-tosh," she said. "Away with that."

I could not resist glancing past her. The first Sister repositioned Mr. G's testicle as though placing a golf tee. Then, *stomp.* I was grinding my teeth.

"I don't want to compromise your position," said Dandine, "but I need to ask you a few questions about NORCO."

Concern—maybe fear—crossed the second Sister's expression like a passing storm cloud. "Oh, *my*," she said. "This *is* serious." With one weather eye on me she added, "We do not like NORCO. The Sisters try to have as little truck as possible with organizations of that caliber. We leave them alone; they leave us alone. Sometimes a disruption in the order, a change, is inevitable . . . alas."

Stomp!

The guard/gardener lifted his hand in farewell as we exited. Dandine had already left a thick envelope on the sterling collection plate that was situated in a small nave within the reception parlor.

"My compliments on the Bordeaux," said Dandine.

"Come again?"

"The wine. Thanks."

Two plus two equals . . . "Wait—you *took* it from my apartment?"

"Didn't you notice?"

"You lugged around a bottle of vino in that rucksack, all night?"

"I didn't have time to shop for the Sisters."

Suddenly I was exhausted all over again. Atmospheric pressure, or something, crushed my shoulders down. My headache resurged. "Well . . . I guess that's better than leaving it as party supplies for those bums who swarmed over my place last night."

"Exactly, that's the spirit." He seemed pleased.

"So the Sisters aren't connected to NORCO?" I asked, recalling the second Sister's dismay.

"Remember all the little competing clubs I sketched out for you?" said Dandine. "Information brokerages exist in a gray zone, with friend-lies and hostiles distributed according to whatever alliances are formed or dissolved within a given time. Like week to week. The Sisters exist outside of NORCO, which makes them especially valuable to me, even though NORCO might use them to gain some other piece of information tomorrow."

"The Sisters wouldn't sell you out to NORCO?"

"I wouldn't completely rule it out. But information spoils very quickly. They would tell NORCO useless truths. Unless NORCO decided to cross the line with them, and that's a bridge you can never un-burn. Put yourself in the position of that fellow in the Cub Scout suit. Sooner or later under such coercion you might change your loyalties."

"So the trick is to utilize the information before the other side can," I said. "And make sure by the time they get the news, it's academic."

The Sisters were like a mom-and-pop boutique, maintaining a safe distance from the Walmart of NORCO.

Right now I really, deeply, and truly wanted to talk to Katy Burgess about her pet politician, G. Johnson Jenks, and I admit that it would be to try to score points with Dandine that might keep me in this puzzling game until I could see something that was really, deeply, and truly a revelation. But it might also be a test of Katy's mettle and grit, and that intrigued me, too. Against the rules of contact, just now. But maybe later . . .

There had to be one single person I could contact that NORCO had not covered. The idea was a devilish itch inside my head. One person from my planet. One resource I could contribute. It was *there* but I couldn't call it up; right on the tip of my brain, making me feel the way you feel when you forget your own phone number.

I saw Dandine's expression click back to combat-neutral. Then his eyes glinted with a light that suggested he was revving up to work fresh, new violence.

A muscular GTO, cherry red under about eighty coats of lacquer, was parked alongside the Town Car, its butt canted upward over fat racing slicks. A well-worn New Balance athletic shoe with gaudy neon-colored treads was sticking out the driver's side window, chocked between eye-searing chrome trim and the rearview mirror. Some metalzoid post-punk madness was churning out of the sound system (the door speakers were blown and frazzled, diluting the effect of the bass) and exhaled smoke rolled out of the cabin. I could see the top of someone's head—dirty blondish hair reaching every which way. At our approach, the head levitated a couple of millimeters so that stark blue eyes could spy on us, through the black leather gap between the top of the dash and the curve of the steering wheel.

"Yo," said the guy behind the wheel.

"Declan Morris Zetts," said Dandine. "He likes people to call him DMZ."

"*The* Zetts?" I asked.

"Mm-hm. Excuse us for a minute, would you? Thanks." He proceeded without waiting whether to see if I'd accommodate him or not. I played it safe and hung back near the Town Car.

Zetts dismounted his charger with a loosey-goosey, *whazzup* attitude I guessed was his normal operating mode. He was wearing ravaged jeans and a NASCAR T-shirt, untucked. When he saw the expression on Dandine's face, incoming, his smile faded and he seemed to contract, like a pet awaiting a thrashing.

"My bad, right?" he said.

Dandine stopped with his nose an inch away from the kid's. Zetts squirmed in place, trying not to look at his master's eyes. Then Dandine grabbed his head in both hands and *lifted* him off the ground, pressing their foreheads together so all Zetts could see was a single, gigantic eye, finding him wanting. I know this because my stepbrother used to do it to me . . . only I was eight, he was seventeen, and my version seemed less physically impressive. Zetts's feet dangled in the air. He might as well have been stuck on a forklift.

"What's the difference between a convertible and a sedan?" asked Dandine. "Let's try something simpler, something even your lump of brain jelly can understand; What's the difference between a *blue* car and a *black* car? Still too tough?"

"It was *dark* in that fuckin garage, hey—

"Shut up. In one single moment of apocalyptic imbecility, you have set off a bomb that can put us all under anonymous headstones. That man standing over there is just one of your victims. I am another. Guess who's going to be the third."

"That would be, uh, me—right?"

"Think carefully before you tell me a story. You've had all night to get it right, and it had better not be a fairy tale."

He released Zetts, who had to grab the door of the GTO to keep from falling. His feet flailed in the dirt and gravel of the lot.

"*Shit,* dude, there was a security guy in one'a those golf cart things there! I had no cover, *nada;* I had to like get under the goddamn car!"

"You'd better have grease on a shirt, to prove it."

"Your fuckin wish is my fuckin command!" Zetts grumbled, trying to save face. He dug his proof out of the backseat of the GTO, a black, long-sleeved tee with a white logo (FUCK FUCKITY FUCK FUCKFUCK)—ruined by his crawl.

"Zetts, did it ever occur to you not to wear a black shirt *with big white letters on it* for a stealth job, a drop job?"

"*You* said it was a sixty-second job, in and out, max! I was under that fuckin car for half a fuckin hour! *Fuck,* man! Besides, nobody in the world would be *stupid* enough to take the key if they like didn't know what it was for!"

I looked around for something else to do while they chatted.

"Zetts, meet Mr., ah, Lamb."

"Meetcha," Zetts said. It took a moment for him to blanch. "Oh . . . shit. You're kidding, right?"

Dandine waited for Zetts's synapses to fire.

"You're not kidding," said Zetts. "Aw, geez . . . fuck *me,* huh?"

"Tell me they haven't bought you," said Dandine. "Whether you remain whole enough to smoke that bag of stinkweed in your glove compartment rather depends on your answer—dude."

"Oh, no, waitaminute, no, no, no, *no*—it ain't like that at all." Now he was making eye contact, earnestly. "Totally no. I work for you. I *so* do not work for anyone else. You might think I'm a moron, but if there's three things I am it's loyal, loyal, and loyal. No. Uh-uh. Negatory, man. I would *never*—"

"Because you know what would happen to you," Dandine interposed.

"Damn fuckin straight, I do. Look, even *I* am not that dumb, okay? You tell me who to hit and I'll fuckin do 'em *myself,* right now, for free."

"Did you bring my kit?"

"Yes, sir, fuckin-A I did, sir."

"Then you and I will talk later."

Zetts retrieved a black Halliburton case from his trunk, still contrite. "Anything else you need," he said. "I mean it. Anything."

Dandine nodded. "I know."

Then he handed the case to me.

"We've got NORCO all the way up our ass, to our scalps," said Dandine. "Alicia Brandenberg is not the target. It appears that *I* am."

I felt as lost as ever. Outside the window of the Town Car, the world of the walking dead drove onward to their fates, doing their best to gridlock the northbound 101.

"According to the Sisters," he said, "NORCO has activated an entire working cell to take me out of the picture. You and me—we both stumbled. You found the hit-kit. I was supposed to be the fall guy for the aborted hit. Together, we messed up NORCO's play, and NORCO usually responds to interference in a totalitarian way." He glanced at me. "Imagine if you inadvertently derailed some oil conglomerate's plan to hike gas prices. They wouldn't be jolly."

"Then, why the brouhaha with our little friend, Choral?"

"Because Alicia Brandenberg is the *excuse*. Because NORCO never pulls a one-way op unless it benefits them somehow."

I took a pull from a sports bottle of water. My sunglasses hurt my head, but the lingering overcast of the day was still too bright to bear without them. "I'm sorry," I said. "Maybe I'm tired. But I still don't follow."

"NORCO is positioning one of their bought puppets for political office, so say the Sisters. In your terms, it's Jenks or Ripkin—one or the other— and they never field puppets without leverage."

"So, Alicia Brandenberg," I said.

"Yes—mixed up with one or both."

"She's Jenks's campaign manager."

"But according to you, and according to the dossier, she's familiar with Ripkin, too. What if it's more than a cordial exchange of evidence, like two lawyers sharing paper for plaintiff and defendant? What if it's deeper?"

Possibly a rhetorical question. Or maybe Dandine was just asking himself, putting the thought out into the air for scrutiny.

"The thing that kills me" (and Dandine said this without a scrap of irony) "is Choral's story. Linda's story. This Brandenberg person does not walk like a NORCO duck. She whiffs more like an indie contractor. Because if NORCO had positioned her just to be set up, that seems wasteful. Choral's description didn't make her sound like an idiot. So now I'm thinking . . ." He paused. Looked at me with that odd head-tilt. Then said, "Tell me what I'm thinking."

Keeping track of this plot had become like finding a needle in a haystack—of needles. I let free association and momentum move my lips, "You're thinking that Alicia Brandenberg is another of your 'random factors.' Aligned with no one. On her own. Working to her own ends. Maybe playing both candidates against each other. But NORCO found out about her, and moved in, made a threat; made a deal, more likely. So she works in their interest, but not *for* them, which would explain a gap or two."

"And she calls them when her fake assassination plot curdles," said Dandine. "Yeah. I'm liking the way you think, Conrad Maddox. Whomever prevails, NORCO can claim they were looking out for his image. They didn't *have* a puppet—they're waiting to move in and claim one or the other."

"With you dead as a by-product? Some kind of diversion?"

"They don't tell anyone to frame me. They tell Alicia to tell Choral to tell Varga to do it. Everyone involved only knows two-thirds of the story, and NORCO makes sure the various pawns never compare notes. And they get rid of me in the bargain, as a bonus."

"But why would NORCO want to get rid of you?"

This was the question for which I could see Dandine steeling himself. "Because I've been a bug up their craw ever since I quit."

My water tried to snort out the wrong tube. "Whoa—back up a second, there, Secret Agent Man. You worked for NORCO? You're, like, a disgruntled ex-employee? I think I need to get out of the car, now, and just go get killed, you know, quietly, by myself."

"I freelanced. When I stopped, I thought all accounts were settled. Turns out NORCO doesn't have a retirement program. They hate losing anything, perceiving it as a gain for a competitor. It's rather like shredding documents."

"Shit, I could've told you that. The ad business works the same way." Hell, the whole *world* worked that way. "If you can't be assimilated, your throat gets cut. Figuratively. Financially. Credibilitywise. The only difference is, we don't blow people up or shoot them in the head." Even as I said it, I knew it was facile and bogus. We *did* kill people—we destroyed their lives with commerce, we sabotaged careers, we pulled our own smug versions of dirty trickery. How many strangers do *you* know whose lives you wouldn't casually sacrifice for ten grand? For five? For a free meal at a fancy restaurant?

Advertising killed people all kinds of ways. We generally just kept the bodies alive. Better spending potential, there.

All Dandine said was, "NORCO doesn't advertise."

"In my field, the Holy Grail is still word-of-mouth." I thumped the armrest out of frustration. "Why didn't you tell me this yesterday?"

"I didn't trust you yesterday," he said. "I was having enough difficulty marshaling your cooperation. Or getting you to believe in NORCO in the first place. I was hoping it wouldn't come up." He shrugged. "It did, just now."

I phased out, not wanting to look at him. Trying to intelligently frame my next question. Five or six car-lengths ahead of us, an LAPD metro cruiser flaunted its privilege in the fast lane. We were stuck behind a laggard, rickety pickup loaded with pool-cleaning gear. Beside me was one of those garishly legended radio station promo vans, the kind that wander the city and give prizes to folks displaying the correct bumper sticker. Its pilot was wearing dense mirrorshades and headphones, lost to the beat of some flavor-of-the-week band. It was one big clashing riot of visible ballyhoo—Web sites, frequencies, call-in numbers, all over it.

"Funny," I said. "Only one of those I ever heard of was in Egypt." It was a long anecdote, a digression. Irrelevant.

Dandine looked over. "What?"

"Station K-AIR. The call letters. Not in Los Angeles. You know, all stations east of the Mississippi have—"

I shut myself up. The sliding door on the starboard side of the van was open, and a man was pointing a riot gun at me. Simultaneously, I heard Dandine mutter *fuck* under his breath as he jogged the Town Car hard left, augering us into an inadequate space between the pool truck and one of the newer Hummers, the parvenu, compact ones. Trim, handles, mirrors crunched all around, with a sound inside my head like breaking teeth. I heard the shotgun say hello, distantly, its sharp boom buffered by traffic roar and our sound-dampened cabin. Dandine's free hand was already on my neck, doubling me over, as all the windows on my side burst into crushed-ice patterns and fell inward, raining jigsaw chunks. Gouges coughed from the dashboard leather.

The Town Car leapt ahead to fox the second shot, which missed its mark and blew off most of our rear bumper. It dragged behind us, sounding like it was holding on by a single bolt. The pool truck sheared right—away from our butt-in—and punched a metallic green SUV right in the guts, driving *it* to the right, in turn. Dominoes, at forty-five miles per hour.

The Hummer swerved away from our intrusion and hunched up on the concrete divider, which was designed to flip cars onto their sides, on impact. It lurched skyward like a rhino stuck in a tar pit and stayed behind, its left wheels hung up on the berm.

Dandine cut hard left and roared ahead in the breakdown zone, close enough to the stone barrier to sand the paint off our car. The K-AIR van tailed us through the temporary gap and bulldogged an ancient Monza out of the way, crumpled its backside, and popped the hatchback glass clean out of its frame, to pulverize on the roadway. I remembered seeing the beefy collision bumpers on the front of the van—Dodge Ram, aptly named.

Buckshot starred our back glass and peppered the trunk with pellets. As the Monza spun out, tires smoking, Dandine veered right and tromped the gas, to rocket us through the hole and steal two lanes. The van followed, butted briefly up on the berm, port wheels leaving the pavement, then barreled through to come up fast on Dandine's left.

It was one of those vans with sliding doors on both sides.

Dandine watched his remaining mirrors and stood on the brakes just as the shooter switched sides and cut loose another shell. The van flew past us and the round destroyed the front fender and tire of a behemoth Ford Explorer, the Eddie Bauer edition with the Arizona beige trim—the vehicle consumer wags had nicknamed the "Exploder." The all-terrain OWL tire seemed to vaporize into snake shuckings and the damned thing skewed and tipped over. I caught an eyeblink glimpse of its occupants tumbling like dice, as the $37,000 vanity toy (base price in 2005) logrolled, spitting parts in all directions. Twenty yards more and the driver would have made the next exit.

The police car, furlonged into the lead, had ass-skidded to a stop, flashbar ignited. But it could not turn around or back up.

The van corrected expertly and cut into a speed-slide that presented its flank and firepower to our oncoming windshield. Dandine folded over on top of me as he hit the accelerator again. The windshield hailstormed in on top of us just before we broadsided the van hard enough to make it shit its own transmission.

Steam gushed from the prow of the Town Car as Dandine came erect again and slammed into reverse. We disengaged from the van with a shriek of tangled steel and I saw the driver with a bloody nose, fighting to grope his way out the passenger door and properly aim a revolver. The shooter had been crushed and jettisoned from the far side, then plowed under by our momentum. The cops were still thirty yards away, dismounted now, running and shouting.

I had to unearth myself from the footwell, where the impact had tried to stuff me like too many clothes into an inadequate suitcase.

People obligingly forked out of Dandine's path as he kept going backward. I could hear the engine starting to labor like an asthmatic. We spent more tread and rubber fishtailing around, and Dandine badgered the crippled auto up the exit ramp.

"Are you damaged?" he shouted.

"What?" I was feeling myself all over, trying to rediscover my original, vertical position.

"Are you hit?!"

"I don't think . . . so."

He mopped his head with the sleeve of his suit. It was black, but I could see the wetness of blood. Air blew rudely on us from all sides as the spewing radiator tried to steam-clean us. Our amputated bumper was still clattering behind, like a wedding train. Dandine slashed quickly toward a turnoff called Harold Way, off the main drag of Hollywood.

"We're gonna need another car," he said.

"I don't think I have another dime," I said.

"To hell with it," Dandine said, shoving another dollar bill into the feed slot. The bus driver looked at him as if to say, *stone waste of money.*

"Give the next passenger a discount or something," said Dandine as we made our way to the rear.

"That's why the fares are weird amounts," I said. "A buck thirty-five, a buck sixty-five. Too much change, to encourage riders to do what you just did. Regular passengers use the Tap cards."

He sat down next to the window, balancing his Halliburton on his knees. He ignored my light panic chatter; at least, didn't rag me about it.

"Okay, *now* I'm pissed off," he said after a few start-stop blocks.

"You're bleeding, too."

"Never mind. I'll deal with it later."

"We'll deal with it *soon,* unless you want to be a walking red sandwich board."

"Point," he said.

I tried to press forward, to think like him. "And speaking of the police, which we sort of were, what about them? Can't you just flash your FBI badge and get all sorts of interdepartmental cooperation?"

"That would work for a fast exchange, but not extended scrutiny. Not because the ID is leaky, but because NORCO is tapped into their computers, their phones, just waiting for a red flag item. Remember, the ID is sourced out of NORCO. If my ID had to be verified, we'd find ourselves very politely thrust into a holding cell, which would end our new career as freeway redecorators."

"Listen," I said. "I have a kind of weird idea. You'll hate it, but hear me out, first."

He was hit in the left arm and possibly the upper chest. His right hand tried to squeeze it all into submission, but he would be in trouble very soon. "Tell me your weird idea," he said, teeth gritting, shock-sweat popping against his will.

The mystery name floating around in my brain had finally bobbed to the surface.

"A long time ago, we're talking years ago, I was friends with this guy named Andrew Collier. He started as a screenwriter; now he's a director—you know, one of those journeymen who keeps working, but nobody has ever really heard of? No hits, no Oscars, but no flops, either."

"I don't go to the movies a lot," said Dandine. "Too unreal."

"Yeah, well, remember when the Twin Towers fell down, all that craziness in New York? The government actually called a little kaffeeklatsch among scenarists—the *Lethal Weapon* guys, the *Die Hard* guys—to use them as a think tank, to see if they could speculate on what a motivated terrorist's next strike might be."

"So a bunch of politicians with no imagination actually consulted a group of guys who possess one." Dandine shook his head. "Shit, maybe there *is* a Santa Claus."

"No, think of it the other way around—they were out of ideas, and they *admitted* it, yet they still needed to do something, show the public they were trying, so they asked the think tank. The expense was certainly an easy sell. It was worth the tax bucks, plus they got to rub up against Hollywood. The politicians were acting like those guys in a movie, the ones that always say *it sounds crazy, but it just might work.*"

"Well, I'm certainly dazzled." He was trying for deadpan, but now he was in obvious pain.

"I met Andrew through some promotional stuff I did years ago, before I joined Kroeger Concepts. I could never keep him in a Rolodex or on a Palm Pilot because the guy changes numbers like you change socks. Always a different production office, always a new gang of assistants. We kept running into each other and promising to sit down and catch up, and the schedules never meshed—you know how it is—and all of a sudden a *decade* had gone by."

"Not even a Christmas card? I'm flabbergasted." But his mouth was slightly open and he was looking at me now. He could already perceive the outer edges of what I was thinking.

"I'd try to nail him for a lunch or something, and it always got cancelled at the last minute, and then rescheduled for another time, and then it would inevitably get cancelled. He invited me to a couple of social things at his house, but I retaliated with the same network of prior commitments. But I was just thinking, All those bits and pieces you can't wire together, or see the whole shape of? Why don't we ask Collier? There's no way anybody would even *think* of him as a connection to me."

"Not your office, not your stuff at home? E-mail?"

"Nope. Plus, Collier knows a lot of people who are, how shall we say, not mainstream."

Dandine bunched up temporarily. "At least you didn't drag me to a veterinarian at gunpoint."

"That's something people only do in the movies."

"Oww, don't make me laugh." He considered all his rapidly dwindling options and didn't waste time he knew he lacked. "Are you sure? Think."

I nodded. "Just so happens we touched base a couple of weeks ago. I have his number on a Post-it in my wallet. Stuck to the back of one of those credit cards I can't, you know, use for anything right now." Pause for fake suspense. "Did I mention his wife used to be a triage nurse?"

"Ah, the dual career household." He tried to say it lightly but grimaced again. "Would he see you, do you think? I mean, if you left out certain details?"

"Only one way to find out," I said. "But I *am* pretty good at the hard sell."

"So let me get this clear as Windex," said Andrew Collier, settling into a rocking chair older than all three of us, in his office, made over with a lot of money, an orgasm of wood tones that put me in mind of the 1960s frenzy for paneling. Built-in oak bookshelves, designed to support the cinderblock weight of heavy tomes without sagging. Overgrown eucalyptus trees outside of a big picture window. A writing return best described as a nook, now clashing with the contours of assorted computer hardware (outmoded the moment it was reluctantly bought). Framed movie posters; either costly collector's items or a display of Collier's own credits—the classics scuffed against the "big face" compositions that had overrun the film industry's concept of publicity. We were seated in a little conference area, in cozy leather chairs shoplifted from Zane Grey's idea of hunting lodge furniture, and Collier's manner was an amalgam of amusement, fascination, and the avuncular posture of a parent who has just posted bail for two errant children on some forgivable misdemeanor.

Collier was an Americanized Brit with the unruly golden hair, rubescent complexion, and inquiring sapphire gaze of an overgrown child of privilege. It struck me as masklike, his face, channeling emotions according to need. This was the face he used to sweet-talk moneymen while advancing his own objectives, with the surety of a chess master marching pawns toward promotion. I was in no position to lie to him, and I couldn't tell about Dandine . . . but, naturally, you never could tell what Dandine was actually thinking.

Dandine sat across from me, sipping a neat scotch in a crystal glass. A thick wad of gauze dressing bulged his shoulder and upper arm where he had taken five pellets of buckshot, recently extracted by Collier's wife, Elise, a slim, tall woman with an impressive jaw line and cheekbones—breeding, there—professionally framed in an efficient, auburn bob with bangs. She talked down all of Dandine's tough-guy protests, packed him in drains and antibiotics, fed him painkillers, and instructed him to shut up and avoid exertion. Then she had tendered apologies and sped away in a Jag to cover some shift at the hospital in the Valley where she spent most of her work time. Her ministrations suggested this had not been the first time she had been called upon to perform a bit of patch-up off the books, and I wondered about that. We had walked boldly into Collier's world, frankly needing a measure of blind trust that neither of us would ever request, in the world of the walking dead. Now it was our turn, to repay generosity with the truth, and spieling out such truths, unvarnished, and hoping for the best had always struck me as the emotional equivalent of puking in public.

Elise's theorized that the nasty M&M'S of buckshot had penetrated Dandine after ricocheting from the door frame of the Town Car. Dandine had concurred. Otherwise, and he would have come to Collier's roost more deeply handicapped. As it was, he could barely move his arm.

His shooting arm, I realized. Dandine was a southpaw. Another pellet had skimmed his neck; flirted with his carotid artery. Damn. Once again I tasted mild nausea at the notion of actually stopping a bullet.

I caught a shower in Collier's guest room while Dandine was being taped up. The stink of fear was all over me in the form of evacuated toxins, and it was a relief to consign it to the drain. Dandine had been given a T-shirt with the sleeves cut off, to accommodate the dressings. In jagged red letters, the shirt read: I DON'T HATE EVERYONE, I JUST HATE YOU. And we had come to the part of our show which Collier would no doubt call the "expositional lump." The dialogue that spells it out clear for the audience, like when the embittered dad tells his daughter, in the first two minutes of some feel-good movie, *"you know it's been two years since your mother died . . ."*

Hence, Collier, running his own lines about window cleaner around in his mouth for rhythm. Hell, he'd probably used that one in a script already. He set us up with another one, about bikers.

"About two years ago, this mate of mine shows up out of the blue," (Collier told us). "Behind him, blocking out the sun, are two enormous mofos in biker leathers—the shredded denim, chaps, everything. Members of the Devil Hogs, out of San Bernardino. One bald, black; the other, a white guy with close-cut silver hair and beard, not old, though. Both higher than six-five, each. They had been poisoned. Somehow, somebody was passing crystal meth polluted with mercury. Elise helped leach that stuff out of their systems. They weren't speed demons, but they, you know, knew a lot of guys who were tweakers, who ran accelerant labs. Elise did what she does, then we talked. I ever need a favor below the law, well, I've got Devil Hogs to call, yes? You never know when you might need a biker escort to LAX. Sweet guys, past the persona. One was called Able and one was called Rex. Rex had just kicked drinking, I remember—nothing stronger than coffee. How my mate knew them, I'll never know. Rather like now."

That was our cue.

It was a near-classic ploy—offer disposable information in hopes of gaining similar, but more valuable, disclosure in return. Fake honesty. Like an actor might use.

Collier and I had become distant friends through his need to research what he called "other people, other lives," for purposes of veracity when it came to scriptwriting. He'd scored some panic rewrite on a green-lit movie called *The Worst Job in the World,* and needed to know trivia on the ad industry. Enter, me, ten years ago. I was tickled at being consulted for a movie. He grilled me and fed me a lot of expensive dinners; I think the movie was eventually released as *Jasmine Junction,* and I've never seen it. I don't even think Collier got credit. He was acting as a script doctor for another friend, who, in turn, had called in a favor. Script doctors get paid obscenely well when a movie is green-lit, and rolling down the tracks like a runaway train burning money instead of coal. But their presence in the finished product is often stealthy. I remember Collier telling me that the guy who drives the crew shitwagon gets screen credit, but "participating writers" never do.

More subterranean machinations, unsuspected by the world at large. Deals most internecine, as Dandine would say. And let's face it, Collier enjoyed these little opportunities. And now he had a guy like Dandine beholden to him; not a raw deal at all.

So, in the interests of crystal clarity, I laid the last twenty-four hours down for our host, abetted by an occasional nod from Dandine.

"I've seen those cameras," said Collier, pushing back in his seat to indicate his digestion of our input. "At a shop in Burbank. Cameras that can be hidden anywhere, and shoot information to anywhere else. I got a bug-sweeper there; that's how I keep my environment bug-free. See those windows? Seventy grand worth of refractive-index hardball glass, my lads."

"Stray bullets," said Dandine, who appeared comfortably buzzed.

"Hey, no joke, up here," said Collier. "Pillocks shooting their guns in the air on New Year's and the Fourth? Forget about it. Lady got killed in Disneyland once, from a slug that just dropped out of the blue. Some homeboy in O.C. discharges his piece into the night sky and a lady standing outside of the Fantasyland castle keels over. Can you imagine dying while that 'When You Wish Upon a Star' music plays? Or worse, 'It's a Small World'?"

"Do you trust your wife?" said Dandine, his focus out the window.

Collier's expression went Rushmore-serious. "Yes. If you're referring to your situation, and that of our chum Connie, here, the answer is yes."

Dandine nodded. That seemed to be the answer he was looking for.

"Again, Andy," I said. "I don't know how we can thank you for—

He waved it off. "Feh. Don't pull gratitude on me, Mad Dog; it's disgusting."

Dandine's eyes swiveled toward me. "Mad Dog?"

I felt myself blushing. "Maddox. Mad Dogs. You know."

"I don't get it."

He held for a beat, or at least until Collier started laughing. Then he smiled—*gotcha*—and put his nose back into his glass, smug as a fifth-grader who has succeeded in making a dirty pun out of your name.

"Yeah, terrific, everybody have a bigass laugh at the expense of the pathetic advertising guy. You're not supposed to have a sense of humor, you know."

"I'd think you'd need a keenly developed one, in your line," said Collier, to Dandine. "That steely-cold operative jazz if strictly for the movies. Think Miguel Ferrer. Tom Jane."

This was pleasant, but Dandine could tell I was itching. He said, "Phone calls, to answer your question."

"What question?" I hate having my mind read.

"The question you were going to ask about what we're supposed to do next. Stop me when I'm wrong. Phone calls. It's time to make a little strategic contact. But not from this location."

"Not on a damned cellphone, that's for sure," said Collier. "Elise says you need to convalesce, and you're in no shape to dance back out into the world for the next action scene. Rest up a bit. I know you probably rail at the idea of doing nothing, but nothing is what you need to do next."

"Actually," said Dandine, almost murmuring, "it's kinda nice." He was falling asleep, on the precipice of nodding off, right there in the chair.

"Help me get this guy into his bunk," said Collier.

Five minutes later, I stood there, thinking, *nobody ever sees Dandine's bare feet.*

Divestment of shoes made him vulnerable. Snoozing in the guest bed with his feet hanging off one end, Dandine looked like a normal guy, sleeping, not some kind of merciless death machine.

He had once worked for NORCO. He had worked for the people who really ran everything. He had quit them. Wasn't that a character point in his favor? Was it compensation enough, against the blacker things he had probably done over the course of his career?

I wondered what he had done *before*. Whether he had ever been a paperboy, or a Boy Scout, or some other frilly, happy-families bullshit.

In the movies, hitmen were iguanas—completely cold-blooded and hindbrain-motivated. Or they listened to opera and quoted fine literature. Or they were Family thugs, lip-deep in all that *Sopranos* pasta fazoole. Not like this guy, for real. That was how he did what he did, while the walking dead . . . walked on, oblivious, uncaring, cluelessly innocent.

"Jesus, we've got us a trigger," said Collier, freshening up his drink in the living room. He paused to consider his own reflection in vast glass, ghostly against his great, panoramic view of a cutback valley dotted with very few house lights.

"He's not a *pet*," I said. "Howevermuch of his story is true, all I know is the bullets being shot at me seemed real. Real things, blowing up. Real people, acting like people—"

"People in spy movies?" Collier said this with a toasting gesture. "Welcome to the real world of the unreal. It's not so weird, when you think about it." He raked his hair, as though tired by deduction. "But, you know what? If I was a producer and this was a movie, I'd be asking one question."

I had to ask.

"Where's the girl?" said Collier. "No female lead. Strictly a guy story."

"What about little Miss Butcher? A.k.a. 'Choral'? What about the lady ninja that crushed all the nerves in my forehead? What about—" I wiggled Alicia Brandenberg's dossier at him. Dandine had left it on the coffee table in the office while we had hacked and slashed through a slightly modified version of our thrilling narrative. "What about her?"

"Bit parts," said Collier. "Supporting characters. Background furniture. Look at the beats you've got." He ticked them off on his fingers, and I had a feeling he was upshifting into pitch mode. "You pick up a hit-kit and become a target. Except the real target is the hitter, and the whole plot seems to be a fake. The fake hit is a subcontracted job, to exonerate some big secret cabal."

"NORCO."

"Yeah, right, NORCO. So what does that tell you?"

"I don't know."

"NORCO set it all up in the first place, and covered their butts with maximum deniability, in case Dandine lived long enough to come after them for payback. Unless . . ."

"Stop doing that," I said. "Unless *what?*"

"Unless Dandine made up NORCO, to cover some larger agenda. He can explain it in ephemeral terms, and you'd buy it."

"Then, if it's all about Dandine, are you saying that Alicia Brandenberg is a completely random factor?" I was recycling the jazz Dandine and I had brainstormed on our way here. I wanted Collier's reaction to it. Needed it, in fact.

"Hence, ancillary to NORCO," Collier said. "Not top echelon, but connected enough to seek help from NORCO when she gets out of her depth. Or maybe she's a NORCO contractee not privy to the internal workings of the big clock itself. Or trained by them as a one-shot capable enough to keep the political fellows in hock to the organization. Any of those would do. You don't have to tell the audience every damned thing in simpleton language; you do have to provide a crumb or two of backstory for the viewers intelligent enough to see layers, yes?"

"So Alicia's just a symptom," I said. "Like a dead-end plot thread."

"Unless she, too, expires in some revelatory way. Collier smiled and spread his hands, palms up. "Hence, *where's the girl?* Why don't you just go and ask this Alicia person?"

Good question. Dandine had kept me so busy ducking and running, over the past day, that it seemed a possibility both remote and unattainable.

"And I've got a better question than that one, Connie. Why are you hanging around? This doesn't even involve you. If it's all about Dandine, nobody gives a toss about you. The shadow warriors *don't care* about you. You're not a target. You only were a target because they mistook you for Dandine, or you were hanging in Dandine's orbit. Why don't you just go home, file a burglary report—that's what it'll go down as, trust me—and get some quality sleep time?"

That let the air out my balloon, double-quick. Collier was right. What in hell was I doing here, I mean, *really?*

"You're like the guy in the flying saucer movies. The one who sees the alien, or discovers the monster, first. Normally, he would hand his information over to experts, and drop out of the picture. Not in a movie, though. The audience needs to uncover the threat alongside the protagonist. Then they stick with him, or her, because he or she is their entrée to the rest of the subsurface plot. That character is the audience point of view, just like Roger O. Thornhill, in *North by Northwest.*"

Collier's words burned me on the inside. It was truth, and it smarted. What the hell *was* I doing here?

(1) I had been given an opportunity to escape my life, indulge in some risky acrobatics, and pretend none of it was my fault. That meant: (2) I had a life that I needed to escape *from,* because (3) it was mostly a calcified, rote bore.

Now I was surrounded by colorful eccentrics and bizarre misfits. I was exactly like those losers you glimpse at airports, pretending they're cooler than they actually are, pretending to be someone else when they're in the company of strangers, all en route to places other than here. An exotic destination, a titillating rendezvous. When you're stuck in an airport, it seems that *everybody* is headed somewhere more interesting than you, and you and I both take this feeling for granted.

We *all* play spy at the airport.

As Roger O. Thornhill had pointed out, in the person of Cary Grant, his initials stood for *rot.* My life, as a crock of same.

Collier was right. I had tailed along at Dandine's behest because I wanted to believe I was essential to his investigation. So far, there was nothing he could not have done, quite ably, solo. I had taken his word for it. For all I knew, his latticework of facts was just more expertly deployed bullshit, for purposes I would never be capable of understanding . . . unless he was merely holding me in reserve as a human shield for some crucial combat.

Dandine had *sold* me on the whole package, goddammit.

Unless . . .

. . . unless it was *all* me. Once I had been plucked from the universe of the walking dead, and was on the outside, looking in, I hated what I saw. I wanted to test my own resilience, to prove myself in some obscure way, to acid-test those theoretical qualities to which we all bow, yet are rarely called upon to demonstrate. I wanted to jump into the predator pool and swim, and find out if my own grit was bona fide, or merely another civilized illusion. There were tons of phony risks available for moral chickenshits to jerk off pretend bravery—skydiving, whitewater rafting, driving a Hummer. Reading *Soldier of Fortune.* Climbing a fence. Crossing against the light.

"My, *that's* an introspective look," said Collier.

"Sorry," I said. I bolted too much single malt and almost gagged it out the wrong tube. "Andy, I think he's for real. He's in trouble and I helped get him there. Maybe it's as simple as that."

He shrugged. "If you enjoy gambling with your own arse."

"It's not that. It's necessary."

"God help us, a romantic idiot. I never would have called you that, before. But what the hell—the worst they can do is kill you, right?"

"Why are *you* helping us, then?"

Collier grinned. Big, honest, broad. "Because when I do things like this, dear boy, I learn things I never knew before, and sometimes reap unimagined benefits."

"Then, I rest my case." I folded my arms.

His grin split even wider. "You're drunk, lad."

I smiled back at him. "Not nearly drunk enough. Hit me again."

"You're dangerously close to expressing a genuine emotion," he said. "Feels weird, doesn't it?"

Yeah, it did. That was the really scary part.

Collier's eyrie was halfway up Nichols Canyon, from the Hollywood side. The serpentine mountain road crested at Mulholland Drive and from there, dropped down into the San Fernando Valley. From anywhere on his tract of property, you'd think you were vacationing in some sylvan retreat or ashram, not maintaining an illusion of frontier hominess less than a five-minute drive from the heart of the tourist district—Grauman's, the Kodak Theatre, all that.

Walking down took considerably more than five minutes. It was cooler in the hills than in what are locally called the "flats." Damp. Morning would bring cushions of fog to compromise all the newly washed cars. I encountered several people in jogging suits or sweats, huffing uphill, or walking their dogs. They all nodded at me in cautious neighborliness, then pressed onward and forgot about me. A private security car on patrol didn't even slow down for review. I looked more or less like I belonged here, and I wasn't lugging anyone's stolen silverware.

Urban noise began to surge toward me from below. Nichols Canyon elbowed onto Franklin Avenue, and suddenly, I was back in the city again. Neat trick. I felt energized from my wandering, legs thrumming, and decided to do my cardio a favor and hike all the way to Sunset Boulevard, where I bought some mints and a pack of smokes at a gas station. The smiling Albanian guy at the counter gave me a free butane lighter, and past the snacks and frozen beverages, I could see a couple of pay phone carrels outside, near the locked, customers-only restrooms.

I returned the counterman's smile and used the advantage to talk him out of a whole fistful of pocket change. In my jacket, on one folded sheet of the dossier, were more phone numbers for Alicia Brandenberg than I had fingers. I figured her direct cell was the best first bet.

Traffic rushed past in all directions, like platelets through an arterial junction jamming up, switching lanes, suddenly busting loose, careening around each other with inches to spare. It was good cover noise; I could be calling from anywhere in the city. I fired up a cigarette, willing myself to look cool—I was Mr. Lamb, the Man from Ad.

I wished I'd felt this certain whenever I was in Vegas, because the voice that answered my very first call said, "This is Linda Grimes."

Alias "Choral." Bingo, blackjack, we've got a winner. She had answered in the middle of the third ring, as assistants are instructed to do, all business.

"Hi, Linda. Listen, I need to talk to the boss-lady."

"Who's calling, and what is this regarding?"

"Well, Linda, first I should say that I hope our abuse of your credit card doesn't piss off Citibank."

I heard her suck in a tiny breath before whispering, *oh shit.*

"May I call you 'Choral'? I hope so."

"What do you want?" There were mufflings and shufflings on her end, as if she was stuck in a crowd, looking nervously around for a sniper, trying to play normal for the company she was in.

"I want Alicia Brandenberg to drop whatever the hell she's doing and meet with me. Right now. I wouldn't ask if it wasn't important, but then, I'm not really asking."

"I can't do that. Listen—"

"You listen! I can see you, from where I am, but you can't see me." How would she know? "Here's what I want. You can either put her on the phone right now, and watch her squirm, or you can pull her aside and talk in her ear like a good assistant, bringing up an essential item of business. Your call."

Big exhalation. "Just a minute."

"Twenty more seconds and I hang up."

"Just a *minute,* dammit. Geez."

I racked the phone. It felt . . . wonderful. I finished my cigarette—my first in three years—had a mint, and called her back from the drugstore pay phone across the intersection. This time, the call was snapped up on the first ring.

"Hey, Choral."

"Jesus—why'd you hang up?"

"Yes or no?"

She frittered. "Yes, yes, goddammit, but we can't just—"

"Yes, you can." I kept her on the ropes, interposing. "Here we go. You know the movie theatre near what used to be the Virgin on Sunset?"

Everything in Los Angeles used to be something else. The titanic complex at Sunset and Crescent Heights had been erected on the grave of the original location of Schwab's Drugstore to house a Virgin Megastore, which of course had gone belly-up after the turn of the century. There's a Trader Joe's there now. Nothing endured.

She wanted to say a dozen other things, but she said, "Yeah. Across from what used to be the Teazer."

"Try to make the nine-thirty show of a movie called *Spiderweb.*"

"But what if—?"

I hung up again. I could walk to the theatre from where I was. Even stop for coffee.

Wolfgang Puck's restaurant had also died around the time the Virgin store vacated its prime real estate. Outdoor escalators still fed up toward the movie theatre complex on the second level, but the place had a besieged, abandoned air, as though the big players had pulled out amidst conflict and disgrace. It wasn't as populous as I would have liked; fewer crowds meant less cover. An espresso joint was tucked into one corner like an afterthought, trapped in a bustle of hazard tape. When new businesses moved into old slots, sometimes the tenants even replaced the damned sidewalks. It was cosmetic surgery for the face of the city—nips, smoothing, tightening—and it held the scary plastic sheen of the new and the transitory. Exteriors mattered. Never mind that they'd warp in sunlight or decompose in mere weeks. They were meant to be replaced again, and that obsolescence, that upkeep, had become what passed for evolution on the face of the city.

In a world such as this, how could any sane person expect to do a single job for a number of decades and then enjoy some kind of retirement where their safeties and investments were protected? People had to morph, too, or risk being recycled into something more useful.

It was happening to me, right now.

The person I had been was not the man who growled threats into a phone, who assigned meet-ups by force, who pushed pawns around. Who was now checking stairs and escalators for escape routes. Nope, not me.

Of course I had done each of those things before, many times, in the course of my work. But then I had enjoyed ameliorative language and the protection of business-class excuses. I was erasing my old identity. I was becoming something new, a "work in progress."

Whether it was a skin-deep makeover—fake, false—or a fundamental change in my own DNA, I had no idea . . . but I was about to find out.

* * *

At exactly nine-twenty I saw Choral Anne Grimes and Alica Branden-berg exit the south bank of elevators directly connected to the upper level where the movie theatre was located. If there were bodyguards, they were hanging back, out of sight in public. From my view there were plenty of getaways to street level.

I handed my prebought ticket to an usher and scooted inside, ten minutes after the feature had already begun. Slap my hand, I'd even lied about the start time.

I was able to monitor the two of them most of the way. Choral was suited up in efficient evening chic and black heels. Her legs turned heads in the courtyard.

Alicia Brandenberg's photo did not do much justice to her allure, or maybe she just naturally exuded magnetism, the way the best politicians do. She was wearing a smart suede jacket and calfskin pants; she knew how to stride in heels, almost imperiously. She led; Choral followed, or rather, kept up. They could have been wealthy, attractive mother and daughter. Alicia was wearing glasses, no doubt costly designer items. Auburn hair, restyled since her headshot. Very pale skin, probably Irish-German. Minimalist jewelry. Matte lip gloss. All top-drawer. Choral eyed the milling consumers in the forecourt and acted frustrated. Alicia kept eyes-front all the way.

I stood in the back corner near the curtains, invisible, with a full view of the multiplex auditorium. *Spiderweb* was a movie about double crosses. The kickoff scene took place in an airport, at night, as twenty or thirty special agents and security watchdogs try to prevent a Chinese fugitive from escaping on an outbound flight. They descend like locusts on their target . . . who turns out to be the wrong man. They reset and realize they've been diverted, and hustle to another terminal, where they are just in time to nail another decoy . . . as the real guy boards yet a third flight, in drag. It was one of those movies seemingly shot all at night. No bright scenes to illuminate the auditorium, at least not for half an hour or so.

Alicia and Choral entered, scanning around uncertainly in the darkness while the forty-plus people in the theatre were engrossed in the onscreen terminal-to-terminal rabbit hunt. The paying customers were clustered within the frontmost two-thirds of seating. Alicia and Choral settled down near the rear, two seats together, not far from the east exit door. I crossed behind them and sat down.

"Ladies."

They both tried to turn and unleash accusations. I placed a hand on each shoulder to deter them. "Watch the movie."

"What do you want?" said Alicia, softly enough not to be shushed by the people in the theatre. Her accent was lilted and vaguely European.

"Nice to see you again, Choral," I said.

"Fuck you," she said.

"No, I think it's fuck *you*," Alicia hissed at her assistant. "After tonight, you and I are no longer related, you dumb little squiff."

That froze Choral into a blank, standby state.

"Be forgiving," I said. Bounce images from the movie reflected off Alicia's glasses, upside down, as in a camera lens. "She didn't have any choice. Choral, remember when we were on the train?"

Choral nodded.

"Remember what I told you on the train, about being covered?"

She nodded again. Tears brightened her eyes in the lurid glare from the screen. Her nascent career had just turned into sewage.

And I was becoming more and more comfortable with using violence—even bluff violence—as a tool. No drug can equal the narcotic effect.

"Same deal," I said. "Now it's Q and A time."

"How much?" said Alicia.

"Beg pardon?"

"How. Much," she said. "How much do you want?"

"That's very kind of you," I said, just above a whisper. "But that's a question, and I'll be asking the questions. First question, How did you get mixed up with NORCO?"

Alicia stiffened and tried to bluff. "I don't know what you're talking abou—"

I tapped her gently on the back of the head. Her hair was thick and genuine. This kind of woman would hate physical prodding, most of all.

"Licia," I said, using Choral's nickname for her. "Do you really want to sit through this entire movie?"

"They came to me," she said, after a bit of soul-searching.

"See, that wasn't so hard. What did they want?"

"If I tell you, they'll kill me."

"If you don't tell me, I'll kill you right now." God, was that ever easy to say. Rather, for "Mr. Lamb" to say.

On the screen, one of the Chinese malefactor's decoys got roughly bulldogged to the floor and handcuffed. Choral kept her attention on the action.

Alicia swallowed a lump. "The whole thing was a third-party action. Nobody was supposed to get killed, not for real."

"Except maybe the guy you selected to do the job."

"That was NORCO's call. Nothing to do with me."

"You didn't answer my question. About what NORCO wanted."

"I met with them one time. One single time. They suggested the setup. But it had to come from outside. Third party."

"But they suggested whomever. And you sent Choral to make the arrangements?"

"Yes." She bit off the word. "I should have done it myself." She turned to Choral. "God, you are *so* fired."

"Eat shit, you fucking *bitch,*" Choral muttered, still watching the screen.

"Choral, shut up. Watch the movie."

"I don't have to put up with this shit," Choral said. "I did what she asked me to. And now, every five minutes, someone is threatening to kill me. So fuck you, fuck her, fuck y'all."

"I know how you feel," I said. The way her Southern accent leaked when she was stressed was just too cute. "I'm not supposed to be mixed up in this either, but here we all are. I want to know what you think is supposed to happen."

Alicia tried to turn again. Eye contact is important for offensive maneuvers. I tapped her on the head and she startled back to her original position. "Right now, you die, she dies, I'm happy and I can go back to dinner."

"You said you had a meeting." I had a firm grasp on Alicia's shoulder, now. "There must be a name."

"Don't you fucking touch me," she said.

I reached around to squeeze the nerve in her right armpit. It was something I'd learned by accident, while being tormented by my once-upon-a-time half brother, Clay. He had hoisted me into the air (the way Dandine had lifted Zetts) to begin some mayhem, and while I was flailing, I grabbed his armpit and hit the nerve bundle there. Grab just so, and the whole arm goes numb. That's what brothers and sisters were for, I guess—practice. Alicia arched slightly, then bulled down against the pain.

"Oww, goddammit!"

"Wrong answer, Licia."

"Geraldis. Or Gerald Something. That won't do you any good; they all have fake names anyway; *let go of my arm!*"

She was pissed off, but she still kept her voice down, and that was when I knew I had her. I pulled a Pilot pen out of my jacket pocket and pressed it into the hollow of her throat, from behind, while releasing her arm. "Feel that? This little toy can make you nerve-dead in less time than it will take your body to touch the ground."

"Gerardis. His name was Gerardis."

(Dandine to Choral, yesterday, right before we boarded the cab to the airport: *You don't happen to know a gentleman who might have given his name as Gerardis, do you?"*)

"And Mr. Gerardis was your friendly NORCO representative?"

"I already told you that."

"Tell me again." I was aware of consciously making my own voice deeper. A bad-guy purr.

She dealt with her breath as though expelling cigarette smoke. "Mister Gerardis was from NORCO."

"And what did NORCO want with you?"

During the skirmish of thoughts warring in Alica's brain, Choral spoke up, "She's fucking the next governor of California."

That would be the honorable Theodore Ripkin, per the dossier. The opponent of G. Johnson Jenks, the man who employed her as campaign manager.

"Thanks, honey," Alicia said acidly.

"She's also fucking some guy, some industrialist who also wants to be governor. Garrett Stradling."

I knew that name, too, and not just from the dossier. Stradling had been the CEO of Futuristics, Inc. The subway builders. The man behind the corporate curtain. Futuristics had been involved with my firm, Kroeger Concepts, for publicity purposes when the initial train tunnels collapsed during drilling, and sinkholes had bloomed in the middle of Hollywood Boulevard.

"Wait a minute—Stradling wants to be governor, too?" I asked. Alicia was trysting on both sides of the political fence. That took organization, not to mention sheer nerve.

"He changed his name," said Choral.

"That's *enough,* Choral." Alicia said.

"Changed his name to Jenks, five years ago."

My heart said, *coronary? Think I'll try it!* My mouth was hanging open.

Garrett Stradling had changed his name to G. Johnson Jenks. That was why Stradling had stepped down from the big-business limelight. Now he was re-created, with political aspirations and probably all the help NORCO could provide, as a breath-of-fresh-air candidate named Jenks . . .

. . . who had just become a client of my lust-object and co-worker at Kroeger, Katy Burgess. Katy and I had talked about the guy for nearly an hour while I was focused on her legs. My company was in line to sell this man as gubernatorial timber, and all the evidence suggested he was a NORCO puppet.

"Do you get it, now?" said Alicia. "Or do I have to drag a blackboard and pointer in here?"

She was making the beast with *both* candidates, waiting to see which would nose forward. You had to cut her some honest awe. Behind every great man was a good woman, so went the saying. In this case, the same woman. To consider the blackmail she had already stockpiled made me feel dizzy.

But I did not wish to allow a transfer of power to her, because she was already too comfortable in her anger. Immediately, I looked around for intruders. New patrons.

I already had Choral by the arm. "How many backups?"

She sighed. "Two in the parking garage, two in the forecourt, one more in the lobby, by now."

"Alicia, you sit right there for five more minutes. If I don't call my partner and tell him I'm clear in that time, you're done, am I clear?"

She nodded, envisioning checkmate. "I have to make a call."

"Do it."

She unlimbered her cellphone and punched a predesignated number. "This is A for Alpha. Have Marion stand down; I'm all right."

Pause. Then her expression smoldered.

"This is a fucking command override, numbnuts! On my authority. Do it." She clicked off.

I was already hustling Choral to the exit doors behind the screen. With luck, she'd be home in time to feed her cat, the unfortunately named Horace. As Andrew Collier might have said, Where's the girl? *Here,* then, was the girl.

We left the parking garage at the Laurel egress, on foot, moving downhill and southward, shrouded by the cover of residential trees and sidewalk. Not strolling; it was more a matter of my impulsion and Choral's lack of resistance. Our only noise was the crisp click of her heels on the pavement.

"Sorry about your job," I said.

"You didn't really have a gun on us back there, did you?" She asked this without looking at me. Watching her step.

"No."

"Great. I try to help out the boss, and here I am, look at me—fired." She stopped and balled her fists, growling loud enough to almost be a scream, *"Goddammiiiiiiiiit!"*

I braced her quickly. "Don't." She sagged in my grasp. "Don't do that."

"I'm sorry," she said. "Sometimes you just have to *yell,* you know? God, it's all so pointless . . ." Then some internal mirth caused her to start laughing.

"What?"

"Funny," she said, resuming our little couple's walk. "Without me, Licia is going to have a hell of a time keeping her *affairs* in order, right?"

"Her lovers."

"Like, half my goddamn day was scheduling things to keep one guy out of sight of the other guy. Let's see her juggle *those* balls on her own."

"Another pun?"

"Maybe. Her leverage tapes fill up two of those rolling fileboxes you get at Staples."

"Leverage tapes?"

"You know—tapes. Discs. Not suitable for YouTube."

"Are you talking about—" it seemed so lowbrow I had a hard time appreciating its simplicity and inevitability "—*sex* tapes?"

"My, my. Don't tell me you're *offended*. What a joke. Of course, tapes. Of sex. With politicians. For leverage. Is this a new concept to you?" She sniffed, almost haughty.

Why, yes—if Mr. Jenks, current Kroeger client under Katy Burgess's stewardship, also happened to be the selfsame Mr. Stradling, after a name change and wash-rinse of his old identity—yes, it could be, as they say in the business, an item of note. Voters are much more incensed by the concept of copulation than by warfare, but never mind that—here was a link between Dandine's universe and mine, at last.

Choral sighed, then made a tiny sound of defeat or release. "In a way, it's a relief. I shoulda known, the minute I had to start doing covert ops for her. All that *lying* and bullshit."

I thought, *well what did you* think *you were signing up for?* But I already knew the answer: Many people who worked honest lives in what Thoreau called "quiet desperation" often spent entire careers waiting for that one small chance at illicit advancement—that one happy accident or confluence of fates that equals embarrassment to some, but opportunity to others. Catching the boss in the lurch; covering his or her ass. Saving their kid from a hit-and-run. Being a fly on the right wall. Taking a bullet for a superior and not asking for recompense, but expecting it nonetheless. If you insider-traded, or went slightly sublegal *just this one time,* you might be able to buy a better car, or get out of your dingy apartment and into a real house. If you helped cover up or expose selected character quirks, some power person might enable the support of your entire family with a touch of the scepter. By such luck are people promoted. It had been Choral's turn. She had drawn the duty and done the deed, strictly for her own self-interest, lying to herself that she was spotless while others were vile. Your life is always somebody *else's* fault.

She had left her shell to perform one task, as a gamble.

"Like hiring hit men?" I said.

"Hey, she just gave me a contact, and I contacted that guy, Varga. If it was all a setup, she probably knew about Varga from those other guys, those narco guys."

"NORCO guys."

"Yeah, like you said."

"No, wait." Adrenaline blowback from my theatre drama was making me dizzy and slightly sick. "You said *guys,* before. Alicia said she met with just one guy. The business-suited guys; remember, you mentioned them?"

"Yeah, there were three or four of them." We had reached the corner of Laurel and Fountain avenues, which crosscut Hollywood between Sunset and Santa Monica boulevards. When neophyte actors asked Bette Davis for advice, she had been famously quoted as responding, "Take Fountain."

"Am I still a hostage?" she asked, watching the crosswalk light, giving us what was known locally as the Curse of the Blinky Hand.

"You're not a hostage," I said, trying to invoke the tone Dandine had used on me when he was trying to convince me of the same thing "I just need to figure a couple of things out."

She shrugged at that, digging in her shoulder bag for a Kleenex. "Great. You don't know any more about this than I do. I don't suppose *you're* hiring?"

I couldn't help but smile as I shook my head no.

"Because," she said, "normally I wouldn't be this way. I mean, you didn't hurt me or anything. But two fucking *days* in a row . . . my credit cards . . . this terrorist horseshit . . . like, everybody has a limit, right?"

"You don't know how right you are," I said.

"I *work* for a living," she protested. "I don't have time for all this rich-guy gamesmanship, this stupid pawn-pushing. Nothing ever changes anyway." Her Southern accent was leaking forth again. "The deck is so stacked, and the guys at the top always get away with everything. What's the point of ever caring, or trying?"

Idiot me, I almost wanted to hug her.

Before the light turned green, Choral gave me a full shot of Mace, right in the face, from the canister attached to her keybunch, while screaming epithets at me and kicking my ribs with her pointy high-heeled shoes as I fell to one knee and banged the back of my head against the light pole.

That's how I wound up getting arrested.

DAY THREE

J ust so you'll know, this is what happens while you're waiting to be
  booked at the Santa Monica sheriff's station . . .

It's cold in the holding cell. Colder, because they keep the tempera-
ture low to discourage hot-bloodedness, and because you're not wearing
your shoes. Your hands stink of the blue-gel industrial cleanser which
was the only option for cleaning off the fingerprint ink. They seem to
make sure your hair is in disarray when they snap the mug shots, and
they compel you to hold up your own little letterpress board with name,
date, crime code, and some of your important numbers. You are not
coerced. Your act of holding up the board is as plain as a confession.
The officer who runs you through the fingerprint procedure acts weary,
as though he has been doing this one task for a century, a penance in
Purgatory. He's chatty, "So, your story is that this isn't a rape, it's a misunderstanding?" His manner is so casual that it crushes your ego—the
guy is not worried you'll flip out or try to get away. You're already behind too many locked doors. The officer's breath smells like coffee
laced with bourbon. Being a WeHo sheriff (as you recall the joke),
there's a fifty-fifty probability the guy is gay. He isolates you nice and
tight into the holding cell, where there is a plank bench bolted to the
wall, and two pay telephones, in plain view of the cops' common room
from windows inlaid with wire and shielded by thick, overpainted
hurricane mesh. But you don't have any spare change; they've already
confiscated that and sealed it into a personal possessions envelope with
your name, misspelled in black marker.

Blinded by the Mace, your face raked open in furrows by Choral's
acrylic nails, your skull throbbing from its rough introduction to a protruding metal object (the crosswalk button on the lamppost), your breath
rawed and ribs aching from repeated kicks by Choral's pointy-toed,

patent leather high heels, the next sensation you felt was a cop's square-muzzled autopistol, kissing your kidney as somebody kneeled on your back and cuffed your hands. Choral must have spotted the sheriff's cruiser an instant before you did, and formulated her scenario with flashbulb speed. When you last glimpsed her on the street, she had managed to rip her pantyhose and bloody her own lip with admirable haste. "Glimpsed," because a uniformed officer named Bambra (according to his tag) made sure to guide your face right into the door frame as he was "helping" you into the rear seat, the one without door handles on the inside. *Bang,* stars, and no Miranda bullshit to waste anybody's time, either. Bambra's partner would cover that teeny procedural slip, if anybody ever asked, and nobody would.

You don't protest. You don't talk to the officers. You don't talk to the garrulous fingerprint guy. Anything you say, no matter how innocuous, will wind up in a written report as "spontaneously volunteered" information. Any protest counts as resisting arrest, and could land you in the hospital, or the morgue. You don't know your rights, but the police know what rights they wish to grant you—another luminous deception that adds glitter to the veneer of civilization we all pretend to know by heart.

En route to the sheriff's station, your arresting officers indulged in manly running commentary about what a fucking scumbag you are, you rapist clot of dogshit, you caveboy, you social degenerate. It's all sculpted to make you blow your cool, get a rise out of you, so you'll say or do something that justifies a little pit stop for coffee, with a side of energetic, professional brutality. *We just pulled over and he attempted to escape, so we shot him thirty or forty times. Hard, you know, to hit a moving target in the dark, and this prick's a public menace. We're doing the public a favor.* You sat on your hands, numb already, hurt all over, knowing that for the cops, this was the best time. Inbound to the station, committed to deliver a miscreant—therefore unavailable for other calls, barring an outright emergency. Another hour of guaranteed life, which time might have been spent cutting you down in the line of duty.

For this, they pay law enforcers an embarrassingly low wage, and you figure they have to get their perks where they can find them, according to mood. Fiscal inequity is not your burning preoccupation, anyway.

Numbers are. Access numbers, phonecard numbers, any string you can summon in order to profitably employ the pay phones, which will otherwise mock you with their stoic, recorded admonitions. Wrapped around your thoughts like hazard tape is Dandine's warning about the police, and "red light items." *We'd find ourselves very politely thrust into a holding cell, which would end our new career . . .*

Which is where you have landed, minus the courtesy. You take the rough processing by the police as a feeble sign that perhaps they don't know—exactly—who they have netted. Yet.

Public phone. Time a-wastin'. Maybe worth the risk. Maybe, in five more minutes, they'll haul your butt out of here and extinguish the option.

You decide to take a fool's chance, and using the access code assigned to your office phone, you call Katy Burgess's machine. Katy never answers her telephone, instead using her machine as a call screener, since she does not have a secretary (and everyone who pesters her about not answering, does).

"Katy, this is Conrad. Listen, I know this is going to sound strange but I'm in a tight spot. I need you to call this number—" you spiel off the number you remember for Andrew Collier's latest production office, somewhere in Culver City—"and just say that it's a personal message for the boss, and then say that Mad Dog is in jail. Remember, Mad Dog is in jail. I really need your help, kiddo. Thanks."

Personally, you remonstrate yourself for every bad thought and throwaway sexual fantasy you've ever had about good ole Katy. Your cry for help makes you sound like a five-year-old in need of an adult authority figure, and you indulge in a flash of self-pity that is quite out of character for you. Normally, you are the one who cuts loose selected bursts of power to achieve targeted goals. Can't you come up with anything better than this squalid, weak-kneed, hat-in-hand routine?

You can't recall the number you used to phone Collier directly at his house. You can't think of anyone else whose day needs ruination. Friends? None that apply. Acquaintances? Plenty; none of any use or worth, now. Relatives? Oh, please, gimme a break. You could ring up your ex-wife, if you wanted to hear her laugh and hang up.

There is no time for a second chance, anyway, since the bulky officer from the fingerprint adventure is pointing at you through the shatter-proof glass, and jingling a big ring of keys in his hand. Cell time.

Ruefully, you remember that Collier's home number is still on the Post-it note stuck to the useless credit card inside your now-confiscated billfold. So much for poor old Andrew.

The common bullpen is a big, brightly lit room stinking of disinfectant and bum stench (organic decay, sweat-rot, B.O., filthy socks). It looks about forty by forty feet with a twenty-foot ceiling, and is entirely without edges. Hard rubber is layered over the walls and floor, sealed over with durable canvas, painted bright yellow. One cushioned, pillbox-style peephole for monitoring prisoners (glassed in triple-thick Plexi that's smudged and fingerprinty on the inside), and one padded cell-block door—the only way in or out. Backed into the wall housing the door is a single, stand-alone institutional toilet of stainless steel with a push-button sink in the tank's top. No seat, no handles; half a roll of cheap TP balanced on the sink's lip. The mildly yielding canvas floor around the toilet is spattered with dried piss and what must be traces of vomit (after identifying a corn kernel, you don't want to look at it anymore).

After five minutes locked in this room, you're extremely glad that you cannot see all the odors roiling in the air. This is where the dregs land, in a room that can be easily hosed down.

The rounded corners (to prevent prisoners from damaging themselves) and the searing yellow above you, below you, all around you, make it simple to imagine yourself inside a giant, plastic child's toy. In here, the lights never go out. They blaze 24/7, from protective insets beyond reach, on the ceiling.

One more thing: You are not by yourself.

Nope, no solitary confinement for you. Right now you are a file number in general bullpen pop, until someone shows up with money or other just cause for your readmission to the world of the walking dead. After being issued a square of "blanket" about as effective against the cold as a thin towel, you are conducted through the padded door with the padded edges and then forgotten, phone call or not.

Tonight's other guests include three guys on the floor, curled the way you see derelicts sleeping on the sidewalk. They smell so apocalyptically awful that the more wakeful inmates have mustered them to one corner of the room, and one of them is lying sidewise, so the window guards won't see the blood on his face. This one is not asleep, he's unconscious after being punched out and discarded. He's the only one with no socks, and his Caucasian feet resemble soot-blackened wood from a prematurely expired fire.

Four others have been tanked tonight, before you, and they're still awake, though not moving much in the cold. Everybody still has their inadequate blanket, which means so far nobody has opted to play King of the Cell and collect them all to form layers for himself, with a fist in the face for any protestors. Two of them look haggard and resigned, like you. One looks like a biker, and the fourth is a Mexican who never utters a sound the whole time you're in the cell.

You'd sell a substantial portion of your stock portfolio to have a book to read, any book, anything with words on pages to free at least part of you from this world. Because once that door slams behind you (it's airtight enough to hurt your ears when it closes), and time does its rubbery elongation trick, you quickly become convinced that your stay is open-ended. In here, an hour seems like a day, with nothing to do except look at your own hands, and maybe pluck fabric pills from your socks. You have no urge to engage your fellow evildoers in small talk, or to bitch about the cops, or compare crimes. You don't dare talk to yourself, or nod off for very long, which is a shame because sleeping is the only way to plow through time in here. You realize the others feel the same way. They're sunk into themselves, huddled like Apaches, waiting, remaining alert enough to radiate a sense of warning to anyone who might pester them.

You're in the *bullpen,* you abruptly realize; with the other fuckups for this calendar date. Which means that the sheriffs don't know about Dandine, or any of the rest of it, at least, not yet.

Back against the wall, you pull up your knees, imitating the others. Your feet are already frozen. No meal here, till breakfast. You try half-baked mental counting games, or remembering the lyrics to songs. *That one ran two minutes, forty-two seconds on radio play; if I recite the lyrics, I will have passed nearly three more minutes.* You waste about ten minutes this way before you decide to risk a threadbare nap.

But your mind is too alive with other input. Such as, *Working backward, who, then, hired Dandine?*

Or how about, *Is NORCO blackmailing Alicia Brandenberg?* Did they propose some sort of fake hit to her, to help her credibility somehow . . . and then carry through without telling her? Or did someone leak the fake to Alicia?

That would mean a missing character in the chain, as Andrew Collier might propose. A go-between who contacts Alica, but *leaves out* the part about the hit being fake, then stands back to watch all the dominoes fall.

But to what benefit?

There were rich, time-consuming veins of worry to mine here, deductions to which you might apply your usually sharp intellect. No good, because there just isn't enough basic information. It was like being stuck with a fresh pad of paper and a pen with no ink.

You have never been in jail before. Ridiculously, you feel you have achieved some sort of watershed of manliness, by being stupid and unaware enough to get foxed by Choral, or, as Dandine might put it, "man-trapped." From now on, you can speak with authority on having been "inside." That is, if you don't get killed in here, if you ever make it back "outside."

If this was a movie about your predicament, some editor, by now, would have had the mercy to *Cross-cut Sharp to Simultaneous Action*—what was up with Dandine, concurrently, or Collier, or Choral, or Alicia; maybe even a bleak peek into the goings-on at NORCO. Anything to dispel the monotony of being stuck in this cell, one character, doing not much, from one boring angle; no action, no interstitial footage to achieve what cinemaphiles call "cutting rate" or "cutting tone"—editorial colorations that confer pace and rhythm to what the audience sees. Moviegoers never think about shit like this. They merely sponge up imagery for entertainment. They never think about how it's all put together; how complicated the process is of their transient little diversions. By now, if this was a movie, the audience would be getting bored of looking at this one poor-ass motherfucker sitting in a cell.

Get in line, assholes, you think. I have to *live* it.

Choral certainly worked you over well when you weren't hitting back. Trying to rest your head on your folded arms, atop your knees, makes your neck throb. Your bowels want to move, but no way you're going to drop trou in this shitpit, letting seven guys watch you take a dump and then, probably, pound the hell out of you for stinking up the room.

No wonder men become rapists, drug addicts, and chain-smokers in prison. Nothing else to do. You've been here half an hour and already you'd gladly chain-smoke a pack, igniting one off the other due to the prohibition on matches. The option does not exist: no smokes, no belts, no buckles, no change, no keys, nothing. Rising on numb feet and chancing a sip of water from the fountain button on top of the toilet tank constitutes a major excursion.

The introduction of yet another scumbag is a benchmark event. He gets tanked while you're still standing, so he looks at you first. As soon as the door thunks shut and the bolts clank, he says, "What the fuck *you* looking at, fagboy?"

No way he's speaking to anyone other than you.

He's not big—five-eight, maybe, with his shoes off—but he's broad enough to suggest he enjoys knife fights in parking lots as dessert when bars evict him at closing time. Wide, deep-set, piggy eyes below unwashed hair raked straight back and gleaming like shellac. Thick stubble outlines his jaw; you think of Fred Flintstone's permanent five o'clock shadow. Stressed-out gray T-shirt with pit stains in large wet-dry-wet rings. Jeans with road grease on the knees. A beer-gutted weekend warrior with rage to spare, still burning off his latest bender. He scopes the talent of the room and refocuses on making your life hell.

"Think you're better'n me, boah? Well we're both in the same fucking cell, so you better watch what you lookin' at."

Your mouth barely moves as you return to your warm spot on the floor. "I'm not looking at anything."

Silver glints appear in his eyes and he moves. "Whadjou say? Whadjou say, faggot?!"

You're turning, ready to duck, or maybe catch his fist one time, just to see his surprise at your defiance before you get mutilated. Your heartbeat is slamming and your adrenaline pumping, and you don't need any of it, because the biker-looking dude—who hasn't moved or uttered a syllable since you got here—appears as if by ghostly magic behind the new arrival, rising up to full looming height. He grabs the guy by the hair and the back of his jeans and propels him right past you, close enough to smell, face-first into the padded wall.

The plumper guy sags in the biker's grasp long enough for your savior to ram him into the wall one more time, for good measure. When he pulls him back the second time, there's blood leaking from his nose, and his eyeballs are rolled up to the whites. *Closed. Sorry we missed you.*

The biker-looking dude zombie-marches the insensate newcomer to the derelict end of the pen, and dumps him in a bone-free sprawl on top of the other unconscious occupants. Then he heads back to his original spot. You think of Andrew Collier's on-call, two-wheeler death squad, and even though you have no idea how to say a simple thanks to this stranger, you start to speak anyway, your tongue running ahead of your brain, as usual.

The biker-looking dude interrupts his trip to bug-board you, dead bang, with a glare. He has a lazy eye.

"Shhh," he says, holding a finger to his lips.

You nod, like one bad homie acknowledging another as they pass on a street. You sit as he sits.

The whole drama has sucked up another two minutes, tops.

Just like everyone else in the bullpen, I looked up, too hopeful, at the sound of the door unbolting. Some undifferentiated amount of time must have elapsed, because now I was freezing, and groggy, as though I had captured a swatch of thin sleep somewhere along the line. The grit and odor of the cell seemed embedded in my pores.

It was a new officer, a replacement for the burly fingerprint cop, cut from the same world-weary pattern. "Maddox," he said.

I just stared at him, from the floor, from my little tent of blanket around my knees.

The officer grimaced as if from a gas pain. "Yeah, you." He crooked a finger. "Come on."

My feet were on ice, in another country, and my legs were asleep. When I wobbled upright I was keenly aware of how stupid I looked. I could not walk, but managed a meandering shuffle toward the door. I tried another nod at the biker-sorta guy, who merely closed his eyes and put his head back down on his folded arms. That would have to play, for gratitude.

Thunk, and the cell was a universe away. "What happened?" I said.

The cop was marching me by a forearm. "Just come on."

I could see his wristwatch. Just after eleven o'clock, but A.M. or P.M.? "I don't understand," I said. "Am I out, or is this another—?"

The cop did not look at me, but offered another intestinal-stitch grunt. "Don't you know how this works?"

No, I didn't.

I found out, however, that it takes a fuck of a long time to get out of jail; just as much time as it does to get in. The downfall of our civilization won't be starvation or nuclear catastrophe or pollution or a stray asteroid; it'll be due to *processing.* I fully expected to be hand-delivered into the clutches of some anonymous and threateningly bland NORCO operatives. About the time the sheriff handed me my brown, string-clasp envelope and told me to *sign again,* my brain began to toy with the idea that maybe I was not walking my last mile, but had made bail.

Thanks to benefactors unknown.

Envelope in hand, personals accounted for, I was shown a door and the cops forgot all about me. I had to open it and walk through by myself. It was an unmarked exit that pooted you back into the front of the station, near the soft drink machines and another door, farther down a short hallway, labeled MEN. The thought of an actual, functioning restroom seemed like a gift from the gods. It was so weird—the more I thought about that, the more innovative and special it seemed, as though a restroom was an obvious convenience no one had ever bothered to invent. Phony, cheap hope flooded me. I wanted to spend a long time dunking my head in a basin of hot water, with real soap. Or, possibly, try to scrub my humiliation off my still-stinking hands. I realized I was still pulled into myself, shutters folded. My consciousness was still back in the cell.

"Yo, wrong way," said a voice behind me.

I turned, joints grinding. In the sickly greenish light of the station fluorescents I saw the gangly figure, dirty-blondish hair, SMOKING CAT

T-shirt, worn-in athletic shoes . . . but my brain was still on time-delay.

"Zetts," I said. It felt like test-driving a new mouth. "DMZ."

"At your service. Can we please get the fuck outta here?" *Getthefuck-outtahere* was all one word. "I fuckin *hate* police stations, dude."

I was lamely searching for some flip rejoinder when I caught the expression in his eyes, *We go like your life depends on it. Now.*

The deputy on desk duty was already looking at a screen, then at me, then back at the screen.

When he looked up again to triple-check, Zetts had already hustled me out the nearest door. "Go, go, go, don't stop, don't look back, keep going, before they—

I figured it out. Red flag.

Zetts's midnight-blue GTO waited in the visitor lot in all its jacked-up, muscle-car splendor. Something seemed strange about it, but Zetts was in a hurry. "Get in—we gotta fly."

Fly where? Why? My mouth still wasn't working right.

His gaze darted down when I sank into the passenger bucket. "Seat belt," he said. When he fired the engine the whole car shook, grumbling, a bomber revving up to takeoff speed. The "seat belts" were the type of harness that crossed over *both* shoulders. Competition grade; I should have guessed.

He did not have to tell me to hang on.

The GTO nosed harshly down as Zetts spun the leather-wrapped steering wheel and we backed furiously out . . . and continued, in reverse, down the canted drive marked ENTRANCE. We piled ass-first into the street and I heard civilian brakes whine as collision was averted. Deputies were already boiling out of the exit door we'd just used, shouting stuff, unholstering sidearms.

Zetts worked the five-speed shift and mashed me with acceleration, slip-sliding around the nearest corner and cutting off a line of right-turn-only mall fodder at San Vicente.

"Zetts!" Useless, to object.

"Silence *please!*" He jammed a protruding cassette into its slot and the cabin detonated into the harsh four-four time of (a song I later discovered was) a Pinch oldie called "Brainfuck." We weaved around commuters doing the legal limit and crammed about a light-year of real estate between us and the sheriff's station. The world went past us, too fast. I was scared to look out the windshield.

The hammering music wasn't doing my headache any good, either. It was too loud and I was now, officially, too old. Before I could make an exaggerated, pantomime face to assert my adult disapproval of this, Zetts directed my attention to the glove compartment.

I opened it on the second try as the car gobbled distance. I pulled out a gun, some kind of semiauto pistol heavy enough to be loaded. Zetts shook his head *no* and indicated something else. It was a unit similar to a handheld volt-ohm-meter—little swing needle, LEDs, buttons. I tried to hand it to him but he shook his head vigorously; he was driving, dammit. Using a sporadic sign language of gestures and expressions, I managed to successfully click the thing on. The needle bobbed into the halfway zone. Three of the row of five LEDs glowed vaguely orange. Zetts pointed at the buttons and I began poking them until the needle ebbed and the lights winked green all across. Zetts gave a thumbs-up, and only then did he crank down the volume on the Kickers booming from the rear deck.

"They tied a can to us," he shouted.

"The cops? Back there?"

"No, no! They're just nuisance value. But fifteen more seconds and we wouldn't have made it out the door." He jerked a thumb past his shoulder. "Our NORCO friends are on us."

"What do you mean—a tail?"

"Yeah!" Our speed was climbing again.

"Where?"

"Behind us about two blocks—the SUV and the Mercury Marauder."

"How do you know?"

"Both black, both new, no front plates, dealer plates in back, no trim, wraparound tint, driving in tandem!" His eyes checked the mirrors. He had installed one of those panoramic rearviews that could reveal a Cinemascope version of whatever was behind us.

Yelling was easier than talking, against the stereo and the bullroar of the engine. "Are you kidding?"

"Yeah, sure!"

"How can you tell?"

"A thousand things. Neither of 'em has any shit hanging from the mirror. No stickers. Identical sunglasses. You can just tell. Mostly from their tracking pattern. They know we know, but they *don't* know we've already made them. Newbies, definitely. Who can't hear us, now." He pointed, indicating I should replace the box (and the gun, too) in its compartment.

"Homers? That liquefies their little transistorized minds."

He notched the music up. "Fuck CDs, man, I hate 'em!" He punched the light at La Brea and hooted in triumph. "Hah! Beat that fuckin camera, dude!"

I looked behind and saw the double-strobe of the traffic camera as it photographed both of our pursuers, lagging through the red.

"Don't *look,* man, fuck! Eyes front, keep low, okay?"

"Where're we going?"

"Speed zone, baby!" He let loose a war whoop and laid on the gas. "As soon as we can smoke these chumps . . ."

The GTO's fat road-grabbers hashed a tight turn onto a residential side street . . . then Zetts went even faster, miniaturizing the chase cars in the rearview. His only distraction from his expert wheelmanship was the indulgence of extending a stiff middle finger out his window. "DMZ pops the clutch and tells the dicks to *eat his shit!!*"

As soon as our pursuit was foxed, Zetts stood on the brake and did a two-point backward scoot that was breathtaking to behold. I hadn't even seen the driveway on which he had zeroed-in, with his prescient pilot skills, the mosh-pit version of Zen that contradicted his entire character. He was the first driver I had seen become one with his machine, though I'd heard that expression thousands of times. Hell, I'd even used it, in campaigns to make hapless consumers feel more like bold individualists by purchasing a car. The numbnuts factor I had witnessed at the Sisters' was completely gone, and Zetts was totally in control.

We backed into a clapboard garage at the end of a downscale block. I had no idea where we were. Zetts cut the motor and leapt out to drop the hinged door. Then he resumed his seat and handed me a cold can of beer the way a magician hands a bouquet to the most attractive lady in the front row. I was still trying to fathom the elaborate buckle on the shoulder harness. It was a hooked deal similar to the clasps on a fireman's jacket.

Zetts raked his hair back and depth-charged most of his beer in a series of long, greedy swallows. "Ahhh. Take five."

I was still getting used to gravity. "That was . . . interesting. Don't the cops ever chase you? I mean, isn't this high-speed chase thing sort of illegal?"

He shot me a dour look. "Yeah, if you're a fuckin moron. I never open Trigger up unless I've got their patrol grid, boss." He snapped open brewski number twoski.

"I don't think I understand anything you just said."

He sighed. We had switched ranks—now he was the grown-up, telling the kid why crossing against traffic was bad. "You gotta know where they are, when they are. What their pursuit jurisdictions are. How far they'll chase you and where they'll call in interception or backup. What the cleanest escape route is. *In advance.* Or else you got an assfull of helicopters and your big, smiling bazoo on the news."

"But there were no cop cars at all."

"Sure there were. They were on us five blocks from the station. But they were busy chasing the chasers. Probably still are."

My mouth stalled and I'm afraid a drip-drool of beer escaped. "I didn't hear sirens."

Zetts leaned over to clink cans, with a satanic grin. "It's a rush, ain't it? All your senses change."

I never even saw flashbars, not even when I looked back. In the mirrors. Nowhere. But the beer was absolutely refreshing and delicious. I'd only read about danger and freedom attenuating the senses, and dismissed it as melodramatic ballyhoo. It really was true . . .

. . . unless the whole chase was a custom setup, designed to make me trust Zetts, whom Dandine had named as a potential traitor.

A bubble clogged, halfway down my parched throat.

"Okay," said Zetts. "Flashback: That doodad in the glove compartment? That was to cook the leash they stuck on Trigger back at the sheriff's station, when I was inside. No way to avoid that, so, you know—compensate."

"You call your car *Trigger?*"

"Do *not* mock my wheels." He spent a moment narrowing his gaze, daring me to badmouth my escape chariot.

"By *them* I assume more NORCO guys?"

"Yeah, most likely. Assholes."

"So, who sent you to get me?"

"You know who. Mr. D."

"Is he still at Collier's?"

"Negatory." Zetts shook his head as if this was stale news. "He's gone from that place. Whereabouts currently anybody's guess. We're supposed to wait for, y'know, an update from parts unknown."

I tried to build the scenario in reverse. It wasn't practical for Dandine to have tailed me to the movie theatre. I screwed that up all on my own. Next likelihood was that Katy Burgess had gotten my SOS ("from stir," as we hard-boiled jailbirds say) and executed my foggy instructions gorgeously. I regretted roping her in, but it had been my only way out. Collier had told Dandine. Dandine had figured out what had befallen me, and sent Zetts. All that had required nearly twelve hours, from the time of my arrest.

"We talked about leaving you inside for eight more hours," said Zetts. "So the getaway would be at night. Better odds. But he didn't like the idea of leaving you there with no backstop and no protection. Plus, like you saw, they were five seconds from grabbing you when I showed up. Besides, I fuckin *hate* leaving people in the can; that's like *no* fuckin place to be."

Testify, brother.

"Besides, I owe Mr. D. For, y'know, fuckin up the key thing. I'm sorry as hell, dude."

I had just passed Go without two hundred bucks to un-flush my life, but, strangely, I wasn't mad. I was *part* of something . . . whatever it was. Feeling uprooted and different felt good. I found it difficult to actually complain.

"Well, y'know . . ." I fizzled out.

"Yeah," said Zetts. "We could all have ourselves a good cry, but what's the point?"

"You're a hell of a driver, DMZ."

"Thanks, brah. It ain't me so much as the chaser block in this sweet piece. Trigger can outrun any cop modification, even the hemis. Listen— kill that brewski and help me pull the skins on this thing."

"You lost me again."

Zetts disembarked the GTO and nibbled at the hood with a grimy fingernail. The paint, midnight blue, seemed to peel up in his hand like contact paper, revealing the car's true, glossy crimson coat, beneath. "Skins," he said. "Like on movie cars. Start stripping this shit and I'll switch out the plates."

Doping out the escape route (with a Plan B alternate path, I assumed), plus modifying his car's identity, had all involved a lot of time, preparation, and thought. Thoroughness earmarked it as Dandine's architecture. Rolling out of jail, the car had looked different to me, but the alteration had been elusive because it was so simple—color.

"Zetts, where the heck are we?" I said. "Is this some sort of safe house?"

I almost divined his answer, when I got out of the GTO and got a look at the expensive tools and equipment lining the rear wall of the dim garage.

"Naw," he said. "I live here."

So you stare at the blank blue square of the behemoth TV monitor in the "living room" (process of elimination has named it so). Zetts notes that he always leaves the TV on whether or not there is programming to be downloaded from his bootleg, black-box dish. He likes the warm electronic glow in the room, for company, he tells you.

You see crate furnishings and sprung secondhand chairs with visible afros of stuffing and patches of duct tape, and conclude Zetts spends most of his leisure time somewhere else, or in the garage. The sole decoration is an enormous poster—what used to be called a 24-sheet—for a 1950s movie called *Hot Rod Girl*. It covers one entire wall in the house, which is a small, totally anonymous two-bedroom cottage. No mail is received here.

Zetts shucks his T-shirt one-handed, shrugs at you, and says, "Pitted out." You presume this means the secretions and sheer panic of your special, Speed Racer moment has transferred to Zetts's garment. Kind of like the method you always use, taking something that makes you feel emotionally rotten and transferring it to the nearest available candidate, so you can reassure yourself you're a decent guy, all-around.

You did this to your ex-wife; made her the bad guy. You've done it to most of your girlfriends and will probably do it to Katy Burgess, if you live long enough. You compartmentalize excellently, and don't allow any cross-pollution in the name of something so shabby as someone else's feelings.

Thoughts of Katy Burgess, again. At the very least, Katy had gotten your message to Andrew Collier and thence to Dandine, all without the benefit of a secret decoder ring. Dammit, now you really want to see her. Not to use her, not to get anything out of her. To thank her. You allow yourself a brief side-story on what might have happened if it had been Katy, not you, who had found the locker key. Would she be sitting here right now instead of you? Would she have fared better, or worse? The reasons you think she may have done better, or at least more professionally, make you want to see her face even more.

If you live long enough. Interesting concept. Rather, an old concept with new vitality. The old version helped you procrastinate on things that didn't matter anyway. The new version counts the remaining hours of your life a minute at a time. Everything seems turned up, enriched, amplified. What food you've managed to grab tastes better, more essential, more satisfying. Your Cro-Magnon hunter-gatherer roots are asserting themselves, emphasizing survival, if only for one more day. This attitude, you acknowledge, can help your career. If you live long enough to resume it.

Zetts is in his mid-thirties, at least, and he is still living like some college bum on the slum. He owns a couple of Melmac plates and cups, and a lot of empty beer cans, the latter almost classing as a collection. There are engine parts spread out on newspaper in various corners of the room, and they make the air redolent. There are no curtains and all the shades are pulled down—against burglars, Zetts says, as though it is the most natural response in the world. Why else?

Cool and dim, here in the cave.

You wonder when it happened to you—that moment when the exuberant dedication of your twenties suddenly caved in to the bitter disillusionment of your thirties. And how come nothing comes after that? Just more bitterness, reinforced cynicism, the calcification of your personality into a slick know-it-all who attacks what he wants, pins it to the mat, nails it, and gets the job done. If someone asks if you are happy, in the conventional sense most of the walking dead understood the concept, you'd have to think about an honest answer . . . then say something else, something that sounds great, and changes the subject.

Truth was, the next stage in the program is total paranoia, nearly always. The gradual walling-up of self, until you are entombed in your own fear, like that guy in the Poe story, except without a bottle of decent wine.

If you are to get erased sometime in the next twenty-four, you can think of a couple of people who would say it was a "shame," but nobody who might weep. Your parents, long split, have been taking the big dirt nap for nearly a decade now, reunited in the oddest way. You have a half brother somewhere, to whom you have not spoken since Dad's funeral. Hey, the phone works both ways, right? Not that anyone keeps the same number, anymore, for longer than a free subscription to a magazine nobody wants, anyway.

A couple hundred thousand people disappear off the face of the planet every year, so say the stats. Earth swallowed 'em. Aliens got 'em. Killed in some trackless jungle. Mugged and left for dead under some bridge and never identified. Changed their names, edited their pasts, shucked their baggage, and became new people . . . sort of the way you did, while in college.

Or they got assassinated, by contract. In America, if you know the right contacts, you can arrange to have nearly anyone murdered for a ridiculously low price. Efficiency (and avoiding felony time) costs more. Contractual clauses are infinitely malleable; loopholes are one of the things that help Kroeger Concepts chug so much steam. Nothing is ever ironclad, because there isn't anything that cannot be renegotiated.

Contracts are one illusory way of trying to impose order on a chaotic world—the key word being "illusory." Reality was fluid; as Burt Kroeger once told his staff, the only constant is change. If you rule straight black lines around your reality and get it into a nice, neat box, then you would break, not bend, when changes you could never foresee swooped in to alter your map. And it didn't take something catastrophic, like a terminal disease or an erupting volcano, to catalyze change.

Sometimes all it took was idle curiosity. Like picking up a locker key that's not yours and wondering what might happen if . . .

Here you sit, criticizing your idea of Zetts, the man who just slung your ass from danger, and you really know nothing about the guy. Blond, blue-eyed, stoner, good wrench, good combat driver, who seems more wired into real-reality than you ever were.

You thought you knew everything, then Dandine came along and proved that practically everyone was in on the joke of the world, except you.

You are less worried about your situation, and more concerned with hunger, thirst, food, rest. Safety.

Maybe this is how you change, next.

"Yo," said Zetts, ambling from his dark bedroom wearing a clean T-shirt, soft-old like a furry grocery bag, its silkscreened logo cracked and split with a hundred washings. HOOKER HEADERS RULE. "The man's on the phone, for you."

He handed me a cellphone. The display was a jumble of icon figures, not a number.

"Dandine?"

"Still kicking," said Dandine's voice from the other end. "Guess my first question, why don't you?"

I had thought about this moment, and rehearsed an answer that seemed to lose structural integrity and fall to pieces as it tried to crawl out of my mouth. "You were hurt; I wanted to *do* something."

"You mean like, put us in *more* danger?"

"You know what I mean." I felt nervous and stupid. Futile.

"You mean you wanted to contribute—to bear some load for your situation, become more of an active player? Right? Connie, you're an advertising man, not a black-bag dude. Although I appreciate the effort, you've really balled things up."

I started to ask the obvious questions, then shut up before Dandine could tell me to.

"For starters, you skated out of the police station about five milli-seconds before NORCO drew a bead on you. I didn't think I'd get Zetts down there in time."

"So, I'd still be in jail?"

"No. I would have had to risk the exposure to pull you out my-self."

"With your arm in a sling and your fake ID."

"Imagine casualties," Dandine said. "Then imagine you and me both winding up in a steel room somewhere. You know—a place we're not allowed to send postcards from."

"I had to do something!" I knew Dandine was trying to stoke me into barking, but I couldn't help it. "I feel completely out of con-trol! You were incapacitated! I had to go . . . get out . . . get away. Try to think—"

Slow hiss of air; Dandine sighing into the phone, or perhaps exhal-ing smoke from one of his five-per-day. "Yeah, well, you could have done worse, for a tyro. Tell me the part about Alica Brandenberg."

"First-class monster hellbeast who is currently sleeping with both candidates for the California governorship. She knows about NORCO."

"Hell, NORCO probably groomed her."

"How's your shoulder?"

"Hurts like a sonofabitch," he said.

"How's Collier?"

"Clear," said Dandine. "Vaguely amused at the drama. I thanked him and relocated. You really owe that guy a huge favor, someday."

"Why'd you leave?"

"Didn't want to attract any flies by staying put."

I found I was pacing, tiger-walking the cage of Zetts's living room, gradually and restlessly expanding my arc. Hyped-up, the way a politi-cian must feel as district vote totals trickle in on election night.

"Why didn't little Choral just turn you back over to Alicia Branden-berg's bodyguards? She must've had four or five, dogging her."

I tried to put events in order. "I guess that when she Maced me, the cops were right there on the street. Coincidence."

"Never discount a random factor," said Dandine. "It makes sense. If she lost face with her boss, and delivered you as leverage toward her job and her trustworthiness, NORCO would have you by now. I wonder why she didn't."

"This is kind of hard to explain, but I think she wasn't all that keen on working for Alicia Brandenberg." From my own view, she had begun to see just how deep the sewage was, and had begun to rethink her goals about the time she had told her boss to get fucked. "Which gives her points as a human being."

"Too bad she'll never get a chance to enjoy her moral state of grace. She's off the grid, Conrad. Disappeared. Watch the news and you'll probably see her turn up dead, and if you're very, very unlucky, you will be the fall guy. Prepare for that—murder suspect, dragnet, a crappy snapshot of you on TV. I know what I'm talking about. So don't mourn her for kicking you in the balls and making you infamous."

My voice dried up in my throat. He could have mentioned that up-front. He had not—proving who was still in charge. "How do you know?" I said, dreading the answer.

"Most obvious course of direct action," he said. "You're tailor-made to take the fall. If Choral knew about this little gubernatorial conspiracy, then she clearly knew too much, so purging her would be in the game plan already. That way, no severance, no unemployment. Economy counts. Not your fault—but you pick up the check, see?"

My vision started to swim and I felt like puking.

That meant that Alicia Brandenberg had been a total NORCO puppet, trained well enough to never reference her true puppeteers. They had aimed her at both candidates, Jenks and Ripkin, like a deadly Tomahawk smart missile of sexuality with no fuse. When in doubt, cover both targets, accumulate intel, then choose who you can best advantage. Her machinations had been so complicated that she required a staff, hence Choral Anne Grimes. There was a distinct possibility that Alicia had been jockeying for position, ready to take over for either Ripkin or Jenks, whoever fell first. Alicia could seduce nearly anybody, and had even succeeded in making a confidant out of Choral Anne Grimes . . . until Choral Anne broke character and got uppity as a result of being threatened by guys with guns. Me and Dandine. There was a second distinct possibility that Alicia was grooming Choral Anne as her own manipulative replacement, once she moved more visibly into the sphere of political double-dealing. God, it was an endless downward spiral, a rabbit hole filled with antipersonnel mines that never, ever got to the bottom.

Third possibility, even weirder: Alicia had managed to spin this spiderweb all on her own, and NORCO had found out about it, and a deal had been cut with extra percentage points for initiative.

So, in the official story version, who was supposed to be the architect of Alicia Brandenberg's failed assassination? Answer: Jenks *or* Ripkin— whomever NORCO chose to discredit. It was hermetically brilliant, in its way.

Which made Alicia Brandenberg herself the person who had hired Dandine, using enough stalking horses to cover her culpability. Hired Dandine for a murder attempt that was supposed to fail, thus nourishing her credibility.

But why had Dandine taken the gig, if he had already bailed out of NORCO? That was one I didn't have an answer for, and now was the wrong time to ask. He was running his own playbook, and so far I hadn't been killed.

But others had.

I felt bad. I felt responsible. I wanted to take it all back. I felt like a dry dog turd in a dirt yard. I sat down, heavily, all the starch gone from my legs.

"Where are you?" I said.

"I'll make contact soon. I have to figure some things out, myself. You sit tight at Zetts's. Don't even look out the window."

Click; he was gone, just like that.

Which meant Zetts's assignment was to make sure I did nothing. Which meant that I was still a prisoner. The exterior doors of his home, I now noted, were deadbolted by keyed locks from the inside. The windows were barred. And Zetts probably had an equalizer or two in reserve, just in case I got rowdy.

Zetts was in the kitchen. "What's the word, Thunderbird?"

"We wait," I said.

"I got frozen pizza. Lots of stuff on the tube."

"Yeah." I felt hopelessly out of the loop—superceded, extracted, impotent, and pointless. This was what normal people called despair.

In the cramped corridor leading to Zetts's bathroom, a hallway composed mostly of doorways, I saw one-by-six pine planks had been laid across the tops of the door moldings to form quick and dirty shelves that held wall-to-wall paperbacks. Zetts had every single *Doc Savage* book in print. The newest reprint was fifteen years old; the oldest, older than Zetts by a decade. Doc Savage, Promethean superhero of the thirties and forties. The Man of Bronze. By Lester Dent, and his cronies, writing under the house name Kenneth Robeson.

Nobody was who they said they were.

"You've got to be shitting me," I said, holding up a thin copy of one of the adventures (fans in the know called them "supersagas") titled *Death in Silver.* "How do you even know about these?"

Zetts was pulling on another beer. "Got the whole set off eBay," he said, rather pleased with himself. "I like 'em. They're fun to read. They're *easy* to read. And Doc always wins."

Blackmail is such a vital industry in Mexico that they have hostage hotels. For five hundred dollars per night, faceless men will keep your kidnap victim in a locked room with no escape options, no weak links in the chain. Fed and watered, provisioned with a bed, bathroom, and TV set, bottled up beyond the reach of the world.

The hostage hotel is hermetically secure. Some are in remote locations, others, right in the middle of Mexico City. The police have been bribed into ignorance. *El Cañonazo* is an enormous part of the Mexican economy, so much so that without all the corruption, the state itself would collapse. Every week or so, some minor celebrity's kid or politician's grandpa is abducted; about half the time it is somebody vaguely newsworthy, which feeds the fever-pitch hysteria of tabloid reporters. Usually the victims (Dandine would call them *clients)* of such an exercise only lose two or three fingers before the targets stop fucking around and pony up the cash everyone knows they possess. A sense of general public resentment underlies the drama; sympathy for the plight, yet resentment toward the haves from the have-nots. How dare you have more money than me? See what it gets you? Regional TV news treats it all like a lurid game show, showcasing the returned victims, who invariably smile at the camera and display their mutilated hands, often still bloody or mummified in soaked bandages.

You think: If Mexico has business-planned it so well on the entry-level, what would the whole enterprise be like with ready cash and resources? Americans still preferred to live in a fairyland where graft was publicly condemned as a backroom aberration, not an open, inevitable, necessary evil for doing business.

(Remember that country? The one whose flag flew every night when TV stations ended their broadcast day, back when freedom of speech was more vital than political correctitude? When the Berlin Wall was still standing, and there was no such word as *downsizing*? Yeah, *that* country . . . before it became East Berlin West.)

Dandine could have stashed you under the stewardship of Zetts two days ago, but did not. Why? You conclude that Dandine had: (1) been honest in his urge to unload secret stuff on some outsider, or, more likely (2) wanted to expose you to danger in order to convince you that his rattle about NORCO was real, so that (3) you'd buy his direction with less question, feeling unmoored and out of your element. The paradigm of the babe in the woods is supposed to engender sympathy and warn against naivete. The poor dupe in the hostage hotel is a depletable resource that can be quickly bartered for cash. So what is the lesson, here—what is the goal?

Your golden rule is make the customer sell himself, always advantaging their basic greed, weakness, or self-interest. You're just there to help them get whatever they already want. You just make them more honest, and you are almost never disappointed. Greed, weakness, and self-interest are the baseline for all human behavior.

You let the hot water in Zetts's adequate shower pound your scalp. It feels good to wash off the experience of jail and send it down to meet the sewer . . . even if you're still somebody's inmate, agenda unknown. You consider your fingers, and what it might take to keep them.

Dandine has not surfaced. He has not raced down to hold your hand because it was not necessary. Zetts has gotten you out, and that was all the news Dandine was interested in at this moment. You'll see Dandine again when it is time to do something new, something further, either to compound an elaborate network of lies, or to bring the drama, real or not, closer to its conclusion. Even though, right now, all you want to do is sleep for a week.

"Let me show you something." Zetts beckoned from the dim recess of what I presumed was his bedroom. Toweled off and temporarily installed in one of my host's black T-shirts (silkscreened with a pink pussycat and the logo GAY MAFIA MEMBER), barefoot, and wearing my jail trousers, I entered the aquarium glow of Zetts's computer kingdom. The bed, shoved into a corner and perpetually unmade, was an afterthought. The real deal, here, was the monitors, keyboards, and hard drives. It figured.

He peered at my face. "You shave?"

"Yeah." It had been another way to scrape off the past day. My chin was smooth again. "So?"

"You, uh, didn't, like use the beard trimmer, I hope."

"No."

"I'm just saying . . . um, 'cos I tried using that thing to trim my pubes, and I, uh, kinda shredded my scrotum a little bit." He opened up a metal folding chair for me. It had FIRST CHRISTIAN CHURCH written on the back in Magic Marker.

I closed my eyes, trying to picture his grooming regimen. "Why did you do that?"

His main monitor was opened up to an Internet browser. After a couple of load seconds, an adult homepage displayed itself, all facial come shots and glistening genitalia. "Because that's what *she* likes," Zetts said. He pointed.

A woman appeared on-screen. A naked hooter queen with that beach movie expression of sizzling intellect. She moaned in a repeat cycle as she jammed a gigantic cucumber in and out of her photo-real vagina, cadenced as a windup toy.

"That's Rebecca," said Zetts. "My virtual girlfriend."

"You've got to be kidding." Pause. "You're not kidding, are you?"

"Hey, it's not like I get much of a chance to lounge at the coffee boutique and scope chicks with laptops, fuckin *poetry* books, brah. Look at the shit I do. Not much window there for work-related love affairs. No MOAS."

"Mo' ass?"

"No—*M-O-A-S*. Minimized Option Attraction Syndrome. Some chicks look better to you if they're the only chicks you're ever around, like, in a work environment."

Like Katy Burgess, at Kroeger, for example. Moonstruck romantic that I am, I wondered if I would ever see her again.

"But compare them to the outside world product, and *whoooo* let the dogs out, ya hear that? Now, Beckah here, she can do things. She comes with a hardline voice person to, y'know, get your juices flowing, live, one-on-one."

"On the phone, you mean."

"Fuckin-A on the phone. Safe sex, dude. But anyway, that ain't what I wanted to show you."

"You tried to shave your pubic hair with a clipper because an animated Internet girl with a real, live phone voice *told* you to?"

He bounced a surly look off me. "This is the twenty-first century, blood. Never mind. You wanted to know about NORCO, right?"

"Oh, geez, I should have thought of that right away," I said. "Just go to the NORCO Web site."

"Even people who don't advertise need a database," said Zetts. "Now, check this out; you can't do this on ordinary wireless or even a cable modem or DSL. Has to be a strong-ass digital signal, uplinked to a satellite." He devoted his full attention to entering a URL, which popped up in the proper window:

http//: www.domainhost@neupixel.com/index/html

When he hit RETURN, the www part disappeared from the URL.

"That's when it happened," he said. "When they modified the uniform resource locator because people got tired of manually typing superlong addresses. Now you can just enter the domain name and it routes automatically. Systems always compress; it's like an abbreviation of what's already an abbreviation that sends the same information. One, two, three—protocol, domain name, and hierarchical file name."

"That's when *what* happened?"

"Clone system, based on mirrored signals."

"Please," I said. "My headache wants to come back and I don't have time to run out and get a fucking nerd degree."

"Just watch." He blanked the URL from the window and typed:

h/t/t/p/:::access

The drive noodled for a bit—that "searching" sound which, for me, usually indicated the thing was about to crash. What displayed next was no surprise:

ERROR = 404 DOES NOT EXIST / NOT ON SERVER

Zetts checked his watch (a no-frills Seiko), counted off thirty seconds, then typed:

Route2access:::portal753690

The computer did not crash. It did not say *The Finder Needs Your Attention* or that anything had "unexpectedly quit." Instead, there came a barber-pole roll bar and the legend:

. . . connecting . . .

The new URL that appeared was a complex string of characters, symbols, and numerals that ran right off the menu window. Zetts keyed to starboard to show it to me. "See? It's like two feet long."

"What is it?"

"Internets within the Internet," he said. "Webs inside the Web, like a subterranean data network. The Internet is like a venetian blind—you twirl the thingie, and it looks like a solid barrier. Look at it at an angle, and all you see is cracks, provided by the illusion of solidity."

I had thought of the venetian blind metaphor myself, a day earlier. It was disorienting, as though Zetts had been briefed on my inner musings.

"Ever get cable TV?" he said.

"Once." Way back during the Bronze Age.

"Yeah, right, well, that co-ax they strung into your house is capable of carrying like a hundred times the signal needed for mere TV. The Internet is like that, too, but it would be like trying to see individual molecules in a solid object. A whole big gang of like untapped potential." He pointed at the screen, which now showed a simple white box with a subwindow headed SUBMIT INQUIRY and blinked with the persistence of a tapping foot.

"So . . ." He scooted back from his berth, offering the keyboard to me.

I typed NORCO. The screen shot back AUTHORIZATION REQUIRED / LOGIN. "Strike One," I said.

"Just wait, dude. Jesus." Zetts leaned in and typed NAKEDAPE21, all caps. "Dandine got this from some guy on the inside."

NORCO (NORTH AMERICAN CONSULTANCY, 1990–98)
WELCOME, NAKEDAPE21

A long homepage menu flowered beneath this. Corporate overview. Business plan. Profit history by quarter. Awards and commendations. Resources.

"All bullshit," said Zetts. "Designed to bore you to death if you actually poke in and read it."

I thought of the labyrinthine language of contracts the thickness of a phone book and weight of a dead Rottweiler. Of clauses and codicils, riders and warranties. I thought of people whose tax returns ran to 670 bound pages per year (not *me,* but I did know a few), none of it good subway reading. After the first few lines, you just naturally glaze over. On our planet, Earth, everyone is usually so busy talking that no one actually pays real attention to anyone else. Each talker merely awaits the next lull in the tirade, so he or she can interpose with what they were talking about already, anyway. This catacomb of the Internet was like that—capable of being ignored in plain sight.

"People are dumb and lazy," said Zetts. "They scream about their privacy being invaded, about Big Brother watching them, and the Internet comes along, and whaddaya know—those same people give up all their vital stats *voluntarily.* Which is the only way true surveillance could ever work, since there will never be enough warm bodies, or man-hours, to keep track of everybody else in a meaningful way. Like, now the government can flag anybody they want by just using a keyword. People put their fucking *diaries* online, for god's sake."

"People who feel invisible want attention," I said. I found that I wanted less, as my life wore on.

"Anywhoo, that's the smoke," he said. "Here's the fire." He hit the FUNCTION / ESCAPE keys together and I almost stopped him. All home computers need a key that reads *take it back*. Think of all the times you've hit the wrong thing at the right time and lost an hour of unsaved work, or all the times your machine took you someplace you did not wish to go, due to a mis-stroke. *Take it back.*

The screen read SUBMIT INQUIRY again.

"Look, Zee, we're back where we started."

Zetts shook his head, smug. No we weren't.

The background window was different now. Active. Zetts typed in MADDOX, CONRAD L. and a whole lot of data began to reveal itself.

"There you are," he said, grinning like a coyote.

This part is going to hurt.

Come along with me, as I review the highlights of my existence. You might stop to consider now and then what your own chart of ups and downs might look like; whether you fared better, or worse, or are continuing to lie to yourself.

I hunched my wheelless chair into Zetts's pilot position, and began to scroll as indicated.

> 1966: I come squalling into the world on August 28, a breach birth, the sole genetic issue of Maddox, Carleton Coletrane (1932–1988), and the former Joan Maurine McDermott (1939–1972). My dad's occupation is listed as SALESPERSON with a number of subheadings under <q.v.>

Despite the fact that it was the sixties, my mom is summarily dismissed with the one-liner descriptive *housewife*. From my recollect, she loved me; I was planned. By the time I was four, my father had essayed a number of stopgap jobs to keep his compact family unit afloat—mail carrier, car salesman, assistant manager at a department store. I think he even tried the door-to-door vacuum cleaner sales racket in the last heartbeats of time before that idiom was outmoded. Later he scored a secure position in a large Ford dealership and kept that job for nearly a decade, which is, I guess, why he was forever pegged as *salesperson*.

> 1971 (July): While horsing around in the yard, I accidentally clock a neighborhood crony named Buster in the head with a rake. Buster nearly dies. Blood—I had never seen so much. It freaked me out so badly that as I ran home, to find adults or someone who could help, I stepped into a chuckhole and broke my left ankle. I'm still in a cast when my fifth birthday rolls around.
> See: STRESS TOLERANCE, VIOLENT BEHAVIOR.

That was the only time I'd ever broken a bone in my life, and somebody thought it was important enough to record.

> 1972/April 1: Mother dies.
> SEE: CONDITIONING BEHAVIORS, AUTHORITY FIGURES.

My mother died at age thirty-three of leukemia. It was the first time I ever saw my father cry. When I turned thirty-three, I realized I had about as much clue or preparation as they did, which is to say, no useful training. I forgave my parents a lot after they were both dead, and I was older than they were.

> 1973/June 9: Father remarries Nathalie Mae Wicks—wicked stepmom—and I gain a teenaged stepbrother named Clay. I'm six and just beginning my first summer vacation, from first grade.

> 1976: Fifth grade. I square-dance with a girl for the first time, Suzie Tyler Morrison.

It went on like that in numbing detail, including most of the bruises and scrapes, cross-indexed to arcane referents like RESENTMENT INDEX. Facts and figures, sketching the life of an average nobody. The world's most boring episode of A&E *Biography*. I did learn (to my surprise because the evidence had been there all along) that the reason for my family's abrupt 1976 move from Fort Worth to San Francisco had been due to my father declaring bankruptcy. Money arguments were the reason Nathalie divorced my father when I was twelve. So long, wicked stepmom; farewell, elder, bucolic, not-really-my-brother Clay.

I proceeded to flunk out of high school and rack up the usual misdemeanors for a surly teenager; nothing really toxic. At least I avoided becoming a crack addict, and I earned a driver's license without mangling anyone in an automobile mishap. Academically, I bounced back with a halfhearted interest in becoming a draftsman or architect, mostly due to the brief but fatherly influence of Clay, who was always drawing things. Along came the SATs, and to everyone's surprise I somehow managed to ace the English section of the test, a first for whatever high school I was in that year. (I'm sure if I click in the right place, I'll find a complete listing.) I qualified for one of those entry-level scholarship/loan/grant packages and moved my ass to the University of California at Santa Barbara in the early 1980s. I switched to Business Administration in my second year, which was also the first and only time I've ever paid for an abortion. My girlfriend at the time was a Graphic Arts major named Barbara Stanns, and we broke up soon after I babysat the "therapeutic" D&C. AIDS was still brand-new. I learned to love latex.

The barnacles of my life accreted, slowly, steadily, uninterestingly. Remember, this is the part where we're all supposed to be white-hot with youthful potential, steely-eyed and revolutionary, world-beaters.

Kroeger Concepts was a funky start-up company then, run out of Burt Kroeger's rented house in Venice, back when Venice Beach was still hanging on to its last dregs of coolness. Now Santa Monica is mostly overrun by feckless TV executives with pattern baldness, nuclear families, and leprous overtanning.

Are you nodding off, yet?

It took me the better part of an hour to wade owlishly through my life in black and white, blinking cursor optional. There is something about verification wiping away suspicion; it makes you feel naked and vulnerable, as though the world has not been fooled by your posturing. It makes you afraid to dare. Perhaps that is the rationale for all those tiny forms of surveillance we accept as inevitable or necessary—those nagging instances of prying and disclosure that, ultimately, don't seem as bad as the more horrifying concept of inconvenience. If you don't buy the attitude I'm shoveling here, then check out your hard drive sometime and see how many cookies it has accumulated. All those companies and individuals have a line on you, oh yes they do.

Zetts resumed his command position and rolled through my data. He extended his hand back to me. "Here," he said. "Eyedrops."

It was a small black disc that looked like a key fob. Its middle was a plastic bag of fluid—imagine a Life Saver with a filling—and a lot of microscopic text in Japanese. The logo, in a ragged skatepunk font, read FX NEO. Obviously, you held the flat end of the disc near your eye and squeezed.

"Your eyes are like super-red, dude," he said. I don't know whether I was having a reaction to some allergen in the air, or I was on the verge of tears, weeping as my father had at approximately the same age. For better reasons.

My method has always been to tilt my head back, shut my eye, deposit drops in the shallow depression thus created, open eye to flood, repeat with other eye. I tried to make my face horizontal and did my best. The back of my head bumped the wall; it was still tender from its encounter with the DON'T WALK button. I managed to coax a few drops from the odd little device, and opened my eye.

"*Wow*—holy shit!" I jolted forward almost hard enough to bounce my face off the desk. At first my bare eyeball felt napalmed, then I realized the burning sensation . . . wasn't. It was more as if I'd put an ice cube against it.

"It's a rush, ain't it?" said Zetts. "It's mentholated. Japanese stuff is tit, dude."

"Tit?"

He nodded like a convert. "Tit—good for hangovers, too."

After the initial shock, my dosed eye receded into chilly, relieved bliss. My other, untreated eye was jealous of how this one now felt, so I rapidly dealt out another hit. Once you were used to the bang, this stuff worked superlatively.

"That feels . . . *great,*" I said, still amazed. My eyes were tingling.

"It's a rush—like coke without the migraines or the paranoia. Like espresso for your eyeballs."

"I want a gallon of this."

"What'd you think of your dossier?"

"It makes me want to turn to the index in the back of the Book of My Life, to see where all the racy stuff is."

"This is just keyhole data," said Zetts. "The surface probe. The links will have more. Anything jump out at you?"

I was at a loss for something trenchant to say. "Nothing much."

"Very bad for you, yo," he said, without looking back. "Looks to me like your whole existence adds up to zero, which means you have no threat potential at all."

"Which is bad . . . right?"

"Bad for you. Remember whose files you're stealthing. If you were no threat to them, they'd just purge you, man—simpler, easier, nobody kicks a stench."

My life, as a fart. "But they haven't purged me, Zee." I shrugged helplessly. "I'm still here."

"Thank Dandine. Here's what I think: They would have demoted you at your apartment, except for Mr. D. Because unless you have leverage on them, you like *sooo* don't matter."

Unless I had leverage on them I didn't know about, or had not figured out yet. "You're talking about NORCO," I said.

"Mm-hm. I know what you're thinking: the heat'll blow over. And for sure, if you were to go public right now, rejoin all the citizens, nothing would happen to you. They'd let you go back to your job, lay your ladies, and make a few more payments on your credit cards. Then, like two months later—blammo. You die in some unfortunate mishap. You slip in your tub. You accidentally drink Drano. Whoops, a 'vehicular incident.' Or they gauge your likelihood of a heart attack and proceed accordingly. Who inherits, when you bite the big one?"

"Nobody," I said. "Kroeger has my power of attorney."

"Wives, kids, parents?"

"Divorced, none, and dead."

He turned to face me, constantly reevaluating me. "Like, no relatives?"

I shook my head. "Well, there's always you and Dandine."

Zetts grinned. "Cool. Leave me enough to buy a big-screen TV, wouldja?" I presumed he meant *bigger*.

"Sure. If I ever get out of here."

"Don't get the wrong idea, dude—you're not a prisoner. You want to go, you go. But if I was you, I'd hang tight, like Mr. D says. Just a couple of hours. Give him time to work some angles. Then he shows up and you're either a lot happier, or a lot more depressed. Better than just wandering the streets, right, waiting for the clock on you to start?"

He pointed at the computer. "Let's consider the freak-out scenario, right? Sure, like, we coulda made all this shit up. Nobody who knows nothing about computers might buy it—all these switchbacks and ghost sites, right? This could be a total fake; most of the walking dead wouldn't blink. But there's like an alternate possibility, right?" He got that odd twinkle in his sharp blue eyes. "It might all be for real; what then?"

I felt an invisible anvil lift off my shoulders. I wanted this to be real; I needed it to be real. Everyone assumes they more or less recognize their own endings, and the terminus of their stories always comes as a surprise. For the first time in my apparently colorless life, I had lost that backstop, that surety of how I might wind up.

I could drown in my own life, right here on this monitor. I turned Zetts's attention back to it. "Is Dandine in here?"

"Nahh, I tried that. Total dead end. *Nada*."

"Can I look at this stuff some more?"

"Sure," said Zetts, standing. "Go nuts. I'm gonna go, y'know, smoke a fatty and kick back. Unless you'd care for a taste."

He didn't wait for me to say no.

By now, you're wondering where all this pathetic wallow leads. You check for files on Dandine and Zetts, knowing that Zetts knows you'll try. There is nothing to read. All queries find no such files. You have no idea what alter egos to request. Reckless idiot that you are, you've used your real name your whole life.

You wanted to smack Zetts in the chops, when he jumped ahead, read your mind, and outlined the "freak-out scenario." You feel lame and obvious, your every thought already broadcast on some subnormal frequency that alerts the players of the world to marks and suckers.

But wouldn't Zetts have been instructed to say all that, as a means of allaying your natural suspicion and fear?

Wouldn't Zetts need to act calm and noncommittal, and offer you the option of exit, so you could protest and refuse it?

Wouldn't you like to head off this poisonous, lousy feeling about yourself at the pass, just one time?

You rise from the monitor with a reckless, risky plan already congealing in your slowpoke brain. Zetts sits in the middle of a cloud bank of dope smoke, nursing his version of the five o'clock martini and watching the news.

"Man called it, brah," he says, indicating the TV.

The sound is turned down but you can imagine the hyperbolic play-by-play that accompanies the on-screen image of Linda Grimes, also known as "Choral Anne." You remember the photo from her driver's license. Now some studio munchkin has spent half an hour Photoshopping it to fit an appropriately hysterical logo within the video frame, titled *Southland Woman Missing*. No suspects or persons-of-interest attached to the developing story. Yet.

Leverage, as Zetts had pointed out.

You affect Zetts's own attitude—loose, easy, uncaring—as you ask to read one of his *Doc Savage* paperbacks. Why not, what the hey, we've got time to kill, right? Zetts rises with a that's-the-spirit camaraderie and fetches a title down from his shelf, jabbering about which ones are good to start with, if you haven't read the entire series of 181 books in order. As he stands on a kitchen chair and reaches for a likely volume, you kick the chair out from under him, feeling like a shit but doing it anyway. Zetts cracks the obverse of his skull on the lip of the kitchen sink, during his fall to meet the floor. The chair skitters away and thin paperbacks go flying. You straddle Zetts as he flails about and put him down exactly the way *you* were incapacitated by the so-called Celeste, the mystery ninja who faked you out long enough for you to open your apartment door. You cock your arm back, flat-handed (as though you know what you're doing; as though you're some kind of fucking martial artist), and give Zetts everything you could throw behind the heel of your hand, just as he sits up. It sounds like a slap. Zetts's eyes roll to white and he goes back down hard, legs spasming.

And you do all this thinking, *I'm sorry—really.*

Zetts's pockets yield keys. You grab the cellphone off the kitchen table. There's already a gun in the car. Queer, to think that if there is no backup key ring, you will be locking Zetts into his own house.

You go.

You leave the television on, for company, and ease back out into the world of the walking dead, thinking, *seriously, I really am sorry, man. Really.*

The cellphone was a bust. I tried back-calling Dandine from the memory menu, but only saw a splash of gobbledygook on the screen, like a high-kicking dance line of swear words from some old comic strip. Whatever piece of spy hardware Dandine had used to call Zetts, the damned thing was encrypted, secure, untraceable, and probably patched through landline exchanges in ten different states.

It occurred to me to wonder who I thought I was kidding, trying for slick, pretending I knew what I was doing, trying to outfox foxes.

Then, just like that (imagine the finger snap)...I suddenly knew where I was going.

I thought of wrestling alligators every time I cranked the wheel of Zetts's GTO into a turn. Manual steering. The car grumbled and vibrated in an ominous and unfamiliar way, causing my pampered, automatic-everything reflex to howl and bitch. Working the five-speed shift seemed harder than calculus. I was doing an incredibly stupid thing, according to my rational mind, which warred with my inner cliff dweller, who was hollering about the damned car, barely under human control, and so on.

My navigational head fared slightly better. I remembered enough landmarks to get me back to the Sisters. Between 20th Century–Fox and MGM; right. I abandoned the metal objects on my person and approached the rear gate, carrying only the slim, handled paper bag I'd picked up at a wine shoppe en route. The wizened Mexican I had mistaken for a gardener faced me through the grillwork, his sawed-off, twelve-gauge pump casually resting on his shoulder, his index finger aligned alongside the trigger guard. He smiled.

"*Nombre, por favor.*"

"Mr. Lamb," I said. "They should remember—"

He had already nodded and turned away.

1984/October 13: I lose my virginity to Carla Johnson at age eighteen.

You're a late starter. At eighteen you have technically never dated, not in the sense "dating" is understood by your fellow seniors, regardless of the rules about male-female coupling that have been trashed and inverted by the slide of the late 1960s into the early- to mid-1970s. Nobody provided a handbook, because if they had, you would have understood that Carla Johnson was after a bit of nasty from line one. She simply wants to get drunk and fuck you. You insist on slopping it up with a lot of garbage from books, movies, fantasies, and your own ignorance. Ever since your cross-country wander at age ten, you have been shuffled from one public school to another as your father struggled to cope with his sudden divorce and changeling finances; hence, you have attended a different institution, with a different class of peers, each year from junior high onward. No continuity of friends or neighbors. You lead an unsettled life that prompts you to internalize and not form attachments, since the whole structure will morph, sure enough, before your next semester begins.

Childhood warps of this sort, it is theorized, make for good spies. Operatives to whom emotional discorporation is second nature. It is a survival skill, and a learned behavior.

Carla's recreation is your turning point, despite all the messed up and misfired signals. She sets it up as a movie date, VCR-style, disguised as a homework appointment. While her parents are away golfing or sun-burning or whatever it is they do in Palm Springs, several times a year. You both gobble pizza—her order, your treat.

The area between her legs is alien, speculative territory. It does not resemble the flayed, face-hugger lunchmeat of men's magazines. It looks more like one of those very smooth French pastries, with a crease in the center. It feels, to your virgin fingers, basically like the roof of your own mouth, only slightly more yielding. If you attempt to inject your penis there by dead reckoning, it will wilt faster than a candle in a toaster oven at the first bump of resistance.

She fondles your equipment while you check out hers. After a hurried and hungry make-out session, she jumps directly to pants-off, the point of no return. She interprets your lack of experience as the leisure of someone who has done this before and is in no hurry. She makes you extra-slick with her mouth and pulls you aboard while some videotape plays in the background, a movie you can't even recall.

Abruptly, just like that, you realize you are *inside* her. Rather, that she has *surrounded* you, and she has a helluva grip down there.

The process is all het up and distorted by two bottles of extremely cheap, fruit-flavored vino. You made the mistake of trying to match her swig for swig, and now your vision is plunging and dotting, your head light, your guts broiling. Spicy pepperoni plus fiery alcohol plus over-stress equals . . . emissions. The horrific thought of venting unseemly gas during your first real sexual encounter distracts you so that you don't climax right away, like you feared you would. Below you, Carla is really getting zoned, grabbing your ass and ramming away with her pelvis, digging in with her heels and bucking to the rhythm of her own breathy gasps. She comes quickly and easily, grinding into the next sequence as soon as she achieves the first spike. No downtime. She seems to be an expert at this. Compared to you, at least.

You're busy clenching your ass to keep from farting.

C'mon c'mon baby come in me come in me baby c'mon . . .

It's like she's trying to demonstrate power, to prove she can make you let go, but hearing her hiss this gentle mantra is more than you can bear, and abruptly your groin goes soft and rubbery as your semen glurts into her. You stop thrusting and can feel your heart slamming against your chest, echoing her own beat, which is making one of her adorable breasts wiggle.

Then your stomach clenches into a greasy fist, and you shit all over yourself. Hydrochloric diarrhea shoots from your ass, sideswipes her thigh, stains the floral-patterned sofa. The air goes pungent with the reek of your embarrassment.

You stumble to the kitchen sink in time to throw up still-recognizable pizza into the disposal. It stinks like strawberries, bile, and apples from the wine. Carla is hollering about the sofa, not vulnerable at all despite the fact that she's nude. Her eyes accuse you. It's the fall of 1984, the year Orwell warned everyone about.

Most of your future sexual encounters will reflect the inaugurational paradigm. Without the cleanup phase.

Such catastrophes need only occur a single time to make a lasting impression. You think of this incident every time you and a woman begin the dance that leads to intromission. Even now, your favorite part is the moment at which they accede. The "yes" part. The sex is almost secondary—deft, now; certainly knowledgeable, technically proficient. But the real achievement, for you, has always been selling woman on the *idea* that they want to fuck you. Everything else is leading up to, or going away from, that fleeting moment. This peculiar mind-set was part of your redraft of your own character, after you got to college with a clean slate and no friends, no hangers-on from your past, and no reputation.

Fucking clients—that came later—when you were a pro.

"Por favor, señor, please to enter." The gate buzzed and the man smiled at me with tobacco-edged teeth. This time, I knew I was walking through a metal detector.

I saw a rake leaning against an elm tree. I thought of Buster from Texas, relegated to the fogbanks of childhood, his head split open and bleeding, my fault. If he'd died, I would have heard . . . something, surely.

As I waited in the parlor, I tried to recollect the way Dandine had greeted the Sisters, like a long-lost son, and decided to try and assess their mood before I ventured anything so bold. My ebbing battery of charm, I hoped, had enough juice left to curry a pair of little old men who displayed themselves as little old women. In deference to their delicate sensibilities, I had turned my GAY MAFIA MEMBER T-shirt inside out, and redonned my jacket from the car.

"Ah, my dear Mr. Lamb!" It was the Sister with the clubfoot. "What a pleasant surprise to see you again so soon. I trust our friend Mr. D. is well?"

"Probably in better shape than I am," I said, trying for an honest face.

She shielded a tiny smile behind her equally tiny, beringed hand. "I shouldn't say anything, but . . . you did observe the proper precautions?"

"Nobody knows I'm here," I said. "And nobody followed me."

"Courtesy is often lost, these days. Perhaps our business would better be discussed in chambers. Or perhaps you would prefer to avail yourself of our confessional?"

I immediately pictured restraints and handcuffs. Certainly the talents of the Sisters extended to the science of information extraction. Ball gags and cattleprods. I assumed the second Sister was engaged in the abuse of some policeman or priest, for money to cover operating overhead, or perhaps to maintain this place's excellent soundproofing and charmingly Old World concept of security.

"Oh, and I brought you a little something I hope you might enjoy." I handed over the bottle of Groth Reserve California Cabernet that had taken me fifteen minutes to select, nervous as a sophomore on prom night.

"Oh. Oh! The nineteen ninety-two. There were only fourteen hundred cases of this made, you know. How very, very kind of you. Please come this way."

I knew the Groth had been a sly choice, not a name brand, a truly awesome vintage to gainsay the idea of snob appeal.

"Chambers" turned out to be an office I had not seen on my first trip. It had a parquet floor and was slightly crowded with Italian antiques. The Sister took her place at the helm of a Queen Anne desk and directed me toward a chair with gnurled arms and dark velvet upholstery.

I had no idea how to start. "Sister, I don't wish to seem tactless, but—"

"Tish-tosh," she said, waving it away. "Ask me anything. You're a friend of Mister D's."

"NORCO." I had a hard time getting the word to leave my mouth.

She looked sympathetic. "Oh, yes. They're very interested in acquiring you. So, it seems, are the police—directed by their betters, for nuisance value to you, I would speculate. I know what Mr. D told us, but could you please outline the problem from your own perspective?"

She was all ears and bright, glittering eyes as I told her what I knew. Or what I thought I knew. Occasionally she said, "I see, I see." Halfway through my multidirectional spill of events, she offered me a glass of very substantial Cabernet, almost as though she knew already what I liked. A couple of times she held up a hand, indicating "hold that thought," while she scribbled notations on a pad of vellum.

"My dear boy," she said. "You say you have no leverage, nothing with which to deal with people who detest making deals. You are being far too modest. You possess avenues and options you may not suspect. You really are a true innocent, and it pains me to see you abused in the ways you describe." She folded the page on which she had been writing and handed it across.

"What's this?"

"Your strengths, young man. We Sisters make no recommendations. We provide information."

I started to read it.

"Please," she said. "Not until after you have left us."

I stowed the page in my jacket pocket. "I . . . uh, I'm a little short on a proper offering right now, Sister." I was thinking of that collection plate in the foyer, and the fat envelope Dandine had left in it.

"Tish-tosh," she said. "You will give what you can, when you can, out of the goodness of your heart. Or, like in those motion pictures, we may require a service of *you,* some day." She made a face and shot me a look that reminded me of Rocky, the gangster infant in the Warner Brothers cartoons. She indicated my expensive gift wine, now free of its designer bag. "You were thoughtful enough to bring this, and that is what counts. Courtesy and consideration are always on the verge of being lost, don't you think?"

She actually managed to make me feel as though I was chatting with a matronly older lady who actually gave a damn about me. I haven't had an official mom for decades, and it felt strange. But not unwelcome.

Back in Zetts's "borrowed" GTO I examined the sheet the Sister had given me. Four names, four addresses in Los Angeles.

Alicia Brandenberg/St. Regis Hotel. That was in Century City, on the Avenue of the Stars, and she probably had a suite and a staff.

Theodore Ripkin, Candidate #1. Could most likely be found at a house he owned in Beverly Hills, up near Cielo Drive, not far from the original location of the Tate/LaBianca murders in nineteen sixty-eight.

Garrett Stradling, a.k.a. G. Johnson Jenks, a.k.a. Candidate #2. Was downtown in Park Towers, not far from where Dandine's first automobile had blown up.

Thorvald Gerardis/NORCO. This was the first time I'd seen the proper spelling, but as too many people had advised me already, nobody's name was for real. The Sister's annotation was cryptic: *New access at 1st Interstate Bank bldg.* Just reading the word NORCO was unfairly chilling. Did this mean NORCO had an office, or something, down near Sunset and Vine?

There was no way I could call Dandine. Check his progress, get his advice, hear that Zetts was okay so I could reassure him about the car. Explain that I was a bit out of my head. No way for Dandine to tell me I was acting like a Grade A, USDA-certified rump roast of stupidity.

I brought the beast to roaring life and tried to rein it toward the mouth of the alley. Jenks and Ripkin would be unapproachable. They could be tilted against each other, and against the acidic Ms. Brandenberg, later. A backstop. I still lacked the balls to go knocking on NORCO doors, just yet. I already wanted to check off Alicia first, if for no more cogent reason than I wanted to hear, from her own photogenic lips, the story of how she had fired Choral Grimes, then had her abducted or murdered, and then, probably, had fluttered off to some cocktail party. I didn't have any right to be angry about Choral—I had put her in danger as much as any power-bitch boss or assassin wielding barbiturates. But I *was* angry, goddammit.

I was cheesed at the derailment of my babe-in-the-woods life among the walking dead . . . but I felt stronger for the knowledge. I was pissed off that the ideal of decent people, hard work, and fair play was just another fantasy to which we all paid lip service, like obedient consumers doing their bit for word-of-mouth . . . but I had become less blind. I was livid at my own fear of what might happen, or the things I might have to do . . . but at least, then, I would better know what kind of material I was made from, and whether it was fiber or simple bullshit that strung it all together into the nervous wreck that was me.

If I lived long enough.

Zetts's huge road-grabbing tires bumped the curb as I negotiated the GTO onto Olympic. If I had hung around for five more minutes, I would have been bushwhacked by the four vehicles that arrived outside the Sisters' and stopped in a crescent formation in the lot. I found out about this later. No tags, no trim, dealer plates. Like Zetts had said, no shit hanging from the mirrors. I would have heard the old Mexican's shotgun cut loose. Once.

I might be dead now, or I might have helped.

Alicia Brandenberg's suite at the St. Regis Hotel was the sort of full-amenity perk that charged normal humans upward of $650 per day and offered twenty-four-hour room service and a complimentary fifty-minute massage. It was up top, on a keyed, secure floor, and I didn't feel in a mountaineering mood. (For the record, I *still* don't know how Dandine had gotten onto my balcony in the middle of the night, a couple thousand years ago. Somewhere along the line I have a memory, probably false, of asking him:

("You don't talk about yourself a lot, do you?"

"Who to?" he asked.

"Point." It was my usual [1], [2], [3] . . . and I was getting sick of it.)

Someone with Alicia's supercharged daybook had to cruise the St. Regis lobby several times during an average business day; it was inevitable. The bar was centrally located, and I needed something to eat, not to mention a fairly hefty drink. I was down to my final, post-jail wad of cash, whittled to about a hundred bucks after the hit it took to buy wine to impress the Sisters.

Enough for appetizers and a beverage, in this place. Maybe two. I had to sit and calculate whether I could afford a sandwich. That was a relatively new experience; not thrilling. I had become so accustomed to flipping out the correct piece of plastic, signing for goods, and trusting the bottomless bowl of an expense account, that the only reflex skill I retained was the ability to sum up a 20 percent tip. If the service was lousy enough, perhaps I could get away with fifteen—*that* would certainly get me noticed, here.

More harmful exposure was offered by the TV flat-screens hovering over the bar. Thanks to Dandine, I was dreading the sight of my picture popping up on the news and hearing some blow-dried dimwit say *more as it happens*. There was literally no place in the room where you could *not* see a screen, another footprint of progress that was especially annoying around Oscar night in Hollywood. I devoured a French dip on grilled sourdough bread—it *was* pretty good, even though it set me back about fifty bucks total. Sipping beer would stretch my meager bank more efficiently.

Just like when I was in lockup, I scoped the talent of the room. Every now and then, an imposing dude would cycle the lobby. There were about three different ones, none hotel security. Zetts was right; they were obvious when you knew what to look for.

Playing cheap detective is exactly as dull as watching dust gather on a tabletop. Movies and fiction present the stakeout mode as irretrievably eroding—infinitudes of dead time, as you wait for a bus that is already late—until a moment of hot, scary action. Usually the payoff is threatening enough to make the boring part preferable. But in fiction, the waiting is usually edited out, and characters are able to gird for their instant in the spotlight of danger. They reflect upon what has brought them to this phase of their lives; how the signposts had pointed, all along, to some obvious culmination. Imaginary gumshoes are always *en pointe* and on target, no matter how thuddingly exasperating the wait.

People can sneak up on you and catch you by surprise if your guard is down. Dandine would not approve of laziness on the job.

I was nursing my third beer when somebody tapped on my shoulder, saying, "You have a call, sir."

It was a guy roughly the size of my refrigerator. Lots of neck muscles, his tie more a noose. I'd seen him cruise the lobby about an hour ago. Quarter-inch hair, the back of his head a tuck-and-roll like a package of frankfurters. Big suit that still looked constrictive. A black man with the muddy green eyes of a deep-sea predator.

"If you'll come this way, please."

"Nobody knows to call me here," I said. To try faking tough with this man would be transparently bogus. "What if I want to stay right where I am?"

He smiled, or rather, simulated what humans did when they smiled. He leaned on the bar next to me, his forearm parallel to mine. "In that event, sir, I'd do this." He cocked my wrist, with my elbow nestled into his. When he straightened, I had to stand up, no choice. "Then you'd have to go where I go."

"Okay, okay. Just let me pay the—

"Already taken care of, sir."

"Stop calling me 'sir.'"

"Yes, sir."

That was how it went. He directed me to the elevators. Phone call, my butt.

"Where're we going?"

"Up." He stuck a brass key into the elevator's button panel and accessed a secure floor. When the doors closed, he said, "Arms up, please." He caught my arms on the rise and pulled them straight out, as though arranging a shirt on a hanger, impatient with my geometry. After a swift, professional poke-and-pat, he drew a doodad with a whisper-thin telescoping antenna and indicated I should hold my place, arms out.

"What's that?"

"Scan for bugs," he said, sweeping up-down, left-right, pits and crotch.

He frowned at the display on the scanner. "You're clean. Stand there, please." He indicated the corner of the car, behind me. All I needed was a dunce cap.

"Is this about—

He held a thick finger to his lips. "Shh."

I did that dumb elevator thing where you watch the numbers.

In the corridor, I noticed my keeper walked with his right foot turned slightly outward, hitting harder than the left. It was subtler than a limp. I decided not to mention it. See, I *can* learn new things. And I figured I should savor my own smugness a tiny bit more before I died.

In this world, I would hear the gunshot only *after* I glimpsed my own brains flying out.

We passed another linebacker; Marine Corps buzz cut, a yard of shoulders, shrink-wrapped into a too-tight suit with stretch seams. They traded nods like cannibal elders and I was conducted through double doors with brass-drop handles into a suite that seemed to take up the whole southern side of the hotel floor. Tons of glass and miles of view. Room-service carts with sterling service and barely touched food. Several televisions all going at once, the news feeds and stock quote channels all muted.

"Sit," said my keeper, and I plonked into a straight-backed Louis XIV chair designed to be desperately uncomfortable. He pointed at the tray. "Coffee there, if you want it. They have somebody grind it right before they brew it. It's pretty good." He shrugged.

Then he popped me on the right ear, putting his weight into the jab. My brain heard a loud howitzer noise and bursting purple globes obliterated my vision; errant planets. Before I knew I was falling, I had already landed on the floor and won a rug burn on my cheek. The whole right side of my head was flushed with a waterfall of white noise.

Tears blurred my view of the legs in front of me, but the shoes were at least eight hundred bucks' worth of Italian leather. Stupid, to guess who.

"Thank you, Marion."

I must have looked pretty submissive, one hand hoisting me into doggie position, the other clamped on my macerated ear. It was absurd, but I could almost see up Alicia Brandenberg's brief skirt from my vantage.

The bald behemoth "helped" me into the chair with a complete lack of grace. I tried to will my head not to loll.

Alicia Brandenberg was wearing black today. Black turtleneck, black leather skirt of triple-dyed lambhide. Black belt. Minimal ornamentation that looked like black pearls. "That was for scaring the shit out of me last night," she said, "and for embarrassing me in front of underlings. A no-no."

There were dots of blood on my hand. Blood was leaking out of my ear. If my ear was still on the side of my head, which felt anesthetized—that scary numbness that engulfs your skull if you stay horizontal too long at the dentist, and the xylocaine starts gravitating.

She stood before me, arms folded beneath her breasts. She blew out a nasal breath of disgust. "Now, as for what you did to little Choral . . ."

My hackles scared up. I could feel the thick presence of my chaperone moving in on me for another disciplinary wallop. "Wait!" I ducked instinctively. There he was, all right, fist cocked and everything. "Wait! I *need* my other ear, lady, unless you're going to teach me hand signals!"

"Marion." She waved him off. He solidified into an at-ease stance about two feet behind me, a golem of retribution short-stopped by a magical command.

I was still watching him. "Marion?"

"Mr. Maddox," said Alicia, keeping her distance, as though I smelled bad. She fired up a dark Sobranie; the smoke that unreeled from it seemed thin and toxic. "Since you're acting idiotic, I'll presume you need things explained to you. But no one owes you any such explanation. I am doing you a favor, since you did me the courtesy of delivering yourself. That's quite strategic, really—you knew you could not get past my security, so you made yourself visible and let them bring you to me."

I wanted to say something by way of comeback. You know, *Your gratitude knows no bounds. Oh, I guess I owe you a favor now.* But my mouth wouldn't work right, and my ear was roaring. Yes, to other eyes it might appear that I had gotten to Alicia Brandenberg quite easily . . . except now I had special status, and I was just beginning to realize that counted for something incalculable, in the same way a nightclub goon knows to let you past the rope, cutting you ahead of the riffraff.

"Do you want an aspirin or something? I don't have all day. Marion, get him a goddamned aspirin."

"What happened to Choral?" I said.

She almost laughed. "Why, Mr. Maddox—you raped and murdered her."

There was literally no comeback in the universe I could summon for that one. I swallowed about six times; I could feel my throat swelling up.

She sucked strength from her imported ciggie. "You fucked up my Plan A, Mr. Maddox. So I went to Plan B. God, I almost feel sorry for you; you're so out of the loop. But pity is wasted on the walking dead, isn't it? Listen closely, the thing you *think* you're part of? Over. Done. Terminated. Finished."

"And now we're in . . . Plan B?"

"Good boy." No doggie treat was forthcoming.

"What does Plan B have happening to me?"

"It's your headache now, or will be shortly. Consider it payback for the bad taste you demonstrated by *involving* yourself."

Marion the bodyguard returned with a bottle of aspirin and left it on the service cart, next to the coffee.

"Can I have some water?"

Alicia glanced at her watch. Marion poured from a carafe of sparkling water and I squeezed down five bitter pills. "Hard to believe," I said, pitched so Alicia could "overhear" my doubt.

She opened her hands like an impatient teacher. "Well?"

"I can't believe this all started with you, that you set this all up. A fake hit on yourself to massage the sympathy poll on whichever of your bed-buddies proves more viable."

"I'll take it *that's* the version of the story you got," she said, unruffled. "Don't tell me I have to explain *politics* to you, now. You are naive, my dear. Listen carefully: Any professional politician with an ounce of competence always looks like he's losing his hair and has skin cancer. Zero charisma, and charisma equals sex, and sex is a no-no. That's why they have platoons of geeks to invent images for them, to fabricate personalities, because they *have* no personalities. It's all manufactured. It's all sell." She paused. "You with me, so far?"

"I figure you'll come to a point eventually," I said, still hurting.

"Did Choral Anne Grimes spin you the sex-tape fantasy?" she asked, narrowing her gaze and not liking what she perceived. "Yeah, she did, didn't she? It's a great shorthand for getting the attention; but you know what? It has zero barter value. Nobody cares who fucks whom anymore. It is the *expected* indiscretion, you see? Predictable. These days the public needs *unpredictable* sins to curry their outrage. Sex tapes only have power if you can scare or control the people in the tapes, not the public at large. Joe Sixpack and Joanne BabyFactory need larger transgressions to justify their reactionary no-vote because now they just assume there's always some kind of hanky-panky, which follows from the assumption that their elected representatives are all corrupt—sort of the same way citizens view the police, if they have any sense left."

Her disdainful superiority was making my ass hurt. "Still with you," I said, not caring.

She shook her head. "Vice president of advertising, huh? Impossible. It's a great cover, though. I've seen your travel records. Four or five hops to Europe, two dozen cross-country jumps, frequent flyer miles up the waz, couple of days at each stop? I've even spoken to Burt Kroeger about you. About your attempts to sabotage Katy Burgess's campaign when she wouldn't sleep with you? You're going to have to find a new cover identity, Mr. . . . uh, Maddox?"

The rancid fabrication she was building toward could certainly hold enough water to occupy me for the next twenty years, before a chance of parole. "You mean the way Jenks pulled a shape-change and zap, he's a politician?"

"That was done perfectly legally," she said, all cool. "Unlike attempted blackmail. Which reminds me—there *is* a tape you'd be more interested in. A recording of your threats, hissed at me in that dreary mall. Just so you know."

"Inadmissible evidence." I knew that much without homework.

"Kidnapping. You took her hostage. In a minute you'll be a wanted man, and I've got all the bodyguards." She sure did act like someone who always got her way.

"Don't believe everything you see on the news."

She actually smiled, for the first time, I think. "Why, Mr. Maddox—they couldn't put it on TV if it wasn't *real*. And now, you've arrived to harm me. Stalking. Premeditation. You were bound to show your face to me, eventually."

She was spot-on. But if she was just waiting around to score points off me, why had I been escorted up here . . . and not to the nearest hanging judge, the handiest electric chair?

Because she was in the dark, too.

"You know the quickest way to get rid of you?" she said.

My gaze followed hers to the balcony. The street was so far down it was out of focus. I could count *Die Hard* floors all the way until I splattered like a 170-pound cannelloni dropped twenty stories.

She shook her head again, with a sinister glint in her eyes. "Let you go. I'd be surprised if you last another day out in the *real* world."

"Are those my NORCO odds?"

"Oh." She chuckled. "That fictional, all-powerful shadow organization that you believe secretly runs everything? If I were you, I'd jump out that window voluntarily, or remember where you got that little story from."

Listen to yourself, I told myself. *Victimized by sooper-secret clandestine ops, wrongfully pilloried, a deer in the headlights of media. Poor baby.*

"You don't have a chance, either," I said, trying to follow her tactic of switching tracks. "There's no stronger election pitch money can buy than saying, 'my governor can kick your governor's *ass.*'"

"Almost true," she said. "And if we'd had things in place when our last governor became a pariah . . . well, who knew, right? And we couldn't scare up enough petty cash to buy his replacement. But those people out there—that network share, that lowest common denominator, that majority vote—they love the idea of empowerment. Up by the bootstraps. So we go for that other great American pitch, the underdog. We put Rocky up against the Terminator. But, for myself, I am in love with the American idea of overkill, and we don't know yet which candidate will accrue the most public favor."

"So you're just serving the country."

"In my modest way, yes."

"But none of this was *your* idea."

"That's inappropriate." She scowled.

I ran Andrew Collier's grocery list of alternatives through my memory. Alicia wasn't running anything except her own mission, here, with NORCO's help. She had her eye on the top of the ladder, though. Her profession was seduction followed by sacrifice.

She would never admit that to the likes of me, though, which made her unreachable, a glacier. I turned back to the expressionless bodyguard. "Is your name really Marion?" I said.

His features thunderclouded for a moment, then he hardened up and said, "Yeah. Just like John muthafuckin' Wayne."

I gave him my lame impersonation of the Duke: "Truly this *waz* da Son 'a Godd."

I could see him fighting to stifle a grin, and that's when I knew I had a gnat's chance. Nearby on the bar service tray was a gas cork-popper— one of those cartridge-fed deals with a shaft like an icepick. Inside the cartridge was enough ozone-depleting refrigerant to open about seventy bottles . . . or kill maybe ten people if your aim was true. If I could get a grab on it . . .

But I saw Marion see me seeing it, and he picked it up himself with a strange glint in his gaze, as though he'd just had an inspiration.

Then he sacked my head in a plastic bag until I blacked out on my own carbon dioxide. Through the bag I heard Alica say, "Take him to Room 2250."

The pain brought me back.

My pants were down and one of my testicles was bleeding.

Then I saw Marion holding the hypodermic needle.

It held about 30 cc's of cloudy fluid.

Then I realized how they planned to make the whole "rape" aspect of Choral Anne Grimes's death pass forensic muster.

I was about to wonder how they were going to hide the needle puncture in my left ball when I saw Marion holding that goddamned tetrafluoroethane cork-popper.

"It'll be a defensive stab wound," he said with a grin. "Y'know, as she was fighting you off."

"You don't have to do this," I said like an idiot.

"Oh yeah." He smiled entirely too much. "It's the gig. Nothing personal. But today it sure sucks to be you."

"Hurry up," came Alicia's voice from the anonymous hotel bedroom. "She's getting cold."

The room was a half-suite, and not more than ten feet away laid the mortal remains of Linda Grimes, a.k.a. Choral Anne. Not beaten to death by me, although I was positive the blood on my newly abraded knuckles would match up, thanks to Marion's catalogue of talents. This man was going to use a turkey baster or something on her corpse, then finish me off with "defensive stab wounds."

178

What a riot.

I was frozen and sweating, trying to will myself to move, take some action, do *some* damned thing, guts plummeting, vomit rising. So much for hope.

That's when Marion fell across me like a clumsy lover, emitting a precious little oral fart of a woofing sound as his last gasp on earth.

To her credit, Alicia was already halfway out of the bedroom, aiming a compact, nickel-plated pistol, but a single shot kissed her forehead dead center, and she dropped without a noise. One of her shoes cocked askew and I could finally see her underwear.

Dandine was standing there wearing an ill-fitting bellboy's getup.

Dandine sucked air through his teeth. "Dammit, I wish I hadn't had to do that so quick." He was already disrobing, trying to wrestle his arm sling around the bellboy's outfit. "Pull your pants the rest of the way off," he told me. "Put this on or we don't have a hope in hell of getting out of here."

1994 / July 13: I score a big hit on the up-and-coming roster, and/ or: I sacrifice a friend to climb the ladder.

Chet Favreaux has become the kind of buddy you should have had in high school, but time and geoposition had other plans, so when you meet at a trade show for tech toys, it's like reconnecting with a long-lost brother, the kind you meet for the first time, unexpectedly. Long story short: You're both attracted to the same woman, a busty Irish lass named Kendra. You use your resentment of this vague betrayal to swipe a few ideas Chet has brainstormed with you on his drafting table. He wants to break ice as an architect, you want to get a leg up in advertising, and you submit the ideas you have purloined from him to Burt Kroeger, at the agency. Chet's somewhat wounded phone call comes a year later, when he actually sees the ads in magazines. Kendra is history; she slept with both of you, Chet first. Now she's vanished to obscurity and child-rearing in some unmemorable Midwestern state. Chet says he doesn't care about the goddamned ads, the stupid drawings; he just wants to know what happened to make you stop calling. He is willing to forgive harsh words spoken in anger. You give him smoothly architectured placation talk, short-stop his pain . . . and never call him again, as you get on with your new, improved life.

Sometimes, modest sacrifices are justified.

Scratch "modest" and just make that "sacrifices." I don't know what made me flash on Chet Favreaux as I was scrambling to disrobe. I haven't thought about that guy for, well, over a decade. No idea whatever became of him. He had left the ad business and gone back East somewhere; something to do with his father's business, leaving the shark tank behind, yadda-yadda. I didn't miss him or anything. He'd served his purpose for me. The world is an arena, and the one sight you don't want to see is a thumb pointing toward the ground.

None of this dunning personal history was spelled out in exact language on paper. But if somebody had access to my hidden dossier, they might be able to draw conclusions about my character from it. Somebody like Dandine, for instance, might conclude that I would act a certain way when cornered, either personally or professionally.

Nobody had had enough downtime for that sort of pat solution to apply, though. It was tempting but highly unlikely.

The cork-popper was sticking out of the base of Marion's neck, little fizzy red bubbles accreting around the penetration point. He was deader than God. Ditto his teammate, in the outside room. Dandine had put them down without a noise; the whole bellboy ruse was probably just window dressing. Or maybe he needed a way to carry the outfit up here for me, while keeping his gun hand free. My waistline battled the trousers that Dandine had just shucked. We now shared the suite with four dead bodies, one of which we would shortly be tossing out the window from above the twentieth floor.

"Move it, lardass," Dandine said, after a thorough and professional once-over of the premises. "Jeezum-pete; I can't leave you alone for a fucking *minute*."

He ignored the corpses. I couldn't *not* notice them. Sixty seconds ago, three of them had been breathing. He registered my expression, or perhaps, my hesitation.

"Don't go all moral on me," he warned.

I couldn't help blurting it out: "Have you seen my file? The secret one? The one Zetts knows how to access?"

"Conrad, I haven't had time for homework. Sure, I know about the system. If we're alive half an hour from now, maybe you can walk me through the transgressions of your life, but *not now.*"

He withdrew the cork-popper from Marion's spine. It made a little *fsssss* noise of retreat.

I got dressed in an ill-fitting hurry. Welcome to the service industry. Dandine peeled Marion, the neater of the two male kills. The clothes were twice his size but he somehow made the fit pass muster. Plenty of room to hide . . . guns and things. Like the weapon he'd used, an automatic with a lot of weight on the front end; boxy, vented and baffled. He broke it down and proceeded to stash parts in pockets.

I watched him snatch up Alicia's pistol and check the magazine, then swap out the barrels. He had killed the bodyguards with the same make and caliber, only now it was Alicia's gun that would tell the ballistic lie.

"Is Zetts okay?" I said.

"Later. Help me lift this sonovabitch." Hoisting Marion's clonelike partner, by the arms, to a standing position was obviously less easy than teaching a sofa to waltz. Together, we got him vertical—your standard crucifixion pose. He remained dead. Blood had trickled from both ears to ruin his shirt sufficiently against Dandine's use. His eyes were open, sightless, their sclera crimsoned.

"Police are supposed to be coming," I said, grunting. The dead guy tipped a gym scale at 300, easy, and most of it was above the waist at about 10 percent body fat.

"That's not who we need to worry about." Dandine bumped his chin against air, indicating we should haul our load toward the balcony—the one from which I thought I was going to swan-dive under duress, lifetimes earlier, this same day.

"They had me in another room . . ."

"I know. That made me almost too late."

"We have to go back there."

"For god's sake, why? Haven't you gone rogue enough? Making shit up yourself and, uhh . . . !" He had to rehoist our silent partner. ". . . *floundering* around in the deep end of the pool, when you can't fucking swim?"

I thought of all the movie trailers I'd ever seen: *He's a cop on the edge who plays by his own rules. There's just one problem . . .*

Problem was, that guy wasn't me. But some advertising dude had thought up all that hard sell, and it sure went down smooth as warm molasses. People never pay any real attention to that stuff, right?

"Because there's a couple of cases up there. Next to the flat-screen TV. Those little file-boxes, on trolleys, with pull handles. Choral Anne described them to me. They're full of Alicia's blackmail tapes. We need that stuff."

"More souvenirs?"

"She has a tape of me threatening her in the movie theatre. I'd say that's important enough to go back for."

Then I remembered I was helping Dandine drag a corpse toward an open balcony.

"Are you going to toss this guy out the window?" We were almost to the ledge. "You are *not* going to toss this guy out the window, right?"

"No. *We* are going to toss this guy out the window, et cetera. Unless you want to run around like a lunatic, setting fire to this entire floor as a diversion. If our adversaries were correct about the police, then those police should be looking for an inconvenient parking spot right about now. Our late friend here will delay them, cause a fair amount of disposable panic, and give us better odds on scooting out unnoticed. Here, pick up his feet." He held back a beat. "Unless you can think of something better? In five seconds or less?"

We had the guy seesawed over the railing. Dandine held one leg; I held the other. We gave him to the air at the same time. Teamwork. I didn't hear him hit (didn't see it, either), but the bleats of distressed onlookers started to echo from below. Sure enough, the cops would find themselves swamped by the more immediate excitement. If we had been facing west instead of south, we would have noticed the beginning of a rather gorgeous sunset, courtesy of the distant rim of the ocean and the indigenous photochemical air. It was beginning to smell like rain once more.

I stuffed my jacket into a plastic trashcan liner, to carry it while I was dressed in the bellboy getup.

"Leave it," said Dandine.

"Not with my wallet in it." More importantly, and left unsaid, was *not with what's left of my identity in it.*

We still had to detour and grab Alicia's tapes. I had no idea whether she had lied about recording me, too. It didn't matter. It was enough that Dandine was willing to make the stop.

"Hurry up," said Dandine. He handed me a can of oven cleaner, presumably smuggled in. Normal, commercial oven cleaner. My expression must have looked pretty dopey.

"Spray everything you touched," he said. I noticed he was not wearing the latex gloves normal for his usual break-and-enter routine, which would have given him away to the bodyguards "And let's make like a tree."

Right at the door he held up the syringe so I could see it.

"Is this yours?"

The device NORCO had sneaked onto Zetts's car was known in the trade as a "zombie." It's dead, then it comes to life again. More precisely, it functions on a preset time-delay so scans for active bugs will ignore it. Later, it winks on, and commences sending its signals, an hour, a day, a car chase later. That was what had doomed the Sisters, according to Dandine. The thing had not turned on until long after Zetts had activated his little bug-fryer.

When we exited the fire stairs I noticed Dandine holding his wounded arm stiffly, tolerating moderate pain. He indicated a beige Town Car in visitor parking, and we hit the trail again, with him at the wheel.

"Where'd you pick this up?"

"Doesn't matter."

"Not black?"

"I was in a hurry. Look."

A pair of nondescript SUVs were nosing through the security gate at the far end of the lot, angling around the police cars. Their lack of detail virtually screamed NORCO. I had at least learned that much.

"Where'd you leave Zetts's car?"

"Valet parking, Century Plaza Hotel, next door. Then I walked over."

"Good man. Smart." Dandine tried to maneuver his compromised arm around the shoulder strap, clearly miffed at being less than a hundred percent.

"Your arm bothering you?"

"Yes." Tight, clipped, impatient.

"Are you pissed off at me?"

He tried to get his cigarette case out while steering, and fumbled it onto the seat between us. I intercepted it, withdrew a smoke (there were three left), and lit it for him, taking a single puff that made me dizzy.

He took a long draw; I could see him trying to prioritize. Finally, he said, "Zetts is okay."

"Should I send flowers?" I still felt awful about actually smacking him.

"I hate that," said Dandine, turning east on Santa Monica Boulevard. The traffic in the gauntlet to Rodeo Drive, as usual, sucked. "The act of giving flowers—*here is a pretty thing*—has become totally disenfranchised from its roots."

Was he making a pun?

"You've got a multimillion-dollar worldwide factory industry for perfect flowers," he said. "Disconnected from the primal; reduced to a courting ritual. Someone with a handy reminder program tells their computer to phone a florist in commemoration of a calendar date everybody has forgotten. Flowers are dispatched in picture-perfect catalogue arrangements, like rubber doorstops from a mold. There—now, don't you feel special? Multiply by everybody, and imagine all that rotting vegetable matter. They're dying from the moment they're plucked. A dozen little deaths, delivered to your door. A bouquet of twelve corpses, ebbing their last. They expire while you're supposed to cheer up."

"I always thought of it as a transfer of energy," I said. "The flowers help heal you."

He redirected his ire toward a pokey wandering over the lane stripe. "The pedal on the right makes the car *go*, you fucking knob! Look at this idiot—blithering on his Bluetooth, going twenty miles an hour, telling some other idiot what street he's almost at. Of *course* he's got an American flag sticker; what a goddamned patriot."

"You're really pissed off, aren't you?"

"No, I'm just dehydrated. Had to give myself a B-12 shot. I slugged down so much caffeine, it's making me jittery. No food to soak it up. Got to find a market; get myself a PowerBar and some water. You hungry?"

"No, I ate at the hotel." He *almost* snickered when I said that.

Then he told me the story about how he had instructed Zetts to "permit" me to escape, and I got angrier than I thought Dandine already was.

"When you hit him, he was faking it," Dandine said.

"I *saw* him hit his head on the counter!"

"He wasn't unconscious. He phoned me as soon as you left."

I spluttered. "For fuck's sake . . . *why?!*"

"We had to see what you'd do."

My hands grasped air, fidgeting, trying to strangle some invisible man. When little bubbles crawl up the side of the pot, a hard boil is imminent.

"Connie, everybody in this scenario could be a ringer. The best ringers are seeming victims."

"I'm not a fucking ringer; I don't even know what the fuck is going on!" I didn't have to yell but I yelled anyway.

"A ringer, in the parlance," said Dandine, "would have alerted NORCO directly. Or broken cover to impart vital intel. You were let go on purpose to test this possibility, however remote. I'm sorry if you're ruffled, but every contingency has to be checked out, and you already know why."

"So you're faking it, at Collier's? Zetts is faking it? All to find out if *I'm* faking it? Jesus!"

"Calm down."

"You fucking calm down! Does anything rattle you? *Anything?!*"

"Getting shot in the arm annoys me. For real. Now calm down or I'm going to have to slap you, like in the movies, where the guy who gets slapped goes, *thanks, I needed that.*"

"You said you didn't go to the movies, goddammit!"

"You know what I mean, though, right? So take a deep breath or something, will you?"

I wanted a bump of cocaine or a stiff drink, the way flustered people always do in the movies. *Glug glug, ahh, that's all better.*

"This was a *test?* The Sisters are dead!"

"See? You don't know that for sure. You only know that because I told you. The dead come back to life all the time. More often than on TV shows. Ordinary people just never see what's going on. Here we go."

He pit-stopped at a 7-Eleven to stock up on carbs, and handed me one of those explosively named energy drinks—the kind to which you resort when Red Bull doesn't cut it anymore. Remind me sometime to tell you the story of how Kroeger helped Red Bull destroy a competitor called Blue Thunder, with my help.

He downed a protein bar in two bites, swallowed painkillers at the same time, and washed it down with some fizzy green mega-jolt.

"What's on those tapes?" he said. "The ones you thought were so important to stuff in your pockets at the hotel?"

"I told you."

"No—you took microcassettes *and* a bunch of MiniDVs. So what's on the video?"

"Alicia Brandenberg, naked," I said. "So I've heard."

We had been in and out in fewer than fifteen seconds, Dandine spraying oven cleaner everywhere, me grabbing double handfuls from plastic cases, cryptically labeled. Whatever I could fit in my pockets, since there had been no time to browse. The dictation recorder in her own handbag had been the obvious place to find my own audio.

"Oh. Zetts will be thrilled, then." Three deep breaths, and his refuel seemed to take effect. He rubbed his temples, hard. "So . . . what was in your supersecret NORCO file? Anything good?"

"I'd like to see yours," I said.

"No way. That system has never heard of me, and I make sure to keep it that way."

And off we went, hitting the road again. We ride together . . . we die together.

"Where are we going?"

Dandine chewed. "God, Connie, sometimes you can be so dense. Isn't it obvious?"

It was, painfully. All I needed to have done was check the next name on the Sisters' shopping list, still in my pocket.

The zombie had come to life about the time Zetts began to toke his first postchase doob. It activated to standby, then began transmitting when the motor was engaged, its trip preset for a certain range of vibration. It hadn't switched on until I had started the engine again. That was how my pursuers had bagged the Sisters, but not Zetts's house. As Zetts told us later, he fished the device right out of the reservoir for his window washer, where it was floating, sealed in a ball of latex insulation, like (per Zetts) "a turd that won't flush, wrapped in a rubber."

The "rubber" turned out to be heavily impregnated with aluminum dust, to further fox scanners. It was colored to match the washer fluid and thus escape detection by the hurried eyeball. But the hide was the brilliant part. Surveillance paranoiacs the world over will tell you complex stories about first bug, wheel well; second bug, tire well, third bug. Target vehicles are over-bugged so as to provide the knowledge-able victim with bugs to find, and bugs to overlook. Both Zetts and Dandine noted that they'd never seen a bug stashed in the washer jug, and that it was so simple it was scary-smart.

Nobody thinks about these things.

Nobody thinks about the real statistics in examples like airline crashes, or AIDS infiltration, or our supposed national epidemic of crack babies. News media slant such hot topics at a fever pitch in order to in-still a particular variant of panic that results in people buying more of certain kinds of products. Airline insurance, sexual armor, home secu-rity systems. Fear sells. I know that one by heart. Know how many people, total, have died in airplane mishaps since the dawn of aviation? Thir-teen thousand. Ask a citizen on the street, and chances are he or she will guess that many *per year*. It's all evidence of what they're *not* being told.

Make the customer sell himself.

At leaving out specifics, Dandine was a master manipulator. I had to keep reminding myself of this, every time I automatically accepted his assessments as gospel. But every time I tried to prefigure a move to reassert my own identity, Dandine was ahead of me. *You were supposed to "escape"; it was all in the plan; it was a test.* I was mucking around with chess strategy, and he was playing Go.

We were headed up Beverly Glen, past the Beverly Hills Hotel. Two turns past Cielo Drive.

"We're going to force an audience with Mr. Theodore Ripkin," said Dandine. "You will inform him you are in the possession of certain tapes provided by Alicia Brandenberg in order to secure his cooperation. What Ripkin does or says should tell us pretty quickly whether he's a NORCO tool . . . or his opponent is."

Calle Viuda was one of those streets that was more a glorified driveway with a sign; it was not on the official register of street names in LA County and only led to a single tract of property, a graded mesa of semi-hilltop overloaded with the kind of fauna either storebought, or imported to these climes by rich people. Dogwood trees, lizard's breath, magnolia, and thick carpets of preternaturally green lawn that must have cost a thousand dollars a month to water. No matter what anybody says, Los Angeles is still in the desert.

The compound was classically boring Spanish Mission style, but the security surrounding it was state-of-the-art for, say, 1999. When we arrived, the electric gate was still open halfway, and I saw Dandine's eyes go flat and silver. He muttered *dammit,* sotto voce.

"What's happening?"

"It's already happened," he said, reaching into the rear seat for the black Halliburton Zetts had delivered. Another case packed with cash, firearms, and fake ID. Dandine selected a leatherette jacket containing documentation that he was with the National Security Agency. He checked the magazine on his pistol and then handed me another gun. "Thumb safety on the left side of the slide," he said. "You'll have to stick it in your pants; I don't have another holster." Then he kicked the car into gear and accelerated through the open gate.

"Whoa, wait, wait just a minute! What the hell am I walking into, here?"

"Not now." He didn't look at me, not once, during the serpentine drive uphill. His eyes were scanning the greenery in search of some enemy. "I need you to be Mr. Lamb again, just like before, if what I think is right."

He didn't *think* it, he *knew* it. Sensed it, on some superhuman level of attuned perception. Whatever "it" was, my latest task was to play along, follow his lead. Perhaps he smelled a mishap, borne on the very air we breathed.

I tried to record impressions the way I thought he was: Big lawn, seven-car garage (all doors down), at least sixteen rooms in the house. A Bronco and a limited-edition Mercedes in the cul-de-sac, next to a Ford Focus, which had to be an employee car. The maid. Pool house out back. Cabana. Gigantic front door in carved mahogany, iron knocker, still ajar. Smear of blood on the threshold. A foot sticking out of the door.

Red-tailed hawks circled in the updraft above the house, which had a canyon view all to itself.

"How about we just leave, instead?"

"Listen." Sirens were approaching in a manic Code Three, doppler-ing up the canyon. "Too late. We'd never make the end of the driveway before the cops got here. Let 'em come and we'll tough it out."

I almost protested before I realized he did not mean a shootout with the extremely well-armed minions of the Beverly Hills PD. He should have winked at me or something, but that would have been a beat too far for melodrama.

We could see the convoy threading through the Calle Viuda switch-backs—one van and at least four other units, most unmarked cruisers, speed-drifting on the turns with the surety of aggressive-driving gradu-ates. The sirens were off now. They knew where they were going and we didn't have a back door.

The dead guy sprawled in the entryway was jumpstitched by bullet holes in a jagged row from his left hip to his right shoulder. He had that bodyguard look, and had died with his teeth clenched and fists balled. Dandine gave him a glance—just one—and stepped over him, leading the way with his pistol, muzzle anticipating and covering the unknown space inside the house.

From the grim look of the scenario, NORCO was already aware of Alicia Brandenberg's demise and had begun a general purge. I remembered what Dandine had said about deducing things from the size and pattern of a hit. This was big-time, scorched earth stuff. It looked like Theodore Ripkin had pulled the short straw in the big NORCO choose-up.

The foyer opened to a grand stairway that spiraled lazily up the curve of one of the house's three turrets. Each step was wide enough to park a car lengthwise, and on one of them there was a woman facedown, her arm extended through the wrought iron risers, coagulated blood forming candle-wax stalactites on her fingertips. Simple black blouse and trousers, probably the maid with the Focus. She had been blown completely out of her shoes. Bullet gouges had vandalized the wall, sniffing to take her down, and some nobleman in a huge painting had suffered a hit right in his stern expression. The hole made his face look like a cartoon caricature of surprise, the face Wile E. Coyote makes when he realizes he has fucked up yet again.

The cars kept barreling up Calle Viuda. When I turned back, Dandine had slipped away to continue his investigation. I checked out the kitchen, through swinging double doors. Another domestic and another enforcer-looking guy, both deader than the meat in the fridge. One of them had been two bites into a Monte Cristo when he started catching slugs and stopped breathing. There was spilt coffee on the floor tiles, drying already, similar to the maid's blood on the stairs. When I came out, Dandine was walking down the stairs with that odd grace of his, like a dancer, despite his arm sling.

"Two more," he said. "Nobody that looks like Ripkin. They either took him, or he got out."

"Or he wasn't home," I said, off-balance with the weight of the firearm in my waistband. I was still holding onto the dim hope that this might be an unrelated event at the hands of . . . I didn't know, revolutionaries, terrorists, angry housewives, *something* else. Pointlessly, I said, "Unless *who* took him?"

"Who do you think? Look at the patterns. They came through the door spraying. Probing by fire, with automatic weapons. You see any shell casings on the floor?"

"No."

"They had their hardware boxed and baffled."

"English, please?"

"They used silencers and cartridge-snaggers, like I used back at the hotel. I doubt if anybody upstairs heard anybody downstairs getting bagged. This ain't happening; it's over." He stowed his piece as the first incoming cruiser rutted the gravel outside in a speed-stop. "Put on your sunglasses," he said.

"Like at Varga's?" I said.

"Just like at Varga's."

There was almost enough overcast daylight left to get away with it, too; I could always claim my shades were prescription, but if we got into chitchat on *that* depth . . .

I hung back while Dandine strolled right into the muzzle view of several riot guns and more than a few drawn police .357s. He had never intended to pull a gun. He was going to pull rank instead. You had to admire the sheer balls on the guy.

"Thompson, NSA," he announced, flashing his perfect credentials. I heard somebody shout *stand down*. The same voice, the shouter, said, "Captain Ramses."

By the time I got to the door, they were already shaking hands. Captain Ramses had brought a small army for his armed response, plus a point man in full-bore SWAT Kevlar, and a K9 shepherd. Ramses made a hand sign and the cops stashed their hardware, relieved at not taking fire, irritated at not getting to discharge. An LAPD chopper had settled into a hover pattern overhead, thrumming the air.

"That's Lamb," he said, jerking a thumb toward me. I did my tough-guy single nod and my glasses slid down my nose. Slick. One of the uniformed cops called in a Code 4 from the location; he said "location" instead of "scene," as though he was talking about a movie shoot.

"Whatever your call was," said Dandine, "This was no burglary. Captain, I'm going to have to ask for your discretion on this, and possibly your judgment. Because I believe we've really got a terrorist incident on our hands, right here in the middle of where we're not supposed to *worry* about stuff like that."

"Copy that," said the captain, playing hardcase, all squint and burly set of jaw. He'd seen worse. He eyed Dandine's sling. "What happened to you?"

"Torn rotator cuff," Dandine said.

"What can you tell me?"

"Run a jacket on every one of those dead bodies in there and you'll find Middle Eastern passports for the lot. You can get an evidence van up here double-quick, but that won't change the prognosis. We may be looking at a Yellow Alert for Beverly Hills, and I'm not talking about missing toddlers, if you catch my meaning."

Captain Ramses knew the ramifications. *"Shit,"* he whispered, indicating what his workday had become.

"Every one of your men will have to be debriefed," Dandine said. "Whoever shot up this place wasn't making a pit stop after the Beverly Hills Gun Club, am I right?"

"Oh, thank god, thank god! Oh, god! Oh, no—"

We heard some antique porcelain tchotchke in the house crash into powder as it was blundered from a pedestal.

"Oh . . . *god,* Esteban, god, god, they're all *dead!*"

"Somebody religious?" said Dandine.

Half the response team realigned their weapons on the front door as a disheveled man plummeted out at a dead stumble. His shirt was untucked, there was an unseemly rip in the shoulder of his tailored suit, his face was bright red, and he walked clop-footed, as though he had forgotten how. His clothing was smudged with dust and dirt, and he only seemed partially aware of us, his rheumy blue eyes saccading across us too many times. His hands were jittering with shock, which was deadly, because one of them held a nickel-plated revolver, a whore's gun that had probably spent most of its life in a drawer.

This, then, was the estimable Theodore Ripkin.

"Stand down!" Ramses shouted toward his men. The presence of the helicopter pretty much necessitated that everyone shout. "Sir—I'm going to ask you to stop right where you're standing, and place that weapon on the deck. I do mean right now."

Ripkin skidded to a halt as though he'd smacked into an invisible barrier. "Oh! Oh! Yes! *Of course!* I—oh, thank god you men are here, thank god—"

"He's back on the God thing again," Dandine said to me in aside, already disgusted with the specimen before us.

Ripkin had the kind of big, weathered hands that always appeared strangulated by shirt cuffs. They were red, too, as though he suffered some circulatory problem. He bent butler-style and relinquished his gun, gingerly, as though it was a bomb about to detonate.

"Did you call us, sir?" said Ramses.

"What? Yes! *Yes!* Cellphone! My god, my god . . . they came in these vans, they were all over the grounds before . . . oh my god, they've murdered Esteban, they've killed them *alllll* . . ." His voice degenerated into a bray as he sank to his knees. Tears tracked his face.

"Jesus fucking *christ,*" said Dandine.

Ripkin's glasses were thumbprinty and skewed. He plowed one hand backward through stone-white hair, which he still had most of. His roseate complexion made the fine, ivory hair pop. It was stark, unnatural. He tried to bury his face in his hands in sorrow, as no doubt he had observed people did when genuinely afraid or immolated by grief. Ramses collected the pistol. He tried to help Ripkin to stand, but Ripkin twisted away and swatted the hand, like a surly child.

"Try to tell us what happened, sir."

"No security, none!" Ripkin blubbered. "Bodyguards all dead! They were everywhere, oh, god, they were shooting everyone, oh my god! I ran, I hid, I *had* to, don't you see?"

Dandine stepped in. "Where did you hide?" His expression told me that he was not accustomed to his searches coming up dry, or worse, unprofessional.

"Room," Ripkin said, husking air, dicing his words into moist, breathy chunks. "Special room."

"Like a panic room?"

Ripkin gulped more air and tried to find his persona. "More like a goddamned closet. Small. Off the upstairs bathroom. Nobody knows—"

"I *checked* the upstairs bathrooms," said Dandine, with a petulance only I could appreciate. "All four of them."

"No, it's . . . you can't see it . . . nobody knows it's there . . . it's inside the shower stall . . . we never use that one . . . special . . . custom . . ."

Dandine rolled his eyes. "You ran away to a hide you had in the *shower,* with a gun?"

"They didn't see me . . . I saw 'em through the window . . ."

"And you ran and hid. With a gun."

Obviously, Dandine was going to need this explained to him, at length, and at the risk of huffing away our flimsy cover. I stepped around him and spoke to Captain Ramses. "Captain, if you don't mind, I need this man for two seconds."

Captain Ramses did what I hoped, and cleared a space in deference to my imaginary rank. There was no time so I got right in Rifkin's face. I wanted to start slapping him, exactly the same way Dandine had wanted to slap me moments before. No time, no time for anything.

"Mr. Rifkin," I said, trying to keep my pot from boiling again. "NORCO did this. Tell me if you know NORCO did this."

"What?" said the man who had run away and hid with a gun while everyone else in his house was getting exterminated. "Who?"

His blue eyes had gone bloodshot, and in that very instant I knew I was looking into the eyes of a man who had never heard of some secret cabal called NORCO. My lungs seemed to compress. The guy was a still-living dead end. All he had ever done was get seduced by Alicia Brandenberg.

Dandine saw the reflex distress in my expression, and quickly stepped in, keeping Captain Ramses's attention off of me. "I think this gentleman requires protective custody, Captain . . . instead of exposure, out here in the open."

That jolted Ramses back to his playbook. "All right!" he yelled at his men, pointing. "You two men, escort! You two—wingmen. Keep him low in the vehicle! Get him out of here, now!"

One officer hustled in and threw a SWAT vest over Ripkin's head. Cops swarmed him like pod people.

"Nothing he can tell us here that he can't tell us at the station," said Ramses. "Thanks."

It was nothing. Really. It really *was* nothing.

"How'd you fellas get here ahead of us?" asked Ramses.

"Dumb luck. I caught your air and was closer."

If Ramses checked our car for a radio, we were sunk. But he deferred to the NSA as though he was used to doing it. He and Dandine went 'round and 'round a bit more, then we escaped in a cloud of bullshit. *Our work here is done, stout sidekick.*

We couldn't clear the drive fast enough. We hit Benedict Canyon and Dandine spurred the beige Town Car north. "I know one damned thing," he said.

"What's that?"

"That guy back there really is Ripkin, right? I mean, he's not like a plant, or a double—somebody pretending to be Ripkin?"

"That's Ripkin, believe it or don't. One of our great leadership hopes for the future. And he doesn't know a damned thing about the shit you and I are in. That guy is innocent of just about . . . everything relevant."

"How did you know that?" said Dandine.

"I don't know," I said. I thought of the information sinking into my brain and percolating down through the layers of fissures until it popped a red flag. "I just looked at the guy and it was obvious. Plus, he had no idea in hell who either of us were. If he was in bed with NORCO, he'd know; he would have reacted. If he was in bed with NORCO, then who sent the cleanup crew to his house, and why?"

"That's good," said Dandine. "You're learning." Then he glanced past the tint layer on the upper windshield. "Fuck!"

I shed the sunglasses because they still pinched my not-completely recovered head. Because it was now *dark.* "What?"

"Goddamned helicopter. It's following us."

I kept my mouth shut, because I didn't have to ask *who* one more time.

I knew other things without saying, too. I knew that tracker satellites could only look straight down from Earth orbit, but if the guys in the helo were sharp, they might already have made our stolen plates, or gotten them from one of Captain Ramses's eagle-eyed crew. I knew we were technically in violation of the Benedict Canyon speed limit. I knew Dandine was formulating a plan I probably would not enjoy.

Nothing I knew seemed useful or applicable, anymore. Right past the tip of my nose, the whole world had changed. I needed to shift the balance, and at least delude myself in thinking I had some sort of control. A grip. Cards to play.

"Stop looking up," Dandine said, as he blew the stoplight and careened the car onto Mulholland. We were riding the spine of the snake, now, twisting and turning on the backbone of the Santa Monica ridge, the territory of scenic overlooks in both directions. Make-out spots. The ribbon of road where rich guys came to blow out high-performance driving machines, and park rangers waited in Jeeps to dole out speeding tickets.

Dandine edged the car up to sixty per. In these hills, sixty felt like ninety-five, and there were abundant cutbacks and hairpins, any one of which could shoot us out into space, where we would prove less than weightless. Up here, chances were good that we might round a turn at high speed and paste a deer, or a family of coyotes. Chances were better and more dangerous at night, and as we flew west on this essentially rural road, Dandine was forced to use our high beams. The pursuit 'copter easily paced us, sporadically nailing the Town Car in a UFO-abductee circle of frozen blue light from above.

"Seat belt," said Dandine, unnecessarily.

"This is stupid! This is a car chase, and we're the only fucking car!"

Brief pause to taste the meat of my own heart, as it tried to eject, blocking my throat. Dandine had chosen to fade past an SUV dawdling along ahead of us at the legal limit. To pass it on the *right* side, because we hit a switchback that made the oncoming turn invisible. Dandine applied the brakes for a controlled skid when we hit the dirt shoulder. I slammed both eyes shut and stupidly braced against the dash, imagining impact, fire, my funeral. The khaki-colored Jeep Liberty spun out after getting a macro view of our left rear bumper. The shoulder was not guardrailed and we missed kissing the edge of the cliff by two, maybe two and a half feet. We whip-cracked back onto the pavement and all I could see aft was a billowing cloud of dust-smoke. The guy in the Liberty sat there, honking impotently. Another guy with an American flag sticker.

"Warn me if you're going to do that again?"

"Do what?" said Dandine. He could have added a little exposition about his plan, but as you've seen, he was not the most forthcoming of individuals.

You know the story about the Mulholland Tunnel, right?

In the 1970s, long before anyone dreamed of drilling through the mountains to provide subway tunnels fifty years too late, there was this movie star who bought a lot of property not far east of Stone Canyon Road. He had a cluster of houses up there called the Compound, with a gated private drive off Mulholland (his heirs own it now). The driveway, incidentally, was similar to Calle Viuda in that it was not an official street, but had been phonied up by its master with a name and street sign *not quite* in accordance with municipal statutes. Hence, "Universe Trail." Most of the Compound was on the hilltop—views in both directions, you see—and when the highway had been carved out of the mountain in the early 1920s to connect Hollywood with what was then called the Malibu Colony, city engineers bisected a minor peak in the range to keep the road level. In 1972, after investigating the LA County land registrar's office, the movie star discovered that his property actually fell on *both* sides of the cut in the mountaintop, and instead of raising a ruckus, offered to build *over* it in order to utilize more real estate for adding additional structures. The courtroom fight with the zoning commission dominated local headlines for months before the problem suddenly vanished, whisked away on the winds of bribery, and geologists pronounced the plan sound in record time. Earth was moved back into the gap and the two-lane Mulholland Tunnel was born. Where the movie star failed was in his bid to get the tunnel named after himself. It is a close, radically arched passage like the ones you can see in Griffith Park, its egresses decoratively limned in granite. It is actually shorter in length than the mountain is tall, vented for drainage, built to last.

(William Mulholland, the water and power baron for whom Mulholland Drive was named in 1923, committed suicide in 1935 after one of his dams burst, rather spectacularly, in 1928 . . . but that's another story.)

Know your city. At least know the lies it's built on. Print the legend.

We slipknotted through the turn by Universe Trail at about six bits, and the maw of the Mulholland Tunnel yawned ahead as the pursuit helicopter kept to its watchdog altitude, fading the treetops. The interior of the tunnel was harshly lit by sour yellow sodium lamps pocked into the ceiling about fifty feet above; I wondered how maintenance guys changed the bulbs.

Sitting in the middle of the tunnel, parking lights aglow in the oncoming lane, was Zetts in his GTO. There was somebody with him—two silhouettes, not one.

Trap, I thought. Dandine had been right, days, centuries earlier. Zetts had been bought and we were doomed.

Dandine flashed into the tunnel and stood on the brakes, baking tread and coming in for a landing just past Zetts's monster.

"Let's go," he said, grabbing the Halliburton, already out of the Town Car, fast-fast-fast. I was right behind him.

Zetts's passenger debarked and he and Dandine passed each other like hurried commuters on opposing escalators. A guy with thick glasses and an explosion of dreadlocks, dressed in very colorful, very loose, very *big* clothing.

"Leon," said Dandine, in transit.

"Yo," said Leon, not even looking. "This one makes us even."

"Copy that," said Dandine.

It was all like a really *organized* Chinese fire drill, with me two moves late and no instruction manual.

Leon vaulted into the driver's seat of the Town Car, buckled up, and glared at me. "You wanna close the *door,* man? *Thank* you. Jesus!"

Slam, vroom, and Leon was off, speeding out the far end of the tunnel while my seat was still warm. I was standing there like a dork when Dandine shouted back, his voice echoing in the tunnel.

"Connie—sometime today, all right?"

We could have wasted time debating over who got to ride in front, but I piled in and Zetts, belted and focused, did what he does best. There was no bruise on his forehead, no damage on the back of his skull. He looked fine.

February 25, 1999: My divorce papers are finalized.

The divorce has taken longer than the actual marriage—three and a half years versus a scant ten months. Signed, sealed, no-fault, everybody shakes hands and goes away, the final whimper in a bang-less romantic career. A grand total of no incidents, during the years I waited out and delayed the paperwork. I used the excuse of "distance" when I enacted these legalities, because by the time the papers trickled through, I did not want to feel a single emotion: anger, regret, anything. I did not want this event to have enough power to cause me to react in any way, other than dropping the documents into a folder and doing my best never to look at them again. I bore no grudge. There were abundant avenues for soap opera, but I wasn't interested enough to cultivate extravagant tales of how I had been cheated, how I had been fucked over, all the tabloid details meant to make your personal failings fascinating to greedy out-siders, providing cheap moral lessons to reinforce a status quo of banal-ity. Several friends wanted to get me drunk and hear all the nasty dish, but that wasn't necessary. Really, it wasn't. They countered with reviews of me as a human being. I was closed off, they said. I didn't allow myself to have feelings, they said. It was all bait to lure me into saying things that were not true, or inventing things equally untrue that satiated their need for common drama. Their tactics were transparent and infantile, and I danced around them easily, because when I lie, I do it by choice, and I am much better at lying than they are. You and I both know the difference between the pikers and professionals, when it comes to lying. The amateurs are lame and awkward (and thus reap a surfeit of the drama they crave) while the pros are somehow admirable in their audac-ity. They don't lie capriciously. They lie as part of the system of getting things done, or because the waters in which they swim are so corrupt that a lie is the only way to keep from drowning. If you don't want to swim with the big fish, it's your choice not to get in the river . . . but don't expect to ride a tide, or go anywhere interesting in your life. Be honest. Be safe. You might get a merit badge. You'll definitely get chewed up and shat out by the predators swimming in the river. Guys like me, who sell you things. Who batten off your fear. Who aren't afraid of the dark. Who live in the real world. Who don't feel, unless they choose to.

"What happens to Leon?" Somebody had to say it, so I did.

"Leon drives pell-mell to the Pacific Coast Highway, where he per-mits himself to be pulled over, at which point our wily pursuers discover you and I are not in the target vehicle," said Dandine. "They can't really hold him. And he doesn't know anything. Anything pertinent."

"Fuckin Leon," said Zetts, bobbing and weaving down Coldwater Canyon. He craned around to acknowledge me. "S'it hangin', brah?"

Not for the first time, I felt like an idiot. "Hey, I'm sorry about the whole—"

"No worries," Zetts said. "Part of the game. I ain't hurt. I know how to fall down. And look at *you,* all action hero and shit."

Dandine extended his open hand. "Gun."

I was in the junk-strewn backseat of the GTO. Both men were in front of me. I could easily jam the muzzle into Dandine's ear and demand straight talk . . . if I wanted him to laugh his ass off. I handed the gun back, butt-first. I hadn't even really examined it. Was it loaded? I couldn't remember. His eyes held on me a beat, as though he had already read a printout of my thoughts.

"Where to?" said Zetts.

"Pizza," said Dandine.

"Boy howdy," said Zetts. "Pizza sounds good."

My stomach lurched, or maybe it was the vibration of the car. I never wanted to consume solid food again. I wanted to eat a pound of antacids, washed down with a gallon of coffee, and maybe take up smoking for the third time in my life. Under certain circumstances, tobacco qualifies as food. Maybe an injection of Demerol for dessert. Better, heroin. My head was pounding. Forehead still bruised, wrists still tender with cuts, and my ear felt broken, sundered, dysfunctional. Zetts and Dandine wanted to gobble slices with everything despite a growing mound of corpses. Varga's men. Ripkin's staff. Assorted NORCO casualties. Choral Anne Grimes. Celeste, a.k.a. Marisole. Alicia Brandenberg. Marion, the bodyguard with John Wayne's name, and his cohort. I knew I had to be missing two or three MIAs, but it wasn't a lax body count for two and a half days of random running around LA, even counting traffic delays.

"What about Ripkin?" I said.

"He won't be living anywhere he isn't surrounded by cops," said Dandine. "He's as good as on ice. Not that hard for us to access."

"Getting Jenks will be impossible, now. Jenks has *got* to know what happened, whether he caused it or not."

"You mean the former Mr. Stradling," Dandine said. "You like mushrooms? I like mushrooms."

"Yeah, and double pepperoni," said Zetts.

"*Whatever* the hell his name is, this week! What if this is some kind of vendetta between these two guys? What if NORCO had nothing to do with it?"

"Connie . . ." said Dandine.

"What if we get implicated? What if I get arrested again?! Where does this stop?"

"Connie." Firmer, now.

"*Does this just keep getting worse and worse until we all fucking die?!*"

"Connie, you're going to throw a clot. Relax. Those are all excellent questions. I expect no less, given the way your brain works. But there's a time to work it out, and a time not to. Surely you're aware of dinners at which business must *not* be discussed? Where it would be discourteous, a huge faux pas? Right now, it's time to eat. Okay?"

I slumped back into the seat.

"Fuckin-A it's time to eat," said Zetts.

"No anchovies, okay?" I said. "Just promise me that one tiny thing—no little dead fishes looking back at me."

"Easily done," said Dandine. "Anything else you want?"

We sidled through the batwing inner doors of Ray's New Original West Coast New York Pizza right between a Van Halen oldie and a Poison oldie on the jukebox. We cast shadows from the entryway like the Wild Bunch, minus one. Nobody inside cared. It was just after 8:00 P.M. Dandine had forsaken his arm sling, shucking it and leaving it in the car. It got in the way too much.

"Ever notice that?" said Zetts. "In movies, like when there's a lot of action and chasing around? Like nobody ever stops to eat. They just keep, y'know, actioning."

"The dull stuff never makes the cut," I said, knowing it was monotonous, but needing to speak. "Cut from a day scene to a night scene, and you just have to assume they grabbed a sandwich." I turned to Dandine. "What happens now?"

"First, we sit."

The place was a riot of Mafiosi movie posters and checkered spreads on wobbly tables. False brickwork laminate, empty vino bottles, bunches of plastic grapes that needed dusting. Real candles burned in Chianti bottles snugged in wicker baskets. The present clientele included two enormous bikers who resembled wrestling stars on the slum, destroying a pie with three inches of meat on top. A sad little guy all by his lonesome near the door with a laptop and a "personal serving" pizza with veggies, sipping a watery Diet Coke. Four more men who looked like grunts on leave, or off-duty cops, or professional bowlers, giving the waitress one last leery hassle on their way out. She seemed to be the sole on-duty wage worker, an ash blonde with fried roots, too much mascara, a nose ring, and about fifty more sterling loops punctuating her right ear. She seemed tough, weary, and savvy enough to handle the parking lot at night, by herself. The chef, or cook, or what we could glimpse of him, remained in his citadel of stainless steel behind the pass-through window, a stocky man with a single bushy brow over both eyes, stubble that warned he didn't give a shit, and took none, wearing a T-shirt that appeared to have been vomited on by somebody else, maybe one of his victims. I saw him smoking as he swabbed down his works. There was sawdust on the concrete floor. The red leatherette booths were comfortably sprung, and the beer was served in mugs of genuine glass, the kind with an ice reservoir in the bottom. It was sensibly dark in here, with candle flame and strands of holiday lights, webbed above.

"Don't even think of wasting my time," the waitress said when she caught Zetts trying to read a creased menu in the dodgey light.

Dandine hypnotized her, as usual, ordering curtly for all of us. She smiled at him and gave her name as Jessica.

The draft beer was *very* good, but not distracting enough. I pressed Dandine, "What happens now?"

"Patience," said Dandine. "Not at the table."

Zetts shrugged exaggeratedly at me, as though to say *don't fight it.*

"No. Now."

Dandine's calm mask tightened. "Listen, I don't know yet. I don't like the options. One of them entails using you as live bait, but I haven't decided yet. Talk about something else. Tell us about your job."

I told them about the very first time I had gone to Pittsburgh, representing Kroeger, in October 2001. It was on behalf of an insurance company whose Manhattan offices had been wiped out as collateral damage from the collapse of the Twin Towers. They were rebuilding, and decided to erase the World Trade Center from the establishing shots of their commercial footage for TV ads. I went there personally to talk them out of it. Instead, I told them, *add* footage of the pillars of light, after the catastrophe. Give your customers the idea that your company will endure, no matter what. It was Ghandi-like in its simplicity. Respond not with aggression, but poetry. You'll enjoy a better quality of lump in the throat, and people will *never* forget your ads.

Yeah, that's right—I turned the Trade Center disaster into an advertising gambit. But they went for it, because of what they understood about product recognition . . . so who's the real bad guy, in that scenario?

Besides, it was nearly a decade later, the Twin Towers were still a hole in the ground, and the insurance company was still exploiting the imagery, jerking those heartstrings in the name of quarterly profit. They were one of those companies that routinely denied medical claims from rescue workers—firemen whose teeth were now rotting out of their gums, paramedics with respiratory fibrosis, cops with post-traumatic nightmares. But they had the best, most emotionally wrenching photos of firemen, paramedics, cops, and Memory Walls you'd ever see on TV. My annual strategy sessions with the company had become a ritual, and I had just returned from the latest one when I found the locker key in the car.

"Circumstance turned gold into straw," said Dandine. "You turned it back into gold. That's a talent."

"Not for me," I said. "For Team Kroeger."

"I should be asking *you* for suggestions."

"Okay, first suggestion." I winked. "Bear in mind I am *not* talking about that thing we've agreed not to talk about. We're talking about a whole other bunch of guys in a completely different predicament."

"Fair enough." Dandine smiled, shook his head, sipped his beer. Zetts was all audience.

"Seems to me that we—those other guys—are in danger of being nibbled to death by ducks."

"Whoa," said Zetts.

"Here are these guys," I said, "who operate entirely under the radar. No profiles, no traceable numbers. Very free. But in order to function within a runaway capitalist economy, you have to sacrifice tiny freedoms, like privacy, in order to use things like credit cards. Or you have to go to double the trouble to mock up false identities and records and backstories, which doesn't help you if the credit card blows a gasket. You just shift to the next identity. But what if you can't? What if you only have one credit card, and you *need* it? There's no appeal for you—no way you can just call the boss of the company and make a legitimate complaint. That's what's tripping us up. It's like we're caught in the gears of the system, sweating out the referrals and process and I'll-have-to-transfer-you-to-another-line. We're on hold because of *policy,* the way 'things are done.' All our time is spent sweeping the pawns out of the way, when we should be talking to the boss."

Dandine was rubbing the bridge of his nose, up and down, with his thumb.

"Here's another thing: Alicia Brandenberg tried to rattle my cage by emphasizing how my part in this was *over* and *done!* We're still farting around, sweeping up the dregs of Plan A, when the big, bad *Them* out there has already gone to Plan B. We need to jump ahead of them, for once. End run. An oblique solution, instead of a direct one. Battering directly just wins you dents in your head."

"So why do you suppose the police didn't just scoop us up at Ripkin's?" said Dandine. "Surely they radioed in our ID."

"Dumb luck. Slow computers. Something random." I knew those were three of Dandine's favorite things.

"He's catching on," he said to Zetts. "You should have seen him at Ripkin's."

I was holding a fork as though preparing to invert it into a weapon. My nerves were still singing like violin strings. I couldn't just turn my paranoia on, then off, then on again like these two could . . . and I didn't know what to do with all the surplus nervous energy.

We had to keep running, ducking, laying down cover fire, and trading witty asides about the meanings inside the meanings of things; until we just burned up, I guess, to leave crisp little cigarette-ash husks of ourselves blowing down the nearest gutter.

Fortunately for my state of mind, that was when the three men with shotguns strolled into Ray's.

Really. Truly. Three dudes with shotguns. They came in just as Zetts halved an anchovy with his teeth, almost daintily.

One key, two backups.

They sought us, centered us, and the backups made the mistake of racking their slides to announce serious ass-kicking intent.

Everybody except me was already moving. Time did its treacherous elongation trick. Zetts eeled beneath the booth. Dandine was already gone.

The dim light inside foxed the shooters for a couple of tumbling seconds, as they tried to track and aim.

Dandine was already on the floor, sliding on his back in the sawdust. He remained completely flat as he raised his arms, a pistol in each hand, and—I'm not making this up—shot and killed *both* of the backups at the same time. They crumpled like empty hand puppets, their weapons clattering, leaving their Number One with a perplexed expression, still leveling a streetsweeper that could clip most of us with a single round.

Except that our iron horseman friends from the far end of the gallery had reacted as fast as Dandine. One was adequately shielded by the jukebox and his partner had gone to one knee behind a freestanding table. Both were holding down on the new intruder with revolvers of grotesque size, combat stances, and dead-sure, unwavering aim.

The cook with the unibrow had dropped behind the serving window, as if through a trapdoor. He reappeared with a sawed-off Remington riot gun with a pistol grip. Already racked.

Jessica, obviously a veteran of several armed robbery attempts, had balled into a duck-and-cover on the deck near the cash register. Our sole remaining companion customer had sunk down into his booth, behind the inadequate barrier of his laptop, trying to become invisible the way short people vanish from cars with big headrests, when viewed from behind.

A second of achingly protracted silence, as Dandine's double shot reverberated. Everyone frozen in a still life of possible chaos.

"Think first," said Dandine to the man at the door. He rose in a slow sit-up, keeping his guns trained. "Say, it's . . . it's Cody Conejo, isn't it?"

"Aww, fuck me running," said the intruder, lowering his own shotgun. "You're supposed to be fuckin *dead,* man."

"Stand down, gentlemen," Dandine said to our unwilling audience at large. "I know this guy."

"You're lifting a little out of your weight class, aren't you, Cody?" said Dandine as he wolfed most of a slice in three bites.

Dandine was a good negotiator. Nothing in the restaurant had been destroyed. He paid everyone's tab and salted enough cash around to ensure the police would not be called, for all the good that would have done. En passant, I wondered if the cash was legit or tainted. But by the time five minutes had passed, and a rock 'n' roll couple (a band rat and his front-row wife) had come in with their little girl for dinner, you would have never known that anything bad had happened. Jessica got a huge tip, the laptop man evaporated into the night without waiting for dessert, and the cook collected several new, unpapered firearms and two bodies in his industrial fridge, which he assured us were no problem. The bikers mostly wanted to compare notes with Dandine about pistols, and rode away happy, with extra road beers. It occurred to me that everybody in the place, except me, had a yellow sheet or criminal record. Zetts ate pizza one-handed, holding down on the groin of our new guest with one of Dandine's guns as a cut from Judas Priest's *British Steel* hammered out of the juke, near which the little girl happily played pinball, twisting some English into her flipper moves.

That jukebox was an eighties time machine, apparently. Nobody minded.

"Dumb luck," said Cody Conejo, a big man—big as the bikers—whose mad casserole of genetics presented us with critical Asian eyes, a Mexican complexion, and rich black Navajo hair casually tied back with rawhide. His eyes kept seeking our pizza.

"Go ahead," said Dandine. "We're all just having a social chat. Catching up on who has betrayed who, today. And don't give me that tripe about luck. Even over the music, I could hear your coat rubbing against your body armor, louder than corduroy. Why do you still wear that stuff?"

"That's, like *sooo* twentieth century," said Zetts.

"If the maggots aren't spraying their slugs with Teflon to zip right through the vests, "Dandine advised, "they're coating them in mercury so you'll die slow and painful. Cheapskates just dip them in feces."

"Shit," I said. "How do you know this guy?"

"We worked some ops before we were franchised. Shakedown, test-drive stuff." He made it sound as though NORCO sent recruiters to our nation's better campuses. "You really think you could take me, Cody my boy?"

Cody shook his head while noshing a too-full mouth of pizza. "Not you. Him." He gulped without chewing enough and indicated me with a tilt of his chin. "They're calling him the Ad Man, now." He seemed resigned to whatever retribution Dandine might mete out, yet light about the whole thing, like someone who has lost a game fair and square and hopes not to be killed for coming second.

"Who sent you?" said Dandine.

"Jenks. For payback. For the woman."

"*That* was certainly quick—a bit too quick even for good planning. How?"

Cody Conejo indicated me. "He's broadcasting, man. How else?"

Dandine sprang from the booth, dragging me up in a bowlegged wobble. His eyes told Zetts to keep Cody on hold. With practiced pre-meditation, he searched my collar and cuffs, and discovered a silver disc, dime-sized, inside my left lapel. He tossed it to Zetts, who examined it by candlelight.

"From NORCO, with love," said Zetts. "They might as well start stamping a brand name on these things; they're like so obvious. They must buy 'em by the case." He dropped it in his untouched water glass, where it sank past the crushed ice. "We now *terminate* our broadcast day, dude."

"You file a prelim report back on the op? A green-light sheet?" Dandine asked Cody. It sounded like NORCO was big on paperwork.

"Naw. Was supposed to, after."

"Don't lie to me."

I needed to contribute. "How did that thing get on me? Not in jail. I didn't even have my jacket on at Zetts's place . . ."

They all stared at me, pityingly, until I figured it out.

"At Alicia's," I said. "When Marion patted me down." Specifically, in the elevator, as he scanned me for nonexistent bugs. "But why bug me there? I wasn't supposed to walk out of there."

"See?" said Cody. "Dumb luck."

"They tin-canned you in case something outside the purview of their plan happened," said Dandine. "It did, too. God, I'm losing it. I should have searched you, first thing. I thought the costume change would be enough. I never should have let you keep your coat."

Leave it. He'd told me to leave it, because his senses were that good, and he'd turned out to be right.

"What did they tell you the op was?" said Dandine to Cody, who was working on his second slice of *our* pizza.

"Do him. Walk away. No peripherals. Straight eye-for-an-eye deal, as a favor from NORCO, to Jenks."

"Do you know who Jenks is?"

Cody shook his head. "Couldn't pick him out of a lineup. No idea."

"Then who's supposed to pay you? For Jenks to call in a favor from NORCO that fast, the rubber stamp man had to be Gerardis."

"Yeah, who else?" said Cody.

"Okay . . . NORCO purges Ripkin's staff, but—brilliantly—*misses* Ripkin. Probably the same team travels directly to Alicia's, to purge her. They budget like that; two-for-one. Except Alicia is already neutralized, and Connie and I get out of the parking lot just as the NORCO squad rolls in. Ripkin panics and calls the cops—real cops—who show up right after we do. But Connie is bugged, so when NORCO bags the SOS, they let it ride, figuring we'll take the fall for the shootout. Which means . . . dammit, that really *was* a police helicopter."

"How do you figure?"

"I figure Captain Ramses is a cautious enough man to radio the chopper and say, follow those guys for a bit."

It certainly queered our chances of saying, later, *Hiya, Captain Ramses, old pal, mind if we talk to the guy you have in max-lock custody?*

208

"And Ripkin didn't call NORCO, he called the real police. Somebody in NORCO's pocket wouldn't bother. Either way, I'd say NORCO has decided which candidate they really like."

"I don't get it," I said. "Why all the . . . commotion, agitation? Why now?"

"Because their delicate balance of Jenks-versus-Alicia-versus-Ripkin has been disrupted by our, um, accidental incursion. NORCO likes to jettison liabilities instantaneously; that's one of the things that keeps them subradar. They're called bathwater jobs, as in baby-with-the-bathwater."

"Man, that shit is like them time-travel movies," said Zetts.

"Paradoxical," said Dandine. "Look it up."

"Whatever it is, it's givin' me a headache."

"Sounds to me like I don't even wanna know what kinda panty-twist you guys are into," said Cody. He took a sip of the only available unused water glass, the one with the dead bug in it.

"How do you know it was Jenks that requisitioned your op?" Dandine asked Cody.

"Like I'm trying to tell ya, man, I *don't*. It was an à la carte gig. Gerardis says for me to do the Ad Man, for somebody named Jenks, is all I heard. He prorated for two backups, so I figured, cool—fast cash, not cheap, therefore Jenks has gotta be some rich asshole. I had no idea *you'd* be here—if I had, don't you think I woulda brought a fuckin tank, and twenty guys? Jesus!"

"Holy shit," said Dandine. "You know what that means?" He was talking to Zetts. "It means we can skate. It's not about us, not anymore. It's about Connie, here. It's exactly as he said—everyone has gone to Plan B."

That sounded to me like something really . . . bad. I almost felt as though Dandine and Zetts would finish their meal, leave me at the table with my soon-to-be murderer, and be home in their beds, all snug, while I began the process of decomposition in some Dumpster.

Dandine just looked at me and said, "Don't worry. I know what you're thinking. You're ignoring the significant karmic bill that NORCO has amassed, through its own mismanagement and thuggishness. They have to pick up their own check, and we have to be the instrumentation for that balance, because if we don't—"

"They'll be up your ass, like a sigmoidoscope," chimed Zetts (carefully pronouncing each syllable), "for the rest of your life, until you like drop into your assigned hole, dude."

"Where the hell did you get that word?" asked Dandine. Then he thought about it. "Never mind."

"What about me?" asked Cody, having stealthed a third slice. He looked like he ate a lot.

"You get to live," said Dandine, "because I'm feeling unusually forgiving today. But not if you don't tell us when and where on your pay drop from NORCO."

That caused Cody to woof a chunk of pizza down the wrong tube, and he grabbed for the water glass.

"Don't drink the bug," said Zetts.

Which is how I got to be bait, just after midnight.

DAY FOUR

Ever since the vaguely religious hiccup that hysterical media have shortformed as "9/11," you can see guys in military fatigues, toting M-16s, inside the Bradley Terminal at Los Angeles International Airport. Go there right now and check, if you don't believe me.

The cameras have been doubled; the guards, tripled. Bored employees wipe your baggage down for trace explosives and make you remove your shoes. There are cops with K9 dogs, and everybody is watching everybody else, to make sure some hausfrau from Thousand Oaks doesn't compromise national security by trying to sneak a nail file onto a passenger jet. Or a roll of tape. Or a deadly can of deodorant. Posted signs enumerate lists of words it is forbidden to mention, even jokingly. Joking is illegal there, which means if someone greets a friend by saying, "Hi, Jack!" they'll most likely be detained and beaten with rubber hoses. No one sees the irony of a terrorist government, terrorizing its citizens, to protect them from terrorists.

And this was *before* the passenger-profiling and color-coding fiasco.

It's a great place to hang out if you don't want strangers pulling mysterious shit, which is why Dandine picked it. T-4, christened in honor of ex–LA mayor Ed Bradley (a former police officer), was LAX's showcase for paranoid security measures, and a terrific, live-action exemplar of the difference between liberty and freedom, for those who had never bothered to ponder the distinction.

"Flyover surveillance and tracking devices won't work here," Dandine said, "because their microwave grid over protected airspace is too precious. No bugs, no leashes, no choppers. The terminal is a huge, open area under twenty forms of watchdogging, so no surprise firefights, or, at least, the possibility is minimized. NORCO may be able to selectively hammerlock the police, but there are too many forms of good guy here for them all to be compromised. It's too public."

Even at 1:00 A.M., the international terminal was fairly bustling. Completely different from Terminal One, where we'd rented another getaway car less than forty-eight hours ago. Flights to Sydney and Shanghai take a *long* time, and cannot countenance farmer's hours, the agrarian nine-to-five hellhole inside which most people, the walking dead, persist in living, even a century after the invention of conveniences like electricity. There was a fellow who ran for mayor here in the last election, who proposed putting the city on a twenty-four-hour clock, since telecommuting had become a practical option for over a third of the workforce. This would have destroyed the notion of "rush hour" traffic, freeway gridlock, and a pretty fair amount of road rage (for which our state is particularly infamous). Needless to say, the guy didn't win, because his opponent had looked at the chad-mincing, double-dealing big lie of a recent presidential election and thought, *hey, I can get away with that, too!*

Back in my old life, I had heard people bitching about politics in the normal, air-filling, useless way most citizens prattle on about food or the weather, and more than once I overheard the assertion that maybe the United States wasn't such a swell place to live, anymore, what with basic rights being whittled away almost one per day. Some people groused about becoming expatriates. All I know is, Shanghai sounded pretty good to me, right now, and that place was full of *communists.*

I wasn't taking a political stance, though. I was defaulting to a skin-saving stance.

The Bradley Terminal is the largest at LAX. The booking section is an open area consisting of three enormous free corridors lined with ticket counters. At the far west end, escalators bleed up to bars and restaurants, prior to the gauntlet of gates and X-ray machines. But out in the main booking area there is no overlook, no mezzanine access to customers. If you're looking for a wide-open space in which you'd rather not be caught in the middle, T-4 was ideal.

Picture me and my new friend, Cody Conejo, trying to appear casual as we walked down the slanted ramp and into the main terminal, no different from ordinary citizens, merely two more of the walking dead. My teeth were grinding, and the rest of my body gently urged me to run like hell.

Zetts held a visual on us from the parking garage. We left Dandine next to him, cellphone at the ready.

Cody had to run a lap in place before he had sounded breathless enough to place the call to the NORCO relay line, his next step toward getting paid. I think he may have had a few overdue bills, because he seemed piqued at having to barter his deal upward (or at least, laterally) in order to keep wearing his skin.

Cryptically, Dandine had specified that Cody *not* use a scrambled cellphone. He made the call from a pay phone near baggage claim. When everyone went askance at that, Dandine merely said, "I want to check something." The rest of his instruction menu was pretty pinpoint.

"Tell Gerardis the op got compromised," Dandine instructed. "Tell them the bug was lost and you were forced to grab the principal in a public place, but you can't leverage him out, because a gun in the terminal would expose the op. That's pretty thin ice, but they may skate on it if they believe you were just doing your job, and now you need their help for an extraction. But—this is the important part—tell them you know about Jenks, and that the take-out order could not possibly have come from him. Therefore, the whole delivery is tainted, because something stinks at NORCO. They're always eager to hit their own internal affairs button. Tell them you will only surrender the principal to Gerardis, who is the only guy you know at NORCO."

"Shit, man," said Cody. "He's the only guy *left* at NORCO that I *used* to know . . . before he got promoted."

"I'm laying odds that Gerardis is the guy who pulled your name out of the dormant file," said Dandine. "Because if NORCO had been able to triangulate on Connie's bug, *you'd* be dead right now, too."

Cody pinched the bridge of his broad nose, hard. "They weren't gonna pay me? I don't *believe* this crap. You can't depend on nobody, anymore."

"It's nothing new," I said. "They work you like a pirate on a galleon, then abandon you when they downsize. No future, no benefits."

"Remind me again what we pay taxes for?" piped up Zetts.

Dandine rounded on him with a grunt. "Like you've ever paid taxes in your life, *dude*."

"Look who's talking," Zetts said, mock-aggressive. "Kidding. I'm kidding. Christ . . . Mr. Sensitive."

I was still wearing Zetts's much-cursed GAY MAFIA MEMBER T-shirt—inside out, under my jacket—and wanted very much to just take a nap.

"I hate to ask," said Cody, "but if Gerardis shows—what then?" He was still a little skittish with contriteness.

"We take him," said Dandine. "But that's jumping ahead."

"Oh, yeah. That'll be easy."

According to what I could glean about the mysterious Mr. Gerardis, he was one of NORCO's favored, fair-haired subjects, rather akin to an executive vice president, the kind you can never get directly on the phone. I, too, had begun to enjoy the insulation of the VP mantle at Kroeger, which gave me the right, for example, to text Danielle at the office and have her arrange for a rental car, as I was flying back from Pittsburgh.

Yeah, *that* had worked out like gangbusters.

Easy: Pull NORCO's officer-on-deck out of the press of a posse of handpicked samurai, without pulling a gun, in the middle of an airport bristling with security. Yep, pie.

"I'm counting on them having guns," Dandine said. "Be aware."

"Yes, and what if one of them successfully *shoots* one of us before he's, y'know, detained and searched?"

"They'll know about all the cameras on you, Connie. It'd have to be an irresolvable situation for them to go public with gunfire. Not their style. Gerardis won't risk bringing an army—"

"'Cos he doesn't know *you're* here," said Cody.

I tried my best to nail Dandine directly, "Tell me, in your experience . . . does this have a hope in hell of even working a little bit?"

"I'll admit I have some issues with NORCO right now," Dandine said evenly. "But I am not going to let them simply erase you, and move on." He let his gaze go abstract. "It's the best I've got."

It was no longer a case of *what would you do?* It was now *What the hell else was I going to do?*

I swallowed the boulder on the back of my tongue. "Alternatives?"

"We go to NORCO, fight our way in, and force them to deal with us. You know where they are, Connie—right there on that piece of paper the Sisters gave you."

"What about Ripkin? Couldn't he help us, I don't know . . . expose them?"

"Expose them how? Go to the *Times*? To *Rolling Stone*? Out them on the Internet? That shit only works in the movies, Connie."

It was true. Unveiling a conspiracy was not the same thing as *eliminating* the conspiracy. It was like pleading injustice to a bribed cop. NORCO was one of those chameleonic malefactors that simply adapted in response to threat, changing its cellular structure to render any irritant subpotent . . . until the truth would not set the stoutest of heroes free. The truth didn't cut it anymore. You also needed backstops, armament, allies, evack, safe houses, cash drops, and bogus identities. Today, Woodward and Bernstein would be eaten alive—discredited, defrocked, unmanned, professionally ridiculed, and cinder-blocked into a drowning pool of disinformation.

As Alicia had sniped at me, right before her death, *Why, Mr. Maddox—they couldn't put it on TV if it wasn't* real.

Which put Cody and I in the middle of the terminal, in the middle of the night, feeling stupid and sore-thumb obvious because we had no suitcases, no props. I confess I wanted to look the enemy right in the eye, to at least see these NORCO drones, these bad-boy enforcers. They had been shadow figures, these past few eventful days, always seen at a distance maddening for its imprecision. When the enemy is faceless and remote, you tend to credit them with superhuman abilities—that's one significator of true paranoia, as a medical condition. The kind for which you take medication . . . so you won't see the enemy anymore.

The entrance of the NORCO phalanx stirred no notice among the forty or so travelers in the terminal at this hour. To me, from my newly enlightened vantage, they seemed as obvious as if they'd come decked out in Roman battle armor and plumed helmets, fanfare guard and all.

"Gerardis was bald the last time I saw him," said Cody. (So much for "fair-haired!")

My heartbeat began to redline. "There's at least *ten* of them."

"Oh, fuck *us*," muttered Cody. "Dandine said he wouldn't bring an army."

"Guess a *platoon* is okay, though," I said.

They had dismounted from two vans still in the loading zone, hazard flashers blinking. Add two drivers to their number. They were all clad in casual clothing—chinos, Banana Republic shirts, Bass Weejuns, windbreakers—but each of them had the hard-ass carriage of an ex-Ranger or bulky prison guard. Four were women, walking arm-in-arm with their mock partners. They had sling bags, briefcases, and rucksacks. But the way they scanned the perimeter and casually fanned to cover each other, moving all the time, betrayed them. This, then, was where all social mutants, decommissioned Berets, psychos, and Visigoths wound up when there was no juicy war on which to feed. They wound up under the wing of NORCO, which cherished your thousand-yard stare; saw it as an asset.

"Stay or go?" said Cody. "I say abort."

"Hang on," I said. "Let's see what they've got."

Their "principal"—as Dandine would say—was a large bald man in a business suit whose own passage vectored the movements of the entire team. He was clean-bald, probably shaven, practically polished. He wore steel-rimmed glasses and was at least six two, but the dramatic profile of his shiny head was adulterated by his lack of an equally strong jawline. His chin seemed to curve softly into his neck, and surplus flesh bulged from his tight, high collar. His head hung forward, rather than projecting up from his backbone; he had what is called a "dowager's hump" below the back of his neck. His sharp eyes seemed silver behind his glasses, and he made Cody and I the instant he saw us. He wasted no time, walking directly to within discreet speaking distance while his hunter-killers arranged themselves into a rough semicircle of protection.

This, then, was the face of NORCO. It didn't seem very compassionate.

"Mr. Conejo," he said, smiling. "And you would be Mr. Maddox, is that correct? My name is Thorvald Gerardis."

"No, it ain't," whispered Cody, to me. We both startled at the tinkle of breaking glass.

Then the bald man's inadequate jaw ripped free of his head and flew away like a home run, in a spray of blood.

Cody swept me back with a forearm as the NORCO team unlimbered their hardware from all the breakaway sling bags, briefcases, and rucksacks—an instant arsenal of weapons with extralarge mags and obnoxiously protuberant silencers. They moved to employ available cover while trying to fix the trajectory from which had come the high-velocity shot that took the bald man's face off.

It was surreal. No one screamed, but all the ordinary citizens scattered or kissed the floor. I fell on my ass and Cody dragged me up, to hug the Northwest ticketing counter next to a businesswoman who looked ready for a coronary . . . but that was not going to make her put down her mobile device, by god. Her fingers trembled as she tried to capture images of the action to send to . . . somebody . . . from her phone's tiny screen.

The average person now appears on a minimum of a thousand cameras per week, just in the course of a normal day. Cash register video. Security cams. Traffic lights. Everybody else's cellphones. I recalled Zetts's archaic mention of Big Brother—an outmoded fear, now, since most people accepted that they were being watched all the time, usually by each other.

A lot of insistent, no-nonsense voices were yelling now. *Weapons down, surrender immediately, lace your fingers behind your heads.* Not us. The NORCO crew wasn't even aiming at us, because we were unarmed. No. I saw an M16 muzzle snake out from behind the counter, just above our heads. Across the way I could see a lot of men in fatigues, drawing down alongside uniformed cops and airport police. More guys on the second level, with guns. *Now! Now! Now!*

I'm sure Dandine, in the car, was laughing his ass off.

The NORCO shooters looked to each other like befuddled lab animals, trying to intuit a group consensus on whether they should exit our realm in a blaze of glory. Then, collectively, they laid down their guns with almost reverent exactitude. Went to knees. Open palms. Laced fingers. Trusted Dad to make bail. As they flattened out, as the soldiers and cops crept toward them (using that one-two advance step so ingrained for people with tactical training—never crossing one leg in front of the other), one of them scooted laterally to avoid the spreading amoeba of crimson pumping from the dead man's shattered skull.

People were talking now, and watching, raising the noise level to a cafeteria fusillade while the various authority figures yelled louder to make their orders heard. Cody was crab-walking, against the counter; back another step, back another step, always nudging me ahead of him. We totally fumbled our attempt at nonchalance once the downward escalators were in sight. A minute later, we were piling into the GTO at baggage claim—our prearranged pickup—trusting Zetts to magick us from harm's blast radius.

First we'd experienced a car chase with only one car; now we had just foxed out of a gunfight with no shooting—except that single, surgical discharge. There was only one other partial casualty resulting from our trip to the airport.

By the time we hit the out-route to Aviation Boulevard, LAX had flash-frozen into its usual terrorist lockdown, and a sentry at a brand-new roadblock asked to see credentials above and beyond Dandine's NSA jacket. Dandine smiled and shot the guy in the chest with a Taser, and we were off. Nobody apologized.

I was so adrenalated at this point, I wanted to shoot the dumb fuck myself, with a *real* gun, because he was an impediment. But that was just heat-of-the-moment; I'm not really like that, at all. I hoped he woke up okay.

Nobody chased us. Dandine and I sat in the back of the GTO, with Cody and Zetts up front, as we blitzed north on La Cienega.

Nobody talked, for several tense miles, until I said, "All right, I'll start. What the *hell* was *that* all about?"

Cody had not uttered a sound since jumping into the car. Zetts was in his own head, the driving zone.

Dandine pulled a pack of smokes from his Halliburton and slotted five into his slim cigarette case. It was after midnight, therefore time to reload for the new day. He lit the straggler from the previous day's stock and drew a deep hit of ghostly smoke that swirled around the cabin of the car and dissipated into the night.

"You guys did perfect," Dandine said. "Exactly what was needed."

"Gee, thanks, Pop." I was angry and scared, and not about to let it all pass without comment. "I just saw a guy get his face blown off for basically no reason, and the first thing I thought of was you, sitting in this car with some big, fancy rifle, deciding whether to take me, or Cody, to see how many accurate shots you could fit into a five-second window."

"Not me," said Dandine. "That's the beauty of it. Look, NORCO expects us to be scared, and panicked, therefore reckless. Cody calling for Gerardis directly, by name? That's the act of a scared and panicked man."

"I wasn't scared," Cody said, with no verve.

"I know." Dandine talked placatingly, to keep us, as dupes, level. "They responded predictably, the way I thought they might. And I found out some important things we all needed to know. And in the bargain, we managed to bite them back, for a change."

"Wait," I said. "Go back to the second part—the part about the stuff we needed to know."

"Remember when I told you about all those organizational rivalries? Everybody nipping at everybody else's heels?"

"Predators predating on predators."

"Right. I used Cody so the call would sound valid. You don't mind, do you, Cody?"

He had slipped into sales pitch mode again. *Eye contact, first names, pretend to be interested in the welfare of the client.*

"Whatever." Cody was still sour.

"NORCO has enemies. Pretenders, rather, who do the job more soullessly as a selling point of their ruthless efficiency. Zetts and I watched a carload of them roll up while you were inside. Which is why I had you use the pay phone, Cody. Somebody else is out there, listening, too—just like NORCO does. Somebody else has a red-flag system, too. And when they heard Mr. Gerardis was about to make an in-person appearance, they very well couldn't *not* send a couple of assassins, you follow?"

"It wasn't Gerardis," Cody said. "They sent a ringer."

"Of course they did, but our mystery guests have no way of knowing that, and probably don't even know what Gerardis really looks like. *You* know, *I* know, but very few people in the country know that privileged trivium."

"A what?" said Zetts.

"You've lost me already," I said.

"Oh . . . *shit,*" Cody said.

"He's got it." Dandine smiled. "Tell Connie what I'm talking about."

"This proves there's another organization." Cody twisted around in his seat, suddenly excited. "Another club, but *this* one is interested in damaging NORCO."

"And whoever they are, they're hot," said Dandine. "Zetts and I watched them do the surgery. Two guys with silenced rifles. One to break the glass for the other to shoot through. One shot each. Capped off and done. They were gone before the echo died; very slick."

"Plus you neutralize ten NORCO hound dogs as icing," I said. "Don't tell me all those soldiers and airport cops work for another secret company."

"No. As soon as you were inside, I called airport security and simply told them that a group of nondescript men and women were about to waltz into their terminal, en masse, with loaded, concealed firearms." He exhaled smoke, satisfied. "In these sensitive political times, all you have to do is cry wolf, or rather, say the sky is falling, and they'll buy it. Terrorism works if you keep everyone afraid. We just made the police and the Army do us a huge favor. The best kind, because they don't *know* they did it. We verified there are interests out there whose agenda includes disrupting or crippling NORCO. And we tilted the situation so that we—"

"Chomped a big wet bite outta their ass!" said Zetts, grinning like a lunatic.

"You could've let us in on it." I spoke for Cody as much as myself.

"Wouldn't've played," Cody said. "We'd've tipped the game, if we knew."

"See, Connie? It's a game. It has occasionally dreadful consequences, but it's a game to them, and it has to be a game to you, to us, if we want to win."

"Yeah, except none of this is real!" I hated the way that sounded, even as it dumped out of my face. The "real" world, versus this internecine world. Those on the outside and those on the inside. The people who *know,* and the rest of the people, who never suspect—the walking dead. "It's all a lie."

"And how do you make a lie go down smooth, Connie?"

I answered almost automatically. "You make it attractive. Appealing. What you want, or fear not having. You make it superficially logical, so no rational person could disagree with the sentiment." My whole face went dead. Crap! He was right! "So you promise them the real Gerardis, when you know they're listening, and set them against the guys who are making our lives hell."

"Bravo. And not a single bystander got hurt. Reel back your own ego long enough to see that we just stung NORCO, badly, for free."

"Terrific. Now they'll *really* be pissed off."

"They don't know we did it. You saw those bodyguards. Not one of them made you. The lower rank and file doesn't even know your face—it hasn't trickled down far enough to be a priority to the grunts. It's probably just Gerardis, and the guys *above* him. It's need-to-know stuff, because they're trying to control the orbital decay of their original situation. And that gives us a number that we can fight."

Damn him, he was selling *me*. I was really starting to despise the profession of huckster.

"So what do we do now?" I said. "That frontal assault on NORCO you were talking about?" I had a vertiginous glimpse of us suiting up in black nylon, weighing ourselves down with firepower from some deadly trunk-load of weaponry, and rappelling down out of a Huey in the dark. First time for everything, as the cliché goes.

"No. Now we go for Jenks. Just like on your list."

"You have . . . thir-ty sev-en . . . new messages. First message . . . sent . . ."

Nearly ten messages per day. Subtract Burt Kroeger, playing hale and hearty, joking about my heroic binge, my sexual appetites, and my long-suspected double life as a porn film producer. Subtract Katy Burgess, calling from a different and slightly more intimate attack vantage, concerned about the jail thing, the MIA thing, *just call me anytime, Connie—okay?* Some of her ploys were almost intimate. Half the incoming messages were from her.

Red flag, I thought, hating myself for it.

Subtract five from Danielle, also in the office, mostly questions about pending contracts, and one lengthy message about setting up a face-to-face with an attorney who was vetting the most sensitive of those. *He really needs you to call him right away, and if you need anything, Connie . . .* Her tone struck me as bullshit, too.

That left seven calls, none of them from friends, pals, exes, or business acquaintances.

Number 29 was a winner, and whoever they used to do the voice needs an Academy Award, right now. It was a perfect blend of urgency and discomfort at speaking to a stranger's machine.

"Mr. Maddox, you don't know me, but my name is Mr. Shannon, and I . . . well, this is a little difficult. Uh, sensitive, I mean. It's a kind of mutual interest thing, covering the events of the past few days, and . . . well, listen, I would really appreciate a callback at your earliest convenience to discuss this matter, and, y'know, work out some kind of resolution I hope makes us both happy, okay? Like I said, my name is Jaime Shannon . . ."

"Never heard of him," I said.

Dandine tilted his head away from the secure cellphone. "Too bad we can't turn ourselves into electronic signals, dial up this Jaime fellow, and transmit ourselves right into NORCO."

"That's charming, but I hope there's a backup plan that takes place in, you know, the real world." It was too much to hope that NORCO had a customer service line.

"Which one?" he said, more to himself than me, with a half-smile. He drew a neat sip of his single malt, then drank half a glass of his seltzer.

We were bending the rail at a dimly lit venue called the Wily Toucan—believe me, where it was located isn't important—which had no last call, no restrictions on smoking, and no listing in the LA phonebook. Neither one of us had ever been there before tonight. I was the guy with the address, and more important, the code word for the door. The Wily Toucan was a cocaine speakeasy, as well—no locks on the restroom doors, and a back room in which live music was played and tables-full of people tapped their feet and drummed their fingers, though their movements had little to do with the tunes. Farther back was an iron door like that of a bank vault, with a food slot through which you could buy a twenty-buck hit of blow in a press-sealed coin envelope. There was another room back there, somewhere, in which customers could aspirate their purchases. I got the impression that few people came for the bar, which was decent. No fronds. No sports. Dandine seemed oddly pleased.

"How do you know about this place?"

"Well . . . sometimes clients have special needs." I tried a sheepish shrug. "It isn't that hard to find if you're motivated. There's, what, forty people back there right now, and it's three in the goddamn morning." I finished off a scotch with a battery-acid afterburn. Stick to beer, I thought. I had decided I needed a drink, *wanted* a drink as a single note of sanity. Dandine had ordered better stuff and was playing it out, making it last.

"How long has this been here?"

"Eight years, at least." Enough time for the owners to paint the joint's name in a fancy design on the inside wall (with a cartoon of, what else, a wily toucan), and outfit the bar with excellent stools.

He did that vague, almost-shake of the head. "The pay-down must be astronomical."

"Yeah, but look at the traffic, and think of the gross."

"Point."

"You want another?" The barkeep refreshed me; all he needed was a glance.

"No," said Dandine. "But I'll finish this one." He took another sip. "I'm a lousy drinker on my best day. My stomach's not built for it. Enough to get tipsy is enough to screw my insides up for two days, so I don't, generally."

"You wouldn't, anyway," I said, taking a long pull of beer and lighting a smoke. "That whole loss-of-control thing."

"Hm." He was not in a lectorial mood. He seemed to be contracting in upon himself, engaging in another whole conversation, somewhere deep inside his head. "You did very well tonight."

"Not bad, for a tyro." I held up my glass and he stared at it for a beat, then realized it was a small toast. I thought, how often does this guy clink glasses with anybody? "You don't go to a lot of birthday parties, do you?"

"Come again?"

"Anniversaries. National holidays. Christmas and Thanksgiving dinners."

He smiled again. (I keep hammering that because I need to empha-size how goddamned *strange* it was to see him smile, when there was no ploy to be pursued by smiling. A smile is one of the most lethal weap-ons in advertising.)

"What I'm saying is, you probably don't sponsor 'guy night' at your house, or apartment, or wherever you live, right? Don't know super-market checkers or waiters by name, because you don't repeat. You don't have a pattern. You're an ad man's worst fucking nightmare—we can't sell you *anything,* can we?"

"What you seem to be attempting to say, in your maladroit way, Connie, is that I don't 'have' anybody, yes?"

"What about Zetts?"

He stifled some internal joke. "Are you asking me if I'm gay?"

I came close to doing a classic spit-take.

"Is there something wrong with being gay?"

I spluttered. "No, of course not, it's just—"

"Stop. I'm not. I wish you could see your face right now. You're blushing."

"Yeah, right, make fun of the straight guy."

"Zetts is just a wheel. An independent contractor who's reliable. Most of the time."

"I thought maybe it was a surrogate son thing."

"That's ridiculous. Cheers."

We had ferried Cody Conejo to an address in Compton. He didn't have to be told to lay low for a while. After we procured another vehicle and performed the license plate trick, Zetts signed off with his usual jaunty salute and headed home to collapse. I passed the tapes I had sto-len from Alicia Brandenberg's suite to Zetts, who was sure to review them at leisure. It was a surer thing than waiting for a chance to do it myself; besides, if there was lascivious humping to be exploited, with Alicia making sure the camera could see faces, Zetts would pay atten-tion. As "evidence," it didn't really matter. You'd be amazed what can be accomplished with digital forgery today.

Our "anonymous" carjack was somebody's Audi A6; our options were limited, and we were pressed for time. It turned out to be one of the 4.2 models with the 300 horsepower engine. While I tried to guess the shape of the option package, Zetts and Dandine went at the car like swarming wasps, and within fifteen seconds (I'm not exaggerating), both the LoJack and the alarms were useless. Dandine could drive a stick as expertly as he helmed the yachtlike Town Cars he seemed to favor; the Audi ate glassphalt like a fighter plane with no wings. (All over Los Angeles, the slurry-sealing on the better roads is embedded with tiny bits of sparkling glass, hence, "glassphalt.") I was sitting in the suicide seat when the idea of the Wily Toucan surged into my brain the way a recovered memory surfaces after years buried in the mental marl.

As proof of my fuzziness, I tried a different tack: "Do you live in LA?"

Dandine put his glass down, empty now. "No, I don't live in the city." Pause. "I was seeing a woman. Up until about a year ago."

I tried to visualize what sort of girlfriend Dandine might court. *Where's the girl?* I was crazy to see what one of those deep-dish files on Dandine would look like, *before* NORCO. Where were the low points and embarrassments and failures in *his* life-line?

Closed book. No further information was forthcoming. He turned to me directly and said, "You game for Jenks?"

"Why . . . you going to cut me loose? Don't answer that. Yeah, I'm in. Whither-ever thou goest—"

"Don't drink any more tonight."

"Sorry."

We had made it through the day, to the cocktail hour. In a hysterical, perverse way, it was almost normal. *Normal.* As if any of us has a right to define it.

The Wily Toucan wasn't the only place in LA that was open dusk to dawn. Dandine next shuttled us to the residence of a gentleman he referred to as Rook, who lived high in the switchbacks of Hollywood Boulevard, west of Laurel Canyon, where it abruptly becomes residential. Celebrities you'll never find on any Star Map live up there, hiding in plain sight. Rook's place was a split-level, ranch-style house built sometime in the fifties; basically a huge rectangle anchored into the sheer drop of a bluff that overlooked the Sunset Strip, which lost a considerable degree of its charm when right-thinking petitioners managed to pull down the billboard of the Marlboro Man. As I have said, more than any other city, Los Angeles gleefully demolishes its own architecture—a holdover lust from the early days, when it needed to prove it was the most progressive city on the West Coast. The Strip isn't what you think you remember from that old TV show. Now it's a riot of sushi bars and trendoid neon. The Trocadero is still there, but it's no longer a nightclub, has been remodeled front to back, and has operated under different managements for decades. I should have said the three original front steps of the Trocadero are still there; that's all that remains of its original incarnation. Nowadays, most drones on the sniff venture into this neck of the enchanted forest to go to the House of Blues, or leer at the women who sleep behind the plate glass in back of the registration desk at the Standard. The Brown Derby, which used to be on Vine Street (it opened on Valentine's Day, 1929, and was the nightspot where Clark Gable proposed to Carole Lombard a decade later), has been moved so many times even I can't tell you where the hell it is today.

And nobody in Hollywood can tell you who the hell Daeida Beveridge was.

To the narrow street, our destination presented only a wall with an iron-banded door that looked imported from some castle keep, and a modern comm panel with touchtone buttons, gently illuminated for night owls. I didn't hear a buzzer or bell when Dandine entered a number sequence on the keypad, but I could hear dogs barking. Not small dogs. I could also hear an annoying, almost subaural whistling—canine frequency?—that cut through my gray matter like a migraine spike, and made me squeeze my left eye shut.

"Did you hear that?" I asked.

"Hear what?" Dandine leaned close to the speaker grille and said, "The word of the day is 'miasmata.'"

"Is that Spanish for 'my asthma'?" I asked.

"Plural of 'miasma,'" said Dandine, not amused. "Look it up."

A low dialtonelike sound emitted from the speaker as relays withdrew the gate bolts.

"Is that what you heard?" said Dandine.

"No," I said. "And I can still hear it. Maybe I need one of your sinus pills."

We stopped midway inside a claustrophobic walkway between the featureless outer wall of the house, and the obverse of the security wall.

"Cover your ear," he said. "Still hear it?"

Distressingly, I did.

"Your bodyguard friend may have busted your eardrum," he said. "You'll have to give it a day to clear, then we'll see." We arrived at the terminus, about thirty feet away, and a rustic door, rounded at the top and surrounded by ivy. It would not have looked out of place on a Hobbit hole, especially since both of us were taller by at least a foot and a half.

It was a suitable height and width for someone in a wheelchair, and guess what?

"Now there's a face that hasn't darkened my stoop for a bit of a while," said the occupant, who I took to be Rook. He was a large gray-beard who reminded me of an old-school biker after a spill, or maybe Santa Claus gone to seed as the result of a tragic sleigh wreck. He was flanked by a pair of German shepherds incapable of being distracted when they were on the job. Their coffin-shaped heads came up to about his shoulders as we peered downward through the absurd little door, because, yes, he was in a wheelchair. Every surface on the chair, save for the rubber on the wheels, was chromed. "Let the kids get a whiff of ya, then come on in. Be sure to duck." He pointed out the dogs, one pure black, the other equally white, both with massive chests. "That's Gunner, and that's Klaus."

"Hey, Klaus," said Dandine, going first. "Long time." He extended his hand slowly, palm down, and the white dog sniffed, then looked to his master. "What happened to Dutch?"

"Ole Dutchie took the big dirt nap about two years ago, amigo," said the man who had to be "Rook." "Which proves you're shit at staying in touch. Gunner there is the newbie."

Gunner—the black one—sampled my scent and looked for a go-ahead sign. If the man gave it, I never saw it. But both dogs broke away at the same time.

"Rook, meet my new compadre Mr. Lamb. Mr. Lamb, say hello to the one and only Rook."

I hadn't had anyone whip a power handshake on me in a long time.

We stooped through the low-bridge lintel of the door and Dandine pushed it shut. I heard at least three electronic bolts slide into the jamb, automatically. I kept covering my ear and experimenting with the new sound that lived inside my skull. Dammit.

"Give you a hand?" asked Dandine, moving forward as if for a repeated handshake. I thought it was another goofy code, but Rook clasped firmly, hoisted himself out of the wheelchair, and stood up.

"Sorry 'bout that," Rook said to me with an evil grin. "Being a cripple can give ya an edge, when you're dealing with certain people." His voice was soft, yet deep and arid, one that could cut under noise and still be heard. It came from the anterior of the throat, and was hollow but not resonant, as though his nasal tones had been deactivated or compromised. It was like a "cemetery" voice.

I accepted the beer he offered; imported German stuff that had to be poured into a pilsner glass to mix properly. Dandine took a club soda. The house was essentially four gigantic rooms stacked one on top of the other, connected by a descending zigzag of long stairways. We stood amid a strew of comfortable furniture, suborganized into more intimate groupings of chairs around low tables. Most of the tables were stacked with books. The theme of this room seemed to be war memorabilia—display cases of painstakingly rendered miniatures: model tanks, other vehicles, and battle scenes. Framed documents—including ones signed by Omar Bradley, Curtis LeMay, Oliver North, Abraham Lincoln and, sure enough, Adolf Hitler—hung on the walls.

"It's real," Rook said, noting my interest. "It's an official letter to SS Sturmbannführer Dr. Ing Wilhelm Brandt, commending him for his design of 'disruptive pattern material,' and recommending that Hermann Goering use the Waffen SS design for his regiment's uniforms; which Goering did, in 1942."

"Disruptive—?"

"Camouflaged uniforms. The Germans invented them. Rather, they made practical tests of it in the late thirties, and discovered their field casualties went down by fifteen percent. So they were the first to introduce camo gear. Some of their designs are still used today, by NATO armies."

On the second floor what appeared to be original paintings—

mostly real pigment on antique canvas—crowded all the available wall space. Rook must have caught my quizzical expression as I did a double take at Monet's *The Houses of Parliament, Sunset.*

"It's a forgery, but a good one," said Rook. "Not as good as the one that still hangs in the National Gallery. Most of the authentic firsts went out of public circulation in the early fifties—thefts, switcheroos, private auctions."

The third floor down was a multimedia library with a lot of high-end tech gear; black boxes patch-wired into disc burners, and a fly-vision bank of flat wall monitors. "Ask me for any movie you can think of," said Rook, "and I can rip ya a copy. New, old, released, unreleased. I dare ya."

"*London After Midnight,*" I said.

"Oww, the cineaste goes right for number one on the hit list!" He slapped my shoulder. "It's got to *exist*, first, my man." To Dandine, he said, "Where'd you find this guy?"

"You wouldn't believe me if I told you," Dandine said. "I just sort of dropped in on him."

The fourth floor was mazed into a lot of worktable space interspersed with enough photo, duplication, and printing gear to run a full-service Kinko's. He even had an old Linotype machine dominating one corner, as well as drum scanners, laminating machines, and a darkroom.

"I could do ya a French passport," Rook said. "And you're gonna say, why not a U.S. passport, and I'd say, think more globally, because we're not living in America anymore." He shrugged, massively. Standing, he was now taller than either of us. "And I could show off like this all night, but I bet my man here wants to cut past the chit and the chat."

"First," said Dandine, "I want to thank you for this." He handed over the NSA identification he had used at Ripkin's house. "It served us well."

Rook dropped it into a shredder that automatically obliterated it, with a coffee-grinder noise. "These are kind of like subway passes; they run out of credibility the more they're exposed. Hey, I could make ya a special subway card, if you like—one that never expires?"

"I need NORCO IDs for two."

Rook returned a slightly comic squint. "Hairy," he said. "But doable. To get into NORCO?"

"Possibly. To fade us past one of NORCO's tools. But they should pass muster in the scanners, if you can manage that."

"Slightly harder." Rook rummaged through a card file on one desk and held up a sample. "This is what ya want. They change the design—"

"Several times a month, random dates. How old is that one?"

"Day before yesterday."

Dandine inspected the card. Photo, name, optical fingerprint, barcode, security striping. It reminded me of our mutant twenty-dollar bill.

"See the embedded tape? It's platinum. They've coded their scanners to read for *platinum*, for god's sake. How paranoid can ya get?" He turned to me. "Mr. Lamb, is it? Take a seat on that stool right there and prepare to get immortalized. Ya might wanna run a comb through your hair."

After Rook photographed us, he led the way to a bungalow that waited on the far side of the pool terrace, outside the lowest floor of the main house. The area was engirded with pine and fir trees and, I'm sure, was bristling with security. "Ya know the drill," Rook said to Dandine, "so show Mr. Lamb the amenities. I should have these items polished off by the time you wake up."

"I thought we were going to hit them tonight," I said. "What about all that crap you told me about *hit them at night, when they're tired or stressed?*"

"No longer applies," said Dandine. "We're too far up the food chain for that, now. The people we need from now on are such hard targets . . ."

"That they never sleep?"

"Basically."

In the parlance, a "hard target" was traditionally one shielded by every conceivable form of protection, and a "soft target," with an almost Japanese simplicity, was "a hard target plucked from its shell." In Rook's guesthouse, I felt secure for the first time. Perhaps I was just running games on myself, but I found it insanely easy to drop off to sleep there in my own little room, with Dandine across the living room, doing his mental exercises or pre–power nap, Doc Savage calisthenics, or whatever he did to unwind. If he ever unwound.

And just below us, the head-and-taillight snake of the Strip slithered onward, completely unaware.

The wife of a man named Horace H. Wilcox gave Hollywood its name in 1887. Daeida Wilcox Beveridge was known as "the mother of Hollywood" when she died in her home near the Boulevard and Wilcox Avenue (named after her husband) in 1914. "Hollywood" was the name of the country home of a woman Daeida spoke to during a train trip back east. Daeida was so enamored of the name that she used it for her own home . . . and Hollywood was born. The city has never honored or accredited her in any way, but there's a plaque, if you know where to look, put up privately.

You think we remember anything, or learn from our past mistakes, ever? Think again. Think the way I was learning to, and say to yourself, what would *I* do?

Rook's guest bathroom was provisioned much like a hotel one-shot—disposable everything. I no longer needed to bandage my wrists and my forehead had cleared of damage, but the keen of tinnitus in my right ear was distracting, pestersome, and still mildly painful. I had hoped it would heal down while I slept. Maybe I just didn't sleep enough. I probed in there with a cotton swab and did not extract the blood crusts I feared.

On the sofa I found a fresh dress shirt still in crisp plastic packaging, and a silk tie that must have cost eighty bucks. Finally, I could retire from my stint in the Gay Mafia.

Dandine, per usual, appeared to have been up and functioning for six hours already. I imagined him stretching and kicking head-high at the door moldings for practice, then using a lava stone to sand off his outer layer of skin in an ice-cold shower, scrubbing right over the melted-wax, nerve-dead skin patches where his nipples used to be, feeling nothing there. I wondered what other blind spots he had; what other places in mind or body that had been scoured of the ability to feel anything. No looking back, there.

His black Halliburton was open, the center of a compact workspace. He had nasty looking bullets lined up in a row on the coffee table. Disassembled gun parts were scattered around, as well as cloths, plungers, cleaner, and lubricant. Arcane, specialized tools in a layout similar to field surgery.

"You might need to know about these, later," he said, holding up one of the cartridges for my inspection. It was a little carbon-colored missile, with virtually no bullet head—just a flat steel dimple—and a yellow hazard stripe around the casing. "Minimal charge. It transports explosive over a short distance, then blows up when it strikes. Good if you want to throw light and concussion across a room. Like the firebacks in strength, but these impact the target, not the shooter. Sometimes it's useful to plug these into a clip as a final shot. A full mag of these and you could make a lot of sound and thunder. The rest of the slugs are full-charge hollow points, government strength, max stopping power."

He handed over what appeared to be a featureless pewter cartridge. "Is this—?"

"Fireback," he said. "Instead of gunpowder and a bullet head, it's a fake shell packed with what is called 'fuel-air explosive' made by the Austrian company that makes Kaurit, which is your basic plastique. This has a small flash primary and the enclosed case multiplies the explosive effect by a factor of about seventy-five times. Little but big."

When "Celeste," a.k.a. Marisole, had experienced the joy of getting her face and hand blown off, the damage had looked (to my virgin eyes) the same as the blast from a small grenade. I was immediately wary of dropping the bullet.

"What the hell is that thing?" I was pointing at another pistol, but leery of picking it up, or even touching it. The clip hung out far below the butt. A scary looking, sharp jut of metal was mounted beneath the trigger guard, under the barrel. The stretch muzzle was vented. "Looks like a Beretta."

"It is," said Dandine, lifting it. "The M93R, built as an antiterrorist sidearm, basically a bodyguard gun for rich Italians who kept getting kidnapped in the eighties. This thing—" he swiveled the hinged metal piece until it locked into position "—is a handle, to stabilize the gun while you fire three-shot bursts, on full auto. Dumb idea."

"You mean like a machine gun?"

"Just like a machine gun. Twenty-round mag. Otherwise it's your basic nine-mil, except without the internal safety . . . so don't drop it when it's loaded."

"I don't think I'll even touch it."

He busied himself removing the metal handle. This required partial disassembly of the pistol, which Dandine accomplished with the swift deftness of a stage magician executing the Linking Rings trick—in reverse. In no time the handle was divorced from the gun.

"So much for stability," I said.

Dandine did not look up. "It adds weight and bulk. Snags on clothing. Tempts you to blow off your index finger. Pointless if you have decent trigger control." He demonstrated. "If you can't hold down one-handed, then you just aim for the lower torso, and the kick from the second and third shots carries your cluster right up into the triangle." He traced an imaginary pyramid in the air, framing my pectorals to my nose. "Sniper's triangle; the sweet spot." I noticed the wooden handles on the gun frame were nicked and worn smooth. As Dandine replaced them with rubber grips, he added, "Heavier than the Glock 18s the DEA uses; I like this better. More familiar in the hand. They don't make these anymore."

"Why? Was everybody killed?"

His gaze became abstracted again. I was getting used to this, whenever he seemed to phase out to some other plane, where he was having a whole separate conversation with beings I could not perceive. "Do you always do that?" he asked. "Change the subject with humor?"

"Sorry. It's one of *my* weapons. Strictly defensive."

"Connie, pardon me for saying so, but you haven't *done* that much that you'd have to dissemble about."

"You think I'm boring, right?"

He extracted the "big stick" clip and put the reassembled Beretta on a clean cloth. "I didn't say that. You're smart, and you're sharp, so why are you so afraid of what people will think of you? Who *cares* what anybody thinks of you? Where do you get off being insecure? You've got more grit than most normal people I've ever met."

"Thanks . . . I think."

"Seriously. You did well in gunfire, you did well at the airport, and you haven't shit yourself once. Stand up."

I thought he was going to demonstrate some kung fu on my poor, beleaguered corpus. I hate it when people who have taken martial arts courses insist on "showing you something." (It nearly always mean bruises, cocked wrists, inconvenience.) Instead, he wired a shoulder holster around me the way anyone else would help you on with your coat. Then he took it off.

"We're going to have to adjust this to reach your belt," he said.

"Wait a minute—"

"That one's yours," he said, indicating another of the guns on the table. It was a matte-finish SIG SAUER, exactly like the ones I'd seen in the Halliburton case from the airport. "It's chambered for Smith and Wesson .40s. With twelve rounds, that means we're hanging about two pounds under your arm. You should find that manageable."

"You mean I'm packing real, live heat that I might have to shoot people with?" I was sweating already.

"It's mostly for show," he conceded. Then he grinned. "Just in case. You are now an official fake NORCO agent. Congratulations."

"Does this have one of those explody-rocket things in it?"

"Last round. Just in case you need to call it a day."

"You mean go out with a bang . . . or commit suicide?"

"Your call." He was having too much fun at this. He pulled the gun out of my hand. "Jesus, Connie, don't fall *too* in love with this thing. You don't get to wear it, yet."

Damn, but he was right. My hand almost refused to release the weapon; I stared at it as though mortified at one of those possessed, monster hands from some horror movie. I didn't want to turn loose of the gun because it made me feel safe. Good. More in control.

"Guns aren't the answer," Dandine said, as if reading my mind (again!). "They're just tools."

"You seem comfy enough with them."

"No. I'm afraid of them. Say it, They're just tools."

He wasn't ribbing me. "They are just tools," I said, like a dutiful student."

"Now remember it. And remember this, if I close both my eyes and nod at you like this—" he demonstrated "—you follow my lead, no matter what I do, no matter how weird it seems. Copy?"

"Roger that."

"I'm not fucking around, Connie. You buckle now, and we might as well use these guns on ourselves."

"I understand," I said, a bit testy. "What's next?"

"Get yourself some coffee, because it's going to be a very trying Monday."

He might as well have said, *snipers are standing by to fill your order.*

I found a breakfast tray—apparently Rook was a full-service host, or did this a lot—and had a cigarette afterward. It raced my heart and shortened my breath. I was a complete phony, now. A nonexistent human named Mr. Lamb, who smoked and consorted with guns, threatened strangers guilelessly, and occasionally hastened the injury, or death, of others; a man whose most potent currency was not the lie, but the half-truth. Substitute "ad budget" for "guns," and I was taken aback by how little I had changed. Same game, new players. *I can do this,* I thought, prevaricating even to myself. *I can do this.*

"I don't think we should do this," I said, eyeing the handcuffs. We were in our stolen Audi, headed downtown, trying to cope with the spilled-marble chaos of the southbound 101. Destination: Park Towers, per the third name on the list given to me by the presumed-dead Sisters.

Dandine had performed another license plate switcheroo. Right now, he was sucking on a wintergreen Life Saver. "What part of this— exactly—do you *not* understand?"

"The part where you throw me to the wolves in handcuffs; that's a fair start."

"The cuffs are just for show. I might not go that way. It depends on what we find downtown."

"Indulge me and detail the 'maybe' scenario," I said. I already felt trapped by the locked door, the seat belt, and hints of worse, to come.

"If it's a stone wall, I walk you in as my prisoner," Dandine said. He was using that too-patient parent tone with me again. "If it's permeable, we improvise. That's why Rook made you the backup NORCO ID."

"Why don't we just march in and bullshit them?" I sulked. I liked the second plan better. It meant I'd get to carry a gun. Right now my snappy shoulder holster hung empty, as useful as a ventilated condom. It, too, was strapping me down, holding me back, preconfining me.

"Because Jenks will know your face, especially if he's as tight with NORCO as I suspect he is."

I was getting hysterical. "Suspect? You don't *know?*"

"Connie, what is this thing with you and planning? Is this some psychological block I should know about?"

That threw me. It was no doubt intended to derail my irritation, but sounded of pure non sequitur. "Okay, okay—peace. Pretend I'm an idiot child and tell me what the fuck you're talking about."

"Well, you seem to want the whole menu laid out in absolute black and white before we do anything. Understand that rigid plans, if they're too rigid, shatter and cave in on you. We need flexibility. I don't know exactly what I am going to do, or precisely when I am going to do it, and that drives you nuts, doesn't it?"

Ruefully, I recalled instructions I had once given to my assistant, Danielle, regarding appointments made by telephone. Pencil them in, I had said. Don't ink them. Writing in ink curses it to change. We all have our little superstitions.

It was hopeless, but I said, "I just want to know the plan."

"The plan has to have the flexibility to totally change at a moment's notice. One option is we fake our way in. One option is I present you as my prisoner to gain special-circumstances access to Jenks. There might be other paths. It all depends on force of opposing numbers, what doors are open or locked, hell, which way the wind is blowing. That's why I asked you to follow my lead, and you agreed."

All the armament I had seen back at Rook's was stashed in the black Halliburton . . . which he had left behind, save for one piece—the monster Beretta—nestled under Dandine's left arm, the arm I thought was still recuperating. He had ceased making any noises that indicated his arm still bothered him, and I knew it hadn't had time to heal . . . much.

I had wanted a bull session, a confab, but clearly Dandine was still in charge, and my job was to duck if somebody started shooting. This was not a democracy. Precious few things *were,* anymore.

The abrasive notion was that I—like many of you—naturally assumed I knew how things worked. There's the lie and the lip service, then there's the coexistent truth. We all accept this; we joke about it constantly. We think we all know what's *really* going on, but this never expresses as anything other than a distant, dunning idea that we're all being eternally hoodwinked. Rarely do people have to stick their snoots into the messy details, and risk the ripe, rotten taste of what has been bothering and handicapping them all along.

The bastille of G. Johnson Jenks (the former Garrett Stradling) was taller than City Hall but shorter than Library Tower, shunted into the huddle of overpriced apartment and condo skyscrapers mere blocks from downtown's own version of skid row. Park Tower had no park attached. It was more accurately a layover roost for executives on the company tit, who needed to be in town for, say, a month at a time, and required more amenities than most hotels offered. If there had been a "park," there would have been homeless people making a tent city out of it. The front cul-de-sac featured a sloping scab of turf—the sole greenery—in front of an imposing fountain that was all minimalist metal angles and cultured rust. The main entry was inch-thick tinted glass two stories tall. Reception desk, waiting area, and uniformed staff with badgelike medallions embroidered onto their jackets, over the left breast. I had never been in this building in my life, but knew some Kroeger clients who had sworn by its security. Great. They could probably flood the air filtration system with knockout gas if anything untoward happened.

One of the staff, smoking outside, pitched his butt and stood right in the path of our car as Dandine turned in. This Hitler Youth poster child unbuttoned his jacket as he stepped over to the driver's window. Faster cross-draw, that way. He had neon-blue eyes and colorless hair cropped so short you could almost hear it screaming.

Dandine flashed his NORCO jacket. "Here for Jenks."

The guy pointed with a finger knotty from extreme weight lifting. "Park in the red."

Point: NORCO ID gets you access. I wish Dandine had mentioned that, but I guess he was counting on my powers of observation, as retarded as they can sometimes be.

The lobby was library-quiet, and the whine in my right ear seemed to amp up, as though from a change in pressure. Maybe it was my sunglasses—my "disguise"—pinching my head. I could hear every fabric movement of the deskman's suit. His gaze ricocheted from Dandine's ID to his jacket, which he was holding open to display his gun.

"I understand," the deskman said. "But I can't allow you to take a weapon up the elevator. Mr. Jenks is on his way down to the garage. I'll call his people and advise?"

"Yes," said Dandine. "Quickly. This is a Class Three situation and I don't want it to get complicated."

"Understood, sir."

Point: Class Three was NORCO double-talk for urgency, or *no bullshit, now*. God, I was learning new things left and right.

The deskman punched a line and spoke with his head turned aside. "They acknowledge and will be stopping the car outside the lobby."

I saw Dandine take stock of the available manpower. Two men near the elevators. Two near the desk. Nazi-Boy, outside. Plus whatever brutes Jenks had flanking his every move. Remember when politicians actually went out in public without bulletproof shields?

Yeah—me neither.

Dandine motioned me away from the desk and put the car keys in my hand. He nodded and closed his eyes. *Like this*. "Garage," he said. "Block the exit. Do it now." He moved off to a midway point between the lobby desk and the elevators. If he went farther, the guards there would prick up.

I was glad no one could see my eyes. I experienced that gut-plunge of exploded time you feel when your body *knows* the dam is about to bust. Nazi-Boy watched me like a falcon as I got into the Audi and gunned the motor, thinking that the sunroof would be shit for stopping bullets.

I pulled smoothly and nonobviously (I hoped) to the slanted concrete ramp that fed into the dim garage, noting that I'd have to drive around the perimeter to get to the exit, which was on the opposite side of the building. I had a little trouble with the stick shift, and wished I had grilled Zetts (or even Dandine) for pointers. The clutch didn't clutch, and I almost stalled out. A black stretch limo was on hold near the elevator bank. Liveried driver at the wheel, and one bodyguard on standby at the open rear door. I decided to wait until someone emerged from the elevator before zooming forth to barricade the exit ramp.

Ding.

The burnished aluminum doors calved and a big guy in an ill-fitting black suit tumbled out like a falling tree, stiff-legged, his mouth open, as though he had been unplugged in midthought. He crashed bonelessly to the floor and I saw another pair of sprawled feet inside the elevator. Then Dandine bulled out, holding Jenks by the scruff of the neck and using the larger man's shoulder to balance his pistol as he took the guard by the limo door dead bang, a burst of three slugs from his Adam's apple up through the "vermilion line," the sure-stop zone between his chin and eyebrows. The hollow acoustics of the garage made the single shot–barrage sound like a blown tire. The guard gobbled thickly, hit his knees, and then unfolded forward onto his face, his own half-drawn weapon skittering free.

Two minds, one thought: The limo driver tried to goose his big ride toward the exit, but I was closer. I gave him my starboard side, cutting off the ramp in a squeal of tires that made my back teeth hurt. He trod his brake so hard the limo nosed down and the trunk lid seesawed open. The back door flapped like a broken wing and rebounded shut.

Jenks did not have a face. Then I realized the man's toupee had come unmoored and was hanging the wrong way, fringing everything above his nose in a curtain of brown hair that looked dyed, anyway. Blood threaded from his nose as bright, fresh, red punctuation.

Still collaring Jenks, Dandine drew down on the driver. "Out."

The driver scrambled, hands up, just an employee, not an operative. He tried to babble assorted reasons why he should be allowed to live.

"Quiet," said Dandine. "Leave the cap."

The driver doffed his hat, pitched it into the limo, and backed away, hands high. Thinking passionately, no doubt, about Jesus.

"Clear the ramp!" Dandine shouted at me. He shoved the wayward-haired Jenks into the back of the limousine, not really caring whether he banged his head on the jamb, then stood with one foot out the door as I tried to catch up. I didn't have a chance to ask about our "plan." What about fingerprints in the Audi? What about the cameras in the lobby, covering the elevator and garage? What about—?

"You're driving," he said, slamming his door behind him.

Now I realized why he'd gotten me the tie.

I let gravity and momentum drop me into the driver's seat; acceleration threw my door shut. Good thing, too: Nazi-Boy was already at the head of the exit ramp, pointing a gun in an excellent, two-handed "profile" firing stance. Firing at me.

So much for my second theoretical question. The spear-carriers of Park Tower had (possibly) witnessed the nasty action in the elevator (unless Dandine had killed the lens there) and responded in about twenty seconds, during which time Dandine had cleared the lift (to avoid a remote lockdown), isolated his principal (by "maximally demoting" all three of his security men), and captured the limousine (with my help, I should point out).

Nazi-Boy's first triple-tap skinned off the windshield right in front of my face, making hard white scratches, but not fracturing the glass. I ducked down anyway, inadvertently jerking my foot off the pedal. Dandine would not approve. Dandine would say, *mow the fucker down.* Dandine was unavailable for consultation. There was quite a bit of thumping noise coming from the limo cabin behind me, beyond the barrier of the privacy shutter. I don't know in what order the truths sifted through my brain; all I knew was: (1) the car was armored, naturally, (2) escape was imperative, before the garage could be compromised, and (3) that dipshit, Nazi-Boy, had just tried to cancel my ticket.

The rearview revealed more guys with more guns, spilling out of the stairway behind us, near the elevators. The crash-proof, latticed gate was already rolling to batten down the exit. More shooting.

Nazi-Boy's expression unscrewed satisfyingly when I reappeared at the wheel. The limo lunged forward like a cigarette boat in choppy water, and it became a race to see if he could empty his magazine before I made him eat the grille. No contest. He tried to vault free but my wing mirror caught him right in the kidneys; it was a narrow egress. He twirled and dropped out of sight; I might have run over his foot (I never found out). Vehicular assault; another first for me. The limousine catapulted over the ramp lip with all the grace of a falling safe. I felt the undercarriage bang against pavement, and all of a sudden I was fighting the wheel, cutting off a number of honking cars. I didn't know it at the time, but Park Tower security had also sprung the tire-cutters below the gate. I didn't know that because the limo was outfitted with solid rubber tires, and as soon as I straightened the monster out to fit inside a lane, the race was on.

"Sorry!" I blurted out, for the benefit of the lady whose Toyota biffed my rear bumper. She lost a headlight, at least. Dare I admit that I'd never driven a limousine before? Another first. Probably a nice lady, whose day had just been tossed into the hellpit of insurance claims. Probably shaking her fist, right now, at all luxury cars, everywhere, while very important phone calls were being exchanged between Park Tower, NORCO, and the police.

Whatever our clock was, it didn't leave much wiggle room.

The privacy shutter was keyed down from the other side. I saw Jenks, balled on the floor with his jacket yanked over his head, snuffing nasally, abused into paralysis.

"Where?!" I yelled at the mirror.

"You know where," said Dandine, coming up in the viewport, inches from my face. "Turn for Sunset, right here. The old First Interstate Bank building. Put on the goddamned hat."

Okay—Sunset and Vine. We had maybe a fifteen-minute drive if the traffic was merciful.

The limo driver's cap fit, more or less. Dandine mopped his face with a paper napkin from the traveling bar and kicked Jenks in the ribs, rolling him over like a turtle as he tried to rise. His hairpiece was clinging to the carpet near the back door. He started to say something and Dandine punctuated him on the jawbone with the muzzle of the Beretta. *Clank!*—an almost porcelain sound.

"No more," Jenks gasped. "Stop. No more. Please."

Dandine double-wound Jenks's tie in his fist and rousted him into a window seat. Jenks's legs were akimbo, displaying pale, bony calves and drooping socks, and he sucked air like an asthmatic, blearily battling for composure. His teeth were outlined in blood and he tried to grab for a napkin, which Dandine slapped out of his hand.

"Leave it," Dandine said. "You piece of shit."

Somehow, I thought, this savage mistreatment of a highly placed public figure might not weigh in our favor, later. Dandine read my mind again. "Shut up, Connie, and watch the fucking road. Don't waste any sympathy on this asshole. In fact, just on general principle . . ." Dandine lunged, pressing the muzzle of his gun into Jenks's forehead hard enough to leave a keyhole dent. He cocked the hammer and Jenks braced for an inglorious finish.

"*Don't!* Don't! Just . . . stop . . . please, don't!"

"I need a better speech than that," said Dandine. "*C'mon,* G. Johnson, make something up."

"*What the hell do you want with me?!*"

Dandine's tactics had rendered his captive submissive; cueing flight instead of fight. "You called NORCO and sent home delivery to scoop us."

"No! No! Just Ripkin! Ripkin and Alicia!"

"Nigga *please,*" said Dandine. "Spare us the histrionics, because you have all the warmth and compassion of a Gila monster."

I had to assemble my impression of Jenks in chapters, via snippets from the rearview. He was a tall, broad man (bigger than Dandine, as I had noticed) with a sunlamp tan and a facial topography that limned him as top-drawer executive material. His slightly bulbed nose and the worry lines etched into his strong forehead would confer a sense of stability and character. With his wig in place, he would seem craggy and solid, a workingman's friend, a man of the people. I had seen photos of him, but the genuine article exuded the cocksure manner of a boardroom veteran . . . even though right now he was about to piss himself in fear. If Dandine let this man regain his center, we'd both have a fight on our hands.

"I need water," Jenks said petulantly. Dandine let him reach for one of the plastic bottles on the bar. Jenks rinsed his mouth and spat on the floor. Then he focused on what he could see of me—the reverse angle on my own mirror point of view. "*You,*" he said. "You caused all this."

"Worry about me, not him," Dandine said.

"To hell with it," said Jenks. "Your days are numbered. Turns out your little à la carte op didn't fly so well. You're running out of time, aren't you?"

"What's he talking about?" I was trying to divide my attention between the road and the revelations Jenks might provide.

"*You*, you asshole." Jenks dabbed his chin with a cocktail napkin. I could almost smell him building resistance, and Dandine, preparing to shut him down. He pointed at Dandine. "This man's job was to develop and turn a civilian asset—a total stranger—feed him a completely fabricated story, and within a few days, convince him to murder another total stranger."

"Complete horseshit," said Dandine.

"Is it? Consider all the casualties of your last couple of days. You certainly strewed a lot of corpses around, getting to one simple target."

"Who was the target supposed to be?" I said.

"Isn't it obvious?"

"He's talking about Alicia Brandenberg," said Dandine.

"And you did it, too, didn't you . . . you repulsive little shit." Jenks was talking about *me*. "And you let this . . . this *assassin* sweet-talk you into it."

"Negative," said Dandine. He let Jenks see the gun again, then jammed it into the hollow of his chin, nearly lifting the bigger man off the leather seat. "I threat-assessed that bitch myself, per contract. So you owe *me*. Bit of a conundrum, for you."

"You didn't do Alicia," said Jenks, with no verve, as though his neat cosmic order had been plunged into partial gray.

"Yes. I did."

Both Jenks's eyeballs rolled and refocused. He was trying to see the hidden trapdoor in what Dandine said. "No, you didn't."

"Yes, I did!" Dandine shot me a look that said *can you believe this guy?!*

"No. No, that doesn't suss out, at all." Jenks seemed legitimately confused. "All the others—Varga's soldiers, Choral Grimes, Ripkin's watchdogs—they were all rookies, seconded to your team. They were told it was a training op and played dead when you needed them to. Guess they washed out when you decided to use live ammo, eh, sport?"

The whine in my head was subsumed by all my skin alarms, shrieking. *Say what?!*

"It doesn't matter who stamped Alicia paid in full," said Jenks. "That usurious cunt died right on schedule, just like her pocket boyfriend. I signed off on both of them. They had outlived their value. But the local laws were supposed to scoop you two idiots, but *that* didn't work out because *you keep fucking around with the program!*"

Dandine was shaking his head no.

Jenks made a hissing sound of dismissal. "Hey, driver? Don't believe me? Read the goddamned dossiers. I've got them in my office. Interested in how this creature selected you as his patsy? Guess what: It involves somebody you work with, at Kroeger." He snorted. "At least one of us already knows what Katy Burgess looks like, all naked and sweaty."

"Shut up," I said.

"My office gets you proof." Jenks was positing one of those lady-or-the-tiger propositions. "NORCO just gets you body bags."

Dandine pegged his temple with the pistol. Jenks yelped, collapsed to one knee, and saw his own blood again; too many times for one day. He shouted at me, enraged, imploring.

"Don't you get it, you moron? You're supposed to die! You take this man back to his buddies at NORCO, and you can smooch your brainless ass goodbye!"

I couldn't arrange the facts in my mind, and Dandine could already see doubt polluting my expression. Jenks was wresting control. Even beaten and bloodied, he sounded like a man telling the truth, because there was nothing left to lose, and he knew it. He hadn't begged or tried to bribe us. He hadn't acted like a politician at all. But I knew why his claims struck me as a symphony of false notes . . .

. . . because I was a professional liar, too.

"What about *your* little buddies at NORCO?" I said.

"That's what I'm telling you. We worked a straight-across swap deal: They get Alicia out of my hair; I get the gunslinger, here, out of theirs." (Pretty surreal, considering that most of Jenks's hair was on the floor.) "Deliver me intact to NORCO, and I'll prove it's the truth. Deliver *him* to NORCO, and you'll suffer what we used to call 'death by friendly fire.'"

"He just *added* the part about how his competition could also get incidentally neutralized," said Dandine. "Kind of like an extra dessert, not on the bill."

Jenks drew what might be his last breath, and made sure I noticed. "Well, what's it to be? You can believe this man if you want to, but let me remind you of how many people are already dead, because of him."

Dandine, as thoroughly fed up as I'd ever seen him, sat back in his seat. "Yeah, Connie—what's it to be?" He sounded the same as a smooth lover, saying *have I ever lied to you?*

The First Interstate Bank building was within sight, within moments.

I couldn't find my voice anymore.

"Get that fucking gun out of my face," Jenks said. "Don't you know who I am?"

"I know one thing you don't, G. Johnson," said Dandine. "Ripkin is alive. Think about that, very carefully."

I witnessed Jenks's cocksure expression melt into horror just as I rolled the privacy shutter back up. I heard the gunshots (muffled, three more tightly packed *bangs* in a row), but did not see them. Somehow, that helped keep it unreal.

In the fifteen minutes since we had escaped Park Tower, massive deployments ensued, and I still believe, to this day, that Dandine knew precisely what would happen. This wasn't a "plan"; it was an antiplan, as graceful as callow youth, rushing in, gung ho, bang-bang. The velocity of what had taken place kept my brain stunned and detoured enough that I couldn't see how hopeless a frontal assault would be. In the end, it did the one thing it was designed to do: It got us noticed.

The persistent, high-pitched whine now living in my right ear hadn't helped my logic processes, either. So, when the stolen limousine I was driving took the first hit, it scared the starch right out of my bones because it seemed to come from the ether, from nowhere, a total shock.

I knew from the moment Dandine buzzed the security partition down that I was going to squander valuable minutes, just yelling. I couldn't help it. I had to get it out of me, or at least throw it somewhere else, because my composure had been gnawed down to a ribbon of shredded nerve endings, and the bite of small, sharp teeth on my stability now had little objective, apart from the delivery of more pain, and more . . .

G. Johnson Jenks, political hopeful (the former Garrett Stradling, corporate ramrod for big oil), was facedown in a pile of himself on the cabin floor, no longer soiling his lungs with our polluted Southern California air.

"What's the best way to sell bullshit, Connie?"

"We're fucked. We're doubly-fucked. That guy was supposed to walk us into NORCO," I said.

Dandine had dots of Jenks's blood on his face. Before he had rolled down the partition, he had lit up a cigarette. "The best way to sell bullshit is to eat a big scoop yourself, and go *yum, yum!* right in front of the disbeliever's eyes."

"You killed him," I said. "You let him get under your skin, and you just fucking killed him."

"Yeah. Shooting that dick was a pleasure."

"But you don't *kill* people. You demote them. You neutralize them. You take them out of the game. You make them subpotent. You 'un-plug' them. But you don't get anybody *killed*—including *me!*"

"What are you talking about?"

Nervous stomach and all, I felt all the symptoms of an itchy employee girding to piss in his superior's face. "You're the only one who ever walks away."

"Connie, watch the goddamned road, would you?"

"Stop telling me what to do!"

"Listen: Jenks was as skilled in his bullshit specialty as you are in yours. He was making that stuff up to save his hide."

"Yeah, like those dossiers," I said, teeth clenched. "Yours may be in fantasyland, but mine is sure-as-shit real, because I saw it on Zetts's computer!"

He snorted smoke and looked away. "Look, goddammit, I know you're upset, but look at all the live ammo that's been thrown at us in the past couple of days, and think about this: I've been on the hide for a solid *year* from these motherfuckers! So what, exactly, are you trying to get off your chest, here?"

"What was all that crap about your 'mission'? 'Developing an asset'? Pegging all the deaths on *me?!* Is that what I'm for?! The designated scapegoat?"

Was that how Dandine could slip, wraithlike, through the world of the walking dead? Because innocent bystanders would never do any-thing 'in the moment'? It was as useful as plausible deniability. Normal people react on time-delay, and only take action if they think they might get on the news, or collect a cash settlement. Otherwise, they're blind, and sometimes, they got in the firing line and became anonymous ex-people. In the moment, they freeze to see what everyone else is doing. I'd seen it at the airport. And the *other* kind of people—people like Dandine—existed in the spaces *between* those moments. Which is how this kind of madness could transpire on public streets, in broad day-light, and you or I would never hear or read about it . . .

. . . which meant that I wasn't one of Dandine's ilk. I was one of *them,* a single-use, disposable asset no different from a vial of hotel shampoo.

"You were going to throw me to the wolves at NORCO," I said. "That's why the handcuffs."

"Pretty close, but not completely . . ." He made a conscious effort not to shout me down. He was attempting reason. "Look, there's nothing hidden under the First Interstate Bank building."

"Then why are we driving there?!"

"Because for some reason, Jenks believed NORCO was there. Take it from me, they're not."

"You're saying the Sisters had it wrong?"

"I'm saying the Sisters had outdated information. If you'll just calm down for a second—"

He maintained his placating tone to the end of our conversation, still trying to get me to buy his product. Our duel was postponed by a huge vehicle veering in from the left and ramming the limousine, driving us up onto the sidewalk midway across the Sunset overpass to the 101 Free-way. We obliterated a bus stop bench and a litter basket, then got wedged between a streetlamp pole and the concrete berm that looked down to the freeway. It felt as though all my teeth had been pried loose with pli-ers, rearranged, and shoved back into the wrong sockets. I banged my upper lip hard on the top of the steering wheel, and Dandine shot half-way through the divider window, like toothpaste spurting from a dropped tube.

I got an impression of a big truck, or an armored courier transport with a snowplow on the front, bumping onto the sidewalk and angling in front of us. Then another of the same type of vehicle, a wingman we hadn't seen, piled in from behind, hoisting the tail of the limo off the pavement and cranking us hard right. The rear glass starred but did not burst. We fell from one side of the cabin to the other. My face mashed hard against the passenger side window and I got a close-up view of the hurricane fence above the berm, all that separated us from an ungainly plummet to the busy roadway fifty feet below. We were damned close to where Dandine had sacrificed a previous Town Car to the van shoot-out—about half a block. Through the canted, Dutch angle of the windows, I could see many men. Men in uniforms, men with guns. Cops and plainclothesmen. Shotguns and automatics. The jet-wash of a helicopter shuddered the limousine as it thundered above us, near enough to make loose parts trickle off the car. We were completely surrounded.

"You okay? Connie!"

My lip ached and my front teeth felt wobbly. My peripheral vision had become a nimbus of dust. Dandine hauled head and shoulders through the divider. An errant line of blood from his nose made a rivermap pattern on his face.

"Those slugs can't pass through this car," he said. "Not even the glass. They'll have to crowbar us out of here. What do you want to do?"

"I think . . . we should fight 'em," I said, sounding like a drunk.

I have a faraway impression that I threw up, then, tasting breakfast stuff, made vile by my stomach juices. As the dust cloud irised shut across my vision, I thought, *there aren't any innocent bystanders out there, not one.*

THE DAY AFTER NEXT

S top me if you've heard this one before: the gag where I turn out to be in a lunatic asylum, having made all this up; a benign, nondescript life, thrust headlong into adventure and danger. As Andrew Collier would say, *what, all violence and no sex? You just lost half your audience. Put the girl back in.*

Strictly speaking, from a sales standpoint, I understand the option. If this was my movie, I'd be screaming about studio interference. But it was never mine, I'm not even the protagonist of my own first-person narrative.

When the biggest lies are laid down, the liar usually says, *may God strike me dead if I lie,* or *I swear to God,* and the biggest liars are all atheists, anyway. Remember that when somebody swears fealty to you based on their dear departed mother's soul, or the lives of his or her dent-headed, mutant children, "God" is merely a useful expletive. It conforms nicely with "dammit" to put enough consonants in your mouth to indicate how piqued you are.

Dandine had never sworn he was telling the truth. He didn't care. Whether the walking dead believed him or not was inconsequential.

"Mr. Maddox? Conrad? I see you're back with us."

Someone was using my name, trying to goad me into some kind of revelatory flashback. No, thank you.

"Conrad? Come on, open your eyes just a little bit. I've pulled the blinds so the light won't hurt your eyes."

Steady beeping. The dial tone in my skull had subsided to a vacancy, an absence of sound in my right ear.

A woman's voice, "Don't be like that. The machines say you just woke up."

My eyes slitted. Sterile white linens. TV set. Vital signs monitors. A food tray. Hoses and IV tubes. Good. I could skip the part where I asked *where am I?*

"Who are you?" The cold engine block of my voice stalled out.

"My name is Vanessa." The ID tag on her nurse's uniform read *Strock.* I was flatbacking it in a semiprivate ward with my privacy curtain drawn. I was wearing a hospital johnnie and my feet were cold. The television burbled faintly, aimed at whoever shared the room with me, on the far side of my curtain. Some old black-and-white show, regularly interrupted by color commercials at a substantially higher volume. Right before we fell into the twenty-first century, the Federal Communications Commission had shattered the so-called "15-minute ceiling" by sanctioning a total of 15 minutes, 44 seconds of advertising per broadcast hour. More than a quarter of each hour now equaled ads. Good for me, not so good for you.

"Vanessa Strock," I said. "Nice."

"Good, you can understand me."

"What happened?"

"I'm here to fill you in," she said. She was willowy and long, that is, tall. Thick brunette hair pinned up. An appealing shape, for her length. She smelled wonderful. "You've had a rather gnarly concussion, and it's not the first in the past few days, is it?"

"I hit my head." Not a lie, exactly, nor the full-disclosure truth.

"Mm. A lot of shattered capillaries in your forehead."

"I hit my head." My mouth was extremely dry. She had a paper cup of water all ready.

"Just sip," she said. "Don't gulp. Now let me do the flashlight thing, okay?" Penlight beams knifed into each of my eyes as she checked my pupils. "We might be able to risk giving you a painkiller. You hurting?"

"Head feels bad." Another partial lie. My body felt fresh off the torture rack. My neck muscles had turned to molten lead. I was wearing a foam collar. I was glad they hadn't locked me in one of those radar-dishes vets put on animals, to keep me from licking myself or gnawing at stitches.

"You're going to be a bit disoriented for a while," Nurse Vanessa told me.

"What else?"

"You have two cracked ribs. Good for you for wearing your seat belt, otherwise the steering wheel would have caved in your chest."

So far, so dire: The anvil weight on my chest, crushing my breath to a rasp, was a stabilizing wrap of tape. "I was in an accident." It wasn't a question; it was a summation of my past few days. "How long?"

"Yesterday," she said. "We were afraid for a moment that you might not wake up and talk to us."

Demon thoughts of coma and vegetation jabbed my mind. "What happened to the man I was . . . driving?"

"I don't know about that. I do know they brought you in, solo."

"Who brought me in?"

"Fire department paramedics. Don't try to move that left arm too much, because your wrist is fractured. I'm more concerned about that one-two blow to the head. We're going to take it very easy at first. A light Demerol drip, just so everything doesn't ache so much. The plastic shield on your front teeth is just to stabilize them. You're lucky; you didn't lose any."

"Where are we?"

"Cedars-Sinai."

Terrific; I could order a cheeseburger from the Hard Rock Cafe.

"Mind if I ask you a question?" she asked. "You were wearing a shoulder holster. Are you a detective or something?"

"I keep my cigarettes in it," I said. How embarrassing: I'd been collected while wearing an empty shoulder holster. *Somebody playing tough guy.*

"Who sent me flowers?" There were several carded bouquets on the bureau against the wall.

"Well, let's see . . . Kroeger Concepts . . . this one is from someone named Katy [she pronounced it "Katie"] . . . lady friend?"

Katy. My dream solution, my much-missed potential soul mate. Far in the background but never far from my thoughts. And, if Jenks was to be believed, some kind of player in the whole NORCO fantasy. I had shared cocktails with her, obsessing about the briefcase. If she was in on the whole deal it would cause me to seriously revamp my definition of irony. If she was not innocent, then about a hundred reasons for her to keep her distance lined up in an orderly fashion. It was a paranoid's worst wet dream.

"My head is cold."

"We have an ice strip up there for the swelling."

"Oh. Got a mirror?"

"All you'll see is bandages." Vanessa seemed mildly perturbed that I wouldn't just take her word for everything. She retrieved a hand mirror from the bureau.

I had a clear plastic tube feeding into my left nostril; a bite wing, making my speech mushy. Big, gauzed, Frankensteinian forehead. Whiplash collar. Two black eyes, from the drainage. I looked like a fearful Cretaceous mammal peering out of a cave. More hoses, for waste, and a saline drip. I was catheterized. Left forearm encased in a fresh plaster cast. Visible contusions on my chest, above the tape mummifying my rib cage. I coughed and felt an ice axe drive into my sternum.

"Try not to do that," she admonished.

"Okay. Good idea."

"Are you hungry?"

"No, not a bit."

"Maybe later. We'll try again later, how's that? Now, I'm here to keep an eye on you until eight A.M. The call button is on the rail next to your right hand if you need anything, or feel any distress. Otherwise it's bedrest for you, mister. You're not going anywhere for a while. You should feel that Demerol sneaking up on the back of your head about now."

I tried to grab her arm with my good hand and the motion sent hot coals cascading down my back. Nerve pain, muscle spasms. "Eight o'clock?"

"No sudden movements. It probably hurts, right?"

I slumped back to neutral; that hurt just as much. "Yeah. You're here till eight in the morning? What time is it now?"

She didn't wear a wristwatch. She consulted a vintage railroad watch, tucked into her smock on the end of a fob chain. It was deeply charming. "Ten at night. Ten-oh-six, precisely."

God, the limousine with me and Dandine inside had been rammed *yesterday afternoon.*

"Nobody else came in with me, or at the same time?" She'd already answered this, I knew, but I was hoping I had been delirious, and misheard.

She shook her head. Nope. "But it's nice to have *you* back with us."

"Nobody named Dandine?" *That* was hopeless, but I ventured it, regardless.

Another negative. She had to go do other stuff. "Remember—call button's next to your right hand."

On the television, two mad scientists were apparently exchanging brains, through the intermediary of a tarted-up lab full of blinking lights. *Remember,* she'd said. As I floated into a rather luxurious, chemically enhanced doze, I tried to remember.

"Ever notice that?" Zetts had said. "In movies, like when there's a lot of action and chasing around? Like nobody ever stops to eat. They just keep, y'know, actioning."

Ever notice, in thrillers, how the hero can be on the run for days without a snack, and how they're so cool they can get hit in the face with a shovel, and keep right on chasing the bad guy?

I mean, have you ever been hit in the face with a shovel? It would flush your whole day, minimum. You've got trauma, bleeding, fractures, concussion, maybe a busted nose. Boxers shrug off busted noses, sure, but that doesn't mean they don't *feel* them. You'd think taking a home-run swing in the face with a large metal garden implement would at least give you a heartbeat of pause. You've got to be an alien (or have a shitload of animal tranquilizer in your system) not to feel that. Hell, if I stub my toe in the morning, I *think* about that all day. You walk funny, your shoes hurt, you're leery of stubbing it again. Even a fellow the likes of Dandine could only Zen away so much of that inconvenience. I've never met anyone totally inured to physical pain, and if I have, they're probably dead now.

Essentially, I had stubbed my *whole body* . . .

And I was alone in this hospital, insofar as fellow casualties were concerned. No Dandine. Maybe he was under another name. But no one had come in the same time as I had. I already knew in my gut that he wasn't here, and my brain was too fatigued to worry about proof.

My wife, Sophie, was the most important thing that ever happened to me. Don't laugh. I know I said "thing." Life, I found out, was something that happened to other people, while I was busy selling them . . . things. Facts and figures are things—quantifiable data that can be formed into lists. What the lists of things cannot encompass (and indeed, what dossiers kept by the minions of NORCO could never assess) is the emotional *tone* of those statistics. The coloring, the shading, the important stuff, which cannot cohere to the militaristic dominion of ones and zeros. So, while certain nefarious conglomerates might have bunches of numbers about me, they didn't have a hope in hell of *knowing* anything that was truly vital. I suddenly felt cushioned, remarkably safe.

I didn't wake up until lunchtime.

THE FOLLOWING DAY

The older you get, the more you know, and the less you're sure of. Selected shoot-outs and vehicular entanglements never make it onto the news—ever notice that? You come home to find your neighborhood cordoned off by police, and after they withdraw there's no update. Nothing really happened. Terribly unlikely, but no one ever says anything.

I needed to fill my blanks with bigger and better blanks, and once Katy Burgess visited me, I wound up knowing considerably less than I had scant days ago.

"Burt would have come, but . . . you know Burt," Katy said, finding a chair and dragging it close enough to hold my good hand. My god, she looked spectacular; my ingrained boy-coding made me watch her sit, watch her skirt ride up over silk hosiery. It made a heartbreaking sound. "My god, Connie, what the *hell* is going on in your life?"

"Thanks for making that call when I was . . . you know."

"In the slammer?" She grinned and her blue-gray eyes sparkled. "Your message was so cute. You acted like I was the last person in the world who would know the number of a bail bondsman."

"I couldn't think of anyone else to call."

"Should I take that as a compliment, or a sad assessment of your personal character?"

"Talk about something else," I said, my spine and legs throbbing from so much horizontal time. "Anything else. Talk about work."

"Maggie's baby is due. Burt gave her French time off, practically."

"Which means Burt has got to repurpose three warm bodies from the hottie pool to cover Maggie," I said. Maggie was Burt's executive assistant. The hottie pool was a rotating corral of incompetents Kroeger kept hiring with something like endless optimism, giving them about a month each to burn out. Maggie was also Burt's hit woman; if you were getting married and Burt didn't show for the wedding, you'd get a voicemail from Maggie explaining why and tendering all regrets.

"Okay," I said, "I meant talk about *your* work." I was trying to pick up from where we left off . . . before.

"Boring. I've been doing vendors and designers ever since we had our not-quite-a-date. Know how much G. Johnson Jenks has in his campaign fund? Over five mil, nonapplicable to the matching fund. That means *major*—"

"Katy!" I almost jumped too fast. Bad idea, to jolt things loose, inside and out. "Sorry, but . . . when was the last time you saw Jenks?"

"Day before yesterday. He's out in the world somewhere, pressing the flesh and minting the cash."

No, he's supine on a slab in the morgue that might otherwise be needed by a real, dead human being, I thought, *if NORCO hadn't taken his body and simply mulched it into cat snacks.* I didn't want to ponder what had become of Dandine. Nor did I want to bring up to Katy the way that sonofabitch Jenks had talked about her . . . but I chose the lesser of two rotten options.

"Don't take this the wrong way," I said. "Please. I don't mean this to sound like it does. But did you have anything going on with Jenks, I mean, besides the business relationship?"

She arched one contrail eyebrow. "Connie, I do believe you're blushing." She put her fist on her knee, her elbow on her fist, her other fist on her chin. She appeared to be puzzling out an intricate math problem. "You mean, like a *relationship?*"

"I apologize. It's stupid. I don't have any right to—"

"Shut up. You've already stepped in it, and it ain't apple pie. All you have to do is *look* at the guy. He's half a century older than me. He wears a for-god-sake toupee. How much class do you think I *don't* have?"

"You're right, I—"

"Shut up," she said. "I'm talking. Now, I think the only reason an otherwise sane man might ask an obnoxious, *insulting,* prying question such as that, is if said man perhaps felt threatened, in some way."

Threatened, by Jenks. Oh Katy, I thought, *you have no friggin' idea.*

"No, more like unbalanced by an overdose of unreality," I said. I tried to find ways to encapsulate the past few days for Katy's benefit and could conjure no explanation that would not sound completely insane. Not only was I stuck with my story; I was stuck with it *alone.*

Gesturing was tough, so I had to push out words: "Katy, when this madness is done, I promise I'll regale you with a tale such as you've never heard. You alone. I owe you at least that much, and I guarantee you will not get the minimum consideration. You took a chance on me. You went to bat for me. Nobody else did. And that gets you in deeper than most of the walking dead out there. But not until it's over, and I promise, also, that I'm not just trying to be mysterious."

"You forgot rule number one." She smiled. "Never try to hustle a hustler . . . and you're laying it on with a trowel."

"Blame the meds." I felt myself sinking into the adjustable mattress. Tar, trying to engulf me. "Okay. Very shortly now, you're going to find out that G. Johnson Jenks is out of the running, permanently." At this point I would have raised my hand for dramatic emphasis, to cut short her protest. I had to give it to her no-frills, sans semaphore. "Don't ask. That's the 'later' part. Yes, it is for your own safety. I'm serious. Here's what you can do: Find Ripkin, if you can. The Beverly Hills cops have got him squirreled away somewhere because Jenks tried to have him killed. I found out, and that's why I'm here, convalescing."

To her credit, she did not immediately call for the psycho-ward orderlies. But her aura of tolerant humor had dissipated. "You're saying that you're not finished, yet, with whatever it is?"

I nodded, practically immobilized, strapped into a bed, full up with thoughts of continuing a battle against phantoms, even after I had been so definitively benched. I could return to my apartment, now; show up for work after a brief sick leave, and it would all be as Dandine had told me—my life, spackled over, refinished and painted, leaving no evidence whatsoever of mishap. And right now, I hated that inevitability. I was furious for my glimpse behind reality and angered that I was now supposed to ignore what was real.

Then, after that first day back at work, once I'd gotten up to speed on my job and my obligations, I was supposed to have cocktails, recreations, and dalliances, and return home to my security building, lock my door, put down my briefcase . . . and then what? Look at myself in the mirror and confirm the truth: *You are one of the walking dead.*

And then, one day down the line, I quite incidentally get clicked off like a switch and nobody notices.

I couldn't do that, and I think Katy *saw* that I couldn't do that, which said a lot for her as an ally. I did not have to ask her, what would *you* do?

(Perhaps you are shaking your head at this point, and thinking, *What the fuck is wrong with this guy?* Give it up, for christ's sake, before they pummel you into mud. Haven't you learned anything? You don't stick your dick where it isn't wanted. You indulged your wild, fancy abandon and look where it landed you; and it could have been lots worse. Cut your losses, fool. Play the game the way you're supposed to. You got a get-out-of-jail-free card and you're just squandering it. Keep your high-paying sinecure, your toys and fancy ladies, and stop messing about with the system. You're eating, and millions aren't. God, you've got it made, and you're bitching about how it's not enough because the "truth" is wobbly. Who cares?

(Or perhaps you can understand why the same simple list of items kept reverberating inside my head: [1] It's not enough. [2] It's not finished, and [3] I hate being forced, to do anything. Period.)

"Therefore," she continued, "what you are *really* saying is that I shouldn't ask, and you can't tell. But you will."

"I promise."

"You'd better, if you know what's good for you."

I had no idea what was good for me, other than staying alive.

Katy was standing at the closet where my street clothes were stashed. My shirt was bloodstained. She held up the shoulder holster as though she'd discovered a strap-on dildo amongst my stuff. "Is this part of what you're *not* telling me?"

"Call it a bad idea."

"That's a good nonanswer. You packing, now? A taste of urban paranoia?"

"It belongs to a guy nobody will admit exists."

"Your imaginary friend?"

"Katy," I said, trying to act more like an invalid. "Not right now, okay?"

"Then what do you want me to do?" she said. Her tone was clipped; all flirtation was cancelled, and she resented being left out. I wanted to tell her, but I did not want to watch the resultant vacuum suck her into a black hole.

"Find Ripkin if you can," I said. "Play everything normal. It won't be long, now. Bring back some folding cash, if you can. And above all—assume you're being watched. Don't act paranoid or alter your routine. Just . . . *know.* Okay?"

"I'd better get a hell of a dinner for this. Two dinners, at least. It'll take you that long to make up a good story . . . so I can pick it apart."

"Thank Burt for the flowers; I know how gay he thinks that is."

"You have another admirer, too," she said, examining the cards on the bouquets. "DMZ? Lady friend?"

Funny, Nurse Vanessa had said almost the same thing, but I could not gauge how long ago.

"Not nearly," I said. "And far from competition with you." I was aware that while I was enjoying Katy's company and the sound of her voice, I was trying to repel her, to get her out of my range in case something drastic was scheduled to happen inside the hospital. At least I'd gotten her to stand, as a prelude to exit. But she kissed me on the cheek before she departed and it caused my heart to ice up with sorrow. *Rotten timing,* I thought. *Rotten all around.* All my fault.

My mind had become a sieve. I reviewed benchmarks and came up lame. My memory could not approximate a likely location for Rook's eyrie, west of Laurel Canyon. The Sisters no longer existed. Varga's crew would have run to Earth and erased their tracks. My pal Andrew Collier would wink at me . . . and deny everything to anyone else. The too-tempting First Interstate address given for NORCO had been a blind, according to Dandine. Everyone else who might help me or clear away clouds was dead or under deep cover. I couldn't guess at where Zetts's house had been, and even if I could, it might not be there *now.*

My memory was behaving almost as though I had been given a drug to obliterate precise types of recall.

And while I was at it, what about Dandine? What solid proof did I possess that he wasn't, in all boring predictability, my own version of Mr. Hyde? Was there some impartial third party I could use to verify his existence? People I loved? People I trusted? None, none, and none.

Dandine was the sort of creature who ceased to exist between missions. But that did not mean he stopped existing altogether. You had to know how to tune your perceptions, to tilt your vision so you could perceive him there in the background, blending unobtrusively, where he'd been all along. Kind of like those moments where you enter a room and immediately forget what you were looking for; that doesn't mean you weren't in the room in the first place. Or those times when you have to concentrate *away* from something, in order to call up some vagrant, lost fact.

Ripkin, I thought, again. Supposedly the police still have him. That was not for me, but something on which I could reasonably sic Katy.

"One last thing, Katy, and this is important: Do you know about, or have you ever heard of, an outfit called NORCO?"

She thought about it. "Other than a drug company, I don't think so. You know—pharmaceuticals."

"Also known as the North American Consultancy?"

"No."

And then, out of the ether, out of pure nothingness, I came up with someone else to ask, someone who had nothing to do with Dandine. My own resource. Mine.

Life is a bottle of wine. If you don't sip with deliberation, you slurp blindly. Connoisseur versus addict. Or, like me, you try to float above it all because you want to put up a good front, without actually knowing or caring about chapter and verse on vintages and "nose." I even faked Dandine out. I even impressed the Sisters, right before they died. That's me, a dusty, respectable-looking bottle of *Faux de Merde.* Sip with me, and try to ignore the earthy afterbite of the *merde.* Everything in life boils down to this sort of blind corner-turning—your pivotal event is not intrinsically momentous or earth-shattering; most often it simply *happens* and you feel no tingle, no vibration indicating the world is about to change. Consider, then, how rare and special it is when you are fully aware of an apocalyptic course-change in your life *in the moment,* as it befalls you. (Consider, also, how many people you know only perceive the best days of their lives in retrospect, with the insulation of time. Some sainted wiseass said that once.)

I was fully aware I was planning to sashay back into the world of the walking dead, oblivious to sniperscopes, and utterly without resources of any kind. Dandine had been a crutch, an expert to whom it was too easy to defer. Now I was making a conscious choice to exacerbate a situation that a hundred other people would have the common sense to leave alone. I think the part that bothered me the most was "common." Few of those imaginary hundred people would wish to be dismissed as common. But then, what was the difference between them and me?

Katy duly delivered some rolling cash, fresh clothing, and a private cellphone number I promised not to utilize. She even kissed me on the cheek again, asked not to know what was going on until it was over, and left. Her special scent—spicy, not floral—lingered in the hospital room after her. I thought, *my God, if she's for real, I am a dead man, in a good way.* And if she had never heard of NORCO, and not been poisoned by their tendrils, I had to accept her as genuine.

(Unless, of course, she was smoothly lying for some future advantage, which is, I'm sure, the first thing you thought of, too. Nurse Strock? They could easily have cast her because she would remind me of my ex-wife. Katy? A familiar face to buffer the lies; a friendly. My medication? Mixed to order, to drop my guard and increase my fear. It would have been child's play to infect me with a low-grade flu that would keep me a-dangle on the edge of hallucination. There were probably homing devices in the cast on my wrist. Where do you stop, once you start dropping impediments in your own way?)

Everything else, I did on my own. Have you ever pulled an IV tap out of the back of your hand, and discovered how much it bleeds? *Not* recommended. I'll bet you've never de-catheterized yourself, either, but I'll spare you that joy.

I shucked the foam collar (no way to work around it) and the sinews in my freed neck gave a spookshow creak. I buttoned up the shirt Katy had delivered, my eyes avoiding the tape on my chest. The best I could manage for hiding my kohled eyes was to wear my sunglasses, my Mr.

Lamb "disguise." My tongue firmed the bite wing against my loose teeth. I could stash it in my pocket if I needed to smile at anyone. Or snarl.

Sneaking out of a hospital is easy if you're dressed in civilian clothing. Merely jump one floor up or down and wander the halls. If a staff member eyeballs you, ask about visiting hours, and inevitably you'll be told they're over and you have to leave the building. Cedars-Sinai was half a block from the Beverly Center, on the buffer zone leading to the Beverly Hills shopping district, Rodeo Drive, and all that. People, anonymity.

An hour to wire my act together. An hour to slip into the world, too loud, too blaring (except to my stunned right eardrum), moving cautiously, my joints like broken glass held together by razor wire. Most of an hour to pace my breathing and find a rental car. If I had known what had been going on while I was in the hospital, I would have tried to move with more alacrity, even though I already missed that cushy bed, and the ministrations of the lovely Vanessa Strock.

Less than an hour, considerably, to initiate the complicated process of back-calling and message drops I ordinarily used to contact the individual known only as the Mole Man.

"You look like you mighta-could use some legally vague narcotics, there," the Mole Man told me. "Say the word and the Mole Man can fix you up on that number. He would say it's good to see you, but—can we be candid? You look like thirteen miles of donkey road, my friend."

"It's been an interesting week," I said. I had already thanked him for coming—twice—and he had waved it off. And I had already warned him that some of the questions I had for him might prompt him to leave our table and make for a fast exit. He seemed unconcerned, and I thought to myself, *I haven't seen this guy for two years, at least.*

We met in the Mole Man's usual corner slot at Vermeer's Dome, an overpriced Santa Monica eatery; to this day I don't know why it's called that. Perhaps I'm not cool enough to plumb the agenda of a fine food boutique that name-drops one of the world's most famous Dutchmen without having a scrap of his artwork in evidence anywhere; perhaps that was the elegant point of it all. The trend factor, here, consisted in the absence of anything a conventional Earthling would interpret as a "table." Beneath arching skylights—hence the "dome" aspect—flowed amorphous islets of stainless steel conformed into uncomfortable, booth-style seating arrangements, and organized around nervous scatterings of little alabaster pedestals of varying height, like outcrops of flat-top mushrooms, underlit by blue neon. These served as staggered surfaces upon which food was offered, if not precisely "served," from machine-stamped aluminum menus that specified "beef," "shrimp," "spud," "sprout," and so on—monosyllables with no hyper-adjectival descriptives. "Meat." "Drink." Illumination on their preparation was left to the waitstaff, which was comprised of young, blemish-free acting hopefuls, regimented into starched white linen and instructed not to be intrusive, not to butt in too often, and not to show much emotion, especially the phony kind designed to enhance tips. It was a place in which it was easy to spot newcomers, who usually mistook the mushrooms for some kind of bizarre seating. The bar was potent and open to special requests. No prices were listed on the metal menus, either.

This was the second or third time I'd met the Mole Man at this place. I think his theory was that all the patrons here were in vampire mode, on the prowl for celebrities, and once we were recognized as not being some hot personality or other, we thereafter became completely invisible.

The Mole Man lived up north; Santa Barbara or Montecito, I think, where (he mentioned once) he had bought the former home of the director who had done the film version of *War of the Worlds* in 1953. He drove down to Los Angeles to conduct face-to-face meetings with various clients, never on a set schedule. I knew his number from our dealings at Kroeger (it was a voice mailbox), and I had used it. The man would not have shown up at all, had he not been: (1) intrigued, (2) bored, or (3) in the mood for a bit of secondhand adventure that would surely reap him a healthy payoff. Our dealings had always been cordial and productive; now I was trying to push it all two steps further. I didn't necessarily want him to know how much I was counting on him, right now.

"It's strange," I said, "but I don't think I've ever asked your name. Too much of a hot button."

"Oh, you asked, matey. More than once. Last time you asked was in '02, when the Mole Man came down to help with that grocery strike thing—putting the nice-face corporate spin on the poor bosses? Yeah, you asked him, then. He didn't tell you. But if you want, now, since it's just you and him here and we're sorta, y'know, deepening the relationship, he might be able to give you a name to use. I mean, a name that's not, y'know, a nickname."

The Mole Man had always done that, I remembered—spoke of himself in the third person, as though the man sitting across from me was a simple intermediary for a more shadowy master. As I have said before, he was soft and round and inoffensively furry, with lightly downed cheeks and a ruler-straight line of baldness extending directly back from his thick eyebrows. Above that latitude, not a follicle. He emphasized the demarcation by wearing glasses in heavy black frames that lent his head (and therefore his gaze) a sense of direction, an "aim" for his attention. He had those wayward, extralong stray hairs at the peaks of his eyebrows. They quested past the glasses like antennae, or curb feelers.

Whenever the Mole Man spoke, he tended to overtalk, and occupied his hands with a lot of stage business—refolding his napkin, fiddling with his wristwatch and a couple of thick gold rings, stirring his drink unnecessarily. He lapsed into a more intimate, first-person address, which had the effect of drawing me into a closer confidence, as it was no doubt intended to do. "I mean, excuse me if I'm wrong, but this smells personal, am I right?"

"Yeah. As personal as it gets."

"Then the Mole Man has advised that you may call me Mr. Tiburón."

"That's funny—a guy I got involved with insisted on giving me a code name. Mr. Lamb. In fact, no one I've encountered over the past week has used a real name. It's all a swamp of fake identities."

"Oh, that's like cover fire," Tiburón said. "Throw enough pseudos into the mix, and if something real comes along, it just gets lost in all the noise. Standard diversionary stuff."

"Thank you for talking that way. It makes me feel less insane, like someone else comprehends all this spy-versus-spy crap and hidden language." He had also tactfully refrained from comment on my black eyes, or the cast on my left arm.

"Please. The Mole Man, as you know, does not judge. He merely arranges information. He does not supply; he suggests. And he never demands, especially of those who respect his protocols. And he would not have answered your call, if not for the pleasure of renewing your acquaintance. He has always suspected there was more to you than meets the eye, Mr. . . . . Lamb." Tiburón winked. "There. See how easy it is to be someone else? Now, before we begin, the Mole Man has a request of you. Not daunting. More of a social thing."

"Name it," I said.

"The Mole Man would enjoy it very much if you were to schedule some time, in the future, say, when you are not so preoccupied, and engage in some investigation into the ins and outs of the finer red wines, something in which he has recently acquired an interest. Rather, attenuated the interest that was already there."

"Sure." I was going to have to do a lot of homework to sound credible, but who was I to refuse this man?

"Splendid. That will please him," said Tiburón. "Now, let's refresh our drinks and address *your* needs."

"I don't quite know how to begin. I guess I should just say the word—NORCO—and see how you react."

He didn't.

To my credit, I was able to lay out the backstory for him in less than ten minutes. He nodded and paid attention. I finished by saying, "I suppose I need two things: Where to find them, and something to use as leverage so I don't get shot the instant I show up on their doorstep." It felt as though all I was asking for was simple—wealth *and* fame.

Tiburón steepled his fingers; then spoke from behind them. "That First Interstate address that you had? Not what you need. That is a facility they call *Processing*. You need *Administrative*. That is item number one. You have mentioned a name that might provide you with the bargaining power you seek; that is item number two. What is important is the connection between the two—the fact that gives power to the knowledge. That is item number three."

Have I mentioned that the Mole Man's custom was to bill per item?

He wrote down a few notations in cribbed, almost miniaturized print, on a perfect square of white paper he had materialized from some pocket, then left it atop one of the smaller mushroom tables after tapping it with his finger. The name he had listed as item #2 came as a shock, and I'm glad I didn't have a mouthful of liquid when I read it. I turned the page back for his scrutiny.

"Then I need to find this person," I said, tapping the name.

"Ah. That would be item number four. My information is twenty-four hours new. And the Mole Man shall assume that you and he have a deal?"

"Positively," I said. "Wine included."

I don't know which sensation tickled me more—feeling reconnected after talking to the Mole Man, or having gotten away with lying my ass off to him about the wine.

All I really had to do was look for the car cover. Odd, how obvious it seemed. My old eyes would never have noticed it.

I dry-swallowed two more of the painkillers provided by the Mole Man's pet pharmacist—item #5 on my coronary-inducing bill. Driving one-handed, I looped my rental Taurus through the slightly illegal U-turn at Sunset and La Cienega. About a half-block east, a cluster of two-story bungalows were grouped behind sad, dying trees near a municipal bus stop. The buildings looked rain-blistered, their faded olive paint flaking. They still had the shake-shingle roofing that had been demonized as a Southern California fire hazard. The garden area up-front, off the sidewalk, was a barren pond of damp dirt where decorative flora had given up growing. A posted sign spieled off details of the complex's imminent demolition for "commercial development."

Over the hump of sidewalk, a bumpy, hot-patched drive tilted south at a sixty degree angle to a madly uneven parking lot, gouged out of leftover hill-space below. Here, the bigger, older trees still held dominion, buckling the pavement, but generous with their shade. One of the cars down there had that "parked without a pass" look; another seemed as though it had been in its slot for months since it was mottled with grime and pigeon shit. Next to that, back in the far corner of the lot, I found the automobile with the protective cover lashed down tight, almost a grunt tuck.

Zetts's GTO. I checked anyway.

"Hey, brah, how's yer hammer hanging?"

It was as stupid as a slasher movie cliché. Zetts was perched in the tree above the car, a cartoon vulture staking out a cheap laugh. It startled me. Afternoon light glinted off his tong shades. He was wearing a big-ass lumberjack shirt and was halfway through a virulent-yellow doob.

"Sorry, dude," he said, all friendly. "You just looked so determined, like, serious, right?" He levered from the crotch of the tree and dropped about ten feet to earth. Then he got a good look at me and wiggled his head. "Ho! Nothin' personal, but you look like rat scat."

"You should see the other guy." It was a weary joke, not as good as what Dandine might have said.

He peered closer at my eyes, in hollowed purple. "Makes you look kinda goth. Want me to sign your cast?"

"Maybe later. Thanks for the flowers. That was sweet."

"Yeah, yeah, eat me." He searched past me. "You don't have like bad guys on your tail or anything, I hope?"

"Just me," I said.

"Then I won't ask how you knew how to find me."

"Why not?"

"Sheee-it, man, you ever try asking Mr. D something like that? Waste of breath."

I moved back to my own car. "Here. Brought you something. Peace offering."

He sniffed and watched, all eyes, as I handed him a plastic-bagged T-shirt. He unfurled it so he could read the logo: MEIN HERZ BRENNT. "Cool. Dude, I don't think I've had a *new* T-shirt in like forever."

"Least I could do for clobbering you on the head."

"Naaah, let's sweat that minimally, man—Mr. D warned me; it was part of the plan."

I knew better than to pursue that one . . . especially considering what I had in mind for Zetts's immediate future. "What became of your house?"

He narrowed his lips and shook his head; a goofy dog with a passing pester. "History. You guessed, right?"

"I hope it wasn't my fault."

"Nah. Blame sucks. Let's skip it. Besides—check out my new hide. Defini-nootly superior and majorly cool." He pointed the way toward a security-gated rear entrance to one of the supposedly condemned bungalows. "Shit came down the pipe, I had a good two-four to evack. A buck and a quarter of time, right? That was right after that heinous action scene at Park Tower. I got in there long enough to mop your wheels; that was my job for that day, according to Mr. D."

"You got to that car we had? The Audi?"

"Affirmative. Sprayed it; got the fuck outta there."

"Where's Dandine?"

"I was kinda hoping you could tell me, boss. I'm like incognito since I had to, y'know, relocate."

"You mean 'incommunicado.'" As Dandine would have said, *look it up.*

"Yeah, whatever. I knew you were in the hospital. That wasn't part of the plan that Mr. D laid down. So I guess he got misfiled. We might as well be comfy while we wait to hear." He ambled to the door in his accustomed hipshot stride and punched a key code that made the gate buzz. "Sexy, huh?"

Inside, Zetts apparently had the entire structure to himself. Strewn inside the entry were motorcycle and car parts. The next room appeared to be wallpapered in what resembled fine-mesh, brass-colored chainlink. It was even on the ceiling. Into this room, Zetts's computer setup had been transplanted intact.

"No hard wires," he said. "Totally electronically secure. No lines in, no lines out. All encrypted microwave at fifty-two hundred characters— better than what the NSA has."

Upstairs was Zetts's flop: futon, kitchen, weight gym, a lot of high-end entertainment gear. His cherished megaposter for *Hot Rod Girl* finally had enough wall space.

"Wicked boss, yes?" he said, eyebrows up. "Y'want a Hot Pocket or something? How 'bout a draft?" Next to his fridge was another, smaller, older unit, with a beer spigot sticking directly out of the middle of the door.

I had to crack a smile at this hog heaven. "But this place is supposed to be condemned. Says so, outside."

"That's the beauty part. The signs are for show. Special arrangement. This place will be standing for the next ten years, minimum."

"Thanks again for the flowers."

"Aw, dude. You stood up for me with Dandine. You know Doc Savage. You helped out. You got me this swell T-shirt. And I owe ya for those tapes, bro. Superiorly sexy stuff. All that oral-anal action gave me some ideas about, y'know, Beckah? Sweeeeeet."

He was talking about his virtual girlfriend. Not an actual person who could be compromised or murdered. Maybe he had something, there. Maybe Zetts was wiser than all of us.

"It's all on its own drive," said Zetts. "I uploaded everything, basically in chronological order." His new crib had plasma screens at almost every vantage. He diddled a keyboard and there was the late Alicia Brandenberg, doing it with Jenks, doing it with Ripkin, and doing it with several other marks I didn't even know. Zetts had been playing with editing software, and had assembled a sort of greatest-hits reel that was pretty assaultive. Naturally, he had tracked it with his favorite big-hair metal bands—a totally eighties soundtrack for Alicia Brandenberg's idea of ritual native dance.

Sitting on a chair near an Ikea-flavored dinette group was Dandine's black Halliburton—the one we *hadn't* taken to Park Tower.

"So what'd the hospital guys say?"

"I left on my own recognizance," I said. "I had to get out. Had to do something about . . . you know, Dandine."

"Do what? What's to do? He's under—like, way under. He'll surface when he has to."

"Did you see what happened? With the limo?"

"Nah. I cleared your car, then I got this priority beep. Coded message from Mr. D, saying get your ass out. This place was prepped and I landed here. So now I'm sorta waiting, like you."

"Prepped by who?"

Zetts shrugged. Who really knew? Who cared?

It was a weird inversion—I actually felt as though for the first time,

I knew more than he did. I knew how the fallback hide had been set up, because of what the Mole Man told me. Zetts knew, too, but he'd never say.

I looked down at the floor and tried to make my play as casual as I could. "I think Dandine is in trouble. I'm going to need your help."

"Nah—he's *under,* dude. That's it."

"I don't think he's under. I think NORCO has him."

Zetts made a face, as though tasting a sour, acidic burp. "Aww . . . *crap.* Ya think?" He fidgeted and punched at the air. "That *sucks.*" He opened his fridge door, then closed it. He looked around as though seeing his immutable environment for the first time. "Shit on a pogo stick."

This next part was negotiatively painful. "You like Dandine, don't you? I said. "He means a lot to you."

"Uhyeah!" The way Zetts said it was a almost a cough—*huh-yeah-huh*—which suggested I was illuminating the obvious.

"You've been together for a long time?"

"Pretty much." There was a new wariness in his tone.

I showed him the paper the Mole Man had given me. His expression crumpled, like an origami bird changing into the shape of something that hunts and eats origami birds.

"Awww, *man* . . ." His expression seemed completely betrayed. "Only Dandine and one other person are supposed to know that."

Good old item #2, the most expensive charge on the Mole Man's shopping list. The thing that made Zetts valuable to NORCO, believe it or don't.

"I don't suppose you have any kind of a plan?" he said sheepishly.

I didn't want to admit that my plan was a steal, a simple modification of what Dandine had proposed, so I said, "Yeah. And it all pivots on you." Then I tossed my recently purchased set of handcuffs on the table, mostly just to see the expression on his face. Dandine had thought of handcuffs and not used them. I had better handcuffs.

"Okayyyyyy . . ." he said tentatively. "You're not gonna hit me again, are you?"

We were back in the game.

THE FINAL DAY

You'd never believe me if I told you where NORCO was really hiding. You'd laugh and say, no way. It's twelve stories beneath a famous Hollywood landmark. The complex was considerably augmented during the endless Metro Rail construction for which Futuristics, Inc. had been the primary contractor. That's right—the company I helped to promote, which at one time was run by Garrett J. Stradling, alias the late G. Johnson Jenks.

The aboveground structures have been restored to their original vintage glory, but the interior of the building was also heavily renovated around the turn of the century, when 2000 became 2001. Guess which company had a big slice of *that* deal, too. Some marketing genius (not me) thought it would be a swell idea to connect Universal Studios City-Walk with Hollywood Boulevard, via the train, so that tourists and other potential consumers could experience a less threatening, wallet-loosening environment. Today, you'll see billboards that desperately proclaim *Hollywood Is Back!* in reference to the mercantile monstrosity erected at the corner of the Boulevard and Highland Avenue. It is called the Kodak Center. It is a sterile, beige, jumped-up mall fashioned after the overblown sets constructed by D. W. Griffith for his movie, *Intolerance*—you know, that silent epic starring Lillian Gish, hailed as one of the greatest motion pictures ever filmed, which neither one of us, you or I, has ever bothered to sit through? Imagine a PG-rated Babylon dotted with "fun kiosks," and you've basically got the mall. It also houses the Kodak Theatre, the place where the Academy Awards landed after a waterfall of payola . . . much to the consternation of anyone who ever has to drive anywhere on Hollywood, or Highland.

But the "restoration" aspect I mentioned was applied to the Chinese Theatre—originally Grauman's, then Mann's, and now Grauman's again in name only . . . and they're already thinking about selling it again. The box office was eliminated from the forecourt—it was a modern add-on to begin with—which had the added fiscal garnish of freeing up additional forecourt space for more premium hand- and footprint deals. (Did you know such "honorees" have to pay for the cost of cleaning up the sidewalk and "framing" the concrete, once the press conference is over? It's all deducted as advertising. And don't even get me started on those stars on the Walk of Fame, and how easily they're bought. Bob Hope has *four* of them.)

All that sound and fury—erection of the bogus Babylonian mall, earthquake-proofing the theatre before its face-lift, and adding a cathedral-sized underground station for the subway—not only consumed a lot of time, but covered up a lot of extracurricular activity. A new, state-of-the-art roost for NORCO was the least of it, as Zetts and I were about to witness.

Now you have to shoulder-and-elbow among milling tourists in order to belly up to the booth and attempt to figure out which movie is playing in the actual Chinese, versus the other six features that are filed in the multiplex closets that are part of the Babylonian mall. Today, the Chinese boasted the opening weekend run of something called *Confirmed Kill,* what *Variety* would designate an "actioner"—one of those flamboyant train wrecks that big-screen-TV emporia always use to demonstrate the coolness of their in-store surround-sound systems.

(Ever notice that? Walk into a rental joint or an electronics discount mart, and a hundred screens magnify the technocarnage and gun porn of some CGI-loaded visual extravaganza. It's never a Merchant-Ivory film or a meaningful human drama, or anything offering surcease of occasional silence; it's usually some endless director's cut of exploding spaceships or volcanic cataclysm, comic books colliding loudly with video games, the better to rumble those subwoofers . . . and sell the rubes.)

You can't get into the Chinese Theatre unless you buy a ticket. That's the single most prevalent question, answered a thousand and one times per day by the crimson-uniformed ushers. *No, ma'am, this is not a museum; it's a movie theatre.*

"Yo, it's fuckin Mason Stone, dude," said Zetts, grinning at the poster, which depicted our hero dangling one-handed from a black helicopter and blowing the undies off a skyscraper penthouse full of baddies. He was holding an M-60 one-handed, his shirt shredded (just like Doc Savage), with blood marring one side of his supercool, spiky haircut. "Did you see *Human Weapon 4?*"

"Was it better than *Human Weapon 3?*"

Have you ever been hit in the face with a shovel? I abruptly realized the fundamental difference between reality and realism: In action movies, the reckless, risk-addicted hotshots always survive. In reality, their corpses got mulched in secret by outfits like NORCO. In movies, we *win* against terrorists. In reality . . . well, we know better now, don't we?

"Popcorn?" asked Zetts. I could tell he was half-serious, looking for a last-minute out.

"No time."

"Kind of a waste."

"You still up for this? Because if you're not, I need to know now."

I was wearing the shoulder holster that Dandine had fitted to me. Sheathed within was the gun Dandine had chosen for me—the SIG Super .40 he had cleaned and lubed back at Rook's, which had patiently awaited me in the black Halliburton recovered by Zetts. The chamber was empty and the magazine held twelve rounds, just as Dandine had left it . . . sort of. While fooling around, I jacked the slide and a cartridge already "in the pipe" (as they say) came flying out. I chased it and had to pick it up off the floor. It was one of the hazard-striped ones, the minirockets. The kind that explode. Dandine had racked it as the *first* shot; not a pleasant portent to consider. Instead of trying to reload it, I put it in my pocket.

I was the least qualified person in the world to go gunslinging after NORCO. If anything begged to be shot with a real bullet, I had to click off the thumb safety, rack the slide, aim the gun, and actually squeeze a live trigger. I hoped I could remember those four things, in order, if the day turned pessimistic. Fancy moves and special applications were for guys in movies, not me. The last time I had fired a weapon—pardon me, *discharged a firearm*—was at the Beverly Hills Gun Club (of which I was not a member) in 1998, or '97. Nothing in the situation there seemed applicable to my current state of mind. I was leery and nervous about the casual gun owner's often-fatal shortcoming: the nerve to shoot at a living human target. *If you pull it, you must be prepared to use it.* Too many people's lives had been ruined by the gap of will between the former and the latter. The issue was not competence, but resolve. Dandine always had a full house of resolve; I wished there was a pill I could take that would bump up mine so I could at least stop shaking.

"Yeah," said Zetts. "I mean, otherwise, we might as well see if the flick is any good, right?"

We got our tickets torn and entered the lobby of the Chinese. Zetts had been right; it was a waste, considering how admission prices had pole-vaulted since the last time I had gone to a movie theatre . . . which had been about the last time I was on a shooting range.

According to the Mole Man, there was a curtained niche near the narrow stairs leading down to the men's restroom. Inside was a door labeled EMPLOYEES ONLY. Instead of a keyed lock, there was a cardswipe slot mounted next to the door.

We ducked inside the curtain; it was a close fit for two men. "Okay. Put 'em on and remember—"

"Dude, I got it, okay?" Zetts cuffed himself with the bracelets I had provided.

I popped the snap closure on the shoulder holster that secured the gun, then ran my fake NORCO ID through the card slot. The LED blinked red, then green, and the door gave you about as much time to enter as the average key-carded hotel room, which meant I had to run the card twice.

Inside, metal stairs led down about two stories, judging by what we could see from the landing.

Zetts held both hands up to point, and I acknowledged the camera lens angled down at us, out of reach in the concrete shadows. We switched positions so he could move down the steps ahead of me, since he was supposedly my prisoner. He was playing my part, from Dandine's backup plan for the First Interstate building, where NORCO . . . wasn't.

Below was more bare cement—buttressing, foundations, heavy rebar and bolting, and foam-insulated pipes. Nothing more mysterious than what you'd see in a newly constructed parking garage. Something was amiss but I couldn't place it. Left of the foot of the stairs was a single bank of elevator doors and a bored-looking theatre usher, leaning against the wall, reading a comic book.

Not reading, not really. Watching us approach. Not an usher. Too big. His jacket was unbuttoned.

I flashed the ID prepared for me by the (obviously talented) Rook. Then I opened my jacket to display the gun in my armpit, the same way Dandine had at Park Tower. The man nodded coolly, twigging up one eyebrow at the sight of my cast, then produced another key card. His and mine were required to scan through double slots next to the elevator doors, the way a safety deposit box needs two keys. The doors slid back and he resumed not-reading his comic.

Not an elevator, not yet. It was a short corridor with an identical set of doors about fifteen feet distant. Once the doors behind us closed, the others opened. It was like an airlock, or a great place to rabbit-trap a possible threat. When I crossed under the threshold, a two-note beep sounded.

The next room was a reception area with no attempt at charm. A grizzled man with a fairly lush handlebar moustache was stationed at an aluminum console full of TV monitors and phone lines. Off to his left, two security men sat browsing magazines in a punishingly severe waiting area—stone table, glass top, vinyl furniture. I was conscious of moving my hand *very slowly* to my pocket to exhibit my ID. The man with the moustache barely glanced at it, but nodded. He resembled an old cowboy gone corporate, or a retired stuntman.

"Reference?" he said.

"This is Declan Morris Zetts," I said. "But Gerardis will want to see me."

"What's this?" He was looking at Zetts, noting the handcuffs.

"I wound up with a detainee. That's why Gerardis will want to know about it."

"Armament?"

"Standard sig Super .40, from inventory."

The man typed a few instructions and waited to see something he didn't like on a screen, or hear it in his phone headset. "One of ours, plus one guest," he reported into his mike. "Reference was Declan Morris

Zetts. Requesting Gerardis." He listened as someone in his ear delivered quite a long sentence. His eyebrows went up.

"You guys must be important," he said. The two men across the room stood up as though snapping to attention. "You need escort?"

"No," I said. "Situation's not dynamic."

"Remove your glasses, please."

I showed him my damage and he blew a little whistle of awe. "You can see, though, right?"

"No problem."

"All-righty." He pointed idly toward the three sets of elevator-style doors on the far side of the chamber. "Know how this works?"

"I'm not really used to it yet."

"Yeah, most of us aren't, and there's still some bugs in the system. Take the first set of doors. You've got a priority tag. Good luck."

The doors parted. Awaiting us was a sleek capsule that resembled a private subway car, or one of those minimonorails used by some airports. To his credit, Zetts waited until we were inside, and the doors had hissed shut, before he said *what the fuck?!* under his breath.

The car bumped smoothly into motion. The tunnel was illuminated by twin rows of blue lights, which we could see blur past fore and aft, through Lexan windows, as we felt the slight press of acceleration. Our conveyance could have accommodated about six people.

"You've never seen any of this?" I asked.

"News to me, boss." He looked around as though we had just been abducted into a flying saucer. "It's like a secret subway."

"You've got it." The proposition was so huge and obvious that my mind had trouble encompassing it. But I already knew when it had been built . . . and who had built it. It was a practical underworld, not in the gangster sense, more in the Dantean mold. Our travel time was thirty seconds, tops.

We were remanded to another detail-deprived waiting room, and virtual clone of the first, but with more humorless sentries filling it, in a huddle pattern that reminded me of the catastrophic fumble at the airport. I finally recognized what seemed "off" about the whole matrix: No signs, anywhere. No framed pictures. No company logos—not on the consoles, not on the walls or the doors. No stickers advising what not to do, nor warnings, nor danger symbols or hazard/restricted iconography. No admonitions to *keep your hands in the car,* or *do not attempt to force the doors,* or *use your damned seat belt.* We're so surrounded and engulfed by signs and symbols that our brains are now tuned to register an alarm if they are absent. Even day-to-day clothing is drowning in logos, and it's all pitch-meistering, the constant low undertone of sell-sell-sell. Think of the product placement all over your sunglasses, your wristwatch, your running shoes. Under normal circumstances, we're all mobile billboards for a variety of preferred products and services. NORCO didn't even bother to acknowledge itself. It seemed transient and tentative, as though waiting to be labeled, and hence, stamped into real-world validity.

There weren't even big numbers differentiating walls and rooms and doors. I suppose I expected them, like deck and catwalk levels in a starship movie, the better to keep track of geography during the chase scene. The absence of benchmarks suggested a kind of vaunting arrogance to me, a superiority to the world of the walking dead that oozed from every crevice—almost a programmed psychological intimidation, very subtle, very potent.

When our little bullet car stopped, we found ourselves staring through another Lexan airlock at another sentry, sitting console. If not for the fact that the man did not have the handlebar moustache of his predecessor, we might have just whizzed around a closed track in a big circle. The door slid back with a soft, pneumatic exhalation.

"What do you think?" said Zetts.

"I think we can't outthink these guys."

We sat there like dopes for a couple of beats, until the man at the console waved us in. *Hey, c'mon, what are you waiting for?*

I let the pistol drop from the holster into my grasp. I cut the safety and chambered the debut round. Then I decocked—I didn't want to sneeze or something and accidentally put a bullet into good old Zetts. Difficult enough, to do all this one-handed; impossible if my fractured wrist had been my shooting hand. We stood up together and I let the console man see me snug the gun into Zetts's neck as we moved forward. His expression went wary and he extended a hand, fingers splayed, as if to imply *that's not necessary; be careful.*

A group of men stood in the Naugahyde nightmare of the waiting area: three gymsteak meatballs twitching in place, eager for attack commands, and their keeper, a tall man in a double-breasted suit with a pricetag that was easily north of two large. He was one of those follicle-free bald men whose pates appeared buffed, and seemed quite pink under the uncomplimentary fluorescent lighting. He had watery lavender eyes, an almost lipless mouth like a deft incision in his face, and large, powerful hands. When his enforcers saw my gun, all three moved as though Bob Fosse had choreographed them—they widened their stances and reached for their armpits. One of the bald man's big hands came up to belay their action.

"Mr. Maddox," he said.

"You're Gerardis?" I asked.

"Thorvald Gerardis, yes. It's a pleasure to meet you at last."

Oh, boy, his tone was enough to make me want to start shooting indiscriminately.

"Skip the butter," I said. "Please tell those gentlemen behind you to sit down and put their hands on their knees so I can see them."

My own armpits felt cold. I fought not to blush. I could feel Zetts go guitar-string tense. My position did not allow me to track the bulldogs and hope to keep an eye on the console man at the same time; I already felt outgunned and outclassed.

The bald man jerked his head to one side; his sentries immediately complied. "As you wish. Incidentally, Mr. Maddox, we have permitted you to keep that weapon as a sign of our good faith. I'll presume you are here to negotiate." He shrugged as though none of this was any big deal to him. "So . . . let's bargain. Let's exchange information for our mutual benefit. There's no need for any unpleasantness—"

"Stop it," I said. "Please shove that paternal politician act straight up your ass." I had had a lifetime's fill of politicians and their placating schmooze.

He closed his eyes and gently shook his head at my misbehavior. "What do you want? Or rather, what do you want us to do?"

I exhaled, imagining I could smell the stink of adrenaline and fear on my own breath. "I want a secure room; no bugs, no cameras. Then I want Dandine. I want you to bring Dandine to the secure room."

The bald man frowned and pursed his non-lips, which were slightly darker than the rest of his complexion, and as unappetizing as two animated strips of liver. "Why?"

"Because I don't know if you're really Gerardis or not."

"Do you know what you're asking?"

"Do you know what you're risking? I was at the airport, so stop trying to sweet-talk me."

"Don't fuck with this guy!" Zetts blurted, with perfect timing. "This dude is *not* the lame you think he is!"

The bald man snapped his fingers toward the man at the console. "Do it," he said. "Call Processing." Then he targeted Zetts with his unforgiving gaze. "You're the last person I expected to see here."

"Yeah," grumbled Zetts. "Eat me."

The possibly-not-real Gerardis kept on Zetts. I recognized the tactic. He was trying to force us into a defensive posture. "Perhaps you should ask your little friend here what *really*—"

I overrode him before his words could get a grip. "I'm not stupid enough to believe that anything you say will let me walk out of here, now that I'm trapped," I said. "This is pretty much a one-way trip no matter how we play it. So tell your men to stand down and lead us to the secret room. Please."

There had to be a secret room. There is always a secret room. I was toast if there *wasn't* a secret room.

"What you request will take a while," said Gerardis, if that's who he was. "You can appreciate that we're dealing with sensitive issues. I don't suppose you would lower that weapon?"

"No chance. Mr. Zetts, here, is my asset, and he's the only thing keeping you from erasing me right now."

Our host seemed amused by that.

"One more thing," I said. "Open up your jacket. Hike it up and show me the back of your waistband. Then pull up your pantlegs, one at a time, and do it slowly." I backed up, keeping Zetts in front of me, trying to better cover the room while the bald man complied. His aura of weary tolerance reminded me of Jenks, in the limo, and I was aching to hit him in the face.

"Satisfied?" he asked.

"Okay. Now, find us that room. One where we aren't monitored."

He nodded again at the console man, who entered some data and spoke low into his headset. The center set of elevator doors rolled open.

"After you," I said.

The bald man abandoned his entourage. "Would you like some coffee?"

"Shut up."

It was impossible to walk down the featureless corridor with anything akin to adequate cover. I settled on making the bald man lead, while I kept Zetts in rein and put my back to the wall, scooting along one step at a time so I could watch the doors at both ends of the passage. Our host walked ahead (hands in pockets, as I had instructed) and never turned to address us directly, although that did not stop him from comment.

"I know it sounds crazy, Mr. Maddox," he said, "but really, this is unnecessary. You are inside a completely secure facility and I doubt if you have any idea of the layout, ingresses, exits, anything. If our intention was simply to kill you, that could have been accomplished multiple times on the outside, with no fuss. We merely wish to work out a situation that has clearly become infected and is out of control. Once we discuss this, you'll see how much of it has been a simple misunderstanding—on our part, as well as yours."

"The magic word," I said.

Dandine's warning to me, on the night we first met, was blooming to full, rancid life: . . . *if an important-looking functionary smiles and tells you it's all just a 'misunderstanding,' then brace yourself for a bullet to the head.*

But it was even better, more horrible. Everything the bald man said stank of speechwriting, multiple drafts, polished and honed. He spoke to lull. He reasserted that he was the power, and I was alive only through his good graces. Then he proffered attractive-sounding solutions and opportunities for negotiation. It was all no big deal, a mere line of annoyance to be crossed out on a contract or covered by a handy rider clause. Then he had used the M-word.

"Tell me something," he said. "I'm curious as to how you forced one of our most elusive decommissions to resurface."

"Dandine?"

"If that's what he calls himself these days. It's one of those happenstances that amazes me. We've been looking for him for the better part of a year. No luck. Then you stumble into the mix, and bang—there he is. You accomplished this by complete accident?"

"He came into my house," I said. "You said 'we.' Why don't you say NORCO?"

"Hm. We never say that. It doesn't exist. Don't you *know* that by now? You really are hanging on a twig and a prayer, aren't you?"

"Don't make him mad," said Zetts, daring a wink at me.

After another set of doors and a duplicate set of watchdogs waved off by the bald man, we arrived at a room within a room. The effect was of a rectangle of tempered glass about twelve by fourteen, suspended in midair, equidistant from the concrete walls and ceiling. It was supported by a fragile looking crosshatch of aluminum girders and accessed by a small catwalk. Even if you were seated at the minimal conference table and chairs within, the illusion of floating would be unnerving. Two squat, black air handlers were stationed in opposite corners, cycling exhaust to secure vents. No obvious wires or intercoms; it reminded me of Zetts's electronics cage, turned inside out. The only solidity to the arrangement came from the steel doors for the sole access, which required another, different keycard to open.

I was wasting time being dazzled. This wasn't an after-hours tour behind the workings of some chic hot spot.

"Another thing," I said. "I want the man who holds your leash. You keep talking like you've already won some sort of victory, but you don't say anything."

"I assure you, Mr. Maddox—"

"Don't assure me of dick. I want Dandine here, and I want your boss—somebody who can actually make a decision. Offer expires very soon, now. Guess what expires after that? I just might shoot you first, on general principles."

"You would never have a chance of leaving this complex," said the bald man dryly. Our voices did not echo in the chamber, but seemed absorbed by the filtered air. Soundproofing.

"You don't get it yet. I don't care what *order* I shoot you in. And after that? Know what? I don't give a fuck what happens after that."

I startled myself because it was true. Even if my life was not over, my old life was gone. And even if I rejoined the world of the walking dead and went through the motions at my former job, I would be dead inside because my concept of the world had just been murdered by the actualities of the *true* world.

The bald man permitted himself a nasal snort of indignation. "My superior has been advised. As you can see, he is not here. Does that apprise you of your worth? I'm just here to do business."

My hands had stopped shaking. All of a sudden, I felt right at home. Two more bully-boys waited, chests out, chins up, near the catwalk. I wondered what NORCO's per annum payout for muscle was. What the sliding wage rate might be for those helpless, pissed off dupes we had bagged at the airport. The bonus scale for the shooters in the van on the freeway, or at Varga's, or the assassins who had tried to nail Theodore Ripkin at his own house. Did they get health benefits? Vacations? Was it a cop-flavored come-on: *You get to kill people?* Were there that many embittered sociopaths and disgruntled triggermen that NORCO could afford to use them expendably?

"We're *all* here to do business," I said. "Please tell those two men to stand back from the door."

"Outside," the bald man directed them. "This won't take long." He had one foot on the catwalk.

That's when something hit me in the neck like a jab from a prize-fighter, something hot and rattlesnake-fast that caused my vision to white-out. My nerves locked before I had the time to fall down, the gun in my hand was a million miles distant, and I was history long before I completed my graceless descent to the floor.

Do you expect me to talk?

No, Mr. Bond—I expect you to die!

Please pardon my little filmic flashback, my mental bullet-quote from the middle of *Goldfinger*. My system had been battered for the past few days on sedatives, nutrients, then the Mole Man's illicit stimulants— soak, rinse, repeat—and so my memory was backing up and slopping over into a delightful bathroom comedy subtitled "Get the Mop." You go up and down enough times, and eventually you climax or flame out. What I knew, or observed, versus what I thought I had seen, or heard, was running together into a bilious soup of images, as time sped up, slowed to a crawl, and folded back on itself altogether.

About to enter the glass chamber, I had thought: This is where it all gets explained, where the bad guy wastes valuable time in spieling off his master plan so the good guy can prevail. Why? For the benefit of the audience, who presumes motive even for the senseless crimes committed every day. Somebody's baby dies in a banger drive-by, then somebody else on the news says it was because the shooters were really after the teenage delinquent in the same house, and everybody relaxes and thinks, *oh, so that was the reason.* Then the incident can be filed and forgotten. Some senator crashes and burns with his pants down and no one asks for the cost-benefit analysis of assassination; normal citizens look at the death, stack it against their own conceptions of morality, and shut the file, thinking, *he got what he deserved.*

Real life, as it turned out, was not one of those count-to-three scenes.

"Dude, wake up, we're in deep shit!"

Okay, so Zetts was still alive. *Dood.*

I pried my left eye open and saw Dandine. He had burn marks on his scalp and one of his eyes was rimed in dry blood. He was cantilevered into one of the chairs on the far side of the conference table inside the glass cube, his legs splayed dumbly, insensate. His shirt had blood on it. His hands were bloody. The belt was gone from his trousers and he had no shoes. He appeared vaguely alive.

The bald man—Gerardis, although I was now cunning enough to await verification of his identity—stood a safe distance away from where the three of us were grouped. Me, Dandine, and Zetts.

"Dart's still hanging out your neck, brah," said Zetts. It felt more like a drafting pencil was shoved halfway through to my esophagus.

I got my right eye open in time to see Gerardis glance back at his two sentries, who were outside the secure room, near the catwalk. I wondered why they weren't inside with us, beating us up, acting hard. Two guns were on the table: Dandine's frightening Beretta and the SIG SAUER I had brought in. Gerardis lifted the SIG and thumb-checked the chamber. A repulsive half-smile jerked up one corner of his lipless mouth, like paper curling to fire. He drew down on Dandine from about seven feet away.

Dandine was looking at me. His expression said, *it doesn't matter . . . it's okay . . .*

He had obviously been beaten or tortured to within a thread of death. I wondered if he had lost any other body parts.

Zetts was seated on my other side. I could see his cuffed hands behind the chair. He, too, was watching me, and made sure I noticed when he gave his wrists a twist and smoothly jerked the cuffs apart. I had bought the break-aways at the Hollywood Magic Shop—part of the plan—but Zetts was too far away from Gerardis to deter him. Zetts kept his freed hands behind the chair, waiting for an opening, a mistake, something we might advantage.

"You okay?" Dandine asked.

"So-so," I said.

At this point, Gerardis should have butted in with a snide recrimination like *oh, how sweet,* or a pithy quip such as *you two will have all the time in the world to chat in Hell.* That was how it was going, right now, aboveground, in the world of *Confirmed Kill* and Mason Stone's superheroics. Once again: Reality. Fantasy. Not the same.

Gerardis's finger tightened on the trigger, confident in his headshot.

My legs were asleep, but I could still tell them what to do. I lunged out of my chair and got in front of Dandine.

In that moment, my job didn't matter. My apartment didn't matter. My equity and net worth did not matter. Nor did washing my car, paying my debts, or settling my satellite bill. Maybe getting a pet, some goldfish or a dog—unimportant. All my loves and false loves, done well or botched badly, meant nothing. Fantasies for my future; regrets for my past. Movies I had not seen, nor far ports yet untraveled. It did not matter that I would never again enjoy my comfort foods, or driving fast, or sinking a ball in a dicey, three-rail combo shot. All my conditional triumphs, all my abject failures; null sum. Katy Burgess and my imaginary future with her were irrelevant. Nothing mattered in that moment, which was blissfully free of all history and all thought.

Free. I was free. Finally.

The confinement of the secure room made the gun sound like a howitzer going off. I fell across Dandine's body and dumped us both to the floor with all the grace of a pair of winos in a bum-fight. The muzzle-flash of the gunshot blinded me; I was staring right down the bore. The end.

There was a great deal of blood. So much blood that it struck the far glass wall and coated it as though bombed by a paint balloon. Ever see those antacid commercials that boast about pink goo coating your clear glass stomach? Like that.

I humped to hands and knees, my limbs numb as the ticking in a stuffed panda, spellbound by the spray of crimson dripping down the wall. The *far* wall.

The wall *behind* Gerardis.

Gerardis was still standing. Well, some of his bones were still holding him upright. Chunks of his vaporized gun hand spattered the glass in wet gobbets, as though a vulture had dropped part of a snack in midflight. All of his face and parts of his head accounted for the bloody mush oozing down the entry wall. When his body fell forward, his shoulder hit the conference table and flipped him onto his back. His corpse hit the glass floor and began making a puddle.

"Got you," said Dandine. "Prick."

Zetts dived forward, surfing on his butt across the conference table in a home-run slide. He stripped off one of his dummy cuffs and jammed the prong into the card-access slot for the door. It made an alarming noise of malfunction and the LED remained red.

On the other side of the door, the two sentries were trying to get in. They were specters limned in haze, rendered faint by speckles of scarlet spray paint. One of them hit the door with a fist in frustration.

Zetts collected the Beretta and checked the loads before rejoining us. He helped me get vertical, back into my chair. Dandine refused assistance. Zetts left him on the floor, then sat on the edge of the table, facing us.

"Trust me, it feels better down here," said Dandine. His voice sounded cracked, more a whisper. Maybe they had burned his vocal cords.

"What happens now?" I said.

"No gunplay, I hope," said Zetts. "I don't shoot guns."

"It's like a rule," croaked Dandine. "He doesn't shoot guns. Never ever."

A wave of nausea tried to bend me. My eyes bulged as though they were about to emergency-eject like pimentos sucked from two olives. My gorge swelled and I gulped hot acid. The dart was still dangling from my neck. I yanked it out. Nasty golden thing, aerodynamic, a tiny hypo of the sort delivered by a gas gun.

Red shadows moved outside as the guards tried to un-fuck the door. Zetts would know how to compromise a computer-controlled entry-way. He could drive, he could hack, and he could anticipate what lesser talents might attempt in the realm of electronic security.

"You're fucking unbelievable," I said to Dandine. "You gave me a gun that blows up."

"I knew you'd never shoot anybody," said Dandine, from the floor. "You're not a guy who shoots people. You don't have the wiring for it."

This seemed mildly insulting. "The damned thing was a fireback, wasn't it?"

Dandine gave a weary thumbs-up. "Kept it. Sorry I had to give it to you. But that was the only way I could get it in here. Good thing you jacked out the first round, or my head would be on fire right now." He pursed his lips. "I knew you would."

Dandine had intentionally loaded one of the hazard-striped rocket rounds so I would see it, and in a semipanic, not reinsert it. Leaving his own special fireback round up second. He had known it would rest there, waiting, because I wouldn't pull the trigger. He had *known*.

"Gerardis was gonna shoot you with his gun, and him with your gun," said Zetts. "Done deal. Then I think he wanted to shoot *me,* and somehow blame one of you. He had about fifteen seconds to decide on a plan, before the higher powers at NORCO came along to close his window of opportunity." He nodded at me. "You were only out for about two minutes, tops. Gerardis had his boys deliver Mr. D's gun and stick us in the chairs. Then he kicked them out. What, no security, in a top-security room? It was his chance to pull something shady and wash a lot of old laundry, so he had to make up his mind in a hurry."

"What'd they do to you?" I asked Dandine.

He sniffed. "Processing. At the bank, remember? I had no idea they'd really built new offices." Another reason the renovation of the

First Interstate building had taken more than two long years. He held up one hand. "Look—they did my nails."

I had read an article somewhere about how prisoners of war had had their fingernails yanked out with pliers during various wars. The trick was to get a positive grip on the entire nail, and apply slow, steady force to remove it intact. Dandine's tormentors had completed the left hand and begun on the right when Gerardis's summons had come down through channels.

"They burned him," said Zetts. "Electroshock. Then they beat him up with those canvas tubes full of iron filings? Purees your insides."

"Why? What did they want to know?"

"They didn't want to *know* anything," said Dandine, almost scolding. "That was just . . . Gerardis, being a prick." A laugh tried to bubble up from deep inside, but it hurt too much. "Hm. Fucker's retired *now*."

"That was the real guy? Not a stand-in, like at the airport?" The only people I knew who could ID the real Gerardis were Cody Conejo, who had made the stand-in at LAX, and Dandine, who now appeared semiconscious at best.

"That was the real guy. We finally got him."

"Yeah . . . and now we're trapped in a bulletproof room." I thought, *If the guards can't get in, maybe I can take a nap on the table . . .*

"Not for too long," said Zetts. "Just until El Chingón gets here. Remember, you asked for Gerardis's boss?"

I already knew the reason, but I let Zetts announce it anyway.

"Well, he's coming. He'll show up. He has to. Because he's my dad."

I tried to glare Zetts into a confession. He fidgeted. All the while, indistinct bad guys tried to breach the secure door to the secure room, banging and chipping and prying. It was slightly comic. Exasperated, Zetts came across loudly, trying too hard to make his point, now that he had blurted out a very intriguing bit of information indeed—a fact that occupied no database anywhere, a truth that only guys like the Mole Man would know, because such facts can have great value, and accrue massive cost.

"Look, it's not like I have a beeper number for him or somesuch shit," Zetts said. "I don't know how to get in touch with him. Let's just say we don't have like the greatest goddamned relationship in the world, okay?"

I looked at Dandine, and Dandine looked away, because he was aware of his own failure to provide full disclosure. I hadn't been far wrong, back at the Wily Toucan, when I'd divined a weird father-son vibe between Dandine and Zetts. They weren't lovers. And Dandine was nobody's surrogate father.

Babysitter, I thought. *Guardian angel.*

"Your father . . . runs NORCO." I wanted everything to be declarative; gemstone-pure.

"Yeah. Basically. Whatever. Listen, brah, that totally doesn't mean that I wasn't—"

"And Dandine knew this," I interposed. "All the time, he knew."

"It doesn't work the way you think it does," Dandine said from the floor, staring at the ceiling, at the universe, praying for strength. His voice was still low, and delivered through clenched teeth. "Just hope he gets here before those idiots outside break through and murder us."

Murder. Dandine was using kill-words, now. To anyone but us, our deaths would be called something else.

"I was down with your whole plan, right?" Zetts butted in. "Right? Even when you told me . . . I said like, fuckin-A, let's go get him back? I did that because contact with my father is not part of the deal. Never was. Isn't, now."

"What did you do?" asked Dandine.

"When I found out Zetts's little secret, I marched him in here like a hostage. Just like your plan for getting into NORCO, but with a huge advantage: Nobody here is going to let anybody kill this kid. But *your* plan . . ." I shook my head. "What would've happened if I needed to start shooting?" I imagined my own face, sticking somewhere else besides my head. I was not smiling.

"If we had gone into NORCO," countered Dandine, "Gerardis would have dropped everything, to do me on the sly. He would have taken your weapon. And he wouldn't have been able to resist trying to kill me, right there, especially with a non-NORCO weapon and you, standing right there, as the best scapegoat in the world."

"Except you didn't know that NORCO had decentralized. It wasn't hidden in the First Interstate Bank building. That's just a branch called Processing."

"I know it *now*," said Dandine.

"They've got this train setup," Zetts told Dandine. "It's like a whole second subway system; secret, private. I mean, like it could be all over the whole city!"

"Besides," said Dandine. "If I got in using Jenks as a hostage, I was going to cut you loose. Using you was a fallback contingency. At which point, I would have worn the booby-trapped gun. See? That's why I never cuffed you."

"But you were going to," I said. "You lost your temper and killed Jenks in the limo. So, Plan B. What happened?"

"I surrendered," said Dandine. "I told them to tell Gerardis that I'd surrender directly to him . . . if they let you go and laundered your debits. Gerardis agreed, but decided to fuck me up first, by sending me through Processing."

The whole time I'd been goldbricking on clean sheets, and ogling Nurse Vanessa, minions of NORCO had been torturing Dandine. Andrew Collier's prediction had come true: Once they had Dandine, they didn't give a damn about me, and had more or less returned me to where I'd begun on the timeline. Deactivated my pending bogus murder charge, for Choral Anne Grimes. Whipped up a fresh owlshit story for the hospital. Restored my credit and un-besmirched my name. While Dandine was hemorrhaging, accreting trauma, and losing his fingernails.

"How'd you know where to come in?"

"Trade secret," I said. "You have your subterraneans; I have mine."

A tiny laugh wheezed out of him. "Bravo."

The drones of Security had stopped trying to bust down the door to the safe room. Nothing at all happened for several unnervingly quiet moments.

"You jumped in front of a gun for me, Connie," said Dandine. "That was very stupid. It was very courageous."

"No," I said. "It was very stupid; I agree. Not like me; agreed. But if you had died, who would explain all this crap to me?"

"Help me up."

"Why?"

"Because they're about to torch the door mechanism with a burning bar. Magnesium rods at nine thousand degrees. That'll liquefy the polymer, the lockdown brace, the frame, everything."

As Dandine spoke, a fan of slag-hot sparks sputtered from the underside of the key-card box Zetts had sabotaged. It sounded like extremely loud static. Sizzling white droplets and chunks landed on the far end of the floor and conference table, where they settled into melt patterns as they destroyed whatever they touched.

"It'll make tempered steel drip like orange juice on contact," said Dandine. He took up the Beretta M93R that Gerardis had intended to use on me, steadied his bloody, two-handed grip on the tabletop, and got ready to give the door a few three-shot bursts.

Zetts and I looked around. Having nothing more intelligent to do, we crouched behind Dandine. You know, to hold him up if he sagged.

The entire door assembly fell into the room. It's edges were molten and glowing. We felt the superheated air it pushed as it crashed down and began to burn the floor. Gravid clouds of white smoke fogged through the entry, drifting low. A pair of men in hazmat suits put down a hundred tiny fires with dry-chemical extinguishers. I learned later that CO_2 would not work on magnesium fires.

"Don't inhale that shit," said Zetts, of the fog.

We anticipated facing a brace of state-of-the-art killing technology, but instead a single man stepped through the breach, holding a handkerchief to his face and ineffectually batting away the billows of retardant. Under his other arm he carried a soft leather document holder, half a step down from a briefcase, but capacious enough for a phonebook.

He was tall and slightly top-heavy. He looked like a Danish film producer, with a young face and an old neck. His ruddy cheeks shined, and I suspected more than a bit of plastic surgery, to tighten out age lines. His hair appeared authentic—gray-blond, backswept, thinning but not receding. He tried to keep from coughing as he used his handkerchief to fan the air in a gesture of capitulation that was almost droll.

"Rainstone," said Dandine. "Thank the Fates." He angled his gun up, off-target.

"Could I prevail upon you to unload that weapon?" the man asked Dandine.

"I'd really be a fuckup if I did." Dandine was sounding a degree more like his old self.

The man—Rainstone—seemed to accept this as a correct response, and acknowledged Zetts. "Declan. It's good to see you."

Almost subaurally, Zetts mumbled, "Yeah, whatever."

"And this would be . . . Mr. Maddox, yes?"

He already knew it. Behind him, visibly holding back, were several NORCO suits with Bushmaster M-17s, chopped for military use and fed by ugly 99-round magazines. That was thirty-three bullets earmarked for each of us . . . by *each* gun. I felt proud of being that threatening.

"We need to talk," I said, "and I don't want to fence with you."

"This is my expert at bullshit," said Dandine, meaning me. He had lowered his weapon but not decocked it. "Watch what you say."

Rainstone dispensed with façade. "Fair enough. We don't talk in here. This place is compromised." He turned to the men behind him. "Stand down and clear out. I don't want to see anybody in the main corridor. Nobody on the platform, not even security. That's a direct order."

The men withdrew soundlessly.

"Good?" asked Rainstone.

"Search him," said Dandine, and Zetts hustled over to perform a pat down, never once meeting the taller man's gaze. He checked the leather bag and gave us an all clear.

"Help me stand up," Dandine whispered to me. I grabbed the back of his pants and assisted; the move looked pretty natural. To Rainstone, he said, "Sorry, but these two are the only men I trust, right now."

Rainstone concurred, forgiving the search. "Understandable." His eyes took stock of the room, inside and out, and hinted at potential ears, all around us. It was the *way* he didn't say it that was convincing.

We moved together down the far side of the table, to avoid stepping over what was left of Gerardis. Zetts backed off two paces, broadcasting that he was with us. The passage beyond Rainstone was clear of staff. Past the open doors at the end—no one.

"Tight group," said Dandine. "No space." He let Rainstone lead. Rainstone kept checking back to ensure he wasn't moving too fast.

"We'll take my car," he said.

The rubber-lipped door went *fsss* and settled into its seam. The blue tracking lights began to pass overhead, and the ride was so smooth that the illusion of standing still while the tunnel moved reminded me of old-fashioned, stage-bound Hollywood, where backgrounds moved on a loop, and you could watch the same tree pass four times if you were diligent. You've experienced the same confusion, if you've ever been inside an airplane or commuter train and something moved past your window, causing your brain and eye to insist that *you* were in motion, instead of the rest of the world.

When Dandine learned I had a pocket full of Percodan, he dry-swallowed two. Rainstone's personal NORCO shuttle was more lavish than the standard-issue cars on the secret subway, slightly wider and definitely shorter than a limousine, with fewer windows Leather appointments, goosenecked halogen lights, a bar. A set of monitors and a comm board. The internal illumination dimmed as we began to travel.

Rainstone was seated in the forward end. Dandine had positioned himself in the middle, on a wing seat. I sat in back and Zetts was in the corner, as though putting the greatest amount of available distance between himself and the man who was supposedly his father. There was a well-thumbed, curly-paged copy of *Los Angeles* magazine on an empty seat.

Rainstone concentrated on Dandine, as though anxious to talk him into a storyline, "Gerardis was old-school, from the seventies gang," he said. "You knew that he could be recklessly, ah, violent."

"Yeah." Dandine looked to me. "He broke my nose the *first* time he tried to kill me."

"It was Gerardis's intent to cleanse the organization of anyone with enough ethics to question his orders," Rainstone said. "It was a pogrom disguised as a recruitment drive. Gradually he filled personnel with the sort of steely-eyed college grads and executive thugs you all saw."

The spear-carriers. The snipers with iffy eyesight at Varga's. The glossy yuppie killers at the airport. The faceless crews in vans who came to sweep and clear in the dead of night. Muscle. Candidates for this sort of work were probably lined up ten deep wherever NORCO recruited. You could kill a hundred of them and twice that would show up the next day. They weren't even pawns. If you knew where to look, you could induct as many bent sociopaths as you needed and sacrifice them willingly, because nobody would ever miss them when they were gone. Large guys who liked packing heat and hurting people. Skilled torturers. Alien pods who could take orders and simulate the behavior of ordinary citizens.

You probably know a few people like this already.

"But specialists, you'd have to train," I said. "You need strategic thinkers and resourceful operatives who can make command decisions in the field, on their own."

"True," said Rainstone. "Gerardis valued those less than I did."

Times were changing, even inside NORCO. Nobody likes to admit to a paradigm shift. They put off the admission for as long as possible. Sweeping changes don't happen all at once. They have to accrete, like barnacles.

I remembered what Dandine had said about no retirement program, and shredding documents. "But you're supposed to be the head guy." The indictment was clear: Why hadn't Rainstone just stepped in and asserted some authority?

"Gerardis had powerful contacts, and was well-entrenched," said Rainstone. "Within the organization he functioned brilliantly. He helped produce results, and made sure people knew that. Things are vastly different now than they were even two months ago. Actually, the . . . ah, interior rot, began to become apparent about the time our friend, here, severed his ties with NORCO."

Never once yet had Rainstone referred to Dandine by name. Any name.

"And Gerardis has been hunting me ever since," said Dandine, rising to his medication. "With the resources of NORCO."

"In another month, there won't be a NORCO," said Rainstone. "It'll be called something else, organized differently. We have a whole new government to deal with now."

Putting a name to a conspiracy doesn't eliminate it. It didn't really matter what the club was called; the aims were always the same. In evolution, the only constant is change, and this truism applied just as relentlessly in the world that ordinary people never saw.

"I think I've got it," said Dandine. "Gerardis cut a deal, a master plan: Jenks gets the California governorship, and Gerardis gets NORCO all to himself."

"That was my conclusion, yes," said Rainstone. "It only recently became undeniable. You must appreciate how much of this transpired without my, ah, knowledge."

It was no different from executives in big oil, or the movie business, enacting their elaborate backstabbing scenarios. The left hand cooperated with the right hand until the prime opportunity arose for one to chop off the other. Then, golden parachute time for the last men standing.

"So the whole deal with Alicia Brandenberg?" asked Dandine. "That never crossed your desk?"

"Not in its true form. All I saw was a leverage play architectured by Gerardis. His plan was to sacrifice a freelancer to confer tension to the triangle of Jenks and the other candidate, Ripkin. That potential blackmail held in reserve, Gerardis could then exert more control, adjusting the tension, publicly and privately, to keep both men beholden to him. I had no idea that he pulled strings to make sure *you* were the . . . ah, freelancer, involved." Rainstone looked toward Zetts, silent and sullen in the far end of the car.

I instantly felt like the biggest dope in the known cosmos. "You're *Jaime Shannon*," I said to Rainstone. "You called my answering machine."

"I made no such call," said Rainstone. "Things have been in a panic here ever since our friend eliminated NORCO's pick for governor. Ripkin, as a sympathy vote, is worse than useless. NORCO hates losing control. Gerardis took an administrative demerit on lousing up what should have been a slam-dunk election. I was charged with securing a workable alternative candidate. That's what I've been doing, and why it took so long for me to arrive here."

"Wait a minute—you didn't call me?"

"I would make no such clumsy attempt at direct contact," said Rainstone. "You had somehow become involved and your situation was only worsening, but, against all textbook odds, you acquired a noteworthy ability to stay out of sight, and duck conventional radar. I'll confess you became so good, so fast, that I feared you were a ringer from a rival organization."

I knew what Rainstone was saying: I mistakenly looked like a pro . . . which would mean even more suspicion, confusion, conflicting signals, and worst of all, squandered time. The past week had involved enormous administrative movement on my behalf, at NORCO, and there is only so much even the most efficient company can accomplish in a day. And that's assuming the quarry is *easy* to track. Dandine had run me deep, and thrown many obstacles and detours into the path of those who sought to acquire us.

"So who left the message on my answering machine?" I asked.

Rainstone, Dandine, and Zetts all glanced at each other. Nobody had any idea.

"What about Zetts?" I asked. "Didn't his involvement mean anything to you? Didn't it clue you to make this whole thing more of a fast-track action item?"

"I was unaware of his involvement," said Rainstone.

"Not now," Dandine said to me.

"Look," said Zetts. "A station." We were approaching another private platform.

"That's Janitorial," said Rainstone. "Near the Kaiser medical center."

We were underneath the pavement near the Sunset Vermont station of the MTA, where Dandine and I and Choral Anne Grimes had caught a cab. We were under the Scientology center. Janitorial had to be the dispatch nexus that assigned vanloads of phantoms to execute all manner of wet work.

"How far does this go?" I asked.

Rainstone rearranged himself on his seat. "You came in at Personnel. Ordnance is underneath Universal City. Administration is downtown. You already know about Processing. But the system is not a closed loop. There are auxiliary branches and routes, a whole substructure for multiple transport, multiple destinations. It's all timed and coordinated by a computer center under the Natural History Museum."

"That means somebody knows where we are, right now," I said.

"I programmed no destination," said Rainstone. "We're just moving at random through the entire system. Traversing every byway, once each, would take, ah, over five hours."

NORCO was decentralized, its brain cells a safe distance from each other. No extravagant enemy complex to demolish in the last act with a big, cleansing explosion. Somebody like Rainstone would have to sign off on a project this huge . . . then somebody like Gerardis could make sure it got done, using someone like Jenks, who had been more than willing to get himself in deeper and deeper with every covert excavation—back when Jenks was still "Stradling," and running the construction company, Futuristics, building LA's top-heavy new tomorrow.

"Why?" asked Dandine.

"Please," said Rainstone, slightly more intolerant. "NORCO required it. Civil unrest and terror alerts were the best thing that ever happened to us. All we had to do, in Los Angeles, was assure the Federals that if something bad happened, and it ultimately will—like a trashcan nuke under City Hall, a biotoxin in the reservoir, or something like that—we could provide a secure and preferred escape contingency in that event. To evacuate the . . . ah, politicians, and, of course, some celebrities. The A-list."

"I think I have to vomit, now," I said.

Andrew Collier would ask, *Where's the ticking clock?* The big race to the finish? We were riding a train for as long as it took to smith together a deal. No bomb to defuse. No building to blow up. This wasn't coming together the way a secret agent ragout was supposed to.

Dandine would no doubt reply, *Didn't you get enough suspense back there in the glass room?* It was true: We might never have made it to the glass room. Rainstone could have been late. But Rainstone would have been notified the instant Zetts walked through the door. That had been the *only* way to direct-line the head of NORCO. Gerardis would have blocked every other option, or at least, snarled traffic until we were all meat for the coroner. See? Suspense is where you find it.

"Bottom line," said Dandine. "What happens after our train ride?"

Rainstone rummaged in his brief and brought out several files. He handed the thickest one to me. "A gift for you, Mr. Maddox."

It was four inches of paper, easy. "What is this?"

"Your data pull under the Freedom of Information Act. You know about that, right? Implemented into law in, ah, 1967. Didn't touch on loosening up potential hot-button matter until '76. FBI files and such were exempt from public scrutiny until then, and the Privacy Act of 1974 exacerbated the potential spill. Think of it: Normal people could find out FBI stuff about themselves. You should have seen the paperwork. They'd dribble out a few pages for every request, with the red flag passages, ah, inked out. Actually, they used a special brown marker designed to photocopy as dead black. Those markers cost the taxpayers $275.50 . . . each."

"Was it a Montblanc?" I said. Nobody laughed.

Rainstone smiled and shook his head. No one present needed to be told that one way or another, the ruling class never compromises its sinecure.

"So the freedom-loving American people now had themselves a handy tool for—"

"Getting all up in their government's shit," said Dandine.

"You're missing the more pertinent point," said Rainstone. "A seeming inequity had been redressed by a new set of subrules. So, the problem had been solved, at the cost of additional bureaucracy. Every request was a special case, requiring special handling. Man-hours. Resources. Until 1982, when Reagan was able to start choking it to death. And again, in, ah, 1986. You see, most people assume that once laws are passed, those rules sit there, inviolate—and they tend to pay less attention to such laws, because Americans love the idea of victory in the short term. The capsule version, the logline, the synopsis. What our citizenry—yours and mine—often overlook is the necessity for periodic maintenance."

"Which is where people like you slip into the gaps," I said, because I knew Rainstone wanted me to say that, to prove I was paying attention. It all sounded too rehearsed to me.

"You seem to disapprove, Mr. Maddox. Surely someone in your line of work can appreciate opportunism. Taking advantage is what made this country great."

"Yeah, and it's what made Exxon rich." Not to mention it was making my head hurt, as Zetts might say.

Rainstone chuckled. *Engage the client on all levels. Appreciate his jokes.* "Love America, Mr. Maddox. You have the right to an independent opinion. To have unpopular ideas. To dissent, politically. The right to be left alone. The Constitution says so. Want to know the difference between you and the man you know as, ah, 'Dandine,' there?" He pointed at my folder. "That is your file. This is *his* file." He held up another folder and let it drop open—empty. "Believe me, you should see your file without the black marker treatment. Which, by the way, is done by computers now, saving America a lot of imaginary money. Your *raw* file is about the girth of a very expensive, ah, dictionary."

There in Rainstone's hand, the fantasy. There in my grasp, the reality. The paper version of what was lurking inside the NORCO database, all the stuff Zetts had shown me on NORCO's incredibly hard-to-access Web site.

If you think you have any privacy, any real secrets, you're crazier than anything I've described.

"You're at a standoff with NORCO," said Dandine, "and we're at a standoff with you. Again, I ask: What now?"

"Your convenient expungement of Mr. Gerardis will have the trickle-down effect of buying time," said Rainstone. "Rather like when an ant-hill is . . . disrupted. Tell me what you want. Propose an arrangement."

"I'm no good at that. Connie is the dealmaker, here." He turned to me, eyebrows up. "You're on."

I took a very deep breath. This was my big performance. The turning point of my life I was only supposed to appreciate years later. The bold knock of opportunity, saying you're on, kid, break a leg, godspeed, don't fuck it up . . .

Except I knew my time had come. The single test of every ability I had ever developed. I knew it, the way Dandine seemed to magically know things. I just *knew* it. And I was ready.

"Okay, Mr. . . . . Rainstone, is it? Good enough. See these files? Files, everywhere. Bits and pieces of you, and me, and us. It's just paper. Facts and figures. See, that's the speed bump. It's a *paper* speed bump. Surely, together, we're strong and secure enough to negotiate a paper speed bump."

"You're saying that none of this, ah, matters to you?"

"Oh, it's all important stuff, I'll give you that. It certainly makes me nervous to consider all the contents. But look at us, here, now—that's the difference between dealing with people as files, and dealing with them as people."

"That's very cute," said Rainstone. "Demoting the end of your life to no big issue in order to curry favor. You've been trained very well."

"All I know is what works best in my field. You guys are all trying pressure, leverage, threats, and I've always found the best way to reach an accord is to let the client sell himself. So—" I turned to Dandine.

He picked up the football. "So, what Mr. Maddox is saying is we want to clear our credit history with NORCO."

"Right."

Dandine went on, "Total unilateral expungement from the database. No red flag items. No black-stripe card alerts. No associational ladders of contact with friends, co-workers, acquaintances. NORCO ignores the fact we even exist. That's what I had until Gerardis superceded your orders. He didn't want me walking around in the world. He wanted to play dog in the manger, and kill anything he could not own. So . . ." He opened his hands—still constricted by his injuries—to give the floor back to me.

"So, simply put," I ventured, "I—we—leave NORCO alone to do its business. NORCO leaves us alone, to do ours."

Rainstone blinked rapidly, several times. "That's all?"

"You have your own problems," I said. "You need to concentrate on the decay curve of an organization you allowed yourself to lose control over." Not grammatical, but certainly pointed. "If you and I and Mr. Dandine and all the worker bees at NORCO merely retreat to our safety positions, we spend a lot of time and resources trying to disrupt each other's lives until one of us finally dies. You don't want that. You want your machine to run without glitches."

"I thought you said this was a, ah, deal," said Rainstone. "You're not offering me anything."

"Go to Ripkin," I said. "Tell him you're responsible for foiling the plot on his life. Think 'spin.' I'll go back to Kroeger—" I swallowed, hard "—and I'll walk that nitwit right into the governorship with a strength-versus-sympathy plan that'll be irresistible. I can solve more promotional problems in advance than you can even think of. You come up with a better substitute candidate, and I'll do you the same deal."

"What about, ah, Katy Burgess?" Rainstone mispronounced her name.

First I gambled, "Katy will help me accomplish the things I say." Then I negotiated, "She has to stay alive and unharmed in order to do this." Then I lied, "I control what *she* does."

"I'm listening, Mr. Maddox."

In that moment, I knew I had him sold. The worst part was that the feeling wasn't new. But he was acting as though he wanted to stall, or win an additional concession.

Dandine sighed. He was pharmacologically better, but medically in severe distress. He brought the heavy Beretta out and rested it on one knee, a chitchat stopper. "It would be crass of me," he said, "to suggest that one day you will receive a Federal Express Courier-Pak containing Zetts's eyeballs."

"Say *what*?" Zetts had been so quiet I had almost forgotten he was in the car with us.

"Don't misunderstand me," said Dandine. "I would never make a threat to anyone as powerful as you. I would merely state a fact. I know what you can do to me. But I also know that you have unusually strong views on the sanctity of family. You're an archetypal American, Mr. Rainstone. You believe in family, even if your family doesn't believe in you, and Zetts is the only blood relative you have left. It is that very belief that made Gerardis consider you an antique, and try to end-run around you. When I left NORCO, you asked me to keep an eye on your son. I kept him pretty close, and never put him in direct jeopardy."

Unlike me, or Zetts under his own power.

"Gerardis obliterated that consideration," Dandine said. "All I would ask is that you reinstate it."

"Fuck *you*," said Zetts. "I can take care of myself." I caught his eye, sidelong, and shook my head. *Not now.*

But the worm of doubt had already begun to squirm in Rainstone's

316

mind. He put down his brief and trued up the ironed seams of his trousers.

"Did our mysterious Mr. . . . ah—"

"Dandine," I said. It wasn't that Rainstone didn't want to say the stage name, or was prevented by some professional code of conduct. He simply could not remember it; one pseudonym among thousands.

"Yes," Rainstone continued. "Did he ever relate the circumstances of his leavetaking from NORCO?" asked Rainstone.

"He never asked," said Dandine.

Sure, like *that* would have gotten me anywhere.

"It's everything you've just experienced, Conrad, over the last couple of days," Dandine told me. "The corporatization, even of NORCO. The top-heaviness. The useless bureaucracy. Its waste, its pointlessness."

The aim of all big business, foremost, is to stay in business. If a cure is discovered tomorrow, you don't think the American Cancer Society is going to voluntarily dis-employ itself, do you?

"Rainstone knew that the new order Gerardis had in mind for NORCO didn't allow for retirement," said Dandine. "They would erase me."

"So while I had supreme executive authority," said Rainstone, "I chartered this man as the steward for my son, in the remote possibility that some pirate force might try to strike at me through Declan." His tone was almost historic—the kind of history written by victors. "With the agreement that Mr., ah, Dandine here would agree not to interfere in NORCO's operation."

"Sort of an emeritus position," Dandine managed weakly.

"A setup," I said. "If he messed with a NORCO program, he would be fair game again. If so, Gerardis could eliminate his headache from the prior administration, with the excuse that he was looking out for NORCO's interests, and you went rogue, thereby proving Gerardis right about you all along."

"Like I said," noted Dandine. "It was a pleasure to shoot him."

"If he broke cover and interfered," said Rainstone, "even I would not be able to deny that he had to be scotched, for the good of the company. That's what Gerardis wanted me to think."

"But that means you're still running this show," I said. "Gerardis called you his superior."

Rainstone laced his fingers around one knee. We were all conversational and buddy-buddy, now. "True, five years ago. Less true today. Increasingly, the position is titular and honorary—only because I'm still breathing. Inevitably, Gerardis would have pulled his coup. Soon, I think. But I am insulated. In addition to which, Gerardis would have known that if he disempowered me . . ."

"Then Dandine would have showed up to lop off his head," I realized. "Hence—eliminate Dandine first, using a subcontract designed to implicate him in the assassination of Alicia Brandenberg, who was operating clearly within the NORCO sphere of influence."

Rainstone seemed to puzzle this in his mind. Slowly, he said, "Yes . . . that is the situation as I . . . understand it."

"So what about the deal?" I asked. "Will you accept this deal?" I photo-recalled what Dandine had laid out; it has always been one of my more dramatic meeting skills. "Unilateral expungement, no flags, no hassle, no surveillance, no leverage, no fallout on us or people we know. NORCO ignores our existence. No files. Period."

Rainstone said, "With the exception of your help in the political campaign, which you've already offered without condition?"

"I can do that without even having to acknowlege NORCO exists. Let me do it on my own."

"Gentlemen, I believe, ah, we may be very close to an accord."

Zetts gave Rainstone an odd look. He thought his father was talking about a car.

Great, I thought—now we were all stuck in unholy wedlock with NORCO (or whatever it metamorphosed into) until the next election was old news. Everybody had been assigned brooms and buckets, and now we had a titanic mess to clean up. Everybody was free. Everybody was obligated. We were stuck in the world of the walking dead, whether this pleased us or not.

"You may keep that." Rainstone indicated the file I held. "I don't suppose you'd be interested in, ah, taking over the position of the late Mr. Gerardis? You've demonstrated quite a range of the skills that are required."

"No, thank you." I was thinking, *that would entail a separate negotia-*

tion. The subdeals were always where the client got nailed, and I was used to holding the hammer.

"A pity. Then I think you both could use some medical attention," Rainstone now ignored his son entirely. "Permit me to, ah, expedite that, shall I?" He punched a couple of buttons on the car's control console.

If he offered us refreshments next, I'd grab Dandine's gun and shoot him myself. Don't doubt it. Not now.

TOMORROW

M *ugged by gangbangers*: That turned out to be my story. Ripping out my IVs had produced subdermal bleeding which resulted in more horrendous bruising. There was some debate over where to reinsert the leads and hoses, until Nurse Vanessa Strock came along and suggested shoving them up my anus, with a smile.

At least the ringing in my ear had subsided.

Perhaps I should have seized Rainstone's offer. The problem with resuming a mundane life is that once a door opens, and you see new things, it's impossible to revert to some program of normalcy without killing part of yourself. Your old life becomes hollow, a walk-through. You feel disconnected and unimportant. Normal, ordinary; bored and marking time. The only other way out was to grab a pen and write it down . . . or use the same pen to perform a lobotomy on myself.

I scrawled down a few notes for Katy Burgess to make pretty, so we could use them to win an election for the honorable (if cowardly) Theodore Ripkin, or whomever the secret masters chose to run against him. The battle plan just bummed me. I finally learned what Poe meant when he wrote about being filled with despair—I mean filled to the rim, slopping over, drowning in it.

I put on an insincere happy face for Katy and Zetts. Apart from them, I had one other visitor. He stumped into my room on a single crutch, ribs taped, hands bandaged, antibiotic gel glistening from the burn patches on his head.

"You wouldn't have a cigarette, would you?" I asked.

"I quit." Dandine inspected my bureau. Three bouquets, just as before—one from Kroeger, one from Katy, one from Zetts. That depressed me, too. It was as though I had time-jumped back to the same hospital room I'd had before. Dandine, on the other hand, found them cheery. He touched a rose with the crude paddle of his left hand, the fingernail-free one. He closed his eyes and inhaled the fragrance. I won't go so far as to say *he stopped to smell the flowers,* but it was an odd thing to witness, especially considering his tirade against floral offerings. He checked the card on a thin, tall vase of purple irises. "Zetts brought these?" he asked, slightly astounded. "Kind of . . . *regal,* for Zetts."

"You want to sit?" I asked.

"No. Too complicated. I have to turn, and put one foot over *here,* and grunt, and go slow, and gasp, and try not to burst any major hoses standing up or sitting down."

"You're in the hospital?"

"Third floor. I'm not going to stay as long as they want me to. Incidentally, this resort is all paid for."

"Damned right, or I'm on the phone to a lawyer on both our behalfs."

"Rainstone is stepping down."

That hung in the air and stank for a while. "Our fault?" I asked.

"It was inevitable. Not only did what happened to you and me *not* happen, but the circumstances under which it happened never existed, either."

"There is no NORCO?"

"Just like I've said, all along."

"So who gets the big, fancy secret subway system under all of LA?"

"The new crew. Hell, maybe the guys who shot the phony Gerardis, at the airport. You can bet your ass *that* was never on the five o'clock news."

Nor the freeway shoot-outs, nor the limo takedown, the firefight at Varga's, the blow-away in the pizza parlor, or my fleeting sideline as a kidnapper. Nothing, anywhere, about Alicia Brandenberg. An appropriately sullen news item on G. Johnson Jenks's unfortunate demise by heart attack. No follow-up on Choral Anne Grimes; it was as though she had never existed, never been spotlit on TV as a possible victim of foul play, since she had been safely refiled as a suicide. The elimination of Zetts's house and the Sisters' compound were random fires so dull they didn't even rate coverage. If it wasn't on TV, it wasn't real.

"What about Zetts?" I asked.

"My deal with Rainstone, when I left the company, was to watch from afar and keep him out of harm's way. I did that. I kept him close and fed him just enough adventure to prevent him from getting damaged for real. Zetts doesn't need me anymore. He is what currently passes for a grown-up. My obligation is fulfilled." He almost bit his lip. "So much for that."

"You'll still see him, right?"

"What are we going to do, Connie? Have a barbecue, go to the movies?"

"Well, maybe he'll still see you."

Dandine snorted. "Maybe."

"What about me?"

He gave me his combat smile. "Maybe."

"I've been going over and over this in my mind, trying to put it in order, in all my leisure time," I said. "I can't track the events. They don't cohere. There's no line of cause and effect. It's not linear, and I like things linear."

"Oh, you want a *story*," he said. "What, are you writing a book?"

I lobbed his own grin back at him. "Maybe."

"What the hell is this?" He picked up the bullet from where it was stationed, upright, on my bedside table—the yellow-striped rocket cartridge, which I had ejected from the (booby-trapped!) gun and stuck in my pocket. It was still with me. I looked at it a lot. "Trophy?"

"Keepsake," I said. More than that, it was my sanity, expressed as a self-contained projectile. Evidence that the things I have told you actually happened. Dandine seemed to understand why it was necessary. "Answer me one thing," I said.

"Depends on what it is," said Dandine.

"The hit-kit. Who doctored it?"

"You should know that by now," Dandine said. "You being all linear and logical and orderly and everything."

"I came up with an answer," I said. "But I'm still having trouble with it."

"*I* doctored the kit," Dandine said. "Before Zetts stuck it in the locker. There—does that save you some trouble?"

One of my little beeping machines started beeping faster. The answer kept bouncing off the inside of my skull like a golf ball in a spin-dryer.

I groped for words and only grunted fragments.

"I doctored the kit," Dandine went on, "and instructed Zetts to hide the key in the wrong car."

My mouth was still working, fishlike. Why? Why?

"Why?" said Dandine. "Because I had you marked out from the first, Mr. Conrad Maddox of Kroeger Concepts, whose data-pull is the thickness of your mattress. I chose you. Out of all the files I reviewed, yours was the best. I would pull you into my world in order to leave a vacancy I could fill. But things did not turn out exactly the way I'd planned. I got to a point where I could not stand by and watch you get killed, or eliminate you myself. Good news for you; not so good for my brilliant plan."

I couldn't really flail about; I was a virtual prisoner in the bed. I was mildly surprised when he didn't click off my monitors, or tweak a hose, or lift a pillow to suffocate me.

"Don't worry," he said. "I'm looking out for you. Don't panic. Just *think* about it all, for a moment."

My reasoning powers had all but evaporated.

"I have to do another round of X-rays at three," he said, preparing his exit. "I just wanted to see how you were doing. And tell you something no one else knows."

"What's that?" My voice had gone arid and I had to clear my throat.

"My name. My real name. Because you're a friend, and you have to promise not to laugh. It's Curtis."

"That's worse than the name of Choral's cat."

"Well, actually, it's Curtis, er . . . Bond."

I laughed, breaking the promise, and to compound the mortal sin, kept laughing. It hurt but was unstoppable. He sniffed and attempted to incinerate me with a look.

"Feel free to indulge yourself," he said, and that just made it worse.

I was still overpowered when he made his good-byes and walked out the door. That was the last I ever saw of him.

AFTERWORD

I was tempted there to go for what they call the Hollywood Ending—
you know, guy triumphs over adversity and gets the female lead; guy
"learns" something and, as a result of his "arc," grows in some unfore-
seen way. But you and I both know that's not how things go down in the
world, hence the gulf between fantasy and reality. Fantasy exists as empowerment parables, wish-fulfillment to make us feel less shitty about
our uneventful lives. We acid-test our value systems by proxy through
the characters presented in books, in movies, in make-believe.

But what if I told you that I lied a little bit, back there during the
part where Conrad Maddox, the dreaded and fabled adman, discovers
hitherto untapped reserves of courage and rises to the challenge?

Maybe you'd prefer a version of the story where poor, angry, mis-
guided Choral Grimes turns out not to be dead, because Connie's knowledge of that death was all hearsay and manipulated media. After the
smoke clears, she makes contact. After a heartwarming meet-cute
redux, they have a terrific sex scene (I probably would not have been
much good at writing *that,* I'll admit). She and Connie eventually get
hitched. Connie leaves Kroeger and starts a consumer advocacy network. They spend their days wisely avoiding the poisoning aspects of
modern advertising, having learned a handy object lesson in the form
of your wacky protagonist, the hit man with a heart. A pat, neatly rib-
boned wrap-up. A story with a palliative moral, easy to swallow, rein-
forcing the status quo of payback and fair play in the world of the
walking dead.

Yeah, Andrew Collier would have *loved* that ending. It paints a ros-
ier worldview than the nihilism of *nobody cares, everyone expects the
worst, and nothing matters.* (A picture that my associate Rook would
instantly peg as a forgery, no doubt.)

Or maybe you'd favor a version of the story that Connie feared the most—that I was a figment of his desperately bored imagination, or a projection of his insecurities. An alter ego, something from a virulent nightmare, or a malign twin, separated at birth. It's astonishing, what some people can talk themselves into.

Or maybe you'd prefer the idea that NORCO wasn't real at all. But I can only tell it from my point of view. Call it authorial license. NORCO no longer exists, anyway. Sometimes it's a new outfit; sometimes a refinement, or evolution, of an extant interest, but whatever it is, it's called something else, today—as Rainstone said. And such people only get better at what they do. Sometimes I think about what a bad shake it would be if they actually *were* running everything, but that's giving them too much credit. Besides, you wouldn't believe it . . . right?

Conrad eventually sorted it out for himself, I'm sure.

And here I am, writing this narrative out in Conrad's voice, as an ultimate test, a sort of final exam. It's up to you to determine how well I've actually captured the man inside the personality.

I was serious when I revealed to Conrad that I had researched him in depth, with the objective of taking his place. I needed a berth in the real world where my skill set would not lie completely fallow.

What surprised me was the letter Burt Kroeger received. It read:

(day) (month), 20__

Mr. Burt Kroeger
Kroeger Concepts
(internal)

Dear Burt:

This letter will introduce Mr. ———— ———— with my highest recommendation as an interim member of the Kroeger team. I'd put him forth for my recently vacated VP slot, but that of course is your call.

Know that ———— is creative, resourceful, and comprehensively experienced in the challenges of ad/pub, with the kind of ability to think out of the box, something I know you value highly. Please review the attached work history and background material at your leisure. I'm positive you'll see what a great potential picture it paints.

Thanks a million for the consideration.

Thanks, too, for your grace and goodwill in letting me out of my contract early, or at least putting it on hiatus. The least I can do is vet you a capable replacement while I'm away resolving a few private matters that have been hanging fire for far too long. You're a pal for not prying.

I love you all and I guarantee you'll be hearing from me.

Sincerely, your friend,

Conrad Maddox
Executive Vice President

The most staggering thing about the letter was that I did not write it. And when I say this, I'm not being what, in fiction, is called the "unreliable narrator." You know—like that movie where the guy whose voice-over you've been listening to for the whole story turns out to be dead when the story begins? Not that at all.

I think Conrad wrote the letter. I think it was exactly what it purports to be. Because Conrad figured out my grand plan, there in his hospital bed, all by his lonesome.

Proof? Who needs it? NORCO? Gone now. Some other head of the Hydra has gained ascension. Databases have changed hands for imaginary cash—think of your own vital statistics—in a yard sale. Anybody can get them. So do names and ominous sounding titles really matter? All it takes is to push the right buttons. What I don't know, Zetts can find out (I'm still not very Internet-friendly, as you might have guessed). As for the skinny on Connie Maddox . . . well, hell, the guy was just begging to be advantaged, he was so bland. But I can't tell my story without telling his, right? And if I had never come along, no one would ever have bothered to talk about Conrad Maddox, in the first place. At all.

Katy Burgess took a liking to me right away. She was prepped for Conrad, but now Conrad was gone, and there I was. Together we worked on the campaign for the new governor. Not Theodore Ripkin, but a senator I think I once saw getting his testicles crushed by the Sisters.

Well, at least I know now who left the provocative message on Conrad's answering machine.

You may have perceived some lack of detail in the sections describing Connie at work. I faked them, hoping to skim past. Sometimes you can sound more credible with less information. But I'm learning as I go.

Needless to say, I got the idea of writing this all down from Conrad himself, back at the hospital.

Gerardis remains dead, and good riddance. Rainstone stepped down with a deal instead of a firefight. I helped him negotiate terms. Zetts still strolls the planet, though now without need of my phantom guardianship.

(It was most likely Zetts who leaked the salacious Alicia Brandenberg home-vids to the Internet, thereby scuttling Theodore Ripkin's aspirations to public office and giving the replacement candidate a running leg up. The scandal thrust Ripkin into exile and I wouldn't be surprised if he has changed *his* name, by now. I haven't verified this, but I suspect it's true.)

That leaves what happened to Conrad.

I wish I could tell you, but honestly, I don't know. He vanished. Disappeared. Went under. In the beginning, my intention was to curry an asset that could be sacrificed so I could conceivably take his place, creating a slot that I could inhabit. By the end, I couldn't countenance that. Against all my understanding of what people do in their own self-interest, Conrad recklessly flew in to rescue me and would have taken a bullet for me. That kind of asset, you don't sacrifice, friends.

Of course, I could be lying. You'll never know.

Instead of my simply taking his place, it appears that we have swapped. Conrad became like one of those dead people who get their Social Security numbers appropriated by con artists. "Dandine" got killed on paper and that was sufficient for certain evil forces to stop dogging the guy.

I come into this world with all the skills and knowledge of my former profession. With acute senses. With abilities that might make you shudder if you really knew anything about me (but then, it's unlikely you'll ever talk to anybody as high up as Rainstone, or even suspect who he really is). In a world where nobody is who they say they are, I fit right in, seamlessly—and you can't perceive the break between fantasy and reality. I can walk among the walking dead without ever being one of them. In my world, the dead come back to life more routinely than they do in drama, or on television. You just never see it happen, or don't recognize what's going on, if it happens right in front of you.

If you were smart, you'd be killing the minions of advertising. Instead, you pay crippling sums of money, tithing the government to kill on your behalf—those rulers who keep you broke, hopeless, and desperate—since you just don't seem to have any spare time, and isn't the pressure of day-to-day living too overwhelming, most ways? Instead, you do virtually everything we tell you to. You wait, breathlessly, eagerly, for the next thing we decide to make you do. Why bother with a frontal attack on individual liberties when you'll give up your most important rights *willingly?* You know that old saying about how everybody is dying to sell out, but there aren't enough buyers? Legislation is clumsy, corrupt, and glacially slow. Not decisive, or surgical, or comfortably subradar.

So what, if I lied, a little bit?

I know this may not be how you were expecting things to turn out, but I ask you, Look at the unprecedented opportunity that was presented here.

I mean, what would *you* do?

Or rather, when your time comes, what *will* you do?

ACKNOWLEDGMENTS

I could reveal the names of many people who profoundly influenced or augmented the production of *Internecine*, but then I'd have to kill you. It sounds mysterious to say that most of the plot sprang full-blown from long rumination on that very word, *internecine* (which by now, I trust, has become part of your vocabulary), but it's the truth insofar as an answer to the eternal questions about story sourcing. That, and—strangely enough—the 1899 poem "Antigonish" by William Hughes Mearns.

Such few participants and champions that can be safely identified are as follows: Charles Ardai of Hard Case Crime; John Schoenfelder of Little, Brown; Brendan Deneen and Thomas Dunne of St. Martins; the ferociously talented Tim Bradstreet and the just-plain ferocious Thomas Jane; and John Silbersack of Trident Media Group.

For long-in-advance read throughs (spanning years) I am indebted to Peter Straub, John Farris, Peter Farris, F. Paul Wilson, Joe R. Lansdale, Michael Marshall Smith, and Duane Swierczynski. My posse!

Even weirder thanks to the late Vernon Green, who as a teenager in 1954 came up with his own oddball term and used it as a lyric in the Medallions' R&B hit "The Letter." Spellings vary but it's another word you need to run off and learn right now: *pizmotality.*

for

KERRY FITZMAURICE

mi pelirroja mejor

and queen of pizmotality

with all my love